The
Getaway

Isabelle Broom was born in Cambridge nine days before the 1980s began and studied Media Arts in London before a 12-year stint at *Heat* magazine. Always happiest when she is off on an adventure, Isabelle now travels all over the world seeking out settings for her escapist novels, as well as making the annual pilgrimage to her second home – the Greek island of Zakynthos. Currently based in Suffolk, where she shares a cottage with her two dogs and approximately 467 spiders, Isabelle fits her writing around a busy freelance career and tries her best not to be crushed to oblivion under her ever-growing pile of to-be-read books.

To find out more about Izzy and her books, read excerpts, view location galleries and gain access to exclusive giveaways, you can sign up to her monthly newsletter via her website, isabellebroom.com.

Also by Isabelle Broom

Hello, Again
My Map of You
A Year and a Day
Then. Now. Always.
The Place We Met
One Thousand Stars and You
One Winter Morning

Isabelle Broom

The Getaway

HODDER

First published in Great Britain in 2021 by Hodder & Stoughton
An Hachette UK company

This paperback edition published in 2021

1

A CIP catalogue record for this title is available from the British Library

Paperback ISBN 978 1 529 32514 0
eBook ISBN 978 1 529 32513 3

Typeset in Plantin Light by Hewer Text UK Ltd, Edinburgh
Printed and bound in Great Britain by Clays Ltd, Elcograf S.p.A.

Hodder & Stoughton policy is to use papers that are natural, renewable
and recyclable products and made from wood grown in sustainable
forests. The logging and manufacturing processes are expected to
conform to the environmental regulations of the country of origin.

Hodder & Stoughton Ltd
Carmelite House
50 Victoria Embankment
London EC4Y 0DZ

www.hodder.co.uk

For my friend, Katie Marsh.

PART ONE

I

Like most people, Kate Nimble was aware that your life was supposed to flash before your eyes in the moments before you died. But she did not know that the opposite was also true. That when you were perhaps more alive than you ever had been before, everything slowed down to a painful crawl.

Every note of the song you had chosen especially.

Every expression on the upturned faces of your friends and family.

And every second that the man you had just asked to marry you did not reply with a 'yes'.

Kate forced herself to focus on James. His mouth was open, unhinged no doubt by a mixture of shock and embarrassment. Like her, he seemed to have lost the ability to speak. If only this particular affliction had come to her earlier – before she had pulled at that chair, clambered onto it and called the room to attention.

'I, er . . .' James gestured around helplessly; his raised arm as flaccid as a sodden flag.

Kate knew that she should move, that she should say something – *anything*; that she should get down from this pedestal of mortification. But she couldn't. Her limbs were leaden, her feet stuck fast.

'I think that . . . What I mean is . . .' James went on. He sounded helpless.

Kate was beginning to shake. The familiar corners of the pub's dingy function room felt as if they were closing in. A number of people had their phones raised; the ramifications of this were too awful to contemplate.

'Excuse me, move aside, coming through.'

Another voice, stern yet soothing. Kate's best friend Robyn had pushed her way past the semicircle of assembled guests and was approaching at speed.

'Come on,' she said, holding out her hand. 'Let's get you down.'

A sob had wedged itself into Kate's throat and she forced it free with a laugh.

'Sorry everyone,' she called out, catching the heel of her shoes on the hem of her skirt as Robyn half-lifted, half-dragged her off the chair. 'I was only joking.'

She braved a glance at James, but her boyfriend was staring at the floor.

'It was just a joke,' she repeated, her voice cracking as Robyn led her out to the hallway.

'Don't cry,' her friend pleaded.

'I'm not,' said Kate, but she could feel the tears building.

'James must not have heard you properly,' Robyn went on, in the robust tone of a woman doing her best not only to convince the person she was talking to, but also herself. 'You just took him by surprise, that's all. He obviously wasn't expecting it. Maybe he had a plan of how he wanted to propose to you, so was overwhelmed with a sudden, speechless regret that he hadn't got there first?'

Kate shivered.

'The good news,' her friend said meaningfully, 'is that he didn't actually say no, did he?' She was twisting a strand of her dark hair around on her finger as she spoke, her pale face pinched with concern. 'Maybe he wanted the moment to be a private one. I mean, he has never been one to draw attention to himself, has he? That must be it – he is simply embarrassed.'

Kate pursed her lips to dam her tears. Horror, like molten lava, was mounting inside her chest.

James had not said no. But he hadn't said yes either.

'Shall I go and get him?' Robyn asked. Then, when Kate did not respond. 'You'll both be laughing about this in a mo, you'll see.'

A leap of faith. That's what Kate had called her plan. She'd allowed herself to believe she would get what she wanted from James if she could only pluck up enough courage to ask him for it. But she hadn't done it right; she should have proposed on the final day of February, during a leap year. Not in the middle of a random April. Those were the rules. She hadn't even been able to get that simple thing right.

Stupid, stupid, stupid.

The door into the corridor opened and James emerged, a rather pained expression on his face.

'Are you all right?' he asked.

'I'm fine,' Kate said, folding her arms. 'You don't need to look at me like that.'

'Like what?' He took a hesitant step closer.

'Like I'm an unexploded bomb that might go off at any second.'

'I just thought that yo—' he began, to which Kate scoffed.

'I told you, I'm fine. OK, so I just stood on a chair in front of practically everyone we know, on my thirtieth birthday, no less, and asked you if you'd like to marry me. To which you said nothing. Not one single coherent word. So, yeah, I'm just peachy, James; I have never been better.'

'Please don't get upset,' he said, as Kate was again forced to fight a treacherous trembling in her upper lip. 'I just wish you'd told me that you were planning this; then I could have—'

'The whole point of a surprise proposal is that it's supposed to come as a surprise,' she countered. 'I wanted it to be romantic.'

'I know, I know.' James seemed unable to look at her; his eyes were darting from the ground, to the radiator on the wall, to his own fingers twisting together in agitation. 'I didn't want to do this now,' he muttered. 'But maybe I should. I don't know.'

Kate couldn't tell if he was addressing her or talking to himself, so she remained silent, studying him as he fought to make sense of whatever internal battle was raging inside him.

'Maybe it's a good thing this has happened,' he said eventually.

'It is?'

Hope bobbed up like a balloon in the space between them.

'Yes,' he replied carefully. 'Because it's made me realise that I need to be honest with you about what's been going on. You know, about how things are with us.'

'What about us?' Kate's stomach churned unpleasantly.

'Well . . .' James paused to inhale deeply. 'Things haven't been right for a while now. Not since we found out abo— Well, the thing is, we've been growing apart since before then.' He was looking not at Kate as he spoke, but at his shoes – those whiter-than-white trainers that he cleaned after every wear, more often than not raiding the bathroom cabinet for her face wipes in order to do so.

'Growing apart?' Kate pulled a face. 'No, we haven't.'

'Come on, Kate – you know we have.'

'And so this is, what?' she countered. 'Your way of saying we need to work on a few things? Of course we do, James – all couples have issues from time to time, and after everything we've been through recently, it's understandable that you might be feeling, I don't know, disconnected from me. Is that it? Because we can fix that.'

James did not say anything; he merely winced.

'Oh my god.' Kate raised a hand to her mouth. 'You're not? This isn't? You're not dumping me?'

A grimace.

'Don't say it like that. You make it sound as if I'm taking you out with the bins.'

'You may as well be.'

Kate's tone was becoming increasingly shrill, but she could no longer control it – no longer wanted to control it. She felt strangely as though she had left her body and was now perched up on the radiator beside them instead, watching but not partaking in this charade. Because that is what it must be. James could not actually be saying these things.

'I'm concerned that neither of us will get the things we want if we stay together,' he said, glancing up when she did not immediately reply. 'You know that as well as I do.'

'I do not. I know no such thing.'

Her disgruntlement might well be as tough as tarmac, but now the anxiety was bulldozing through. Kate found herself abruptly overcome by an unsteadying wave of nausea.

'We don't have to get married,' she hastened, making a grab for his hand. 'We're fine as we are – I just got carried away, what with freaking out about turning thirty and losing another bloody job. I only decided to propose to you about half an hour ago. It didn't even occur to me before then. And I'm honestly happy as we are,' she insisted, cutting across him as he began to interrupt. 'We can work on all the things you think are broken. We can't just give up, James,' she said firmly, squeezing his fingers between her own. 'We've come this far, haven't we? Eight years must count for something.'

'It's not giving up,' he said, removing one of his hands from hers to fuss unconsciously at the rapidly thinning hair on his crown. His 'Prince William patch', Kate called it. It was the only part of her boyfriend that hinted at vulnerability and she loved it – loved him.

'All I'm saying is that I think it's time we accept the facts,' he continued. 'I know you've been trying – we both have; we've both tried really hard for a really long time now. But that's the thing: we shouldn't have to try. It shouldn't be this hard.'

He was speaking so quietly that Kate had to lean forward in order to hear him. The party had continued apparently, despite all the drama she had caused.

'It's not as if either of us has done anything to hurt the other,' James said, sounding as much as if he was trying to persuade himself as he was Kate. 'There's no reason why we can't stay friends.'

He eased his other hand out from her grasp, leaving Kate's cold and clammy.

Who was this man standing here in front of her, saying these things, striking these blows? He looked and sounded and even smelled like James, but how could it be the same person?

'But you are hurting me; you're hurting me right now,' she whispered, thinking in miserable desolation of the plans they had made and of the home they shared, with its collection of framed movie posters, harmonious scatter cushions and colourful spread of kitchen tiles. She pictured the photo on their living-room wall; saw the smiling couple inside the frame – him tall, lean and serious; her round-edged, wild haired and smiling. That captured moment was already becoming less substantial than a memory, their shared love relegated to a past tense.

'But it's my birthday,' she said in a small voice. 'You can't break up with me on my birthday.'

James was looking sheepish. 'I didn't exactly plan this, you know. I was going to wait a few weeks before I said anything.'

Kate watched in silence as he chewed over the next few words.

'But then you got up in there and . . . you know. I definitely didn't see that coming. I mean, how could I? I thought if a woman proposes, she's supposed to do it in a leap year.'

Kate pushed her bottom lip upwards morosely.

'Whatever, anyway,' he went on. 'The point is, I knew as soon as you said the words that I couldn't lie to you anymore. Things just suddenly became very clear.'

'Things?' she prompted faintly, staring with unseeing eyes at a patch of peeling wallpaper.

'All our friends' lives are moving forward and I feel as if we're being left behind,' James said. He seemed to be choosing his words now with delicate care and kept pausing to clear his throat.

Kate was struck by an absurd compulsion to shout at him for not covering his mouth, but knew that if she started yelling, she might never stop.

'I'm not blaming you.'

But he was. Because it was her fault. Of the two of them, it was she who was the failure.

Kate had begun to shake; she could no longer stand still and began to pace up and down the narrow corridor in agitation. There was a window at the far end, the sky beyond the glass as black as ash.

'I think I should stay with my folks tonight,' James said, moving slowly away from her.

Kate swallowed another sob. 'Please don't. Let's at least sleep on it. This isn't the time or place for this conversation – our parents are in the next room, for god's sake. All our friends are here.'

James paused at the door to the function room. The fact that the party was still ongoing felt to Kate like a betrayal. The wider world should have stopped spinning, just as her own had.

'I'm sorry,' he began, but Kate shook her head, dismissing his words. Moistening the tip of her index finger, she began rubbing furiously at a sticky splatter on the windowsill, thinking that if she stayed here in this spot, cleaning this stain, she would not have to watch him leave; would not see him tell their guests what had happened, or know when he headed down the stairs and out into the night without her.

Only when she heard the click of the door closing did Kate stop; only when the muffled sound of voices followed did she crumple, and only when she felt Robyn's arms wrap around her did she finally give in to the tears.

2

Like an errant boulder careering down the side of a mountain, life somehow continued on as it always did. But while the rest of the world's inhabitants went about their daily business of showering, dressing and commuting to their respective places of work, Kate remained where she had fled to the night of her party, back at her parents' house with a duvet pulled up over her face.

A short time ago, when she'd still had a boyfriend, a future, a purpose, Kate had been able to laugh about the fact that she had been made redundant. Again. Now it did not seem funny in the slightest – nothing did. She had done her best to laugh both hard and often for her entire life, believing it to be the simplest cure to most of the things that ailed her, and had always been able to poke fun at herself. But ever since James had walked away from her, abandoning their relationship with what felt like barely a backward glance, Kate could not bear to smile, let alone muster the amount of energy required for a laugh. She missed it; missed laughter.

Kate heard the creak of someone outside the bedroom door and closed her eyes, willing whoever it was not to knock. Pretending to be unaffected was exhausting; she did not know if she had it in her to continue the make-believe act she had portrayed to her parents since moving back in a little over a week ago. Her mother, who was emotionally subdued and overly apologetic by nature, had done little more than

pat Kate rather forlornly on the shoulder and say repeatedly
how sorry she was that things hadn't worked out, while her
father – from whom Kate had inherited determined cheerful-
ness in the face of adversity – relayed joking platitudes about
there being 'plenty more eels in the pond'. Kate appreciated
each of their efforts, but neither had offered her much
comfort. What she really needed was a plan – a scheme to
win back her boyfriend, and therefore her happiness.

'Nims, are you up?'

Kate opened her eyes. Only one person called her by that
abbreviated surname moniker. But he wasn't even in the
country.

The door opened a crack just as she lowered the duvet,
and Kate exclaimed in surprised delight when she saw who
was standing in the gap.

'Toby! What are you . . . How are you here?'

'I don't know if you heard,' her brother replied, 'but there
are these things called planes nowadays. Big cylindrical
machines with wings and engines that fly people from one
country to another.'

'Funny,' she retorted, then promptly burst into tears.

Toby sat on the bed and pulled Kate into a hug. It was
nice, for a moment, to feel swaddled and protected. But
almost as soon as the gratitude came, so did the guilt. She
hated that she was behaving in this way; that she was unable
to get a handle on her emotions.

'I'm fine,' she croaked, pulling gently away from him.
'Honestly, I'm just tired, that's all.'

'You may have fooled Mum and Dad,' he chided, as Kate
wiped sullenly at her cheeks, 'but I can see what's really going
here, Nims – you don't have to put on an act for me.'

'I'm not,' she argued, although without much insistence. 'I
just don't want to worry anyone.'

Toby frowned.

'I'm your big brother, so it kind of comes with the territory.'

'Yes, but—'

'But nothing. You let me worry about me being worried about you.'

'I'm not even sure that makes sense,' she said, to which he laughed.

'Almost certainly not, but at least the confusion has stopped you crying.' Reaching into his jacket pocket, Toby extracted a KitKat. 'Two fingers each?'

Kate, who had barely eaten a morsel since her birthday, shook her head.

'Oh, go on,' he urged, tearing off the wrapper. 'You don't even have to eat them – save them so you can give James a two-finger salute the next time you see him.'

'It's too soon to make jokes,' she told him, bringing her knees up to her chin and wrapping her arms around her legs.

The bedroom that had once been her own was now the guest room; her lipstick-marked posters of Take That and McFly long gone from the walls. Kate's mother, presumably in an attempt to rouse her dejected daughter's spirits, had dug out a My Little Pony duvet cover of old and brought Kate's most treasured soft toys down from the attic. Far from comforting her, however, the whole childish ensemble made her stomach knot together with dismay. She was thirty years old; this should not be the way her life had unfolded.

'I wish I'd been at your party,' Toby said regretfully. 'It's not every day your little sister turns thirty, is it? I should have said to hell with the hostel refurb and flown over. If I had,' he added, his tone hardening, 'then maybe that prat would have thought twice before deciding to break up with you on your birthday. Who does that?'

'It was my fault,' Kate said glumly. 'I'm the one who put him on the spot; I'm the one that pressured him into making a decision he might not have made otherwise. If I hadn't done that, then maybe . . .' She trailed off, knowing there was no point in continuing with the 'what ifs'.

Toby had yet to mention the video, but he must know about it. Kate suspected there was barely a human being in the UK who hadn't seen it. She glanced across at her laptop, which was on the desk where she'd left it, the lid half-closed and the red standby light flickering on and off. She had spent most of the previous evening on Twitter, watching in horror as the retweet number below the #WannabeWife #NorthLondonLoser #ProposalFail #LeftOnTheShelf post steadily increased until it was nudging the 500,000 mark. The replies varied from the sympathetic to the openly hostile, while Kate's direct message inbox – before she'd had time to remove the tag and block unsolicited attention – had received no less than 600 messages from men offering her their own hand in marriage. Kate would have been cheered by these if the majority hadn't also attached a photograph of the part of their anatomy they would like her to kiss by way of a thank you. The most hurtful responses had been the retweets with the word 'cringe' added as explanation – those were the ones that told her what the majority of people really thought. Would a video of someone publicly proposing have made such a splash if it had been a man up on that chair in the pub, she wondered? Of course it wouldn't.

Toby must have followed her gaze, because when she looked away, he said, 'I still can't believe someone did that to you. What kind of person creates click bait from someone else's heartbreak?'

'I have no idea.'

'Your friends would never do something so vile, so it must have been someone James knows,' he added. 'And as far as I'm concerned, that means it's up to him to find out who it was and make them take it down.'

Kate emitted a whimper of protest.

'Well, he should, Nims. I've a good mind to drive over there and tell him so – give him a piece of my mind while I'm at it.'

'No.' Kate looked up in alarm. 'Please don't – you might scare him away for good. There's no point anyway,' she hastened. 'The original post has been shared so many times now that it wouldn't make any difference.'

They both fell silent as the front doorbell chimed, followed by voices and the sound of feet on the stairs. Robyn had visited every single day since Kate had moved home, dedicating each of her lunch hours to checking up on her friend and trying her best to chivvy her back out into the world. When she burst into the room now, a carrier bag dangling from one hand and her car keys clutched in the other, the sight of Toby made her shriek with pleasure.

'Oh my god, Tobes – how are you? How is Croatia? You're so tanned, like a lovely boiled egg! How is married life? How long are you here? You look so well.'

Kate watched them, her best friend and her older brother, trying not to envy the easy way they slipped into an exchange of gossip and banter. This had been her just a few weeks ago, so full of optimism despite everything, so prepared to seize upon every thread of happiness – yet now her heart felt as wizened and dry as a raisin.

Her phone lit up with a message. James.

Please stop calling. You're making this harder than it needs to be.

Kate stared hard at the words, her blood turning to ice in her veins. She was now only vaguely aware of the conversation that was still ongoing between Robyn and Toby.

'She's been getting steadily worse over the past few days,' she heard her friend whisper. 'Ever since that bloody video went viral. Before that, she still seemed hopeful, you know.

But now, it's as if she's been punctured and all that makes her Kate has seeped out of her.'

There was a low hissing sound as Toby drew in a long breath.

The screen of Kate's phone faded and went black.

She had become a burden, an embarrassment – and she wanted it to stop. Ever since the video of her proposing to James had blown up all over the Internet, Kate had felt unable to leave the house. She was convinced that everyone would know; that they would point and laugh at her with scorn. And who could blame them?

'I know you can't see it now,' Toby said, 'but one day you'll realise that James isn't worth any of your tears. The way he's just given up on you – it's unforgivable. Who does that to a person they claim to love?'

'He doesn't love me,' Kate mumbled. 'Not anymore. And why would he?' she added mutinously. 'I'm a joke of a human, a failure in every possible way. I can't even hold down a minimum-wage office job. Is it really any surprise that I've ended up alone? James has just worked out what everyone else has known for years – that I am a nobody who will amount to nothing other than apparently being a national laughing stock.'

'Stop it!' Robyn held up a hand. 'You are *not* a joke or a failure.'

'Erm, I beg to differ,' Kate retorted, sitting up a fraction straighter. 'Let's go through and tick off everything I have tried and failed to do, shall we? Let's see, oh yeah, there's my seven GCSEs in grades D and lower, my barely scraped single A level in English, which has got me, oh, precisely nowhere. After a resounding reply of "thanks, but no thanks" from pretty much every university in England, Scotland and Wales – no, let me finish – I then went on to work as the following: burger flipper, checkout cashier, waitress and lollipop lady, none of which lasted more than a few months each. Then I was a dog groomer for about ten minutes, got sacked from my delivery driving job after reversing into a telegraph pole on my second day, didn't even make it through one shift as a kitchen porter and was let go from that receptionist job I took in the City because I dared to ask for Christmas Eve off.'

'But none of those jobs were right for you,' Robyn insisted. 'And at least you kept trying.'

'Trying and *failing*,' Kate replied, putting extra emphasis on the last word. 'The only thing I've ever been any good at is looking after James and now I've been sacked from that job too – and everyone on Twitter has watched it happen.'

Toby was shaking his head.

'Why don't you do what I do?' Robyn suggested brightly. 'Occupational therapy is all about caring for people – you'd be great at it.'

'She's right, you would,' put in Toby. He was smiling with encouragement, but Kate could see doubt in his eyes. Like hers, they were pale green with flecks of gold, but while her red hair was long and curly, he had shaved his back to the merest fuzz.

If only she had some skills she could trade on. James had handled all the official stuff while they were together, and Kate had accepted her comparative ineptitude in the same way everyone around her always had – by laughing at herself and shrugging it off. James would roll his eyes at her, sure, but he had always done so with affection. He didn't mind what she chose to do for work, because soon enough she would quit to be at home with their children. She knew that many would denounce this attitude as outdated or sexist, but Kate had never let it worry her. It was what she wanted and, if anything, she had felt lucky to be with a man who was eager to take on the more traditional role of provider while she completely embraced full-time mother-and-wifehood. Not once over the past eight years had she considered the possibility that James would change his mind; that he would leave her when the momentum of their relationship did not adhere to his self-imposed timeline.

'I think it might be time for a tea,' Toby, said, getting to his feet. 'Give me a hand, would you, Robyn?'

Kate looked up just in time to catch the two of them exchanging a knowing look. They would now go downstairs to her parents' kitchen and talk about her; discuss the best way to winch her free from the hole of misery she had dug herself into.

'Sure,' said Robyn. 'Oh, and these are for you,' she added to Kate, lowering the carrier bag. 'An entertaining reminder that no matter how bad your life may seem, there is always someone in a far worse situation than you.'

Kate tutted with amused disapproval as a slew of real-life magazines slithered out across the bed.

'See!' said Robyn with enthusiasm, pointing to a headline. 'My husband left me . . . for my mother's ghost. And what about this poor fella? He bought what he thought was a kitten for his girlfriend for Christmas only to realise later that it was bat.'

Toby visibly shuddered.

'That is horrific. Please stop,' he said, as Robyn flicked a second magazine open with her finger. 'Let's leave my poor sister here to wallow in the misery and misguidedness of others while we make a brew. You can fill me in on your latest dating shenanigans.'

Robyn groaned. 'That won't take long.'

Kate waited until they'd gone before snatching up her phone, reading again the curt message James had sent asking her not to call. He had been patient to begin with, willing to talk and to explain, but now it felt as if she was losing him more with each day that passed. She could not think of a single thing to write to him in reply, and that in itself scared her, the notion that two people who had been so intricately linked could suddenly become strangers. She did not want James to become someone she had once known; she wanted him to remain the person she knew best.

Irritated at herself and the situation, Kate pulled the closest magazine towards her and glanced at the cover, her eyes widening as she read the bizarre headlines. She began to leaf through the publications in a listless trance, scanning but not properly reading the articles and features within.

She must find a way to win James back – but how? How could she make him see reason if he was refusing to meet or even speak to her? Kate wanted to respect his request to leave him alone, but she also wanted him to realise how stupid it was to simply throw away everything they had built together. Telling him was not going to work – she needed to show him the error he had made, make him realise how much better his life was with her in it; teach him to miss her somehow.

Kate reached for a second magazine and opened it at random, expecting to be confronted by another story about a cheating spouse or an unusual fetish. Instead, the large black headline that greeted her read: 'Why I write letters to my brother – ten years after he disappeared.' Below it there was a photograph of a grim-faced woman in her thirties, plus another of a young, blond-haired man. His cheeks were hollow, and his eyes cast down, as if he'd been unwilling or unable to meet the gaze of whomever was behind the camera, but there was a defiance in the angle of his shoulders, a challenge in the tilt of his chin. He was broken, yes, but not yet beaten.

It was an expression that she recognised well.

Lifting the magazine a fraction higher, Kate pushed up

her glasses from where they had slid down her nose and
began to read.

*When it comes to tragedy, Angela Dawson has unfortunately had
far more than her fair share. Much more, in fact, than anyone
should have to endure in their lifetime.*

*By the age of just twenty-six, she had lost not only both her
parents, but her younger brother too – a fact that haunts the thirty-
six-year-old dental hygienist to this day.*

*'There's a finality to death that makes it difficult, but not
impossible to deal with,' she tells us, from her two-bedroom terraced
home in Aberystwyth. 'My parents dying was awful, but in many
ways, Josh disappearing was worse. I know my mum and dad
won't arrive back at my door one day; I won't spot either of their
faces in a crowd and be able to run up and greet them, but those
things could happen where Josh is concerned. I know saying "it's
the hope that kill" is a cliché, but it has become one for a reason. I
do feel as if I die a little bit more every day that I don't find him
– every moment that my brother remains lost. It's not just that I
want to know where he is and what happened to him, it's that I
have to know, in order to live.'*

*Angela asks us to stop recording while she composes herself,
which we do, taking in the photos she has of her absent brother on
every available surface of the small living room.*

*'I want him to know that I haven't forgotten him,' she explains.
'That a day does not go by where I don't think about him, wonder
how he is and how much he would have changed in the decade
since I last saw him. Take as many photos as you want,' she urges.
'I want as many people as possible to see them, just in case someone recognises him.'*

*We ask her about the police and missing person charities, but
Angela shakes her head, motioning that we should begin recording
once again.*

'A hundred and eighty thousand people are reported missing

in the UK every year,' she tells us. 'That is one every ninety seconds.'

We both pause for a moment to allow her words to sink in.

'Of those hundred and eighty thousand, fifty-one per cent are men – so, that's ninety-one thousand eight hundred men. Ninety-one thousand eight hundred hearts broken, lives shattered, and families torn apart. And I understand that Josh is just one of those, but he is my one. He was considered to be a "vulnerable person" when he disappeared,' Angela goes on with a slight tremble. 'That meant the authorities took my concerns for his welfare seriously, and through them, I discovered that he'd left the country. He took a train and then boarded a ferry to France. After that, however, the trail went cold; the limited resources available to the official channels ran dry, and the case was filed away. To the police, Josh is now a sheaf of papers, a statistic, another name amongst the list of those who disappear. I don't blame them for not finding him and I understand why they cannot allocate any more resources to the search, but it doesn't deter me. I still believe he is out there somewhere, and I am determined to find him – whatever it takes.'

As we have been talking, Angela has curled herself up into a tight ball, her shoulders hunched and her chin resting on her knees. She is fragile, yet undeniably tough, and the sorrow she feels is palpable.

Josh disappeared following a disagreement with his sister, yet Angela is reluctant to divulge any details about what was said on that terrible day. Instead, we ask her gently to tell us about the letters she writes.

'I don't post them, of course,' she says, laughing without humour. 'But I do imagine him reading them one day, when he decides to come home, and I wanted there to be a record of everything that's happened, all the things he may have missed. Sometimes the letters are nothing more than a list of what I ate that week, while others are a tirade of anger. Being cross is easier than being scared,' she explains. 'Anger is a productive emotion; grief is not.'

Asked what she would like to say to her brother exclusively through the pages of Me Time *magazine, Angela takes a piece of paper from the pocket of her cardigan and unfolds it.*

'Dear Josh,' she begins. 'It has been ten years now since you went missing, and not a single day has passed, from that one to this, when I have not looked for you. I have called every hospital, every hostel and every shelter. I have spoken to the police, to charities, to those living on the streets. I have walked the length of Aberystwyth both day and night and shown your photo to anyone willing to look.

'But despite all that, I have not found so much as a trace of you.

'I remember you, every day. I remember the baby with the pudgy arms who used to ball his fist around my hair and pull it into his mouth to chew; the gap-toothed toddler who would slip into my bed after lights out because he was scared of the witch in the wardrobe. I picture the little boy with the matching scuffed knees who rode his bike into the garden pond; the teenager with the acne who pinched the last of my crisps; the sullen youth who forgot what it was to laugh; the gaunt young man with grime under his nails and the haunted eyes of a human being who has seen too much, hurt too much, felt too much. I remember it all.

'You are still a son, still a friend, still my brother and I still love you, Josh. I do.'

The letter has a powerful effect on the atmosphere in the room, and for a few minutes, the two of us sit in silence, the only sound the clock that we can hear ticking in the kitchen, marking the time, counting all the moments that poor Angela must spend without her brother Josh.

Does she have anything else she wants to say to the readers of Me Time?

Angela nods, her eyes wet with unshed tears.

'Please, help me to find my brother,' she says. 'Help me find Josh.'

3

Kate stared at the photo of the missing man as she furiously wiped the tears off her face. It felt almost cathartic to be crying due to the pain another person was going through, as opposed to herself, but this strange relief did nothing to detract from the tragedy of the story. She tried to put herself in Angela's position, but it was impossible to imagine a world in which her brother would ever choose to run away and never see his family again. Even after he moved to Croatia with his husband Filippo, Toby called or texted daily. He had always been there for her, was here for her again now, down in the kitchen, concocting a plan to cheer her up, and Kate had not even thanked him yet.

That was the problem with family, though – it was easy to take them for granted; to assume they would love and support you unconditionally for as long as they were alive. And not just family. Kate knew that James had taken her for granted – that he most likely still did. And why would he think anything different, when she had spent every day since their break-up begging him to reconsider, telling him how much she loved him and that she would do anything he asked if he would only agree to try again.

Perhaps that was exactly where she was going wrong.

An idea began to nudge its way through her subconscious, elbowing aside the predictable barriers of uncertainty and restraint, hastily erected by the one emotion that had so often let her down in the past: fear. She must not give in to it this time. For this plan to work, Kate was going to need to be both brave and steadfast.

By the time Toby and Robyn returned, three mugs and a plate of orange Club bars on a tray between them, she had read the article through again and was full of conviction.

'You look as if you've been crying again,' observed Toby with concern.

'I was,' Kate admitted, taking a sip of her tea. 'But not about James this time, you'll both be glad to hear.'

'That man has shown his true colours,' declared Robyn, unsheathing her chocolate biscuit. 'And they are the same shit brown as this Club.'

Kate smiled but didn't laugh.

'I have a proposition for you,' she said to Toby, who was happily submerging his own half-eaten biscuit in his tea. 'It's going to sound a bit out there, but I think it's got a good shot of working.'

'OK,' he agreed, somewhat warily. 'When you say working, do you mean—?'

'Getting James to see sense, yes.'

'But I thou—' began Robyn, falling silent as Kate gave her a pleading stare.

'How would you feel about me coming to stay for a while?' she asked her brother.

'What – you mean in Croatia?'

'Well, I know you and Filippo are due to open the hostel this summer, but I also know that the place is nowhere near ready. Mum told me,' she added, as Toby grimaced in reluctant agreement. 'According to her, it will be a miracle if you open in time to make any revenue this year. I thought that if I came to stay for a bit, I could help you out. I did mine and James's place up on my own, so I know my way around a paint roller.'

Toby glanced at Robyn, who started to laugh.

'What?' demanded Kate. 'What aren't you telling me?'

'I'm not laughing at you,' Robyn assured her. 'It's just funny that you've gone and done one better on us. I was all for whisking you away on a spa break or something, and instead you've come up with this far better idea all by yourself. Some distance from James and all this nonsense with the video is exactly what you need – I'm proud of you for realising as much. Out of sight will hopefully become out of mind where he is concerned and—'

'That's not why I want to go,' Kate interrupted. Picking up the magazine, she tossed it across the bed so Robyn could see the article she had been reading.

'What – you're planning to run away?' she asked, clearly confused.

'Well, yes. But not in the way that man did. I just thought that maybe if I wasn't so, you know, available, that James might miss me. For the whole time we were together, he has known exactly where I am, who I'm with, what I'm doing – and I figured that if I took all those things away for a while, it might help him realise that he does still love me after all.'

There was a silence as Robyn and Toby considered this, each of their brows furrowed by a blend of concern and disappointment.

'Don't you think it would be better to try and get over him?' Toby said at last.

'My thoughts exactly.' Robyn screwed up her Club wrapper and lobbed it in the direction of the bin. 'Every day for the past eight years, you've been at that man's beck and call, tending to his every bloody whim. It's about time he had a taste of life with no adoring girlfriend in it – see how he likes them apples.'

Kate got up from the desk to pick the wrapper up off the floor.

'I don't want to do it as some sort of big revenge, though,' she tempered. 'I just want him to miss me for a little while. I know what I want,' she went on, as Robyn relinquished a sigh of frustration.

'I hope you don't mean that all you want is James. This could be an opportunity for you to work out what you want for yourself, not for him.'

Kate thought about saying that they amounted to the same thing, but she didn't dare.

'It would be great to have some help,' put in Toby diplomatically. 'You know me and Filippo have basic aesthetic blindness. We're at the stage now where we're choosing paint colours and furniture for the dorms – I bet you love all that pernickety stuff. Remember that dolls' house you had when we were kids? You decorated every room differently – there was an aquarium room, a farmyard room, even a SuperTed room, if I recall rightly?'

'It's honestly a brilliant idea to get away, even if I don't wholeheartedly agree with your motives for doing so,' said Robyn, who had started flicking through the stack of magazines again. 'I guess the alternative is that you sit here festering in your childhood bedroom all summer, feeling sorry for yourself and clicking the refresh button on Twitter.'

'I'm not festering, I'm hiding from widespread public ridicule.'

Toby gave her a sympathetic smile as he fished his phone out of his jeans pocket.

'I'll just call Filippo and let him know then, shall I? I'm sure there will be a free seat on my flight next week. It's still early in the season.'

'This is so exciting!' Robyn clapped her hands. 'I'm so going to come over and visit too, just as soon as I can get some time off bloody work.'

She called it 'bloody work', but Kate knew her friend was passionate about her job. She always had been, right since the age of fifteen, when she'd decided occupational therapy was what she wanted to do. At the time, Kate had pretended that she had a similar yearning to become a primary school teacher, but that could not have been further from the truth. And even if she had wanted to follow that career path, her grades had never been good enough. Where was the incentive to study if you didn't care about the outcome? It was easier to do the minimum and hope for the best, which she did, although she'd come to accept that her best was always distinctly average.

Still, it had been good enough for James, so it had been good enough for Kate.

Until it wasn't.

The truth was Kate did not want to go to Croatia simply as a ploy to win James back. There was another, deeper reason – one that she could not admit to her brother, or her best friend, or even to herself. The urge to run away, to flee the debilitating pain that had haunted her for far longer than this recent heartbreak, had been building for some time. There were too many reminders of it here, too many emotional landmines liable to blow, and Kate could not face any of it. Not yet.

Perhaps not ever.

4

Six days later . . .

Kate and Toby landed in Split late on a Sunday afternoon, the high tepid sun above the airport not the only warm welcome they received. Filippo was waiting for them in the arrivals lounge, a home-made sign bearing a large red heart clutched in his hands; he hurried forward the moment they emerged, pulling them both into an enthusiastic embrace.

'*I miei amori*,' he gushed, covering Kate's face with kisses before turning to his husband.

'Soppy gits,' Kate remarked, as the two men rubbed noses affectionately. 'Remind me what the Italian for "get a room" is again?'

'This one.' Filippo looped a long slim arm through Kate's, almost toppling her gigantic suitcase in the process. 'Still funny.'

'She's putting on a brave face,' Toby told him. 'Don't be fooled. What she needs from us is TLC – and lots of it.'

'Oh, *povera bambina*,' Filippo crooned. 'Toby told me all about what happened. James is an *idiota*.'

'At least that's one I don't need translating.'

'Come along.' Filippo was drawing Kate away now. 'We will make everything better. Wait until you see the new place, it will make doves flutter inside your heart.'

'My husband is nothing if not poetic,' drawled Toby, who was following them with both sets of luggage.

'Tobe showed me some pictures on the flight,' Kate began, but Filippo was shaking his smooth, dark head.

'Pictures,' he repeated disdainfully, flicking his hand dismissively as he weaved them through a sea of tourists, airport staff and waiting taxi drivers. 'This is your first time in Croatia, *si*?'

Kate nodded.

'Then very soon, you will have a new love in your life. All thoughts of James will be forgotten when you see the clear waters, feel the sun on your face, hear the birds singing in the morning as the church bells ring out across the harbour.'

With each proclamation, he tossed a flamboyant hand out to the side, narrowly missing anyone foolish enough to get too close. They were nearing the exit now, and Kate could see palm fronds set against a sky of the deepest blue. Toby had described Croatia as being 'the best of Italy, Greece, Spain and Eastern Europe all rolled into one', but until she had looked at a map a few weeks ago, Kate had not even been sure exactly where the country was located. She'd never paid much attention in geography lessons at school.

Filippo's rhapsodic praise of the place continued as they walked across the car park, and he barely paused for breath when they reached the jeep and loaded up their bags. After finally letting go of Kate so she could clamber into the passenger seat, he declared her to be '*minuscola*' and switched the subject to dinner instead.

'I hope you like fish,' he said, leaning on the horn as two bewildered-looking old ladies wandered across the road in front of them. Toby, who was laughing in the back seat, chided his husband for being so impatient.

'This is how Italians drive,' he explained to Kate, as Filippo took the second corner so fast that she was flung sideways over the gearstick. 'The first time I ever got in a car with him, I thought it was the end of me.'

Filippo tutted good-naturedly. 'You British are too polite,' he said, mounting a kerb in order to overtake two taxis. 'If you want something in life, push to the front of the queue to get it; if you want to get somewhere quickly, put your foot on the gas.'

'If you want to not be punched on the nose or end up in a ditch, ignore Filippo,' intoned Toby, to a cry of bemused outrage from his husband.

Kate had always admired the dynamic of their relationship, with its teasing and playful banter. Toby was more subdued than his spirited other half, but it was precisely this difference that balanced the two of them out so well. Filippo adored her brother, while Toby loved him back with a fierce passion that felt to Kate all the more powerful because of how rarely she glimpsed it. There was nothing showy about their feelings; they were both secure and mutually besotted, so there was no need to prove anything to the world. Kate had thought she had the same thing with James, that when he told her how much he loved her, he had meant it. Could she really have got it so wrong?

They were hurtling towards the port now, where they would catch a ferry over to Hvar, but Kate barely registered the scenery that was flashing past. Taking out her phone, she switched on her roaming and opened Facebook. Seventy-five people had liked her 'check-in' at Gatwick Airport, sixteen of whom had left comments asking where she was off to and how long she would be away. Kate scanned them all, her pulse accelerating as she searched for James's name. But there was no sign. Either he hadn't seen her update, or he did not care enough to comment. Kate felt the disappointment run like a lance through her chest. She had been convinced her plan would work and that he would be unable to resist getting in touch to find out where she'd gone.

To be sure, she checked all her other messenger apps and platforms, but there was nothing from James. Tears began to threaten, and Kate blinked them furiously away, angry with herself for being so weak, only to veer from that to sudden hope as a text message arrived.

It was from a local mobile network, welcoming her to Croatia.

'Bloody hell!' she grumbled, coinciding her curse words with a particularly hair-raising example of overtaking by Filippo.

'That is the spirit!' he replied happily, tooting the horn with appreciation.

Kate was vaguely aware that her brother was providing an ongoing commentary from the back seat of the jeep, telling her about Split's Roman harbour and the ancient emperor's palace that provided the old town with its intriguing layout of covered lanes and narrow courtyards. It was interesting, but Kate could not work up the required enthusiasm to listen properly. Her mind was solely on James, on the absence of any message, of the big gaping hole that had opened up inside her.

They weren't far from the ferry port now, and Toby had switched from the subject of medieval architecture to calcium carbonate, which he was now earnestly explaining was the elemental magic they had to thank for Croatia's famously blue-green waters.

'You'll see what I mean once we're on the boat,' he went on, pointing through the windscreen. 'Not far now.'

It wasn't until they had driven aboard, parked up, and were standing side by side along the vast car ferry's outer railings that Kate's frantically beating heart began to slow. She had felt trapped inside the jeep, her anxiety filling the small space to such a suffocating degree that she had eventually sat on her hands, unable to trust herself not to fling open the door and leap out onto the tarmac. As the ferry's vast engine shook the boards beneath their feet and salty spray found its way from the sea into the air around them, Kate gazed back towards the city they had just left behind and took it in properly for the first time.

A scatter of white-stone buildings decorated a shoreline dressed up by tall palms, the red rooftops above a punchy hit of colour against the cobalt sweep of the sky. Low-lying clouds were tossed like torn cotton wool across the horizon, while mountains lay further still, as silent and imposing as sleeping lions.

It would be so easy to slip away into one of those labyrinthine streets and lose herself; or set sail and moor up on a distant island – one uninhabited by people or industry; a place where nobody would come looking, where there was nothing on which to snag her fragile emotions. But then, just as rapidly, thoughts of the life she had left behind overtook her.

She must not allow herself to forget the reason why she had come here. The summer stretched out in front of her like an enormous chessboard, and by flying to Croatia, she had moved her first pawn into position. No matter how James responded, or how many strategic moves he made, Kate had to believe that she was capable of taking back her king.

5

Toby and Filippo had named their first business venture Sul Tetto, which was Italian for 'up on the roof', and when Kate was led out onto the hostel's large roof terrace by her proud brother, she immediately understood why. Hvar Town, in all its higgledy-piggledy beauty, tumbled down the hillside towards a sea turned molten gold by the steadily setting sun. Kate gazed out, speechless with awe, and watched as a light evening breeze carried a flock of birds west towards distant clusters of land.

'Those are the Pakleni Islands,' Toby told her, smiling as she continued to gape. 'Well worth a visit for the beaches and restaurants, or to wander off the beaten track for a bit.'

'I can't believe this is where you live now,' said Kate. 'I know you sent photos, but I must not have been paying proper attention. I had no idea Croatia was this . . . well, look at it.'

'I know.' Toby put an arm around her shoulders. 'I fell in love with this place as soon as I set eyes on it.'

'The same as he did with me,' drawled Filippo, who had just appeared behind them carrying a bottle and three small glasses.

'Not for me, thanks,' said Kate, as he eased out the cork. 'Alcohol will only make me maudlin.'

'Nonsense.' Filippo handed her a small glass that he had filled to the brim with the amber liquid. 'It is a Balkan tradition to toast a new guest with *rakija*.'

'What is *rakija*?' she asked nervously, bringing it up to her nose for a sniff and promptly recoiling.

'Grape juice,' put in Toby pragmatically, tapping his own glass against hers. 'Come on, Nims – one shot won't kill you.'

'Fine.' Kate steeled herself. 'But I am doing this purely for you two.'

'One, two, three – *živjeli*!' the men chorused, and before she had time to demur further, Kate swallowed the lot.

The *rakija* burned, but she found the sensation oddly galvanising. It was as if someone had fed her an elixir of courage; she felt switched on – awake suddenly for the first time in more than a fortnight.

'Shall we have another?' asked Filippo, and Kate nodded just as Toby shook his head.

'You're sure?' he checked. 'All right then, if you say so.'

The second shot lifted Kate's spirits even higher and she emitted a small 'whoop' as the fiery liquid dribbled through her insides. Having eaten nothing but a limp croissant all day, she knew there would be no barrier between the alcohol and her bloodstream – but Kate didn't care. She wanted to feel reckless, to be reckless. When she took her phone out of her bag and asked for the hostel's Wi-Fi password, however, Toby pulled a face.

'Later,' he said. 'First, I want to give you the tour.'

They left Filippo grilling whole fresh sea bream on the built-in rooftop barbecue and made their way back down the outer stairs. Toby had insisted that they go straight to the terrace when they arrived, because it was the only part of the hostel they had finished, so Kate had yet to see inside. Like many of the buildings she had glimpsed during their journey from the airport, the hostel was a large stone townhouse. But unlike the detached properties on either side, this one had been converted for purpose, with the ground floor consisting of an open-plan reception area complete with small lift.

'We're one of the only hostels in Hvar to have disabled access,' Toby explained, as he pushed open a door that was peeling paint and led her into an enclosed stairway. The first floor housed the largest of Sul Tetto's six dormitories, plus a kitchen and lounge area that contained little more than piles of rubble and beams of wood.

'Now you see what Mum meant when she told you we were running a bit behind schedule,' Toby said, pushing his foot through the dust only to begin coughing in earnest.

'There are two female dorms, two mixed and two for the boys,' he explained, opening another door on the next floor up and revealing partially constructed bunk beds and a newly installed basin unit below a filthy mirror.

'It's . . . great,' Kate offered lamely. 'I mean, I can see the potential. How long have you got until you open again?'

'Oh, we hope to be ready in a few weeks,' Toby said airily. 'Plenty of time to get everything done.'

Kate pictured neat patterned curtains fixed to bunks, hidden shelves for guests to store their valuables and individual lights for bedtime reading. There was an air-conditioning unit trailing wires in a top corner, but how much better it would be to have a large ceiling fan in here. She wondered how much Toby and Filippo had already planned, and how nice the three of them could get these rooms looking with just a little time and effort.

'Did you mean it when you said you wanted my advice on colour schemes and stuff?' she asked, pausing to catch her breath as they reached the third floor.

'Of course I did. I told you, Nims, this isn't simply a pity party. We need you.'

There was one final dorm room on this level, plus a handful of private bedrooms – one of which Toby proclaimed was for her.

'Where do you and Filippo sleep?' she asked, taking in the pale green walls, clean white sheets pulled taut across a double bed and a wardrobe that she could tell had been purpose-built.

'We have a small apartment over the road. You don't mind staying here, do you?' he checked. 'I would offer you the sofa at ours, but Filippo has started sleepwalking lately – I think due to the stress of getting this place finished – and he prefers to sleep na—'

'Yes, yes – I get it.' Kate raised a hand. 'Say no more. And I really like this room, so don't worry.'

'You do?' Toby sounded proud.

'Yes. I mean, you've made a good start on it. A few finishing touches might be nice, though, to make it a bit more homely.'

'Finishing touches?'

'Some art on the walls, a few plants, maybe? A selection of complimentary toiletries in the bathroom.'

'It's a hostel, not a hotel.'

Kate felt herself deflate.

'Did you make this?' she asked, running an admiring hand across the wardrobe doors.

Toby laughed. 'Yeah, that was me. The man who can't even build a sandcastle. No, our local carpenter did it,' he told her. 'I say carpenter, but he's a decorator as well. And a pretty good fisherman. He also put a new clutch in the jeep last month, which saved us a fortune.'

'Is he on the payroll, this multi-talented individual?' Kate asked, opening the door of the bathroom cabinet and peering inside. 'It looks to me as if you still have rather a lot of bunk beds to build.'

'You're not wrong,' Toby agreed, ushering her out into the stairwell before shouldering ajar the door that led through to the terrace. A delicious aroma of grilled fish wafted out.

'Alex is away at the moment, but he'll no doubt be back soon.'

'You don't sound very sure,' said Kate, recalling the time she and James had booked a local 'friend of a friend' gardener to come and dig their flowerbeds, only for him to continually cancel for the best part of three months. In the end, Kate had borrowed a pitchfork and trowel off the neighbours and done the job herself.

'Alex is a casual sort of bloke,' Toby told her with a shrug, as they followed their noses across the rooftop. 'He'll show up and do a few days' hard graft, then he vanishes for a while.'

'Just like that?' Kate frowned.

'He is a man of mystery,' explained Filippo, passing Kate a plate piled high with fresh tomato salad. 'He was here only yesterday, finishing the bedroom for you, so my guess is that he will not return for another week – perhaps longer.'

'Doesn't that frustrate you?' she asked.

'That is just his way,' Filippo said, busying himself with filleting the sea bream. 'We do not argue because he is the best. We prefer to give him the work if we can; he's a good man.'

'He had better be a bona fide miracle worker,' Kate told them. 'Otherwise, there's no way you'll have this place ready to open in a mere few weeks' time.'

'Ye of little faith,' tempered Toby, conjuring up some cutlery from a pot beside the barbecue as Filippo began to top up their shot glasses for the third time. 'Don't you start stressing about it on top of all your other woes – if Alex says he'll get the work done in time, then he will.'

Kate must have allowed her incredulity to show on her face, because her brother rolled his eyes as he raised a toast.

'To Alex the carpenter,' he said, looking directly across at her. 'The most trustworthy man I have ever met.'

6

It was long after midnight when Toby and Filippo finally began to make noises about heading off to bed. Kate could tell her brother was against the idea of leaving her alone and it took some earnest convincing on her part to shoo him away. How many times could a person claim to be fine inside a single half hour? Kate may easily have set a new world record.

The truth, which she would not so much as contemplate telling him, was that she wanted more than anything to have some time by herself. More than wanting it, she needed it. Thanks to the combined efforts of Toby, her parents and Robyn, Kate had spent the majority of her time since that fateful night in the pub being looked after by one or all of them, and as much as she appreciated their efforts, she was also fatigued – tired of being strong, tired of making jokes, tired of holding back the truth.

Kate ventured back downstairs to her room at the same time as Toby and Filippo departed for the night, but she had no intention of going straight to sleep. Having finally persuaded Toby to give her the Wi-Fi password, Kate immediately opened Twitter and checked on the status of #WannabeWife, discovering that in the space of just a few hours, the retweets were up by several thousand. She had yet to discover who it was who had posted the original clip of her proposing but had believed James when he denied all knowledge. Kate had called him as soon as she'd seen the video, near hysterical with mortification, and he had sounded genuinely angry on her behalf.

Rubbing her eyes, she went through the now-familiar routine of checking all her ex-boyfriend's social media accounts followed by his WhatsApp, so she could see what time he had last been online. It had been recently, she noted. Who had he been messaging long after his usual lights-out time of eleven p.m.? She watched the grey line of text below his name, willing it to turn blue and switch to the word 'online'. It comforted her to see it, made her feel connected to him somehow, even if the two of them weren't exchanging messages anymore. She was gratified to find that his profile picture was still the same one, taken by her in Athens the previous September, of James holding up an ice cream, the Acropolis rising grandly out of the dust behind him.

Again, she was struck by how unfair this situation was, and how wrong. How could they have shared that moment – all those moments of such joy and hope – only to have them amount to nothing? How could he have thrown away everything they'd shared? Kate felt the pain of that loss again, as she did every time she thought about him, and forced herself to stop and breathe deeply

It would not do to sit and dwell – there were too many thoughts clamouring for attention in her head and too much throat-crushing anxiety coursing through her body. To lie down in the dark now would allow all the things that lurked in the shadows to take hold, and she was not sure if she had the energy to fight them, not after so many days of pretence. Instead, she fetched a cardigan from her suitcase, swapped her flip-flops for slippers and headed back up to the roof.

There had been so much to take in since she arrived in Croatia – new sights, new scents, new faces, a new home for however long she decided to stay – that the day felt to Kate as if it had passed by in a blur. Here she was in a different country to the one she had woken up in that morning, yet the sense of being so far away from her everyday life was yet to register fully. She had not given it the space to do so, but now she knew she must try.

The rough stone wall on the far side of the terrace felt warm under Kate's fingers and she pressed her palms flat against it. Faint sounds of chatter were drifting up from the town and the lights from the larger yachts moored down in the harbour were reflected in the water, each one dazzling every bit as brightly as the stars far above. The elements were all in place to soothe her, but Kate could feel agitation knocking from inside her chest, demanding attention from her embattled heart.

Of course, it wasn't just the humiliation with James, and his hostility. There was also the secret she'd been guarding for months now – a truth that she had only shared with James. She hoped he would honour his promise not to mention anything about it to anyone they knew. If he had ever loved her at all, then surely he would do the decent thing.

Kate had been staring at the harbour lights for so long that spots of colour were floating behind her eyes. Tilting her head, she squinted out across the dark expanse of water, over to where the Pakleni Islands rose like slumbering sea beasts from the gloom. Toby had explained that there were beach clubs on some of them, and Kate thought she could just about see signs of life on a few distant shores. Straining her ears, she listened for the thump of bass coming out from a speaker, or the shrill cry of a sozzled group of friends stumbling home from a bar – but there was nothing now. All she could hear was the dancing wind; the whisper of the waves as they kissed the shore.

Loneliness gripped her then, taking hold of her so fast and with such potency that Kate took a few steps backwards, her hands clutching her chest. It felt as if the enormity of everything that had happened was suddenly consuming her, rising like bindweed to choke her resolve. Turning, she slid steadily down into a sitting position, her back pressed against the wall and her head resting on her knees. She tried to focus on the floor below, but her breath was becoming shallow, small gasps in place of measured gulps.

Acknowledging the fact that she could not breathe did nothing to steady her frantically racing heart, and Kate rolled her head back, her eyes darting in desperation for something steady and unmoving, a fixed point upon which she could anchor her fear.

I don't want to be alone. I don't want it to be just me.

She could feel the tears streaming down her cheeks but could not unclasp her fingers to wipe them away. A bright star burned high above her, a constant and beautiful sight, and Kate forced herself to focus on it as she tried to steady her breathing.

In and out, in and out.

It was in this position that she remained, marooned in the darkness and motionless save for the slow rise and fall of her chest, until weariness finally took over, pushing aside her misery long enough for a shellshocked Kate to regain some control, stagger to her feet and wrap her arms around her shoulders, her teeth chattering as the useless adrenalin drained away.

This was the real her, a black biro scribble beneath colourful layers of crayon, the sad face below the painted grin she showed the rest of the world. The truth amidst all the lies.

Far from leaving it behind in England, all she had done by coming here was to make herself feel worse.

But she must not let this sadness consume her. She must repeat the pattern she had followed all her life and soldier on regardless.

Avoid conflict, avoid sorrow, avoid confronting the truth.

Pretending was all Kate knew how to do.

7

Any residual anxiety lingering within Kate was eradicated as soon as she stepped outside the following morning. The low breeze that greeted her felt warm against her skin, and she paused to let it chase around her legs like a child, her face lifted towards a sun turned milky white by clouds.

She had dressed simply, in functional cotton shorts and a honey-coloured vest that James always said brought out her eyes, with her long russet curls tied back. Warned by her brother that the temperature in Hvar was climbing by the day and that the sunshine, whilst obviously welcome, was a fiery opponent to the fair and freckled complexions of the Nimble family, she had covered her exposed skin in sun lotion and brought along her straw hat.

Yesterday's drive from the ferry port to the hostel had afforded her a glimpse of a town that was arranged on the hillside like a marble run, its upward-snaking roads interconnected by a series of steps and narrow alleyways. Kate suspected that there were a hundred different trails she could take to the harbour, but she did not want to wander with her head buried in a map. After all, the sea was visible from where she was standing, so all she really had to do was continue to head downhill.

Setting off along a street strewn with fallen pine needles, she passed the open door of a tiny bakery and turned left, following a sloping stone path that ran alongside a house with shells set into its outer walls. Kate felt her rigid shoulders slacken as she took in each beautiful detail. Ducking under the overhanging branches of a pomegranate tree heavy with ripening fruit, she almost tripped over a black cat that was washing itself on a step.

'You could have warned me,' she chided it a few moments later, when she found herself confronted by a collapsed wall and had to hop over the fallen bricks in order to keep the craggy shoreline in sight. Even at this early hour, the hum of the crickets was shrill and intense, and Kate was surprised not to see clusters of them converging together on every surrounding surface. Squinting into the distance, she saw that the same wind which was blowing jacaranda petals across her sandalled feet was also agitating the surface of the sea below, turning its mirror-like flatness into dappled glass.

Perhaps she should have waited for Toby and Filippo to emerge before venturing out on a solo exploration? Her brother had told her the previous evening that the two of them tended not to get up until mid-morning most days, preferring to indulge in a long, leisurely breakfast before working at the hostel right through lunch and into the early evening, so Kate did not think they would be surprised by her absence. But maybe they would have wanted the opportunity to show her around themselves?

Feeling frustrated, she came to a stop on the path, dithering as she so often seemed to over a seemingly easy decision. It had felt simple when she awoke that morning – she had wanted to go for a walk, and so she did – but now she was riddled by uncertainty. Robyn would tell her to please herself, while James would think her actions impolite. He would point out that Toby was her host, and therefore she should look to him for instruction, just as she looked to James for his when they were at home.

Grumbling audibly, Kate retraced her steps and climbed back over the toppled wall, making it as far as the cat that was still busy washing itself before her indecision halted her once again. Perhaps she ought to just keep going?

'What the hell is the matter with me?' She sighed, sitting down beside the small black moggy. 'Why am I so bloody useless at being a human, eh?'

The cat paused mid-lick and gazed at her through narrow yellow eyes.

'You're quite right,' Kate told it. 'I do deserve nothing but disdain.'

The cat lowered an outstretched paw and showed her a neat set of claws. Either it was offering to shake her hand or wanted to scratch her face off. Kate shuffled away, figuring it was better not to find out which, and heard her phone vibrate inside her bag.

It was Toby, suggesting they meet for breakfast at a place that she discovered, once clicking on the link he had attached to the message, was less than ten minutes away.

'I would have made a decision eventually,' she told the cat as she stood to go. 'Honest.'

There was nobody at the waterside café when she arrived save for a young waitress, who smiled in greeting before showing her to a table that overlooked the harbour. Toby arrived less than five minutes later, announcing himself with a loud 'boo' that frightened several gulls into flight.

'Are you trying to give me even more grey hairs?' she scolded, as her chuckling brother eased himself into the seat opposite hers.

'Sorry,' Toby said, sounding anything but. 'I couldn't resist.'

Kate continued to berate him good-naturedly as he motioned to the waitress to bring menus, her foot tapping away on the ground beneath the chair while they ordered. Breakfast was a simple ham and cheese omelette washed down with fresh orange juice and a rich, deliciously bitter espresso. As she broke off bits of leftover bread from the basket and tossed them out for the birds, Kate's attention was snagged by a shaft of sunlight that had broken through the clouds, falling like an open sail across the white-stone buildings in the distance.

'Not a bad place to stop for a bite to eat, eh?' said Toby. 'This is where the majority of the smaller boats are moored, those used for fishing or rented out to tourists intrepid enough to venture out onto the water without a guide. The main port, where the passenger ferries stop and most of the taxi boats leave from is a short walk away, along the coastal path.'

'I see,' she said, soothed by a full stomach and the gentle lapping of the waves. 'You're up earlier than I thought you'd be,' she added, smiling as Toby yawned in reply.

'Big day today,' he said. 'Got to get the catamaran over to Split to pick up some bits for the hostel.'

'Oh? You never said.'

'It was a last-minute decision,' he said. 'There's a particular shade of powder-blue paint that my husband has set his heart on for the laundry room and it's only available in Split. And, as we have to go anyway, Filippo and I thought we'd make a day of it, see some of our friends for lunch.'

'Sounds nice.'

Kate waited expectantly for her invite to follow.

'I would say come with us,' Toby continued, 'but I doubt there'll be room in the jeep, not with all the stuff we need to pick up. It's not just the paint, we're collecting a whole load of flatpack tables and chairs for the terrace.'

'It's OK,' Kate said, feigning nonchalance as she extracted her phone from her bag. 'I'm sure I can find something to do in your absence.'

'That's why I'm here.' Toby's tone had switched from sleepy to resolute. 'Staring at this all day,' he said, taking the mobile from her and holding it up, 'is not doing you any good.'

'Hey!' Kate made a grab for it and missed.

'I was thinking that maybe I could keep hold of it?' he said. 'Just for today, so you can't keep checking it. This phone has become a ball and chain, dragging you back to London every ten minutes. You need a break from it.'

'No, I don't.' Kate's fingers were inching involuntarily along the table.

'Just for today,' Toby persisted. 'I told you when we came out here that I would support you, so please let me try. I want you to be happy, sis – happier than you are right now. I do see you, you know. I can tell you're only pretending to be OK.'

Kate said nothing.

Toby's second coffee had arrived, and he put down the phone in order to open a sachet of sugar. Knowing this was her opportunity to snatch it back, Kate was surprised to find that she didn't take it.

'OK,' she told him. 'You can take it – but I want you to know that I'm only agreeing to this under duress. I'm doing this purely for you, and I want it back this evening.'

Toby nodded. 'I have the perfect idea of what you can do today to take your mind off things,' he said.

'Oh?'

'I think you should head over there to the beach at Jerolim,' he said. 'It's mine and Filippo's favourite spot in the Pakleni Islands and it's less than ten minutes away by taxi boat.'

Kate stared out towards the direction he was pointing, watching as gulls dived into the shallows in search of scraps.

'The beach there is truly captivating,' Toby went on. 'I honestly think it will help to distract you from this' – he held up Kate's phone again – 'and everything else, for that matter.'

'OK,' Kate agreed, although not without misgivings. His enthusiasm was making her suspicious. 'I'll go if you can tell me what's so special about it?'

Toby took another sip of his coffee and grinned. 'You'll see,' he said.

8

It only took the taxi boat ten minutes to reach Jerolim, but that turned out to be more than enough time to lift Kate's spirits. She had taken off her straw hat to stop it blowing away, and her long red hair rippled out behind her, twisting, curling and whipping across her cheeks as she turned to stare back at the diminishing harbour.

Despite the fact that it was still relatively early in the season, every space on the wooden bench seat inside the boat was taken, while the floor played host to a mess of beach umbrellas, picnic baskets and snorkelling equipment. They were sitting low enough for Kate to reach over the side and trail her fingers through the clear water. It was so blue that she half-expected her hand to re-emerge stained, as if by paint, and felt her mouth tug upwards into a smile.

Having been first on board, she was the last to disembark, and took her time clambering carefully out onto the wide stone jetty. The island had the same craggy shoreline as its larger cousin across the water, but the surrounding trees were more unkempt here than in Hvar. Kate crunched her way over flat white pebbles towards a rustic wooden sign painted with the words 'Welcome to Jerolim'. It appeared to mark the start of a pathway, which she followed through the undergrowth.

It was impossible to hear anything except the collective hum of the crickets. They sounded to Kate as if a thousand tiny pneumatic drills had been switched on all at once. The little insects were always so busy, so insistent, yet she had grown accustomed to them so quickly. When you closed your eyes and listened in London, it was the heavy drone of traffic that filtered through first, while over here it seemed to be the birds, or the wind, or the water.

The scent of pine was rich in the air, the ground below her feet softened by fallen needles and patterned with droplets of sunlight. Kate reached instinctively for her phone to take a photo, only to remember that Toby had it. Why on earth had she agreed to that?

Distracted by her muddled thoughts, she had not been paying proper attention to where the path was heading, but now she glanced up to find that she had made it to the island's beach bar – a small, single-storey building the colour of baked fudge.

Tables and chairs that had been fashioned from fallen trunks and stumps spread from the edge of the trail into the treeline beyond, while to the right was a shallow cove fringed with more sugar-lump stones. As she gazed around now, Kate could understand what her brother had meant about Jerolim being special. But more than that, there was an unspoilt charm to every part of Croatia that she had seen so far; the beauty here felt less contrived than it did in the more traditional resorts in Spain and the Canary Islands, where she and James had holidayed together in the past. James preferred to book an all-inclusive, so he could take advantage of a bottomless bar and buffet, whereas Kate had always secretly wished he would suggest they rent an apartment instead, somewhere with a kitchen so she could cook for him on the nights they chose not to dine out. But she had never said anything. James worked hard – far harder than she ever had – so it was only fair that he got to enjoy his leisure time as he saw fit.

Digging twenty *kunas* out of her purse, Kate went to the open hatch of the bar and bought herself a bottle of water. There weren't many customers around, save for one elderly man who was sucking an iced coffee up through a paper straw, but instead of sitting down at one of the tables, she decided to give in to the lure of the sea.

At first, as she made her delicate way over the smooth pale stones in search of a place to lay down her towel, everything about the beach seemed normal. There were children splashing away happily in the water, a dog panting in the shade of upturned fishing boat and the usual battalion of colourful parasols. It was only as Kate stumbled, her foot slipping sideways out of her sandal, that she spotted the first uncovered bottom.

The first uncovered *male* bottom.

'Oh, I'm so sorry.' Kate assumed she had caught the man changing, but he merely frowned at her, seemingly nonplussed.

It couldn't be? Could it?

Coming to a standstill, she glanced first left, then right, the truth becoming ever more apparent with every naked breast, bum, exposed bush and . . . All the blood drained from Kate's face. She didn't know whether to scream or laugh. What was it that Toby had said? That Jerolim was captivating.

CAPTIVATING?

She was going to kill him. As if he had sent her off unawares to a nudist beach! What kind of brother – or indeed human – did that to a person? Kate wanted to close her eyes to it all, but she could not seem to stop seeing all the bodies, all the flesh, all the dangling bits and pieces. Turning to flee, she stared straight down at a man who had just raised both his knees and watched in horror as his testicles slipped down into the gap between his thighs.

No, death was too good for Toby. She would have to think of something worse.

A woman was heading down to the water now, her sunburnt bottom as red and shiny as a snooker ball, while a

young lithe couple played a game of bat and ball nearby, her
boobs and his penis bouncing about all over the place.

Kate was not a prude, but she had never even sunbathed
topless before, let alone starkers. This was not the place for
her – a fact that bloody Toby would have known only too
well.

In her hurry to retreat to the relative safety of the beach
bar, Kate almost tumbled over on the stones for a second
time only to be caught mid-fall by a man who had just
emerged, dripping wet, from the sea.

'Steady there,' he said, propping her back onto her feet.
'Are you OK?'

'No. I mean, yes.' Kate hooked a finger into her sandal and
pulled it back over her heel.

The man let go of the arm he had grabbed. He wasn't
much taller than her, Kate realised, as she took in a mass
of dark-blond dreadlocks and a long, matted beard. Their
eyes were almost on a level, his the palest ice-blue and so
direct that she felt suddenly unnerved. Dropping her gaze
instinctively downwards, Kate was confronted by broad,
tanned shoulders, a sodden forest of chest hair and deep,
sharp grooves that ran from above his hips down towards
his—

'Oh Jesus,' she said, clapping a hand over her face.

'I get that a lot, what with the facial hair,' he said evenly.

She hadn't seen it. She hadn't. All she had seen was a dark
mass of pubic hair and a flash of pale pink – nothing else.

Kate opened her fingers and peered through the gap.

'I didn't see anything,' she squeaked. 'I didn't – I wasn't'

The man folded his arms. They were thick and solid and
covered in bleached blond hairs.

'Doesn't bother me,' he said.

'Clearly,' she replied, her voice at least six octaves higher
than usual.

'This *is* a nudist beach,' he said, sounding more amused than confused. 'Being naked is kind of the whole point.'

'Yes, I see that.'

Kate wondered if her voice would ever return from that of a tightly corseted mouse to normal adult woman.

'You're not a nudist,' he surmised. He was clearly British-born, that much was clear from his voice, but Kate thought she could detect a slight lilt to his accent.

'So,' he went on, 'I have to ask – why did you come to this beach?'

He was definitely trying his best not to laugh at her. Kate realised then how foolish she must look, standing here with her hand planted over her face, and lowered it gingerly, keeping her eyes determinedly on a point just below his nose.

'My brother,' she muttered, as the corners of the man's mouth twitched. 'He sent me here, told me it would cheer me up. I am going to put earwigs in his shoes as punishment.'

'Brutal,' he said. He had unfolded his arms now but made no move to locate a towel or cover his lower half. 'Earwigs have a nasty bite.'

'Good,' Kate declared. 'I'm going to need plenty of them. Honestly, though – my brother is such a dick.'

At the mention of the word, Kate was suddenly compelled to glance down again, and this time she did not manage to stop herself. The man with the dreadlocks did not so much as shift position. He must have seen her looking – he must, even now, be watching her staring at it – at him. She had to stop. Why couldn't she stop? Oh, hell.

STOP. LOOKING. AT. IT.

'I should go,' she said, finally tearing her eyes away. Kate could feel the heat flooding into her cheeks as the realisation of what she had just seen dawned. She needed to get out of here – and fast.

'Do you want to—' the man started to say, but Kate did not hang around to hear the rest. She was already scrabbling away, half-running, half-tripping over the stones in her haste to escape from him, from this beach, from her own mortification.

Her only comfort, as she hurried back onto the taxi boat twenty minutes later, was that Hvar was a relatively large and busy island. The chances of her ever bumping into the man again were slim, if not non-existent. Life had been unkind enough to her recently, so perhaps on this occasion it would let her off the hook?

She really, *really* hoped so.

9

The hammering woke Kate long before her alarm went off.

Dragged abruptly from a dream where she was being pursued by a yeti wearing James's bright white trainers, Kate sat up so fast that the room started to spin and she had to clutch both hands to her head in an effort to steady it.

What the hell was going on?

Another flurry of bangs echoed up through the floorboards.

Kate groped for her phone. The screen was so bright that it made her eyes water and she had to squint to make out a text from Toby.

Good news. Just heard from Alex – he'll be here in the morning to build bunks.

There was a crash from downstairs, followed by whistling.

Kate flopped back down against the pillows with a groan. Her brother had sent the message in the early hours – hopefully up late tending to all his bruises. Kate had waited on the roof terrace for him and Filippo to return from their day trip to Split, a bag of ice cubes torn open ready to throw at him. Toby, who had smirked with all the contrition of the Cheshire Cat, merely responded with an unrepentant 'you're welcome' before ducking behind his husband to hide. When she had later filled the two men in on her eventful morning – including the part about the naked man she had encountered – her brother had clapped his hands together in delight.

'Retribution will be mine,' she had warned him, before adding, 'Now give me my phone.'

There had been no messages waiting for her from James. Kate was beginning to think that her plan to disappear from England was not having the desired effect, although she had only been gone a couple of days. Surely after a week had passed, he would begin to wonder why she hadn't been in touch?

A drill whirred into noisy life below her and Kate clenched her jaw in irritation. It was five a.m. – what kind of tradesman showed up to start work this early? This Alex bloke wasn't exactly conventional though, not if what Toby and Filippo had told her was true. Perhaps in his weird world, it made perfect sense to fire up the power tools when most people were still sleeping?

Too tired and discombobulated to bother brushing her hair or putting anything on over the shorts and vest she slept in, save for an old hoodie of James's, Kate put on her glasses, dragged herself out of bed and went downstairs, thinking that now she was up, she may as well do the polite thing and offer the hostel's resident carpenter a tea or coffee, even if he was to blame for waking her up.

'Knock, knock,' she called out, pushing open the door to one of the mixed dormitories and walking straight into a cloud of sawdust. There was a man crouched on the floor facing away from her, his face obscured by some sort of plastic mask and his hair – no, his dreadlocks – twisted up in a man-bun.

Kate emitted a small 'oh' of horror, but before she could turn and flee, the drilling stopped and the man sat back on his haunches, removing his protective visor before turning to look at her. If he was surprised to see the strange woman that had barrelled into him on the nudist beach standing agog in the doorway, then he hid it well.

'Hello there.'

'Hi.' Kate pulled her hoodie down over her shorts. 'You must be Alex,' she stuttered. 'I'm Kate. I'm Toby's sister.'

'Is that the same Toby with the sore feet?' he replied, to which Kate could only gawp with incomprehension. 'On account of all the earwig bites,' he added.

'Oh. Yes. I see what you mean.'

Kate laughed a bit too loudly and clasped the door with both hands.

'I thought for a minute there you hadn't recognised me,' he added, brushing sawdust off his arms and standing up. 'You know, what with my clothes on and all.'

'I didn't see anything,' she stated shrilly. Then, noticing the same bemusement creep across his features as had in Jerolim, said hurriedly, 'I was in bed. I mean, I was asleep. The banging – you woke me up.'

'I did?' Alex cocked his head, one hand raised to stroke his beard. 'Sorry about that. Toby said his sister was here, like, but I assumed you'd be over the road.'

'Did you?' she said. 'Only, I thought it was you who finished the bedroom upstairs for me?'

'Right you are,' he agreed with a nod.

'I was just about to put the kettle on,' Kate said faintly.

Why was she was still gripping the door as if she was Kate Winslet at the end of Titanic?

'A tea would be magic,' he said, pulling his visor back down over his face. 'Milk, four sugars.'

'Four?'

'Afraid so.' Alex revved his drill and smiled at her. 'I'm not satisfied unless the spoon can stand straight up.'

'OK . . . So, that'll be one cup of syrup? Coming right up.'

If life had not been so immeasurably cruel to her lately, then Kate might have seen the funny side. Because it was absurd – that much could not be denied – but it was also absolutely bloody typical that it would happen to her, Kate Nimble. Why couldn't she have simply had one embarrassing encounter and never had to have seen the person involved again? Or why couldn't she have been spared the embarrassing encounter altogether? Toby may have sent her off to Jerolim, but she couldn't blame him entirely – it was the universe that was at fault. Fate had long since decided that she was the person to whom all these mishaps must happen, and apparently it did not matter how many thousands of miles she put between herself and her normal life, this determined barrage of ridicule would still find her.

Hadn't the failed proposal been enough? Hadn't the video that followed been the cherry on top of a cake with layers of stupidity in place of jam? Now, she would have to endure who knew how many weeks of Alex, who she had humiliated herself in front of so entirely and would have to pretend that she was not only fine with it, but that she found the whole situation just as entertaining as she knew the three men undoubtedly would.

'Hang on a minute – so you two have already met?'

Toby was predictably delighted.

The shock of finding out that the 'man of mystery' Alex was, in fact, the naked bloke Kate had met on the beach, had not dimmed since that morning. After making and delivering his tea without comment, a drained yet resolute Kate had showered and changed into a decorating ensemble of old leggings and T-shirt, before heading back down to the dorm. To his credit, Alex had accepted her offer of help without a trace of his earlier amusement and promptly directed her towards a tin of varnish and brush.

'If you paint while I build, I reckon we'll have these bunks done in no time.'

Despite Kate's still-burning mortification, the two of them had settled quickly into an easy rhythm after that, and although there wasn't much in the way of conversation happening on account of all the drilling and hammering, Kate found herself beginning to relax.

'Oh, so you two bumped into each other in Jerolim?' Toby went on now, his grin expanding as Alex confirmed that this was indeed the case.

'And you were . . . ?' he added, his eyes wide.

'Let's just say, there are no secrets between us,' Alex said evenly. 'At least, not where my naked arse is concerned.'

'I told you,' Kate interrupted firmly. 'I didn't see anything.'

Toby was looking at each of them in turn. He was enjoying himself far too much for Kate's liking.

'Shall I fire up the barbecue for breakfast?' he suggested. 'I don't know about you two, but I've got a real craving for sausage.'

'Toby,' Kate warned.

'What?' he protested. 'You don't feel like bangers? How about an aubergine?'

'You eat aubergines for breakfast now?' Alex's eyebrows knotted together. 'Am I missing something?'

'The aubergine emoji is the one everyone uses to represent – well, you know,' Toby explained. 'Don't ask me why, though. I have never seen one that colour or that shape before, and I've seen lots of them.'

'Oh my god.' Kate went back to varnishing. 'Please ignore my brother. He is sick – a sick, sick man.'

'I'm afraid I don't speak emoji,' said Alex, reaching into the back pocket of his shorts and producing an ancient Nokia. 'Never been big into gadgets really.'

'Alex here is too much of a free spirit to need anything technological,' Toby told Kate. 'You don't even have an email address, do you mate?'

Alex shook his head.

'Don't really see as how I would need one. I do all my business face-to-face most of the time, and if people such as yourselves want to get hold of me, they can call me on this thing. It still works,' he added, with what Kate took to be a certain amount of pride.

'Don't you ever feel like getting an upgrade?' put in Toby.

'Not really, no.' Alex considered for a moment. 'I don't see the sense in it, of throwing something away that works perfectly well, you know?'

'Not even if you could get something better?' prompted Toby.

'Who says it would be any better?' Alex said, lining up a screw. 'You can't miss something you've never had, and I have never yet had a need for one of those fancy phones.'

Kate, who had fallen silent as she listened to their exchange, turned to her brother.

'I think Alex is right,' she said quietly. 'People throw things away that they shouldn't all the time – even if they don't have any reason to do so.'

It took Toby a beat or two to catch her meaning, and just for a moment, his face fell. 'What did I tell you about this man, sis?' he said, putting his arm around her shoulders. 'Alex here is a good guy – one of the very best.'

10

By late afternoon, Kate was beginning to droop.

Alex had constructed an impressive six bunks since that morning, and she had varnished every one of them. Her elbows throbbed, her back ached and she had a pain in her head that two paracetamols had done little more than wave a white flag at. Putting down her brush and stretching out her arms until her shoulders cracked, she set off in search of Toby. The last time she'd seen him was in one of the en suite bathrooms upstairs, laying tiles with Filippo, but when she pushed open the door, there was no sign of either of them.

'Any idea where my brother is?' she asked Alex, who was measuring up wood for another of his beautiful wardrobes in the next-door bedroom. There was a pink band across his forehead, a souvenir from the visor he'd been wearing most of the day, and the chewed end of a pencil poked out from behind his ear.

'Yeah, he mentioned something about going to see a second-hand coffee machine – did he not tell you he was going?'

'He did not.' Kate sighed. 'To be fair, he probably needed a break from me. I've not exactly been the best company this past week or so.'

'Oh?'

Alex wiped the dust off his wristwatch and looked at her expectantly.

'I've just had, you know, stuff going on. And no couple genuinely enjoys a third wheeler tagging along with them all the time, even if they pretend otherwise.'

'I reckon I'm about done here for the day,' said Alex, surveying the mess of wood chippings that littered the floor. 'I can get out of your way if you want—'

'Oh no,' Kate hastened. 'I wasn't hinting or anything like that. I was actually going to head out myself soon. I haven't been for a walk yet today and I'm about ready to start climbing the peeling wallpaper.'

'Right you are.' Alex folded his arms. 'I guess it is about that time. I'll walk down into town with you – if that's all right with you, like?'

'Er.' Kate looked down at her varnish-stained leggings. 'Sure. Great. I just need ten minutes or so to get changed.'

In the end, it was closer to an hour before she re-emerged, having washed and tamed her dark-red curls, scrubbed the grime off her hands and carefully applied the barest trace of make-up. Kate had yet to venture down into town after dark, having learned that it was hard to separate Filippo from his rooftop barbecue or encourage him to mingle with the tourists.

'They may be my bread and butter,' he had told her the previous evening, 'but that does not mean I have to toast them.'

She found Alex waiting for her on the steps outside, simultaneously reading a battered paperback and tossing a coin up in the air, which he caught without so much as a sideways glance. When he heard Kate approaching, he stood, and she realised he was still wearing the same tattered vest and shorts that he had been all day. His dreadlocked hair, which he had now released from its elastic band, was coated in the same sawdust that she had just spent the past three-quarters of an hour washing off.

'Sorry I took so long,' she said, as Alex slid his book into his back pocket. 'I'm glad you had a something to keep you occupied – is it a good read?'

'Pretty good,' he said, not elaborating. Then, almost as an afterthought, 'You smell nice.'

Kate smiled. 'Much as I like eau de garden fence,' she joked, 'I thought eau de actual perfume might be kinder on the inhabitants of Hvar.'

The sun had long ago vanished and the evening sky above them was a rich navy blue. It was so quiet now that the crickets had fallen silent, and the air that drifted around them carried a faint scent of lavender. Kate led the way and Alex fell into step beside her, apparently content to let her choose the route, even though he must know these backstreets far better than she did.

'So, you're staying for the summer, are you?' he asked, standing to one side to let a thickset Croatian man pass by them.

'I'm not sure . . .' Kate trailed off, unsure for a moment how to continue. 'How much did the guys tell you about why I'm here?'

Alex scratched at his beard. 'Well, let's see. Filippo mentioned that things at home had gone a bit south. Something about you needing a break from it all. Is that about right?'

'I lost my job,' Kate told him. They had reached the point of the journey where she had met the little black cat, but there was no sign of it now. She hoped it had a house to go to.

'And I lost my home,' she went on.

'Right. That doesn't sound ideal.'

'That's not the worst of it.' Kate sighed, debating whether or not to tell him the next part. She didn't want to overshare, but she also desperately wanted an excuse to talk about it – to talk about James in particular.

'I lost my boyfriend, too. I mean, he's not dead or anything,' she said quickly, punctuating her words with a strangled sort of laugh. 'We split up; he dumped me.'

'Right.'

Kate waited for him to say the thing that people always said. The platitudes varied, but in the end they were just empty words, meaningless phrases. But Alex did not express sympathy, or tell her she was 'better off', he merely asked if they had been together long.

'Ages,' she said glumly, punctuating the word with a sigh.

As they started down the long, sloping road that would lead them to the water's edge, Kate filled him in loosely on how she and James had got together, but left out the part about her disastrous proposal. The last thing she wanted was another person watching that bloody video.

'I didn't see it coming,' she said morosely. 'I was blind-sided, and I think – no, I hope he's going to change his mind; that he's just freaking out about things. Everyone does that, right? We're all supposed to be settling down in our thirties, buying houses and picking out wedding dresses. It is a lot of pressure. I can understand why he's scared,' she rattled on. 'I'm not exactly the best wife material.'

She trailed off yet again, her words mingling now with tears that she was adamant would not fall. Alex had not commented at all, merely listened, the hand that was nearest her buried deep in his pocket. Now that they were approaching the hub of Hvar Town, there were more signs of life – strings of yellow bulbs and notes of music. Kate could hear mumbled chatter coming from the restaurants they passed, the clink of cutlery and the soft pop of a cork being eased from a bottle. The sun's warmth had lingered and the stars were out in its place. She lifted her face to stare upwards, drawing resolve from the world's very own light show.

'Sorry,' she mumbled. 'Sorry to drone on about myself.'

'Don't be.'

She could feel the weight of Alex's gaze and dropped her chin towards her chest before braving a look at him. The pale-blue eyes had been turned dark green by the night, but the intensity behind them was the same. It was as if he was trying to tell her something without saying anything at all. Kate did not know him well enough to guess what, but she sensed it would be kind. There was an inherent compassion to Alex; a quality about him that made her feel able to open up as she just had. Or perhaps she was kidding herself and it was purely that she wanted so much to discuss her own life.

'I don't even know where I'm going,' she said, and although she had meant it more figuratively than literally, Alex took it as the latter.

'Are you hungry?' he asked.

'Starving,' she admitted, giving in to a smile as her stomach emitted a serendipitous growl.

'Do you like pizza?'

'Yes!'

'In that case,' he said. 'Follow me.'

Instead of going along the Riva, which Alex told her would be packed with tourists, they turned off the main street and made their way through a complicated jungle of narrow lanes, some of which went up, while others took them down. Within a few minutes, Kate had completely lost her bearings and was trotting to keep up.

'Will this bring us out near the water?' she asked hopefully, as they nipped around some outside tables and descended another flight of wide stone steps. Kate had swapped her heels for flats just before leaving the hostel and was grateful that she had.

'Not the harbour, no,' he called back. 'The restaurants down there are nice, you see, but none of the pizzas you'd get there would be as good as from Lovro's.'

'Is Lovro the name of a place or a person?' Kate queried.

'Both,' he replied. 'Best pizza in Hvar – you can trust me on that.'

Lunch felt like it had been ages ago and Kate's headache, which had retreated temporarily after her shower, was back banging cymbals together in her brain. She needed food. Or sugar. Or preferably both at once.

'Here we are.' Alex had stopped so abruptly that Kate almost walked straight into the back of him. They were on a cobbled lane thrown into shadow by the tall buildings on either side, each one with crumbling wooden shutters behind narrow balconies. Glancing up, Kate saw a red, white and green triangular sign with the word 'Lovro's' scrawled across it in black letters and below it a propped-open doorway from which oozed the most delicious smell of warm cheese. Like many of the eateries in Hvar, it was tiny inside – a single room with space for little more than a tall fridge and a serving counter, behind which were large wheels of pizza cut into gargantuan slices.

As they approached the till, a man bustled out through a door set into the back wall. He was grey-haired, red-cheeked, crinkle-eyed and wearing an apron that bore large smears of tomato sauce. When he saw the two of them standing there, he beamed.

'*Zdravo*. Alex, my friend, how are you? I have not seen you in a very long time.'

As he spoke, he extended both hands over the counter towards them.

'Hello,' muttered Kate, unsure what to do next; whether it was customary to shake Lovro's hand or go in for a kiss on each cheek. She opted for a smile instead.

Alex started chatting away in Croatian, only breaking off when he turned back to find Kate staring at him with incomprehension.

'Sorry,' he said. 'Rude of me. I was just asking Lovro which pizza he recommends.'

For some reason, Lovro seemed to find this comment hilarious and bellowed with laughter, his rotund middle bobbing up and down underneath his apron.

'Am I missing something?' Kate asked, worried suddenly that this Croatian stranger had somehow viewed the #WannabeWife video and recognised her as its star.

'Lovro thinks we are on a date,' Alex explained, as the older man readied two paper bags. 'He was teasing me for bringing such a pretty woman to such a nondescript restaurant.'

'But it's his restaurant,' exclaimed Kate, to which Lovro laughed again. 'We're definitely not on a date,' she told him, reddening as both men turned to her. 'I mean, not because I wouldn't be, just because I have a boyfriend. Or I did. I have someone,' she said with finality. 'Someone I love. A man.'

For a split second, she was sure she saw Lovro's face fall with disappointment, but he quickly recovered, nodding at her and smiling as she followed Alex's lead and selected a slice of the seafood pizza, as well as two bottles of Coke from the fridge.

'I'll get this,' she insisted, scrabbling for her purse before Alex could argue. 'May as well put the redundancy money to good use.'

Alex let her go through the open door ahead of him as Lovro waved them off from behind the counter, and Kate, wishing she knew how to thank him in his own language, asked Alex to teach her the right word.

'It's *hvala*,' he said. 'You say it like the French say *voilà*, only with an "H".'

Kate gave it a try, but only managed an odd mumbling sound.

'Just keep practising – you'll get it.'

'How long did it take you to learn the language?' she asked, peeling back the corner of her paper bag and taking a generous bite of pizza. She had never eaten one topped with octopus tentacles before and spluttered as one of the curly fronds tickled the inside of her nose.

Alex waited until she'd wiped tomato sauce off her face, then said, 'I'm still learning.'

'I was terrible at languages at school,' she confessed. 'Dropped German and failed French with aplomb.'

'Isn't "aplomb" a French word?'

'*Touché.*'

'And that one?'

'*Oui, monsieur.*'

'Now you're just showing off.'

Kate laughed at that. Really laughed. Not at herself for a change, or because she thought she should, but because she had found something genuinely funny. And because right now, in this moment, eating pizza with this man she had just met, in a country that was almost entirely new to her, she experienced a feeling that had been absent for quite some time.

Happiness.

II

'So, what was it you did before you were made redundant?' asked Alex, as he led Kate through yet another warren of back-streets and out into the town square. The piazza was far busier now than it had been when she meandered along the harbour in search of a taxi boat, and almost every outdoor restaurant table was occupied. Behind them, the tower of St Stephen's Cathedral loomed tall and resplendent, while the marble paving slabs below glowed like embers in the lamplight.

'I worked as an assistant in an auto parts office,' she said, grimacing over the memory of her former boss, Jakub Kowalski, giving her the bad news.

'I think this will be good for you,' he had said. 'I can tell that you are bored here. I see you staring off into space and I think to myself, "What is she dreaming about?" I do not think it is accelerator cables or windscreen wipers.'

'I love windscreen wipers,' Kate had mumbled, but Jakub had already made up his mind, telling her encouragingly, 'Don't see this as losing a job, see it as the gift of a fresh start – the push you need to make the changes you want.'

Kate wondered now if Jakub would agree that fleeing the country was an adequate enough life change. When he had paid out her severance package of three months' salary, did he envisage her blowing a sizeable chunk of it on plane tickets?

'It wasn't exactly the most glamorous of jobs,' she told Alex. 'But it was better than being unemployed.'

'That's why I work for myself,' he said. 'That way, I can never be sacked.'

Kate smiled in reply.

'I can't believe how warm it still is,' she said, lifting her heavy sash of curls off her neck. 'I'm tempted to dip my feet into the water over there to cool down.'

'Fun tourist fact for you,' said Alex, stopping not far from a small lavender stall. 'This square was an inlet once; we're standing where the sea used to be.'

Kate looked down, then back up at him.

'I never used to be that fussed about the sea,' she told him, 'but since coming here, I have found myself oddly drawn to it. I guess because of how beautiful it is, and how clean – like something out of a glossy travel brochure. I've never seen sea like it.'

'Have you been in for a swim yet?' he asked.

'No. I was going to go for a paddle in Jerolim,' she said mildly, 'only I was scared off by a load of naked people.'

Alex laughed. 'I was wondering when that was going to come up again.'

Kate almost raised a comical eyebrow at that remark but stopped herself. The two of them had strayed into flirtatious territory and she didn't want him to get the wrong impression.

Pizzas eaten and wrappers binned, they crossed the square and began to stroll along the Riva, a flotilla of super yachts on one side of them and a battalion of ritzy bars and restaurants on the other.

'I wouldn't mind one of these,' she said, gesturing towards a particularly expensive looking vessel. Three storeys high and gleaming black and chrome, it boasted polished wooden decking, built-in bar, a long wraparound leather seating area and a gym on the lower deck. There were two jet skis fixed to the back and – Kate had to blink to be sure she hadn't imagined it – a Land Rover bolted to the floor.

'Who can afford such luxury?' she wondered aloud.

'Sheiks, shipping magnates, film stars,' Alex intoned, sounding unimpressed.

'I wonder what they're like inside,' she went on, running her eyes over mahogany panels and sparkling spotlights.

'They have air conditioning, hot showers, TVs, Internet, king-size beds,' Alex listed. Then, as Kate turned to him in surprise, he carried on, 'I've been on a few. Quite often they're a bit worse for wear by the end of season, so when the passengers fly off home in their private planes, they hire local folk to clean and fix things. One of the yachts I worked on last year had starry sky panels in the bedroom ceilings. Can you believe it? Now why would you need one of those when you're out at sea, with a front-row seat to the real things?'

'Maybe they would rather be in a nice clean bed than in a hammock out on the deck,' Kate mused. 'I know I would.'

For a beat or two, Alex said nothing.

'What's wrong with that?'

'Nothing at all,' he said levelly. 'I'm just surprised, that's all. You seem quite bold to me; a woman who knows what she wants and isn't afraid to go after it.'

Kate had to shake her head at that – he had got her so wrong.

'Are you telling me you're not adventurous?' he pressed, then, when she made no reply, 'You must have done something in your life that scared you a bit?'

Kate's smile withered and died. 'To be honest,' she admitted, staring stoically at her feet, 'most things scare me.'

'None so much as choking on octopus pizza?'

Kate appreciated his attempt to lighten the mood, but she could not quite bring herself to laugh along with him. The single most courageous thing she had ever done was the one thing that had backfired the most spectacularly. What she should have done was remain true to cowardly self and erred on the side of utmost caution. If only she had, then she might not have lost everything that mattered.

'You don't need to walk me all the way back,' she told Alex as they reached the far end of the Riva. 'I know how to get to the hostel from here.'

'It's all right. I would rather see you home, if that's all the same by you. Thought I might catch a kip in one of the dorms – get an early start in tomorrow.'

He sounded unsure all of a sudden and Kate cursed herself for making things awkward. Casting around for something to say to change the subject, she noticed a raggedy old boat bobbing just offshore. It was white – or had been once upon a time – but now the hull was a mess of peeling paint and water stains. The small cabin at the front was buried under all manner of nets, pots of paint, broken planks of wood and stained carrier bags, while yet more pots, tools and unidentifiable objects hung down over the sides. Kate was surprised it was able to stay afloat.

'Would you look at the state of that old thing,' she exclaimed. 'Talk about the Littlest Ho-boat. Who do you think it belongs to, Captain Calamity? Captain Collector of Crap? Someone should do the poor thing a favour and sink it.'

'You mean that boat there?' Alex pointed.

'Of course,' she said with feeling. 'Do you see any other boats here that are about fifty years past being condemned?'

'Well now, I see my boat,' he said.

'Yours?' she repeated. 'Which, er, which one is yours?'

'That one right there,' he said. 'What was it you said, the Littlest Ho-boat? That's the one.'

Kate squirmed. 'You're joking?'

'No, not joking.'

'Oh god. I'm so . . . Oh bloody hell.'

Alex wasn't smiling, but he didn't look offended, more bemused. Kate was about to apologise more coherently when she felt her phone start to vibrate in her bag.

'Saved by the bell,' she joked weakly, only to freeze as her stomach leapt up into her throat.

It was James.

12

All those unanswered messages, all the days that had passed where she hadn't heard so much as a murmur from him, all the times she had stared at her phone, willing it to light up with a call or even a simple notification – and now here he was, wanting her again.

Kate stumbled away from Alex, her fingers swiping hurriedly at the screen.

'Hello? Hello, James? Is that you?'

'Kate – where on earth are you? I got a weird ringtone.'

'I'm—' Kate hesitated. Her plan was never going to work if she gave away her location right away; the whole point of disappearing was to be out of reach, far enough away that he would miss her; that he would realise how much he still loved her.

'Away,' she said. 'I needed a break after everything that you – everything that happened.'

'Away where?' James pressed, and Kate took a deep breath.

'Somewhere I can walk around freely without worrying that someone will point and laugh because they've seen a video of me making a tit of myself on the Internet.'

Even as she said it, Kate quailed. Now was not the time to goad him – not now she finally had his attention.

James let out a long-drawn-out sigh. The sigh of the reluctantly guilty.

'How are you anyway?' she asked, doing her best to sound more conciliatory. 'How is everything there? How's work? And your family?'

'I'm fine,' he said, although she could tell he wasn't. 'It's weird in the house, though. So quiet with just me here.'

Kate swallowed.

'I guess I never realised how much you did around the place,' he admitted. 'You know, keeping everything tidy and doing the garden and that. My mum came over yesterday and almost had a heart attack when she saw the state of the kitchen.'

'I bet she did,' said Kate, feeling slightly cheered. James was not coping well without her; he needed her there with him and perhaps now he had realised as much.

'I saw Robyn the other day,' he went on.

'Oh?' Kate was taken aback. Her friend would surely have been straight on the phone if that were the case.

'Yeah,' muttered James. 'And you know, if you wanted to send one of your mates round to spy on me, you should have chosen someone with a less obvious car.'

Robyn drove a bright yellow Mini painted with daisies. It was undoubtedly bold, but suited her sunny personality perfectly.

'I didn't send her round,' spluttered Kate. 'I haven't sent anyone round – I wouldn't do that.' She had reached the low wall that ran alongside the harbour now and collapsed down onto it. Alex was still standing by the water where she'd left him, his eyes trained not on her but the distant dark shapes of the Pakleni Islands. There was a smear of varnish on the back of his shorts, she noticed absently.

James was mumbling something unintelligible about her and Robyn having some sort of stalkerish scheme up their sleeves.

'Even if I had sent Robyn over there to check up on you – which I didn't, by the way – would it really be such a horrible thing? Just because you decided to throw me out doesn't mean I stopped caring. I still worry about you; still think about you. I still love you, for god's sake.' Her voice cracked as she fought to keep the tears at bay.

James responded with another sigh. 'Listen, you don't need to worry about me. I admit, it is a bit weird you not being here – but that doesn't mean my decision was the wrong one. I do miss you, of course I do, but my feelings haven't changed.'

'Neither have mine,' she protested. 'Does that not count for anything? Does love not count for anything?'

Another sigh.

'I will always care about you,' he told her steadily. 'I don't know what more I can say. I called because I thought you sent Robyn over here, that's all. I'm glad you're OK and that you're apparently abroad somewhere having a holiday. You deserve it, Kate; you deserve to be happy. That's all I want for you; it's all I've ever wanted for both of us.'

'Being with you is what makes me happy,' she said in a small voice. 'Please, James. I know this isn't right, us not being together. It feels wrong; I feel all wrong. I know things got tricky, but surely we could have tried a bit harder. We still had options and—'

'Listen,' said James, more gently this time. 'We shared so many great times and taught each other so much. Just because it's over doesn't mean it was a waste. Don't focus on this part, think about the good times – the happy times.'

'I can't,' she mumbled, fighting a second sob. 'My life feels so empty without you, James. I need you. I don't work properly without you.'

'I don't believe that, Kate,' he said, sounding forlorn. 'And you know I'll always be here for you as a friend. I would come over and give you a hug now, if I could. But I can't, can I? Not when you're in . . . Where did you say you were again?'

'I didn't.' Kate grasped her one remaining trump card. 'And I don't see why I should,' she added firmly. 'You wanted me gone, so I went. The further the better, right?'

'Now you're just being silly,' he grumbled. 'Why won't you tell me where you are? Why all the secrecy?'

Kate could hear a kettle boiling in the background and pictured him in what was once their kitchen. It had been James's grandparents' house, once upon a time, but it had been she who had turned it from sad and dingy to cosy and bright; she who had added all the little touches that made it a home. How could he stay there without her? How could he bear it?

'If I come home, will you see me?' she pleaded. 'There's stuff we need to talk about; things I want to ask you.'

'Kate, we've already been over this. The facts are what they are, and I'm sorry if that sounds harsh, but I have to do what's best for me.'

James had switched the telly on. Kate could hear the *Match of the Day* theme tune. The pain of this, of his apparent disinterest in her continued suffering, almost rendered her mute. Glancing up, she saw that Alex was strolling towards her, a questioning expression on his face. He was concerned about her; worried that she might be upset. A man who was basically a stranger cared about her more than James did.

Rage surged up inside her then, as hot and destructive as lava, and she gripped the phone tighter in her hand.

'Do you know what, James?' she said, hissing the words so that Alex would not hear them. 'Maybe Robyn was right – maybe I'm not the one who should feel sad right now.'

And then Kate did something she had never done to James before. She hung up on him.

13

Robyn responded with predictable indignation.

'I have a patient who lives on that road, for god's sake. Does James honestly assume I have nothing better to do with my time than spy on him? I hope you told him to naff off.'

Toby was gleeful.

'You hung up on him? Oh, well done! I bet you feel even better than those rowers did when they won gold for England.'

Kate, however, felt utterly wretched.

She should never have allowed herself to become so accusatory with James, or to be so rude to him. Once she had calmed down enough to realise quite how big a mistake she'd made, she tried to ring him back to apologise, but he ignored her call. Nor did he reply to the message she sent, telling him how sorry she was and that she had only lashed out because she was hurting.

Half tempted to book a flight back to London and turn up at his door, Kate was only swayed by the one smidgeon of hope she had left: he had called her. He might have pretended it was because he'd spotted Robyn's car and wanted to confront her about it, but the fact was, James missed her. He had said as much. And that was something. It was the only something Kate had.

Today was a Wednesday, and as a reward for all the hard work she had put in at the hostel over the past few days, varnishing bunks, smoothing Polyfilla over cracks and poring over paint charts, Toby and Filippo had hired a speedboat and were taking her out for the day. They had extended the invitation to Alex as well, but he had declined, saying he would rather stay behind at Sul Tetto and supervise the local plumber and electrician, both of whom had arrived to do some last-minute tinkering. Kate hoped he wasn't using it as an excuse to avoid spending time with her. Alex had taken her to the finest pizza parlour in Hvar, chatted to her and kept her company when she was feeling low, and she had repaid his kindnesses by first making fun of his boat, then crying about her ex all the way back to the hostel. He must think she's a complete nightmare.

Still, today was a new day, and the sunshine that greeted them outside the hostel was optimistically bright. Kate took a moment to pause and enjoy the feel of it. In the short time she had been in Croatia, she had gone from being someone who lurked in the shadows to basking like a lizard, her efforts so far earning her the beginnings of a modest tan – or, as Toby had thoughtfully remarked the previous evening, 'a mass coming together of freckles'.

Hvar was dazzling this morning; her white stone walls seemed to gleam from within. Kate looked up to see wooden shutters propped open in welcome behind balconies dripping with plants. Flowers burst like cheerleader pom-poms through cracks in the walls, the blue sky above them paint-splattered with birds. As they drew closer to the harbour, large sprawls of cacti clambered out from the earth, their spiky fronds and paddle-shaped blooms so alien yet at home amongst the swirling dust.

There were many elements on the island that continued to mesmerise Kate, but none more than the sea, so alive as it was with colour. Not only blues, but greens and golds, crests of silver and pockets of the deepest black. It was intriguing yet astounding, stirring and soothing her in equal measure whenever she stared down into its glistening depths.

The slick and expensive-looking boat that Toby had hired for their day out was about as far removed from Alex's beaten-up old craft as it was possible to be, and Kate smiled with excited anticipation as she kicked off her sandals and hopped on board.

Filippo, who was the designated driver, disappeared into the small cabin at the front and re-emerged with a life vest.

'Where's yours?' she asked him, obediently zipping up. The vest was far too big for her and she clasped it to her chest with both hands.

'There are straps at the sides to readjust it,' Filippo instructed. 'Make sure it is on tight, *bambina*. If you were to fall overboard, you don't want the vest to stay on the deck without you.'

'Is that likely?' she replied warily.

'Not if you hold on tight,' quipped Toby, as he pressed a button to bring up the anchor.

'Why do I have to wear one if you two don't?'

'Because you, my darling *bambina*, are far more precious than either of us,' smoothed Filippo. 'And if your brother fell in, he would not sink; he would float like a little satsuma.'

Chuckling, Kate slid onto a seat towards the back of the boat. Every edge of clean wood was soft and rounded, every white leather seat spotlessly clean. The glass windscreen above the steering area had been polished while the chrome fixtures shone. It was all so flawless, she thought, stretching out her legs, a blissful reprieve after several days spent in the chaotic, rubble-strewn hostel.

Filippo tipped the peak of his baseball cap at all the other drivers as he manoeuvred their boat past an array of fishing vessels, rowing boats and dinghies, while Toby busied himself tying ropes and stowing the bags of food and drink below deck. The boat also had a radio, which was soon tuned in and turned up, and shortly after they had cleared the line of buoys that ringed the harbour, Filippo opened the throttle and they sped off across the water.

Kate had thought the taxi boat that she'd taken to Jerolim was fast, but this vessel was in a different league. The boat bounced up out of the sea and scudded forwards so quickly that she yelped in surprised delight, grabbing her hat just in time to stop it blowing off her head. Great clouds of white froth churned out from either side as they cut through the water, flinging salty spray across her glasses until she had no choice but to take them off. As the engine roared and the music pounded, Kate was struck by an invigorating sense of freedom, the rapidly vanishing landscape of Hvar reminding her that she was moving, that she was away from anything and anyone that could harm her. She missed James so much that sometimes she was sure she could feel his absence as one might a severed limb, yet here, in this strangely wonderful moment, she did not want to be anywhere else – not even with him. The exhilaration had temporarily galvanised her heart against the pain and she wished she could somehow keep hold of it.

It took them another half an hour to reach their destination, by which time Kate's emotions had run the full gauntlet from unbridled joy back to confused guilt, although she did not let on as much to the two men, merely pulling a face when Toby explained where they were.

'Krk-whatty?'

'Krknjasi Bay,' he repeated, rolling his tongue easily over the complicated cluster of consonants. 'But people also call it the Blue Lagoon, which is much easier to pronounce.'

'It's certainly popular,' she observed, peering over the side towards where six other boats had moored up in a line, all of them spilling over with passengers. The sea here was darker than it appeared closer to shore on account of the added depth, but it still looked every bit as inviting. Now that they had slowed to a gently lapping crawl, Kate became quickly aware of how hot it was, and how much stronger and scratchier the sun felt out here in the Adriatic. She had applied her usual thick coating of factor thirty before they left, but now she started to lather up for a second time.

'A lot of the tours come through here on the way to the Blue Caves or Vis,' Toby explained. 'It's a good place to stop if you're a fan of snorkelling. Now, shall we swim then eat, or eat then swim?'

'Naughty boy,' tutted Filippo, as he prepared to drop anchor. 'It is always swimming first. If you get into cold water after a meal, it will give you the cramps.'

'I might not swim,' Kate told them, unzipping her life vest and laying it carefully on the floor of the boat. 'It's a bit deep for me.'

'It's the sea, not the Dalai Lama,' joked Toby.

'Funny,' Kate deadpanned. 'I can't anyway, I've just put sun cream on. You pair go ahead – I'll watch.'

Filippo had stopped fussing with bits of rope now and tugged off his shirt and shorts to reveal a waxed chest the colour of strong tea and the smallest pair of red Speedos that Kate had ever seen.

Toby clocked her expression and grinned. 'It's the Italian in him,' he said. 'Exhibitionism runs through their blood like awkwardness does through ours. He can't help it any more than we can help saying sorry to someone when they walk into us.'

'Oh my god!' exclaimed Kate, as Filippo turned and bent to fasten his flippers. 'You could have warned me that it was a thong.'

'Now you know the real reason Alex didn't want to come with us,' cackled Toby, raising an arm to shield himself from the splash as Filippo executed a perfect dive into the water.

'I thought it might have been because he was avoiding me,' Kate confessed, filling her brother in on her boat faux pas from a few days ago. 'I feel so bad about it,' she groaned. 'I had no idea he even had a boat of his own.'

'Oh, don't stress over it,' Toby replied, pinching her bottle of sun cream. 'Alex is a chilled individual. He is not going to care about something as trivial as that.'

'Are you sure he doesn't hate me?' she badgered.

'Don't be daft. Al doesn't have it in him to hate anyone. He's a bit of a happy hippy, but in the good way, you know. Comes and goes when he pleases, lives his life to nobody else's schedule but his own, works when he needs to, travels when he wants to.'

'Where does he live when he's not staying on site some-where?' Kate asked.

Toby chewed on his bottom lip.

'I'm not sure if Alex has a home base, as such,' he said carefully. 'He has that little boat, as you know, so I imagine he spends a fair few nights on that when the weather is behav-ing, and I'm pretty sure he mentioned a tent once.'

'So, what you're saying is that he's homeless?' Kate clarified.

'Not exactly, no.' Toby squirted some lotion onto his hands and rubbed them across the peach fuzz covering his head. 'I wouldn't classify him as homeless. It's more a lifestyle choice – Alex is a nomad because he wants to be, not because he needs to be.'

Kate tried to imagine that way of living, of flitting from place to place, never knowing for sure where you would be from one day to the next; of having no walls to hang photos or drawers and cupboards to fill with the things that you had collected. Then again, a life like that would also mean no Internet bills or council tax, no loan repayments, TV licence or monthly phone tariffs.

'What do you think happened to him?' she said. 'Something must have, to have caused him to leave wherever it was he grew up in England. People aren't just born into nomadity.'

'Pretty sure "nomadity" is not a word,' Toby pointed out. 'To be honest, sis, I've never thought to ask him about his living arrangements. I figured if there was anything that Al wanted to tell us, then he would. I don't see how it's any of our business how he chooses to live or why.'

'I can't help thinking it's a bit sad,' she said wistfully.

'Why sad?' asked Toby, removing his sunglasses in order to clean them with the edge of Kate's towel. 'Alex isn't sad. He has a lot of friends, keeps himself busy. He has a good life, as far as I can tell. Not an ordinary life, perhaps, but then, what is ordinary? And what makes his way wrong and ours right?'

Kate fell silent, stung by his words and by her own need to categorise Alex and his life choices. All it proved was that she was naive at best, small-minded at worst. But there was something about Alex that niggled; a sense she couldn't shake that there was more to him than the version he put out into the world.

What that might be though, Kate had no idea.

14

They lunched on the boat as the sun continued to beat down, Filippo proudly handing out Tupperware boxes still clad in only his small red thong.

Prising off the lid, Kate laughed.

'What is the matter? Have you never eaten octopus before?' asked Filippo, frowning as Toby eased the cork out of a chilled bottle of sparkling rosé.

'It's not that,' Kate said. 'I'm laughing because I've gone from barely encountering octopus to having it twice inside a few days.' She told them about the pizza, to which Filippo looked horrified.

'Cooked? On a pizza? *Buon dio.*'

'What's so bad about that?'

'Octopus is best served cold, as it is in my salad,' he told her. 'The technique is to freeze it, boil it, remove the skin, then chill and chop it. And if you don't freeze it first, it will very quickly become stringy and chewy.'

Kate stared down into her container. As well as chopped purple and white tentacles, the salad consisted of tomato, boiled potato, slices of red onion and finely chopped fresh parsley. Glancing up at the two men, she saw that Toby had already finished his own tubful and was now mopping up the leftover juice with a chunk of bread.

Picking up her plastic wine glass, Kate took a large gulp of the rosé and followed it down with a spoonful of the salad.

'Oh,' she said, when she had chewed and swallowed. 'I see what you mean – it's delicious.'

'It's nice to see you trying new things,' appraised Toby. Then, seeing the look on Kate's face, 'What? It is!'

'You make it sound like I'm a gastronomic heathen who survives on tins of baked beans and McDonald's Happy Meals. I'm not as unadventurous as you think I am.'

'The last five times Filippo and I came for dinner with you and James, he served us the same thing – Spaghetti Bolognese. Every. Single. Time.'

'That's because it's his signature dish,' she said, compelled to leap to her absent boyfriend's defence. 'He knows he can do it well, and he was always so keen to impress the two of you that he didn't want to risk letting me loose in the kitchen. Don't you remember that time I made us a Thai soup using those dried mushrooms I'd bought from a stall in Camden Market and all four of us ended up hallucinating?'

'That was a great night!' said Toby. 'James was convinced that he was a jellyfish and wouldn't let anyone touch him in case he stung them accidentally.'

'See,' she said resolutely. 'He is all heart – even when he's tripping out.'

'He was that night, I grant you,' Toby agreed. 'But after his recent behaviour, I would have to argue that "all heart" is a bit generous.'

Kate lowered her fork, but her rebuttal was interrupted by the sudden arrival of a large, beady-eyed gull, which chose that moment to crash-land in the middle of the foldout picnic table and make a desperate lunge for the remaining chunk of bread.

'Shoo! SHOO!' screeched Filippo, jumping to his feet and flapping his hands at the bird. Startled, the gull hopped from the table onto Kate's lap, sending what was left of her octopus salad over the edge of the boat, along with the tub.

'Bloody hell!' cried Toby, turning red with suppressed laughter as an enraged Filippo dived over the side in pursuit of his Tupperware. Kate, who had jumped up to rid herself of the bird, promptly slipped over in a spilt puddle of rosé and went down hard on her bottom.

'Oof!' she yelped.

'Kate!' exploded Toby.

'I have it!' cried Filippo, and the next second, the empty tub was launched back onto the deck, narrowly missing Kate's head before rebounding off the white leather sofa and landing on Toby's bare foot.

'Shit!' he swore, hopping sideways into the table and knocking over the bottle of sparkling wine. There was a crash, followed by a swift volley of far ruder swear words from Toby. By the time Filippo had pulled himself back up the ladder, he found his husband and sister-in-law laughing so much that they could barely breathe. But no sooner had Kate gained control of her hysterics did she find herself overwhelmed by a flood of tears – a shift so dramatic that it caused the still-hovering gull to squawk in alarm.

'Sorry,' she managed, waving a hand in front of her face. 'I don't know why I'm crying. Just ignore me.'

'Poor little *bambina*,' crooned Filippo, easing himself down slowly in his Speedos so as not to inadvertently flash any escaping body parts. 'Your heart has been broken. Of course there must be tears.'

'He's right,' agreed Toby, who was busy mopping up rosé with Kate's towel. 'The crying stage is a horrible yet unavoidable part of the break-up process.'

'I guess, just for a moment or two there, when we were reminiscing about old times with James, I forgot that I'd lost him. I thought I would turn and find him sitting there, all red in the face because we'd embarrassed him with the jellyfish story. The fact that he isn't here just feels so . . . wrong. I feel guilty that I'm having fun, when what I should be doing is working out how to get him back.'

'Oh, *bambina*, you have nothing to feel guilty about,' Filippo said soothingly.

Kate removed her glasses so she could wipe her eyes. She could never remember feeling so utterly conflicted, so torn between anger and pain, bewilderment and determination. Everything had changed so quickly, and it did not seem real that she was here, on a boat in Croatia, a world away from the life that had, up until just a few weeks ago, felt so set in stone. OK, so there had been a few thickets to scythe through along the way, but nothing bad enough to warrant such adamant rejection.

Even though it hurt to do so, she allowed herself to picture James, to see the two of them laughing together as they prepped the vegetables for a Sunday roast, or scrolled through Netflix looking for a new series to binge over a rainy weekend. He had been for her there on the evenings she came home bemoaning yet another terrible day doing which-ever job she had stumbled into next, frustrated by her lack of skills and the inevitable shunning by colleagues that followed. James had made her see the funny side, pointed out that it hardly mattered if she'd messed up yet again, because to him, she was perfect regardless.

And he had been right. It hadn't mattered to her, not really. Because she'd always had him – had the promise of their future happiness and his unconditional love. But now that both had been snatched away, Kate felt exposed; lost in a way that frightened her. She hadn't been lying when she spoke up for James's big-heartedness – he had showcased this trait time and time again, ever since she had known him – but it was precisely this that made his betrayal so much more difficult to accept. The James she knew would not hurt her in this way; the James she knew was a good person, a loyal person, a courageous person.

There was something he wasn't telling her; Kate could feel it. And if she wanted to win him back, she had to find out what it was.

15

In a bid to distract herself from thoughts about James or from spiralling into Internet searches for a viral video in which she was the unwitting star, Kate spent the next few days throwing herself into the refurbishment project at the hostel.

Sul Tetto was beginning to resemble a tangible residence in which paying customers would be happy to stay, but there remained much to do in the way of decoration. Toby and Filippo were nearing the bottom of their modest budget, but there were still pieces of furniture to source, kitchen crockery and utensils to buy and bedding to order. While the two men were content to leave the walls in the dorm rooms and communal areas blank, Kate harboured a far more aesthetically pleasing plan for the building – a theme that would be in keeping not only with the hostel's owners, but with the island on which it stood, too. She was convinced that with a few small additions here and there, they would be able to transform the interior from something understated and uninspiring to a real home from home.

Toby might have been joking when he talked about the dolls' house Kate had so loved as a child, but it had got her thinking. It was true that she had always been a fan of interior design – an avid viewer of the BBC home makeover series *Changing Rooms* and consumer of glossy tomes such as *Elle*, *Ideal Home* and *Living Etc* – but aside from overhauling her childhood bedroom numerous times and being permitted very limited rein to redecorate the house left to James by his grandparents, she'd not had many opportunities to flex her creative muscles. Kate couldn't even be sure if she had a good eye for such things – all she knew was what she liked, but there was no saying Toby and Filippo would agree. Eventually, she concluded that what she should do was create a mood board of ideas to show them, and it was with this in mind that she had slipped out of the hostel before breakfast that morning and set off on a mission to find inspiration.

After picking up a coffee-to-go from the same café she had visited with her brother on her first morning in Hvar, Kate headed west along the coastal path, only stopping when she had crossed to the opposite side of the town port. The view across the water was enchanting, and she smiled as she took in the terracotta rooftops and spiky palms, sweeps of mountainside blanketed by scrubby trees, and above it all the sky, a propped-open umbrella of the purest blue. Boat masts bobbed with pendulum rhythm in the harbour while crickets sang along from the brush, and all the while the breeze scurried around her, its whispering voice soft as silk.

The pale gold pathway snaked ahead of her and she followed it, tracing the dome of the far horizon down to its distant blurry line. She had awoken not long after dawn, agitated by a bad dream that soured her thoughts, but out here Kate felt calmer, her emotions subdued by the clean air and the promise of a task she would relish getting done.

Hvar had its own small pockets of disorder, but for the most part, it was flawless. Litter was placed in bins, fallen twigs were swept from the streets, and the beaches she had seen were blessedly untainted by trash. London, by comparison, was an assault course of filth and noise, a city that had fallen victim to the general disregard of its residents, so many of whom she watched toss their food wrappers and cigarette butts to the ground. She had lived there all her life, but Kate did not miss the city – not yet anyway. What she missed was the people. Or, she countered internally, the person.

She must not think about James.

Spotting a bountiful heap of driftwood not far from the shore, Kate hopped down off the path and made her way carefully over the rocks towards it, scooping up a few of the split, salt-tarnished logs and stowing them in the tote bag she'd brought along for the purpose. She wondered what Alex would think of her ideas. He had been in situ when she departed that morning, already occupied with building the dormitory vanity units she had mooted as an idea during the eventful day trip to the Blue Lagoon.

'People need an area to get ready,' she had pointed out. 'And with multiple guests, you need to keep the bathrooms free from human traffic. Nobody wants to wait in a queue to dry their hair or put on their mascara.'

'Sounds like a plan to me,' Toby had replied. And to Kate's surprise, it had been as simple as that.

Leaving the beach weighed down by a further collection of stones, shells and some dried remnants of seaweed, she returned to the path and headed on past one of the island's oldest and grandest beach bars, skirting the corner up ahead before dipping inland again, content for now to follow the undulating shape of the coastline. A painted sign told her she'd reached Amfora Bay, and she looked up to where a splendid hotel rose grandly out from between the trees, its enormous poolside terrace dotted with white plastic loungers. Admittedly, this was the kind of holiday establishment she knew James would favour, but Kate preferred the more rustic wooden sunbeds that were chained up in various spots along the rocky shoreline below. She never understood the point of going somewhere beautiful only to sit by a swimming pool that could be anywhere.

Isabelle Broom

Once past the hotel grounds, Kate hesitated. There was a hill leading up to the right that she felt compelled to take, and deciding to trust her gut, she began to climb up it, removing her straw hat and shaking out her curls as she went. It had been blisteringly hot on the main pathway, but here the street was shaded and cool, the vegetation around her alive with insect life. It was only when she remembered the crickets that she heard them once again, and Kate found herself marvelling, as she often did, at how loud the little creatures could be.

She was out of breath by the time she reached the top of the hill and rested for a moment against the edge of a skip that was blocking the pavement. Behind it was what looked to be another hotel, although this one was far smaller and much sadder than the palace she had passed earlier. The garden area at the front was overgrown while several of the shutters had broken and were dangling precariously from a single hinge. Taking a step back, Kate noticed a crude sign that had been written on cardboard and shoved in the skip.

'*Besplatne Stvari,*' she murmured, taking out her phone and typing the words into the translation app she had downloaded. It meant 'free stuff'.

Kate stowed her phone and began to examine the contents of the skip more closely, her eyes widening as they fell across a large gilt-framed mirror, its glass centre shattered into thousands of pieces. Bad luck, but for someone other than her for a change, she thought ruefully, moving aside several broken chairs to get a better look. The mirror was beyond repair, but the frame, although scuffed, was definitely salvageable. She could fill the cracks somehow and respray it with gold paint; hang it up on one of the hostel walls and fill the empty space inside it with blackboard paint so that guests had a place to leave messages for each other, or draw pictures, or sign their names. Kate was sure she'd seen something similar on one of the interior design Instagram accounts she followed.

Snapping a photo of the mirror on her phone, she sent it to her brother, allowing him only a moment or two to view it before pressing the call button.

'What do you think?' she said, as soon as he answered, not giving him a chance to reply before she barrelled on with her idea. As she talked, she continued to rummage, listing her finds with increased enthusiasm as Toby made noises of interest and approval on the other end of the line.

'Sounds like you've stumbled over a bit of a treasure trove,' he said, when he could get a word in edgeways. 'I'll drive over in the jeep and we'll see how much we can load up. Just give me ten minutes or so.'

Kate hung up and began rooting through the skip in earnest, soon coming across a pair of footstools that she guessed might be useful for something or other. Pulling the second one out, however, she discovered that it was missing a leg.

'Bum,' she said, making herself laugh.

Determined now to find the missing piece and restore the little stool to its former, albeit worn and shabby, glory, she tunnelled further, pushing aside a rotting plank of wood only to yelp as a dart of pain shot across her hand. Blood bloomed from a shallow scratch, and Kate sucked it instinctively, wrinkling her nose at the metallic taste. It must have been a splinter, or a nail, or perhaps a shard of the busted mirror.

With her hand still in her mouth, Kate leant over into the skip until her feet were almost off the ground, trying in vain to find out what it was that had injured her.

A high-pitched snarling growl emerged from the depths of rubbish and Kate froze, her heart hammering. Squinting into the dark space between some banister rails and a mini fridge, she spotted yellow eyes, a small black nose and two oversized pink ears.

'Oh, you're a cat.'

At least, it looked like a cat, but this was no average domesticated moggy. As well as its huge, Dumbo-esque ears, the cat had wrinkled grey skin and a long, spindly neck.

'So, you're the one who scratched me,' she went on, doing her best to soothe the creature by making kissy 'come hither' noises. The cat did not move; it simply glared at her, as furiously indignant as any feline Kate had ever encountered.

'Are you lost?' she asked. The cat was not wearing a collar, but it looked to be one of those expensive breeds, the sort that spend all their time indoors, lounging on a padded cushion that had its name embroidered across the front. When Kate reached forward to try and stroke it, however, the cat hissed, and she quickly withdrew her hand. One injury was more than enough, and who knew what this poor abandoned kitty had picked up on its claws?

Very carefully, Kate eased the mini fridge to one side, thinking that she might be able to scoop the cat up more easily if she had more space in which to manoeuvre. She heard the jeep pull up not far away but didn't want to risk turning around in case the cat made a lunge for her again.

'Come on, darling,' she urged, trying the kissy noise again. 'You can't stay in he— aaargh!'

There was a crash of tumbling banisters as the cat scrambled out, using Kate's head as a springboard and knocking her glasses off her face. Hearing a shout of 'whoa', Kate swung round to find Alex right behind her, the keys to the jeep in one of his hands and a very angry, very dirty and very ridiculous cat in the other.

16

'You're not Toby.'

Alex looked at her. 'No,' he agreed. 'Far too hairy.' Then, nodding towards the cat, 'This isn't a mirror.'

'No,' said Kate, digging her glasses out of the skip and putting them back on. 'But it is dangerous, so be on guard.'

'This thing?' he replied, as the cat moved from his arm up onto his shoulder. 'Seems pretty harmless to me.'

'It savaged me,' she said defensively, showing him her still-bleeding hand. 'Although, to be fair to the cat, I did turn up and start rummaging around in its home, so no wonder. Seems to like you, though,' she added, frowning as the cat rubbed its head against Alex's dreadlocks and began to purr. When she reached out once again to stroke it, however, the cat hissed.

'Do you think it's lost?' Kate said, looking on in bemusement as Alex twisted his head to the side in order to examine his new friend in more detail.

'Smells like a yes,' he replied. 'She's looking a little raggedy, a little thin.'

'She?'

'I would say it's a she, yes, but I'm no expert. You'd have to ask a vet to be sure.'

'We should take it – her – to one,' Kate said. 'I would feel awful just leaving her here. Is there a Croatian RSPCA or something?'

'There's a place called Eco-Hvar,' he told her. 'You can try them. She might have one of those microchips in her neck if you're lucky.'

'She hates me,' Kate lamented, as a further attempt to touch the cat was met with an angry swipe of the paw.

'You're trying too hard,' Alex said. 'Cats can sense it, just like people can. You see, I'm not a fan of these things. More of a dog man. There is no way I would ever invite one to sit up on my head, but that's exactly why she chose me, see? She did it purely to spite me.'

Kate smiled at that. 'You really don't like cats? But they're so fluffy and cute.'

'Not this one,' he exclaimed, and they both laughed. 'This one looks like a bat got too friendly with a tortoise.'

'How could you say such a thing?' Kate admonished lightly, although he wasn't far off. The cat was quite extraordinarily ugly, yet there was something undeniably appealing about it at the same time.

When Alex tried to lift the animal down so he could help Kate with the mirror, it whined loudly and dug its claws into the neck of his paint-splattered T-shirt.

'Have it your way then,' he said, and putting a hand on the skip, bounced up and over the side regardless. They got the mirror out first, carefully extracting each broken shard and wrapping the pieces in some discarded newspaper. Alex then helped Kate to clamber over to join him and they both dug around until they located the missing leg of the footstool, plus a set of three chipped and faded garden gnomes.

'Oh, look at them,' enthused Kate, using the bottom of her dress to wipe the dust from their faces. 'Poor little Misters, abandoned in a skip.'

'You seem fonder of this motley crew than you do the cat,' Alex pointed out, to which Kate hit back with, 'Because they didn't attack me!'

'Do you really think Toby and Filippo are going to want all this stuff in the hostel?'

Kate sniffed. 'I hope so. I'm sure between us, we'll find a place for everything.'

'Correct me if I'm wrong about this,' Alex said, as he held up a battered side table for her to inspect, 'but aren't garden gnomes supposed to sit in your garden?'

'Yes, but—'

'And the hostel has no garden.'

'Yes, but—'

'So, that being the case, these three chaps, nice as they are, won't have anywhere to go once you get them there.'

'Ye of tiny imagination,' she chided. 'The first rule of interior design is to have fun with it. Finding things in unexpected places is what it's all about.'

She was sure she had read that somewhere. It sounded right.

'All right, all right.' Alex almost gave in to a smile. 'You might have a good point there.'

Only when every space inside the jeep was taken up with crooked, crumbling and cracked items did Kate agree to stop digging for buried treasures. Worn out and streaked with dirt, she climbed gratefully into the passenger seat and balanced her bag on her lap, while the cat, which had eventually been coaxed down by a patiently insistent Alex, curled up in the footwell on Filippo's designer bomber jacket.

'We just won't tell him,' said Kate.

It didn't take them long to get back to Sul Tetto, and they found Toby waiting for them on the road outside.

'Bloody hell,' were his first words, closely followed by, 'What the hell?' when the cat leapt out of the jeep and streaked straight through the open hostel door behind him.

'I might have got a bit happy,' Kate said sheepishly. 'But it's all going to be brilliant, you'll see. Look at this mirror frame – didn't I tell you it was beautiful? And there are chairs in here as well and check out this old hat stand.'

'What was that thing that just ran past me?' he asked her with a shudder. 'It looked like a giant rat.'

Filippo chose that moment to emerge and Kate cowered as she took in the thunderous expression on his face.

'Can one of you please explain why,' he began, 'there is a hairless, trunkless, angry little elephant sitting upstairs on our pristine new carpet? And what,' he added, reaching into the jeep and picking up a gnome, 'is the meaning of this monstrosity?'

In the end, the cat managed to win over Filippo to such an extent that he insisted on driving with Alex over to the Eco-Hvar animal charity office in Jelsa, on the eastern side of the island, leaving Kate and Toby to sort through all the stuff she had salvaged. When she told her brother rather shyly about her idea for the interior theme, Toby was gratifyingly pleased – especially when she explained that the overall look she was going for would be heavily influenced by Hvar.

'I want to restrict the colour palette we use, but then slide up and down the spectrum scale,' she said. 'I looked up the rules, and if we stick to blue, green, white and pink – on account of all the bougainvillea around here – then we can still have doors painted in the fuchsia or rose, if you want? And we can incorporate dark plants, indigo borders and cream units in the kitchen. Everything I've read says that as long as you don't stray off that basic colour wheel, then whatever decorations you choose and however you place them, the overall look should feel harmonious.'

'I like it,' he said. 'It sounds perfect – exactly what we wanted but had no idea how to articulate properly. You are clever, Nims. How did you even know what to look up?'

'Oh, you know,' she said vaguely. 'I follow a few designers online and I've read a few books on the subject. Trawling around IKEA on a Saturday afternoon used to be James's idea of hell, but I loved it. I could have spent all day in there.'

'Well, I'm impressed,' he said.

'Steady on.' Kate snuffled out a laugh. 'We've barely even started – it might end up looking dreadful in here.'

'I didn't actually mean your surprising amount of interior design knowledge,' he said, 'although that is incredible. I'm impressed because you just spoke about old plonker-features James in the past tense, and that, my darling one, is progress.'

'But I didn't mean . . . I was just saying—'

'I know, I know.' Toby raised both hands in surrender. 'You still love him. But, you know, just because you love James doesn't mean you need him. Don't allow the two things to become confused in your head, because the Kate Nimble I see here now, who is so full of ideas and passion, is a far happier woman than the one I found skulking miserably in her old bedroom a week or so ago. If you want my opinion,' he went on, talking quickly so Kate could not interrupt, 'you are very much capable of a life without James in it – and what's more, it may even be a better one.'

'You're sweet to encourage me,' Kate told him, turning away so he would not see the hurt in her eyes. 'But I know what's best for me. I'm thirty now, Tobes – not thirteen. You should trust me more.'

'I do trust you, sis,' he said, as Kate stared down at her feet. 'It's him I don't trust.'

'Hmm,' she said, deliberately non-committal. 'So, the gnomes – can we keep them? I can repaint them for you, give them shorts in the colours of the Croatian flag or something?'

'If you want Filippo on board,' her brother countered lightly, 'then it had better be an Italian one.'

'Are there any flea markets in Hvar?' she wanted to know. 'Or jumble sales, that sort of thing. I know you said there wasn't much left in the way of budget for extra bits of furniture, but I bet we could pick some pieces up second-hand. There are heaps of upcycling tutorials online that we could follow.'

'I'm sure there are,' Toby said, reaching into a box he had just carried through into the reception area. 'What on earth are all these for?'

Kate snatched back the old curtain tassels defensively. 'They're for dressing up doorknobs and window latches,' she muttered. 'I know the gold is gross, but I can get some dye.'

'And these?' he added, holding up a pair of metal jelly moulds.

'Will apparently make nice vintage-style lamps. I read a how-to on someone's Instagram account about them.'

'Jelly mould light fittings,' he said warily. 'I really have heard it all now.'

'It's just an idea.' Kate faltered. 'I'll take them back to the skip if you hate them.'

'Let's start small, shall we?' he suggested. 'What you said about Hvar being the inspiration behind the design, and how we could incorporate natural materials – that feels right. The only real question is, do you think we can get it all done in time?'

If he had asked her that morning, Kate would have said there was not a chance in heaven, but now, buoyed up by his obvious confidence in her, she felt as if anything was possible.

'We won't know unless we try,' she told him. 'And I say we get started right now.'

They were ferrying the last few items of her haul from the street into the hostel when the jeep reappeared, Filippo's wide grin dazzling Kate even more than the bold midday sun.

'What are you so happy about?' enquired Toby, his voice laced with suspicion. 'You look like the cat who got the cream.'

'Not the cream,' said Filippo, leaning back so Kate and Toby could see the pet carrier balanced across a bemused Alex's knees.

'I am the cat who got the cat.'

17

True to her word, Kate worked tirelessly from dawn through to sundown over the following week, often staying up long after midnight to apply extra coats of clear varnish to upcycled items of furniture or to sew up the hems of curtains for the bunks.

Toby and Filippo had hired a team of local decorators to help paint the walls and wooden floors, but with the two men often out running errands or ensconced in the small office downstairs working on their marketing plans, it fell to Kate to answer all their queries. Given that she spoke barely a word of Croatian and had no experience whatsoever in supervising anything or anyone, she was pleasantly surprised by how nice it felt to have a semblance of responsibility. The more the hostel started to come together, the more her self-confidence grew, and this gave her the boost she needed to step up and make decisions about the design.

Having spent a chunk of the morning trying to find a home for the stack of real-life magazines she'd brought over from England and moving a large, jute rug around in the lounge area, seeing how it looked in different positions, Kate now turned to her next project, which she took up to the roof terrace where it was relatively quiet. Toby had found an old wooden chest at a market in Split, which she was planning to sand down, paint white and use to store the hostel's selection of board games and DVDs. Spreading out a dust sheet and arranging all the pots and brushes she needed on top, Kate sat down cross-legged in her denim shorts and plain vest and was just pulling on her latex gloves when her phone rang.

It was Robyn, calling through FaceTime, and Kate propped the phone up against the front of the chest before answering.

'Hey!' Robyn waved. She was in the front seat of her car, by the looks of things. Kate could see the usual stack of folders, crumpled items of clothing and empty crisp packets piled up on the back seat. Despite almost twenty-five years of friendship, Kate had yet to convince her best friend that being neat and tidy was an endeavour worth pursuing.

'I'm just in between appointments, so thought I'd check in,' Robyn said, unwrapping a Twix with her teeth. 'How's it all going? The photos you sent me are amazing.'

Kate blushed. 'You really think so?'

'I know so,' Robyn confirmed, taking a bite of the chocolate bar. 'Oh, that is heaven,' she said, her mouth half full of biscuit and caramel. 'Sorry – lunch on the go as per. What are you up to?'

Kate held up a brush. 'Painting – what about you?'

'I'm about to see one of my stroke patients. He's been doing well, actually, but we've hit a stumbling block with the writing. My plan today is to help him write a list of all the things he'd buy if he won the lottery; I figure that'd be a good incentive.'

'What would be on your list?' Kate asked, already knowing the answer.

'A house with its own lake, so I could go wild swimming whenever I liked. And a Twix factory,' she added, popping in another morsel of her chocolate bar. 'What about you?'

'Nothing.' Kate grimaced. 'The only thing I want is a time machine, and not even a rollover-week win can pay for something that doesn't exist.'

Robyn looked at her reproachfully. 'You're not entering into the spirit of the game. And we agreed, remember, no talking about You Know Who?'

'Voldemort?' cracked back Kate, earning herself a withering stare.

'So, I'm guessing you and James are still at an impasse?'

Kate nodded.

'And you honestly haven't caved and messaged him?'

'There's been no time,' Kate said truthfully. 'I've been so busy here this past week. The only things I look at online these days are Pinterest boards and YouTube tutorials about Polyfilla.'

She decided not to mention her daily foray onto Twitter, or the fact that a well-known reality star had now retweeted the #WannabeWife video, leading to a fresh influx of snarky comments. Kate had watched herself proposing to James so many times now she almost felt removed from it, as if the small, bespectacled, curly-haired woman standing up on that chair was not her at all, but a poor hapless stranger. Someone she could feel sorry for, but not have to engage with. It must be her mind's attempt at self-protection.

'Talk me through what you've done so far then,' enthused Robyn, her sleek dark bob falling forwards as she wriggled around her car seat trying to get comfortable.

'Well,' began Kate, pausing to take a mental inventory, 'we've gone for two main shades of wall paint in the dorms – white along the bottom and green above – separated by a strip of pink, while the interior doors are this lovely rich bottle green on one side and a sweet taffy on the other.'

'Taffy?' Robyn asked.

'It's a soft pink,' said Kate. 'Then, each of the dorms has a vanity unit, which is the focal point, and the wall space behind that is an even darker green – almost juniper.'

'I love how you speak Farrow and Ball now,' her friend joked, and Kate rolled her eyes.

'That part of the wall had to be darker,' she explained, 'because the units are so beautiful I wanted to help them stand out. Plus, with all those bunks in there, the rooms were in danger of looking too uniform and drab, so anything I could do to draw the eye away, I did.'

'It's nice that you're filling the place with plants,' Robyn told her. 'So good for air quality.'

'That's one of the nicest things about Hvar,' said Kate. 'Everywhere you look, there is foliage of some kind. Toby says it's because the island is so dry. At home, we have forests and rolling green hills to satisfy our craving for nature, whereas here, natural greenery is harder to find, so people make more effort to surround themselves with it. I did want to decoupage the big ugly storage lockers with a cactus-print wallpaper I found online, but Toby wasn't keen on the idea.'

Robyn squinted into the camera and put on her best Detective Columbo voice. 'Decoupage?' she said. 'Who are you – and what have you done with my friend?'

Kate affected surprise. 'Is my disguise not fooling you?'

'You may laugh,' said her friend, 'but I'm serious. This change in you, this new top-notch designer who's emerged recently – it's great. I had no idea you had such a knack for all this stuff.'

'I didn't either,' Kate confessed. 'But honestly, nothing I've done is that difficult. James is the architect, the one with all the design knowhow – he would probably cringe if he saw my mood boards and painted gnomes.'

'If anything,' countered Robyn, starting on a packet of Monster Munch, 'he should have encouraged this passion in you, given his job.'

'He didn't know,' Kate said. 'How could he, if even I didn't?'

'You must have had an inkling?'

'Maybe ... But liking something and being good at it aren't the same thing. I did suggest that we try a feature wall in the bedroom once and James looked at me as if I'd grown an extra head.'

She turned as the terrace door was pushed open and Alex emerged, an enormous carboard box in his hands.

'Tiki lanterns,' he said, in answer to her enquiring expression. 'For the bar.'

'Er who is *that*?' asked Robyn, loudly enough to warrant an interested glance from Alex.

Kate snatched up the phone. 'That's Alex,' she hissed. 'I told you about him – he's the carpenter.'

'He looks like one of the Dothraki from *Game Of Thrones* – only a blond version.'

Kate cringed as Alex put down the box.

'Let me see him again,' pleaded Robyn, laughing as Kate put a finger over the camera.

'Didn't you say you had that appointment soon?'

'I get it.' Robyn gave her an exaggerated wink. 'You want some alone time. I can go.'

'No, no – it's fine. Just wait a min—' But a cackling Robyn had rung off.

'Sorry about that,' Kate said to Alex, wondering as she did so why she ended up apologising to this man so often. 'That was my friend Robyn – aka London's primary wind-up merchant.'

'Right.'

Alex was dressed in his standard ensemble of moth-eaten T-shirt, mangy shorts and a pair of ripped Converse pulled on over bare feet. He had tied a bandana over his dreadlocks, presumably to protect them from flecks of paint, while a colourful pile of woven wristbands pooled together above each of his hands.

'At least I'm not crying after this phone call,' Kate blundered on, picking up a knife and prising the lid off a tin of white paint.

'You seem to like it a lot,' Alex observed, folding his arms as she glanced up at him. 'Your phone, I mean. I see you on it all the time.'

'To check stuff online for the hostel,' she protested. 'I'm in about seven bidding wars on eBay for various things at the moment.'

'I see.'

Kate shuffled closer to the wooden chest and began to apply the first coat. She figured she would need at least three to get the pure-white finish she was after.

'I'm not on it all the time,' she went on, slightly defensively. 'My mum checks in a lot and I like talking to Robyn. She is my best friend, so it's natural that she'd want to make sure I'm OK. The last thing I want to do is worry anyone – especially not my family.'

Something seemed to flicker across Alex's face at her words, and he thought for a moment before replying. 'I guess some folk just do better on their own,' he said. 'I know a bloke like that, met him a long time ago now. He always used to say that only when a person is completely alone are they their true self. He said he found it exhausting, all the pretence that you have to put on around other people, so as far as he was concerned, it was easier to distance himself from everyone else.'

Kate swallowed. Her heart had snagged on the word 'pretence'; she understood the concept better than he realised, and whoever this acquaintance of his was, they must have struggled as she did to be honest about who they really were.

'Why do you think that is?' she asked Alex, the words uttered before she thought to stop them.

He was still standing by the edge of her dust sheet, the arms that had been folded hanging prone by his sides. He didn't answer at first, merely watched her, a struggle of some kind playing out across his features. Stoic was a good word for Alex, she thought – he never gave away so much as a trace of how he was feeling.

Finding Kate's eyes with his own pale-blue pair now, however, he seemed to soften.

'Why what is?'

'Why people are so afraid to be their real selves?'

'Maybe because they don't like what they see on the inside,' he murmured. 'Or because they want to keep that bit of themselves a secret and not share every last part with others. My friend would tell you that – he would say that the lies we tell, that face we put on for the world, is far better, far less ugly, than the truth that we choose to hide.'

'He sounds wise, this friend of yours,' Kate said lightly, uncomfortable suddenly with how close they were straying towards to her own buried truth. 'Is his name Yoda?'

'No.' Alex laughed but didn't smile.

'He's called Josh.'

Dear Josh,

Do you remember what you were like as a child? Because I do.

I have been thinking about the early part of your life a lot lately, wondering about all those odd behaviours that hinted at what was to come. It all seems so obvious now, in hindsight.

As a toddler, you were boisterous and playful at home – but that all changed when you started school. You became so withdrawn and watchful; Mum was told that you resisted attempts to work in groups and would sit in sullen silence on the boundaries.

It was so frustrating, Josh, because you were clever – exceedingly so. You only had to be told something once and you'd remember it. I can recall being astonished by the nuggets of information you would casually impart – our very own little walking, talking encyclopaedia. But at school, you barely spoke.

I realise now that it was anxiety, of course. That awful alarm bell in your stomach, telling you to run, the voice in your ear that whispers cruelties. You weren't being obtuse, as the teachers thought, you were merely scared. Frightened not just of the clutter and chaos of a classroom, but of the undeniable fact that you did not fit in.

It breaks my heart to think of you then, a confused and desperate boy being endlessly reprimanded for not trying hard enough, when it took every bit of strength you had simply to cross the threshold. I can hardly bear to imagine that – imagine you being punished for doing your very best. How did you find the courage to keep going when every fibre of your body must have been urging you to retreat? I wish I had listened better, been there for you more.

Things became worse as you got older, didn't they? I saw you fly into such tempers that you could not recognise us. You started to lock your bedroom door and barely emerge for days, hardly eat, rarely sleep. Your handsome features sunk inwards as the depression pulled you down from the inside out.

Your form teacher assumed you were autistic (not true); one GP blamed anxiety while borderline personality disorder was suggested by another. At no stage did anyone come up with a definitive diagnosis. The information coming to all of us was that you were different, your mental health something that could not be categorised; you were an anomaly.

On your eighteenth birthday, you told me that you'd given up on doctors.

It was another two years before you gave up on me.

I have tortured myself with what ifs and why nots. That is the nature of this vile disease, of anxiety and depression, of all mental health issues – they spread like webs from the sufferer to those closest, holding us fast but rendering us helpless. You and I are connected by more than simply blood, Josh; we are pieces of the same puzzle, shards of the same shattered image.

To feel whole again, I need you back.

Love, Angela

PART TWO

18

In the end, they had named the cat Siva.

According to the both the vet and the results of an extensive Google search, she was a Peterbald, and according to the microchip on the back of her neck, she belonged to an Italian family – or at least she had, once upon a time. The phone number on the file did not connect, and while Filippo had done the honourable thing and sent a handwritten note to the address, nobody thought it likely that Siva would be reunited with her owners. The vet guessed that either she had come over with her previous family on a yacht and been abandoned or forgotten, or she had made the journey across the water as a stowaway. No matter how the plucky little cat had come to be in Hvar, nobody seemed to be clamouring to get her back. So she stayed, much to her brand-new doting Italian father's delight, and set about causing as much trouble as possible.

'She's taking a leaf out of your book,' joked Toby, when Siva strode nonchalantly through a tray of olive-green paint that Kate was using on the legs of a footstool, and left paw prints all over the white floorboards. She was also a shameless thief, stealing every bit of food she could, including buttered slices of toast, cocktail cherries off the bar and even an ice cream, which she swiped clean out of a decorator's hands.

Siva tolerated Kate and Toby and begrudgingly allowed Filippo to pet her occasionally, but her real love was Alex. On the days he didn't work late and unroll his sleeping bag in one of the dorms or up on the roof, she would sit by the downstairs front window after he'd departed and wail forlornly into the night – so loudly that the neighbourhood dogs often joined in. She was also very stubborn, literally chewing up and spitting out the fancy diamanté collar that was bought for her and turning up her snub nose at the dry food recommended by the vet, because she knew Filippo would eventually relent and grill her fresh fish on his beloved barbecue instead.

But despite Siva's many calamities and histrionics, they all adored her – as did many of the locals, more of whom Kate was meeting every day. It was easy to like the people of Hvar, who always seemed so happy to help and never made her feel as if she was being judged. They were friendly without being nosy and kind yet not overbearing. Toby and Filippo had hired an office manager called Nika, who was a few years older than Kate and a good foot taller, with dark hair that she wore in a long plait and eyes the colour and shape of Brazil nuts. Manning the reception desk each day would be Noa, who drove a dilapidated scooter and had a full beard despite only being nineteen, while married couple Ana and Roko were put in charge of the cleaning duties.

'What are you going to let me do to help?' Kate had asked her brother, to which he had tutted affectionately.

'Just keep doing what you're doing,' he said. 'Tart the place up. Make us look good on Instagram or whatever.'

Today she had been tasked with delivering a handful of invitations for Sul Tetto's opening party, which Toby and Filippo were hosting in just a few days' time. As well as friends, guests and staff, Kate had suggested they also add local businesspeople to the list, such as those who ran touring companies or excursions, as well as bar and restaurant owners who might be interested in offering discounted deals for the backpackers who would soon be filling the dorms.

Having followed the coastal path from the centre of town all the way across to Majerovica Bay in the west that afternoon, dropping off printed invites as she went, Kate retraced her steps and ambled through the cobbled backstreets behind St Stephen's Square, pausing to browse at several gift shops and clothing boutiques along the way.

It was the sleepiest part of the day, that lull she had grown to love so much between lunchtime and sundown, when bellies were full, and moods were contented. Kate found herself enraptured as she often was by the sounds and sights of a town that had become like a second home to her, marvelling at how a place that was teeming over with exploring tourists continued to feel so serene. Was it the heat slowing everything down, or the surrounding echoes of the past? Hvar's culture and history fitted together so seamlessly with the moneyed extravagance being flaunted down in the harbour, while the plethora of visitors from every notch along the wealth scale made for an eclectic atmosphere. There was room for all, and all made room for each other, and Kate, who had always felt much like a square peg in a round hole, found that she was completely at ease here.

In London, where the pace was frenetic and her rate of disillusionment had become as insistent as a drumbeat, her jitters had been permitted to flourish. Yet here in Hvar, where life lay sprawled like a sleepy sunbather and where Kate had finally stumbled across a pastime she was actually good at, her anxiety had receded – swept away into the deepest recesses of her mind. The thought of returning home, even to James, was becoming increasingly unfathomable, yet what choice did she have? She could not stay here on this island forever, not if she wanted the future she had set her heart on long ago.

And she did still want it. She must not allow herself to forget that.

Realising that she had ended up in a street she had never walked along before, Kate paused in an attempt to get her bearings and saw a woman she recognised pushing open the door to a pharmacy a few feet away.

'Nika,' she called out, but the dark-haired woman was already in the shop and, for a reason that she would later agonise over, Kate decided to follow her inside.

The pharmacy was brightly lit and smelled faintly of antiseptic. Kate pretended to examine a display of nail varnishes while she waited for Nika to turn around. The hostel's newest recruit was at the counter, chatting away in Croatian to the white-haired female vendor on the opposite side. As Kate listened, comforting herself that it didn't count as eavesdropping if you could not understand a single word being said, the older woman clapped both hands to her cheeks and began to croon in delight.

Kate heard the word *dijete* repeated several times and slipped her phone from her bag.

It took her a few tries to get the spelling right, but eventually the translation app confirmed what she had guessed but did not want to believe.

A sickness engulfed her, tightening her chest and jabbing pins into her eyes. Kate took a breath, then another, aware that she was reeling but unable to pull herself together.

It was just a word. One little word couldn't hurt her.

She stared at the phone in her hand, painfully aware of the hard edge of the shelf digging into her stomach. Her flat stomach. Her empty, hollow, useless insides.

Dijete was the Croatian word for baby.

19

Kate stumbled along the lane, her head down and sandals slipping on the smooth cobbles.

She would not cry. She must not cry.

It was no good, though. There was a tidal wave of despair gathering pace inside her that she knew would soon burst forth, and so she concentrated on getting away, on being alone, on hiding her pain from anyone who might be watching.

She was happy for Nika, of course she was – but she was so very unhappy for herself. Of all the things that Kate had tried and failed to do in her life, falling pregnant was the one that hurt the most. She could have dealt with being made redundant if there was a baby on the way, would have laughed away her ineptitudes if motherhood were wonderfully imminent. But it wasn't. And it likely never would be.

She emerged not far from the church at the bottom end of the town harbour, but instead of heading up the hill towards the hostel, Kate followed the horseshoe shape of the small inlet around and continued on along the coast. She had no idea where she was heading, only that she must keep going, keep moving. To stop would be to collapse, to bash her fists against the ground and rage at the unfairness of it all – of life's decision to withhold from her yet another thing that she wanted.

For a number of years Kate had had no reason to think there was anything amiss regarding her fertility. Ever since coming off the pill in her early twenties, she had always been as regular as clockwork, never had an irregular smear result or caught a sexually transmitted infection, and with these facts had come an assumption that when she was ready, when they were both ready, she would be able to conceive naturally.

Then came the scare.

Kate had always hated that phrase. *The scare.* As if there weren't things far more frightening in life than becoming a parent. As a teenager, she read articles in magazines and letters in advice columns that talked about 'the relief' of finding out that you weren't pregnant after all, as if it was a disease or affliction. It had not felt like a relief to Kate when her 'scare' turned out to be nothing more than a skipped period.

'Most likely caused by stress,' the doctor had reassured her. Kate and James had just moved in together and, a few months prior to that, her granddad had suffered a mild stroke. It made sense biologically that her cycle would have been upset by these external factors, but Kate was still crushingly disappointed to learn that it was a blip and not a baby. There was nothing that made you yearn for something like having it snatched away from you.

The friendly waitress at the waterside café waved at Kate as she hurried past, but still she did not stop, could not stop, was compelled to put more distance between herself and the pharmacy, as if the place itself was tainted by the same cruel misery that was now coursing through her. She knew it made no sense; there was no escaping this kind of sorrow. Yet, she had to do something; had to show her heart a willingness to escape so that it might not break irretrievably.

She wished that she could speak to James, that he were here, or she were there. It seemed ridiculous now to recall how apprehensive she'd been three years ago, when she thought she might be pregnant and that he would be furious about it. James had surprised her then, perhaps for the first of only two times since she had known him and reacted with excitement. They had sat together on the edge of the bath, the test held between them, waiting for those two pink lines to appear as if they were the final winning numbers of the lottery. When it did not happen, with either that or the following two tests from the box Kate had bought, it had been James who insisted that she see the GP.

'These tests are wrong all the time. It's probably too early or something. I know you're pregnant. I have a good feeling about it.'

But it wasn't. And she wasn't.

Afterwards, when she was cradled sodden-cheeked and miserable in his arms, Kate apologised for telling him; for getting his hopes up only to dash them down again. James had said nothing for a long time, his thumb rubbing a circle on the top of her arm; an attempt to soothe that made her feel even more like a burden.

'It will happen one day,' she'd whispered. 'One day I will have your baby – our baby.'

She had felt him smile, felt the vibration of his voice as he spoke.

'What are we waiting for, Kate? Why don't we start trying now?'

There were loose stones beneath her feet now; the road had climbed up away from the sea. Scraggy pines clung to cliff faces bleached white by the sun, the water below a rich blue tapestry threaded with gold. Kate gazed out towards the horizon, seeking comfort from beauty, but today it remained elusive. The darkness, the blackness, was too great, too all-encompassing, too much.

Kate had always thought of James as a traditionalist, assuming he would want to get married before starting a family, but parenthood was the only thing he was proposing back then. When she had queried his decision, making a joke of it as she habitually did whenever she was too timid to tackle a weighty topic, he had disregarded her question with a lift of his shoulders.

'So, we do things the other way around,' he'd said. 'At least then, our kid will be at our wedding. We'll have a ready-made flower girl or page boy.'

She had loved his idealism and believed in his confidence. Agreeing was easy, but what came next would end up breaking both of them.

Almost as if her body somehow knew what she wanted and had decided to withhold it, Kate's periods promptly became as erratic as her frustrated mood and she would veer from panicked to positive every few days. James was patient for the first year, staying on her side and blaming the timing, the stress, the temperature in their bedroom, the angle at which she lay after sex. He downloaded articles, read books, bought thermometers and drew circles on the kitchen calendar around the days he thought she would be most fertile. Kate went along with all of it, in part because she wanted to please him, but mostly it was due to her own desire to have a baby. She had decided that motherhood would be her thing, the role she was destined to have, the reason she could not settle into a job doing anything else. This baby was going to give her a purpose, make her useful at last, change the way that James and her friends and family saw her – no longer an aimless, ambitionless fool, but a someone, a mother to a child.

After eighteen months had passed, Kate returned to the doctor. More tests followed, and eventually, a diagnosis of polycystic ovary syndrome.

'PCSO is a hiccup, not a final nail for fertility,' the gynaecologist assured her, and Kate began her first course of tablets full of renewed optimism. Months passed, and still nothing.

Frustrated with herself and tired of being the one who must continually be poked and prodded, Kate became impatient.

'Maybe you should get tested too?' she had suggested to James, being careful to use the same tone that she might when asking him if they should roast chicken or beef that Sunday. Her boyfriend had frowned, his forehead wrinkling like a book dropped into a bath.

'The issue isn't with me,' he replied, illustrating his annoyance by closing the fridge door so hard that the sauce bottles rattled.

'How can you be so sure?' Kate had demanded. 'It's not as if you've ever got anyone pregnant, is it?'

But, as it turned out, he had.

Her name was Kirsty, and James explained that he had slept with her during Freshers Week at university, on a night when he was too drunk and irresponsible to use protection. The girl had apparently later asked for a chunk of his student loan to pay for an abortion, and James – relieved, he admitted sheepishly, to be let off the hook – did not hesitate to comply. Hearing this story for the first time, Kate had needed to sit down and take long steadying breaths, her emotions in a tangle of sadness for the poor girl, annoyance at her boyfriend for not telling her sooner, and lastly pity, for the younger and presumably scared James who had, after all, lost a child.

'I'll go and see my doctor if you insist,' James had grumbled, relenting, Kate suspected, only because she refused to let the topic drop. 'But I'm telling you, there's no point.'

Kate was not unkind enough to confess the truth to him – that she'd been secretly hoping he was the reason they could not conceive. James was good at everything; he had never failed at anything, whereas she was the opposite. Why couldn't it be his turn for once? Why did it always have to be her who was holding life back from progressing?

True to his word, James did get tested, his triumph suitably muted when he informed her that there was nothing amiss. Kate responded by gathering all the information she could about alternative options, such as IVF, surrogacy and adoption, the last of which James refused to even consider.

'I want my own child,' he said, which she had snappily corrected to, 'You mean *our* own.'

Kate was still walking, and as she diverted her mind back to the present, she became aware of sweat running in rivulets down her back. Her hair beneath the straw hat was damp and itchy, while the tears she had finally allowed to fall were making it impossible to see through her glasses. Kate pulled them off, rubbing at her eyes as her surroundings fell into soft focus. There was a sharp bend ahead and once around it, she could just make out a small cove in the distance, its white-stone beach the shape of a vast grinning mouth. Somewhere to sit for a while in the shade of a tree, pull herself together and find a way to dam this faucet of self-pity.

It was only as she approached the final stretch of the road that Kate replaced her glasses and noticed Alex's boat bobbing not far from the shore, instantly recognisable due to its overflowing cargo of old cans, curls of rope and assorted bags of who knew what. As she stared down at it, the cabin door at the front opened and the man himself emerged, his dreadlocks flattened upwards at the back, as if he had been sleeping. He was wearing a pair of red shorts, but the rest of him was bare.

Not wanting him to see her in such a state, Kate was about to hurry past when Alex looked up and their eyes met, an understanding of sorts passing between them. He did not say anything, nor did he move, but she read concern in his expression; knew that if she requested it of him that he would be there to help her.

But it was wrong of her to ask. The fact was Alex could not help her. Nobody could.

Kate softened her features into what she hoped was a smile, or at least a good imitation of one, then turned to walk away from him.

'Hey.'

Alex raised a hand.

'You want some company?' he called.

And to Kate's complete surprise, she did.

20

'Do you want to talk about it?'

Kate shook her head, unable to look at him.

'Not really, no. Sorry.'

'No need to apologise,' Alex told her. 'As long as you're OK, like?'

Her sigh of reply came from such a depth that it seemed to rattle her insides.

'I will be,' she assured him. 'I just heard . . . Well, actually overheard some news and it reminded me of something sad. I'll be OK,' she said again, with far more confidence than she felt.

Because she had to be, didn't she?

Alex had brought a T-shirt with him from the boat and pulled it on now as they walked on towards the white-stone cove. Kate had become so accustomed to seeing him in baggy, paint-splattered overalls that she had forgotten how tanned he was, how broad his chest and shoulders. The hair and accompanying beard remained unwelcome additions, as far as she was concerned, but for the first time, she could appreciate why Robyn had been so taken by him, and why her friend had compared him to one of the hunky, horse-bound warriors in a fantasy adventure series.

'I'm not a bad listener,' he said now, a final attempt at persuasion. 'Anything you tell me will remain strictly between us. You don't have to worry that I'll go shooting my mouth off to your brother or anything like that.'

'I didn't think you would,' she said, meaning it. She may barely know Alex, but she trusted him – perhaps more than she did a lot of people.

'You're not a big believer in the "a problem shared is a problem halved" philosophy then?' queried Alex, to which Kate shrugged noncommittally.

'Maybe in some cases – but sometimes I think the more you talk about a thing, the more airtime you give it, the bigger it grows. What begins as a tiny scab becomes a nasty scar if you keep picking at it.'

Alex bent the arm nearest Kate and showed her his elbow, which was crisscrossed by white lines.

'Fell off a scooter in Italy years ago,' he said. 'Got myself a nasty tarmac tattoo for my troubles and picked at it for months. Now look at the state of it.'

'Exactly!' she exclaimed, happy to have her point proven. 'And don't you wish now that you'd left it alone?'

'No.' Alex grinned at her scandalised expression. 'Scars that you can see are never as bad as the ones you can't.'

'Ain't that the truth,' she muttered darkly.

They had reached the boundaries of the beach now, but every available space seemed to be taken by sunbathing tourists, sun-cream-caked children and overflowing picnic hampers. There were long queues snaking out from the only two beachside cafés, while a further area had been colonised by a company offering kayaks for hire. Upon spotting Kate and Alex, the man in charge beckoned them over with a wave of his clipboard.

'All right, Al?'

He was British, that much was clear from his accent, but if she'd been asked to guess, Kate would have taken one look at his Billabong board shorts, shoulder-length blond curls and easy manner, and opted for Australian. He and Alex clearly knew each other well, and soon the man was telling them both a long and entertaining story about a pod of dolphins he had followed out so far to sea that he'd got lost.

'One of the Jadros picked me up in the end,' he laughed. 'I'd almost paddled my way right over to Korčula.'

'That's another island south of here,' Alex explained. 'Quite far south of here.'

'You're telling me!' The man laughed. 'Listen, do you two want to take a kayak out? Been a slow day today on account of it being changeover.'

'Changeover?' echoed Kate.

Again, it was Alex who filled her in.

'The day flights depart and arrive,' he said. 'People tend not to book excursions on the days they travel, in case they get held up.'

'Makes sense.'

'So?' prompted the man with the clipboard. 'You can have an hour on me. I owe you anyway, Al, for sorting out that problem with my car the other week.'

'You mean putting oil in the engine?' Alex laughed. 'That doesn't exactly deserve a medal.'

'Not a medal I'm offering you, though, is it?'

Alex looked bemused.

'What do you think?' he asked Kate. 'Feeling brave enough for a paddle?'

And for the second time that day, Kate surprised herself by saying yes.

The man – who it turned out was called Joe – helped the two of them drag one red and one yellow kayak down to the water's edge, returning a few minutes later with life vests, oars, a dry box for valuables and two bizarre-looking garments resembling adult bibs, which Joe explained were spraydecks. Once pulled on over her vest top, the wide ladle-shaped part could be stretched around the kayak seat, providing a barrier against any water that might splash inside. Alex showed her how the foot pedals worked, while Joe gave her a short tutorial on how to turn, stop and reverse using the paddle. It was a lot to take in, but Kate did not feel at all daunted. Besides, she would have Alex with her the whole time.

Satisfied that she was comfortable, Joe ferried both her and the red kayak into waist-height water, giving the elongated canoe a friendly slap on the rump as he headed back to shore. Looking around for Alex, Kate saw him cutting through the water towards her in the yellow kayak, a smile on his face so wide that she felt the corners of her own mouth lift.

'OK?' he asked.

'Great!'

'Right then – follow me.'

Kate gripped her paddle and dipped one end into the water, pulling back so that the kayak was propelled forward, then doing the same thing again on the opposite side.

It was working. She could do it!

After only a few strokes, Kate felt confident enough to speed up, and she stayed close on Alex's tail as he weaved them through the flotilla of boats that had been moored in the cove.

'Where are we going?' she called.

'Anywhere you want,' he called back, and Kate felt a thrill of anticipation. As much as she had loved being on the speedboat with Toby and Filippo, and how ardently she had enjoyed the sensation of rushing air and roaring engine, there was something even better about being in a kayak. The further she and Alex paddled, the quieter it became, and soon the only sounds were the soft splashing of their oars and the gentle whisper of the wind. Kate kept expecting to stare down and no longer be able to see what lay below the water, but the sea was as clear out in the open as it was around the shoreline. She pictured them as a fish might, two dark oblong shapes hundreds of metres above, as tiny to such a creature as a plane in the sky was to her. The thoughts of James, of Nika and her baby, and of her own failure to conceive were all still there, but diminished now, as if rubbed faint by an eraser. Faded like the scars Alex had shown her.

Instead of leading her in the direction of Hvar Town, Alex had headed east as they emerged from the cove, and they were now adjacent to an area of the island that Kate had never seen before.

'Is that the road up there?' she asked, as the distant roof of a car slid past beyond the treeline.

'Yes, but not the main one – that's set inland a bit. All the buildings you can just about see through the branches, those are private homes – expensive ones at that.'

'Oh, to be rich,' she sighed, but Alex did not seem to share her enthusiasm.

Kate paddled faster until she drew level with him. She was not the tidiest of kayakers, and the front of her spraydeck had collected a neat puddle of seawater in the ten or so minutes they'd been afloat.

'What? You're telling me you don't have aspirations of becoming a millionaire?'

'Not really, no.'

'But think of all the good you could do,' she badgered. 'And all the things you could buy.'

'Look around you,' said Alex, drawing a circle in the air with his paddle. 'At the clouds, the trees, the sky, the water, the sunshine – it's all free. It belongs to everyone. I could be the poorest man in the world and still have everything I wanted or needed.'

'Isn't that a bit of an idealistic viewpoint?' she said. 'There are plenty of people that will never have the means to see places as beautiful as this one. We're privileged to be here, to have the ability to travel and visit new places.'

'I would argue that everyone can see sky, everyone can feel the air on their cheeks, the heat and the cold, the rain and the wind.'

'That's all well and good,' she said, as Alex leant back in his seat, 'but you still need to pay your rent and put petrol in your car, buy soap and toothpaste, see a doctor if you're ill. All those things require money.'

'Some money,' he countered. 'Not millions.'

'So, if I were to offer you ten million pounds right now, no strings attached, you're saying you would refuse to accept it?'

Alex considered this for a minute. 'That amount of money would get me an awful lot of attention,' he said. 'And to tell you the truth, I don't much fancy the sound of that. Can you picture me in a sports car, or on one of those ridiculous yachts?'

'I can actually,' Kate said with a laugh. 'And it's the juxtaposition that's amusing me. You could have a gold kayak!'

'A gold kayak, you say?'

'Why not?'

'Because it would sink, you wally.'

Grabbing her paddle in mock offence, Kate used it to flick water across his chest.

'Come on then,' he said challengingly. 'What would you do with ten million quid?'

'Buy a fleet of gold kayaks.'

'Well, yes – that goes without saying. Anything else?'

Kate thought for a moment, steering her mind away from the ridiculous.

'I would probably buy a house – a home, you know? Where I was living before, with Ja – with my ex, it belonged to his grandparents, who left it to his parents. We just rented it from them. And it never felt like ours, not in the way I wanted it to anyway. I still had so much of my stuff in boxes, because it felt so temporary. Turns out my gut feeling was right,' she added, the smile that had followed them right around the next curve of the island drooping under the weight of her sudden despondency.

'You're the opposite of me,' Alex said quietly. 'I don't have much of anything to keep in boxes – and I prefer it that way. The freedom to move around, to get in the boat and go whenever I want to.'

'I wouldn't trust that boat to get you very far,' she quipped, and this time it was Alex's turn to give her a drenching.

With the atmosphere between them restored to one that thrived on the exchange of silly banter, they paddled on along the coastline trading increasingly outlandish ideas of how to spend their imagined millions. Alex pointed out first Mekicevica Beach, then the wildlife refuge of Versteckte Bucht, which he explained was on the outskirts of Milna.

'There's so much of the island I have yet to see,' said Kate. 'I will get around to it, I've just been so busy at the hostel. We both have,' she added. 'In fact, nobody has worked harder than you have this past week.'

'You say that,' Alex tempered, 'but until you arrived, there was no real vision for the place. You should give yourself credit for coming up with so many ideas.'

Kate immediately became coy. 'Oh, I haven't done anything really,' she protested, but Alex was shaking his head. 'What?'

'I should have said this earlier,' he told her, 'when I was talking about how much in life is free – how we so often confuse the things we want with the ones we need.'

'I remember,' said Kate.

'I forgot to mention one more thing, something even more important than all this around us now.'

'What thing?'

Alex lowered his paddle until it was balanced across the seat of his kayak before raising his hands to his chest.

'This, in here,' he said, tapping where Kate knew his heart must be. 'Who we are, the things that make us unique. Those secret parts that nobody else will ever see but us, the thoughts and feelings that only we understand, the talent and belief which are ours and ours alone. I get that you could spend millions learning new skills, but the thing is, you cannot buy natural talent – that is something you're born with, a genetic miracle.'

'Are you saying that my decoration mood boards make me a genetic miracle?' she teased, but Alex was not laughing.

'All I'm saying is that you're you,' he said simply. 'An exceptional, singular, special, inimitable one of a kind. And that,' he added, giving Kate a look that was both impassive yet utterly direct, 'is more important than anything money could ever buy.'

21

The dawn sky that set the scene for the hostel's official opening day was a pale lilac shot through with streamers of golden light, but unfortunately for Kate, she did not get to see it.

For the first time since her arrival in Croatia, she had slept in – and she was horrified.

'Why didn't you wake me?' she complained to Toby, who had the misfortune to be passing her bedroom as she burst out into the stairwell. 'There's so much still to do!'

Toby raised an eyebrow over the crate of beer bottles he was ferrying upstairs to the bar. 'Relax,' he said. 'Everything we need to function has been done, the rest is just decoration.'

'But the decoration *is* everything!' she cried. 'The bedroom chairs still need to be painted, there's a stack of postcards waiting to go in frames, about twenty plants in reception that need repotting, and Alex promised he would put up some utensil hooks in the kitchen.'

'They're next on my list,' called a voice from below.

Kate, who had promptly turned puce with mortification, hurtled back into her room and slammed the door. Cursing her own foolishness – she knew she should have worked on through the night to get all the little jobs done – she yanked on the leggings and old T-shirt that had become her uniform over the past few days, both of which were so encrusted with paint that they practically stood up to attention. There was no time for make-up, but she did clean her teeth and gargle some mouthwash whilst briefly checking her phone for any signs of life from James. There was nothing, of course, but at least the views of the #WannabeWife video had slowed from thousands to hundreds. Kate did not check any of the comments; she was in an edgy enough mood already.

After first pressing her ear to the door to make sure Alex wasn't lurking right outside, Kate stepped back out into the stairwell only to trip over a passing Siva, who hissed in outrage and scratched her ankle.

'You are such a cow,' she muttered, wiping ineffectually at the blood as the cat strode serenely away.

'Wrong species,' said a voice, again from below.

Kate hopped forwards and peered through the banisters, to where Alex was papering the stair risers with some leftover scraps of wallpaper.

'Morning,' he said. 'Or should I say afternoon?'

'Oh don't!' Kate gripped the sides of her face. 'I can't believe it's almost ten. I never sleep late, not ever.'

'Well, I guess there's a first time for everything,' he replied cheerfully, as Kate scoffed with self-vexation.

'Where do you want me?' she asked, only to turn immediately red.

What the hell was wrong with her today?

Alex went back to papering, not looking at her as he said, 'You're the boss, but if you're asking for my opinion, then I would start with the plants. Grab yourself a coffee, take them outside and slow the pace down a bit, right? If you try to do anything too fiddly now, when you're all' – he glanced at her – 'het up, then you'll only go and make a mess of it, won't you? There's hours to go yet; no need to tie yourself up in knots.'

Kate slumped. 'I suppose you're right,' she said sulkily. 'I'll go and do the plants.'

She eased herself up from the banister rail and stepped down the stairs towards him. Alex scooted along to make room, but for some reason, Kate decided to pat him on the head as she passed.

'Sorry.' She snatched back her hand. 'I have no idea why I just did that.'

Alex gave her a questioning look. 'That's all right.'

'It's really not,' she said. 'I patted you like a dog. I don't think of you as a dog, you know. Just in case you were worried. I mean, not that dogs aren't nice – they are. And you're nice. I mean, easily as nice as any dog I've ever met. Probably nicer, in fact. Or definitely. Oh, for god's sake. I'm going to stop talking now.'

'If anyone here is a dog,' Alex told her lightly, 'it's the one who is absolutely barking.'

As much as he wound her up with his teasing, Kate had to allow that Alex had been right about doing the replanting first. Being outside in the sunshine helped her to relax, as did the repetitive action of scooping out compost and patting it down. An hour after she had bolted upright in bed, Kate had finished the first of her tasks and was feeling much better, not least because Filippo had brought her a breakfast of toast and fruit, while Toby had insisted she wash it down with a glass of Bucks Fizz.

'This is a day of celebration,' he said firmly. 'And nobody deserves to celebrate more than you. Honestly, I can't quite believe the place looks as good as it does. I mean, who knew that avocado green was an acceptable wall colour? Or that dirty old garden gnomes would turn out to be such excellent bar ornaments?'

'It was a team effort,' Kate told him, shaking her head as he started to compliment her for all the work she'd put in. 'I barely did a thing.'

In truth, Kate did feel proud of herself. It had felt so nice to be trusted with tasks, even if her employer – if that was the right word – was her brother, and for her ideas to be considered and taken seriously. If only she could have found her way into a career that provided the same amount of happiness – perhaps then, the idea of being a mother would not have become so obsessive, and she would not have ended up driving a wedge between herself and James.

Ever since the day she and Alex had gone out on the kayaks, Kate had managed not to allow her thoughts to stray too far into the murky waters of her recent break-up, but with her list of jobs now dwindling, they were beginning to wade out once again. Desperate for a distraction, she decided to go on a mini tour of the hostel and take photos of all the rooms before the guests started to arrive.

Starting at the Tiki Bar on the terrace, which was the only space that had not required much in the way of her creative input, Kate slipped into the first of the private double bedrooms on the floor below and closed the door. She could still hear the thud of feet on stairs and the occasional shout as her brother and the team of last-minute helpers yelled out instructions to one another, but in here the sounds were muted and the pressure that she had felt all day began to subside.

To save both time and money, Kate had suggested they paint on wood panelling to break up the large empty walls, and in this room she had chosen a bright pine green for the outlines. Mounted inside the central panel was a large landscape painting of Hvar, while on either side, Alex had screwed in hooks from which Kate had hung small clay planters full of baby spider plants. Sourcing those had been easy – there were hundreds of them on the island, streaming out from every other balcony and window ledge she passed.

She snapped a few photos, crouching down so she could fit in part of the room's double bed, its warm thulian throw tossed artfully over the bottom corner. They had bought a cheap batch of fifteen beige blankets and dyed them in the laundry room downstairs. Kate had enjoyed wandering around with the pile heaped over one arm, draping them over the back of chairs and sofas. It did not matter that warm summer nights in the Adriatic had no cause for extra layers – it was about the cosiness of the blankets; how they made a person feel when they walked into a room – invited and at home. Toby and Filippo had told her on the night she arrived that what they wanted more than anything was for their guests to feel as if this was a home-from-home hostel – a concept that fitted their welcoming nature and open hospitality perfectly. Kate hoped these little touches would help to reinforce that idea.

Moving around to the other side of the bed, Kate captured an image of the footstool – one of the sets that she and Alex had rescued from the skip – admiring its ripe-pear paint job and carefully selected stack of second-hand books about Hvar and the neighbouring islands. While the dormitories were stripped back and functional, these private rooms had more scope for adornment, and Kate hoped her attention to detail would be appreciated by whomever came to stay.

There was a knock at the door.

'Nims, are you in there?'

Toby peered through the gap, smiling when he saw her.

'Our first customers have just arrived,' he said. 'I thought you'd want to be there to welcome them with us.'

'Oh, I do!' Kate took one final picture of the huge vase of fake hydrangeas in the bathroom and made her way towards him. 'I was just taking some photos while it's all still perfect.'

'Good idea,' he appraised. 'You should put them all on Instagram – people love all those "swipe right to see the transformation" posts, don't they?'

'Don't you want them on the Sul Tetto account?' she asked.

'We can share. You're the main reason it looks so nice in here anyway. I know you keep pretending that what you've achieved is no big deal, but it is. It's miraculous. You should show it off – should *want* to show it off.'

Kate bit down on a smile of pure pleasure as she followed her brother down the stairs. If she wanted to show off her work, she would need to open another Instagram account. If she put any pictures of the hostel on her personal one, it would immediately reveal her location to James and, for now at least, Kate wanted to remain elusive. She still believed it was her best course of action when it came to getting James's attention. And if she did start a little interior design account of her own, then maybe, just maybe, when James did begin speaking to her again she would have something of value to show him. Something that he would rate, that would help him remember why she was worthy of his love.

She had nothing to lose, after all. Because she had already lost everything.

22

The opening party was scheduled to start at sundown, but in the end, corks started popping as soon as the first ten guests ventured to the terrace, lured up from their respective dorms and bedrooms by sounds of merriment and the smell of barbecuing fish. Toby, who had donned a green shirt and pink bow tie for the occasion, was having a great amount of fun creating experimental cocktails over at the Tiki Bar.

'What the hell is in this?' spluttered Kate, who had just taken a sip of something her brother proudly declared was a 'Toby Le Rone'.

'Oh, you know,' he said. 'Pineapple juice, a splash of orange, some grenadine.'

'And what – petrol?'

'Rum. I put eighty millilitres in – is that too much?'

'A single shot is twenty-five,' Kate exclaimed, her eyes watering. 'That's one thing I actually do remember from my eventful three weeks as a bartender.'

'Did you learn anything else?' he asked eagerly. 'Anything that could help me?'

Kate pushed the offending cocktail away as gingerly as she might a scorpion.

'Well,' she said. 'I learned the hard way that if you decant lemonade into a shaker and make the mistake of shaking it, then it will not end well – not for you or anyone who happens to be within a ten-foot radius. Oh, and if you're going to serve anyone a flaming cocktail, remember to give them a straw and a set of instructions, otherwise you'll spend half the evening icing the lips of a drunk guy named Gary.'

Toby nodded sagely. 'Understood. Now, remind me again why you got the sack from that job . . .'

Kate picked up a bar towel and laughingly swung it in his direction. 'I attempt to kill them with fire, while you douse them in petrol – quite the dangerous duo us Nimbles make.'

They were both still laughing when Nika arrived, flanked by bearded Noa and his girlfriend, a slim and shy girl he introduced as Klimentina. Both staff members had clearly made an effort to look nice for the big day, and Kate tried not to let her gaze rest too long on Nika's abdomen. Nika had not yet told them that she was expecting, but as there was no sign of a bump beneath her form-fitting red dress, Kate concluded that she must still be in the early stages.

She'd chosen her outfit for the party carefully as well, selecting a flattering black top-and-skirt ensemble and understated gold jewellery. Being pale-skinned and red-haired, Kate usually avoided dark and drab colours because they made her appear washed-out, but her modest tan had changed all that. She had also swapped her trusty glasses for her hated contact lenses, even though it had taken her almost twenty minutes to get them in. After weeks spent covered in sawdust, paint and sweat, looking respectable made a nice change.

'Where's Alex?' asked Noa, taking a large sip of the drink Toby had mixed for him. Unlike Kate, he did not seem perturbed by the high alcohol content, and neither did his girlfriend.

'I've no idea,' said Kate, scanning the terrace in search of him. 'He was doing a few last-minute jobs down in the kitchen about an hour ago, but I haven't seen him since then.'

She turned to Nika with an enquiring glance, but the dark-haired woman shook her head.

'Tobes, do you know where Alex has gone?'

Her brother paused mid-shake. He was fully immersed in his Tom Cruise from the film *Cocktail* role now and she feared he might start juggling bottles soon.

'Not sure,' he said. 'I told him it was party time ages ago. I'm sure he'll be up here in a bit. Maybe he went to get changed?'

'Alex? Dress up? I don't think so somehow. That's not really his style, is it?'

'He may yet surprise you,' remarked Toby. 'Come striding in wearing a tux and plant a Hollywood kiss on you.'

'I didn't know that you and Alex were—' began Nika, who had tucked a red cocktail umbrella behind her ear that matched her dress.

'We're not,' Kate corrected. 'My brother is just trying to wind me up. It's what he does best, after dropping bottles.'

'*Bambina*!' came a shout. Filippo was waving at her from the other end of the terrace. 'Bring me some lemons.'

Kate slid off her stool as Toby passed her a handful of the waxy fruits.

'You could do a lot worse, you know,' he mused. 'Than Alex, I mean.'

'Don't be so ridiculous,' protested Kate. 'Dreadlocks and beards are not my thing – and I like tall men, preferably over six foot. Like James,' she added.

Toby went to protest, but she cut across him. 'And anyway, I don't see Alex in a romantic way, and he feels the same about me – we're just friends. Perhaps not even that; more like casual acquaintances. I hardly know the guy. And I love James,' she insisted. 'You know I do. I don't know why you're so keen not to believe me.'

'Oh, I believe you,' said Toby sadly, balancing one final lemon on top of the stack Kate had clasped in her arms. 'I just wish I didn't have to anymore, that's all. I don't think he deserves to be loved by you, although I understand it's not that simple.'

Kate deposited the lemons but didn't return to the bar. Her brother's words had affected her more than she liked to admit, and she was frustrated with him for prompting her into thinking about James again. It occurred to Kate now that this was the first party she had been to since *her* party; the thirtieth birthday celebration that was supposed to end with her engagement. How different her life would look now if James had said yes. Would the two of them have made any wedding plans, or would he have agreed with her suggestion that they have a long engagement, which would allow them to save up for any nuptials once they had got through the first round of IVF? Going private was a must, because she suspected the NHS would insist that they try for longer first, and neither Kate, nor James, could face any further delays. That was one thing they had agreed on in the wake of his test results.

None of it mattered now, of course. Because of her stupidity in pushing him into a decision, Kate had lost both James and her ability to have a baby with him. What was it he had said to her that night? That he'd been thinking about breaking up with her for a while – presumably ever since they found out for certain that it was she, not he, who was the issue when it came to making a baby. That was the horrible, savage truth: he had rejected her because of her failing, because she was a failure.

Taking out her phone, Kate flipped sullenly through her message apps, finding one from Robyn wishing her luck on opening night, which cheered her up marginally, and another from her mum that simply read: *Proud of you.* What was it about mums and kind words, thought Kate? Blinking, she dabbed away the tears that were threatening to ruin her eyeliner. She only had to picture her mother's soft, sympathetic face to feel emotional.

Similarly to Kate, she had never settled on nor had she pursued any kind of real career, staying at home to take up the mantle of that other, less lauded yet far more laudable, full-time role of wife, mother, homemaker. Kate's father was a lot like James, in the way that he naturally took control and made decisions – not in a patronising or belittling way, but because he was a natural caretaker, and because he loved his family. He had said once to Kate that he was happy she had chosen a life partner who would not shy away from responsibility, someone sensible who clearly loved her as much as she deserved.

He had been wrong about that, though. They both had.

It hurt to think about her parents' dashed expectations, and in a bid to distract herself, Kate opened Instagram, her tears drying abruptly as she took in the number of notifications on her brand-new account. How could she have gained so many likes and follows in such a short time? It couldn't be the #WannabeWife connection – Kate had made sure there was no link between that vile video and this creative venture – so it must be the content, helped along perhaps by all the hashtags she'd added. Scrolling down beneath a photo of the hostel lift, the inside walls of which she had papered with vintage postcards of Hvar and the neighbouring islands, she found over a hundred comments, all of them complimentary. Toby had been right – there was a market for this type of before-and-after interior design.

Feeling absurdly touched, Kate emerged from the corner she had retreated into and made her way back over to the barbecue.

'*Zdravo, bambina!*'

As always, Filippo was combining languages with as much panache as he did dressing ingredients for his evermore inventive salads. This evening, he was dolled up in a blue silk shirt, cream shorts and an Italian-flag apron, worn to catch splatters of hot fat from the grill.

'It is nice to see you smiling,' he remarked, squeezing her hand with affection. 'And you look *bellissima* in black.'

'*Grazie*,' said Kate, performing a small curtsey before bestowing her own volley of praise on everything from the bowls of Russian salad he'd prepared to the suede loafers on his feet.

'I don't suppose you know where Alex is either, do you?' she asked, shaking her head as Filippo offered her a bread roll.

'You must eat,' he instructed. 'I thought you were *minuscola* when you arrived, but now, you are even smaller. Like a tiny peppercorn.'

'Hardly!' Kate patted her stomach. 'About Alex – do you know if he's still around? I wanted to show him something. Here,' she went on, 'I uploaded some photos of the furniture he built and there are some nice complimentary comments.'

'Ah, Alex left.'

Filippo's face fell and Kate felt her own do the same.

'Oh. Did he say why?'

'He said to me it is because he was offered a job in Stari Grad, on the other side of the island, at the last moment. But I don't think he is much of a party man. He and Siva have this in common.'

They both glanced over towards where the skinny grey cat was sitting, hunched and furious, on a plastic chair not far from the outer wall of the terrace.

'Siva is nothing like me,' Filippo said happily, flipping two burgers that were beginning to smoke. 'She is a total bitch, but I love her for it.'

'How long is he going for – Alex, I mean?'

Kate's short-lived buoyant mood was disappearing faster than the rum was into Toby's experimental cocktails.

'A few days,' said Filippo. 'I loan him the jeep, because it is quicker for him to drive than to take his boat.'

'I can't believe he's not here. He did so much to make the place look amazing – he should be here to celebrate with the rest of us.'

'*Si.*' Filippo was nodding gravely. 'But if he is not comfortable, then . . .' He lifted both shoulders. 'Perhaps it is better?'

'I wish I could do something nice for him,' said Kate, barely registering what she was saying as she watched Noa's girlfriend Klimentina wobble right off her bar stool and land on the floor. 'Something to say thank you – and sorry for being mean about his tatty old boat.'

More guests were starting to arrive, and Toby had cranked up the volume of the music, gleefully strutting up and down behind the bar as the opening notes of 'Wonderwall' by Oasis began to play. In the far distance, the large red bulb of the sun was about to plant itself into the bed of night, the sea below it a furnace of fiery, flickering light.

Kate stood aside as well-wishers hurried forwards to greet their hosts, watching as hands were shaken and kisses planted on cheeks. She thought about the hostel, and the photos she had taken, and all the comments she had read from strangers compelled to award praise. It was then that an idea came to her – one so perfect that it sent triumphant air whooshing back into her lungs.

There was something she could do for Alex – something kind that needed to be done.

She would start the next morning.

23

Alex's boat was still moored not far offshore in the bay beside Pokonji Dol beach, where Kate had bumped into him just prior to their impromptu kayaking trip. She had hoped it would be a simple case of wading out and clambering over the side, but a quick look at the water told her that was not a viable option – not unless she wanted to swim, fully clothed, somehow carrying her bag of supplies over her head.

When Alex had come across to join her the previous week, he had done so on a small dinghy, and after scouring the beat-up old vessel for taut trailing ropes and following one down to the bottom of the steep cliff upon which she was now standing, Kate spotted the small craft bobbing in the shallows. All she had to do was make her way down to the water, untie the dinghy from its mooring, and use the rope to tow herself out to Alex's boat.

It should be simple; it *was* simple. Except it was anything but.

Kate slithered down the stony slope on her bottom, planting the heels of her palms into the earth to steady her pace. She wasn't worried about the dust that would now be coating the back of her shorts, because the task she had planned for the day was a messy one. Rather than feel intimidated by what lay ahead, she felt eager; this was a challenge she would relish.

Once down at the shoreline, she struggled for at least five minutes with the knots Alex had made to stop his little boat from floating away. There was a single oar clipped into a bracket on the floor, along with a grubby life vest, and Kate fed her arms through it and zipped it up. She was not going to take any chances, not so far from the beach. Squinting towards the distant curve of white pebbles now, she could see only a few figures milling around and no sign at all of Joe and his kayaks. That made sense, though – it was early. Far too early, in fact, for most people to be up and active on a Sunday morning. But Kate had barely slept; she had been too wired after the party, too consumed by treacherous thoughts of James, and too keen to put today's project into action.

Her rucksack of supplies clanked as she lowered it to the floor of the dinghy, and squatting, Kate pushed it under the narrow seat. Once she was sure that both she and her belongings were as safe as they could be, she gripped the sodden rope that connected Alex's larger boat to the metal rung amongst the rocks and began to pull herself along.

It was hard work – harder than she'd imagined – but it would have been even more difficult had she not toned up her arms, chest and back with all the painting, sanding, varnishing and hammering she'd done recently. Kate gritted her teeth, grunting with effort as she dragged the dinghy through the water, her eyes for once focused not on the shimmering depths surrounding her but on the boat up ahead. The closer she drew, the larger it seemed to grow and despite her resolve, Kate found herself daunted.

It would be worth it, though, she thought. Worth it to see the look on Alex's face.

'Oh, you have got to be kidding me,' she said aloud, squinting in dismay at the ladder flopped over the hull. If you could even call it a ladder. From the rusted remains of two metal clips not far from the stern, she presumed Alex's boat had once upon a time had a proper, and presumably sturdy, set of steps. All that was on offer to her now was a slimy tangle of twisted rope that was more seaweed than stairway.

Still, she was not about to quit now – not when she had made it this far.

Taking a deep preparatory breath, Kate secured the dinghy and tossed her rucksack up onto the deck, thanking her instincts for urging her to wear trainers rather than her usual sandals today. The textured soles would hopefully provide a bit of traction on this perilous ladder contraption. The last thing Kate wanted was to lose her footing and end up in the water – even if she was wearing a life vest. She wasn't sure if she'd have the strength to go through the whole rigmarole again whilst soaking wet.

At least Alex was not here to see her flail and hear her grunts, Kate thought, as she heaved and scrambled her way up across the peeling wood. It didn't help that Alex had so many random objects dangling over the side, and she swore as her right knee connected with a paint can for the second time.

'This is why mess is dangerous,' she muttered, only to chuckle at the absurdity of talking to herself. Perhaps she was cracking up? Perhaps the heartbreak, the redundancy, the apparent infertility and the fact that she had become a national laughing stock had finally penetrated her flimsy internal armour, and she would soon be found rocking backwards and forwards in a corner, giggling away like a maniac.

Only when she had finally clambered into the boat and lain like a beached starfish on the floor for a few minutes to catch her breath did Kate begin to look at the interior properly. Alex had told her that he had very little in the way of stuff, but there was stuff everywhere; undiscernible tools packed into plastic bags that were hanging from hooks, dirty rags, ripped strips of beach towel and several watering cans of various shapes and colours, all of which contained holes.

In the small steering area, she found four boxes of different cereal lined up on the floor, three cans of baked beans and two of peaches in syrup, along with a chipped bowl, tin opener and mismatched set of cutlery. To the right of the steps that led down below deck, there was a tiny toilet, the lid of which Kate lifted gingerly and was relieved to find no stains. In fact, for all its detritus, the boat did not smell remotely unclean. The only real scent she could detect was its owner and glancing down into the cabin where she guessed Alex must often sleep, she saw a couple of rolled-up blankets, two thin pillows and a pile of folded clothes, many items of which she recognised.

Was she trespassing?

Kate had been so fixated on her plan to give Alex's boat a makeover that she hadn't considered how presumptuous she was being. This was, by all intents and purposes, his home, and she had just clambered aboard without asking his permission. Now, she was standing in what was essentially his bedroom, having a nosy at all his stuff and preparing to move things, reorder them, throw them away. For a moment, Kate was almost winded by her own audacity, and sat down hard on the steps.

She had stowed her phone in the front compartment of her rucksack, and reached behind for it now, dragging it across the cracked boards and putting through a call to Robyn.

'Hello?'

It had taken her friend a long time to answer, and when she eventually did, her voice sounded croaky, as if she had just woken up. Kate cringed as she realised her error and began to apologise effusively.

'It's all right,' Robyn said with a yawn.

'I keep forgetting about the time difference,' Kate replied, although it was not much of an excuse. 'You said I should call you in an emergency and this sort of is one.'

'Why?' Robyn muttered sleepily. 'What's happened – is it James? What has that tos—'

'No, no – it's nothing to do with James. The thing is, I'm on Alex's boat—'

'Dothraki Alex?' Robyn's tone became perkier. 'Does he have spears mounted on the walls and a stuffed dragon head under his hammock?'

'Funny. No, he's not even here. I kind of broke in. Well, I don't know if it counts as breaking and entering if a boat doesn't have any doors, but anyway, I'm here, and he's not.'

'Maybe it's called floating and entering?' she suggested.

'Very good,' drawled Kate.

'I know, right – and it's, what? Oh, bloody hell, it's only just gone seven. Why are you calling me at such an ungodly hour on a Sunday?'

'I told you,' Kate reminded her. 'An emergency.'

'Emergency means fire, theft or falling into bed with a fit man, so unless you're planning to set that boat alight, steal it and sail off into the blue, or wait there until Alex returns and then seduce him, I don't see how I can help you.'

The idea of a seduction routine involving herself and Alex was so ludicrous that Kate began to laugh, then found she couldn't stop.

'I'm glad you find this whole scenario so amusing,' said Robyn. 'Definitely worth waking me up for so early on my only day off. That's right,' she added, as Kate made a small noise of apology, 'my only day off. Hear it and weep, Nimble-com-poop.'

'Oi!' Kate stopped laughing. 'We agreed you were never going to use that nickname again.'

'You agreed. I said nothing of the sort. It's just been a while since you have done anything that warranted being called a compoop, but today you have. I would go so far as to say that you have outdone yourself on the compoop scale.'

'I'll let you go back to sleep in a minute,' Kate promised. 'I just want someone to tell me that what I'm doing is a nice thing.'

'Right,' said Robyn, sighing as Kate continued to rabbit on about owing Alex a favour. 'But you do realise that you haven't actually told me what it is that you are doing yet?'

Kate explained how she had dissed the boat the first time she set eyes on it, and how Alex was far too busy to spruce it up himself.

'So, correct me if this is wrong,' Robyn said slowly. 'You want to spend the day cleaning Alex's boat for him, basically because you're a weird Mary Poppins-alike who requires things to be neat and tidy at all times, but you're worried you might be overstepping?'

'Yes.'

'And that's all you're going to do – clean it?'

'Well . . .' said Kate, who had already begun to concoct a use for Alex's battered collection of watering cans. 'I thought I might add a few extra touches here and there. Some plants, maybe, a chair of some sort if I can find one. The thing is, I think he lives on this thing a lot of the time and it's just not very . . . homely. It could be so much cosier with just a few additions.'

'It sounds to me,' said Robyn, yawning loudly, 'that you've already made your mind up.'

'Is that a yes?' Kate prompted eagerly, smiling as she heard her friend's small groan of reply.

'You hardly need me to tell you what to do – or anyone for that matter.'

'I know that, but do you think it's a good thing? Do you think he'll be annoyed?'

Robyn sighed. 'I'm sure he won't be. You wouldn't be there if you had any doubts. It's time you learnt to trust that gut of yours – it's your biggest ally.'

'But my gut has been wrong before,' Kate argued. 'What about the proposal?'

At this, Robyn fell silent. Kate imagined that she could almost hear the cogs whirring in her friend's mind as she searched for the right words.

'Sorry,' she said, pre-empting whatever it was that Robyn was preparing to say. 'You must be so bored of me and my histrionics.'

'Nah.' Robyn was careful to keep her tone light. 'You are a lot of things, Kate Nimble – but boring is definitely not one of them. Now get off the phone and let me go back to sleep.'

Kate rang off, cheered by her friend's words and confident, at last, that she was making the right decision.

She was going to transform this boat, and Alex was going to love it.

24

'It certainly looks . . . different.'

Toby folded his arms and put his head on one side.

'Different good?' asked Kate hopefully. 'Or different bad?'

'Can't we just settle on different?'

Kate stole a glance at her brother. He never had been any good at hiding how he felt, and the bemusement she could see on his face now may as well be a flashing illuminated sign.

'I mean,' he began, 'I like the colour scheme you've gone for, the blue, red and white – very Croatian.'

'It was so difficult to paint the front part,' she said. 'I tried standing in the dinghy, but it was impossible to get a steady footing, so I had to hang upside down over the side.'

'Did you give it a name?' he asked. 'Boats are supposed to have names, aren't they?'

'I couldn't do that,' she said aghast. 'It's Alex's boat remember, not mine.'

'Yet despite that, you went ahead and repainted it, sanded and stained the deck, made plant pots out of old watering cans and nailed those up, tossed out all his old tins and put curtains in the windows and oh – somehow fixed a deckchair to the cabin roof.'

'I thought it would be nice for him to sit up there,' she said in a small voice. 'The deckchair didn't fit on the deck – which is ridiculous really, given its name – and it had to go somewhere.'

'You didn't just want to fold it and stow it out of the way?'

'No,' said Kate, who had not thought of that. 'It looks great up there. And now Alex will know which boat is his from miles away – everyone will.'

'I'm amazed you didn't hoist up a Jolly Roger, too,' said Toby, who still had his arms folded.

'A flag is what you expect to find on a boat,' she countered. 'Interior design is all about adding the little things that you don't expect to find.'

'Nothing little about that chair,' he muttered, and Kate groaned.

In the time she and Toby had been talking, a small crowd had started to form around them on the road, as beachgoers and passing locals stopped to see what they were staring at. Kate, who had worked on the boat solidly for two days and was exhausted to the point of collapse, glanced around, smiling nervously when a tall blond man lifted his large camera and began taking photos of her handiwork.

'Did you do this?' he asked, gesturing towards Alex's boat. From his accent, Kate guessed him to be German, or perhaps Dutch. He was so absurdly handsome that she found herself blushing, and stuttered that yes, she had, as he continued to take pictures.

'I think that you must be a natural artist.'

Kate went to protest, but Toby got in first.

'She is,' he said proudly. 'I hired her to do the interior of my new hostel – if you like this, you should come and take a look at that.'

The blond man accepted Toby's proffered business card gladly, slipping it into a wallet that he'd extracted smoothly from his back pocket.

'I'm on Instagram,' Kate said hurriedly, turning an even deeper shade of red than the painted stripe along the bow of Alex's boat. 'There are pictures on there,' she added stupidly, as the man dazzled her with another megawatt smile.

'*Danke*,' he said, when Kate had typed it into his phone. 'And do keep doing what you are doing – you have a gift.'

'Bloody hell, Nims,' whispered Toby, after the man – Finn_@_Freunde, according to his Instagram account – strode away. 'You could write a sermon on the beauty of that German – talk about illegally blond.'

'Shhh,' hissed Kate. 'He might hear you.'

'Straight as a church spire, that one,' he drawled sadly. 'But perfect rebound fun for you. Why don't you invite him over for a drink?'

'I'm not on the rebound,' she said indignantly, stepping aside as a tourist bustled forward to take photos of the boat. 'James and I are on a break – it's a hiatus, that's all.'

'Do you think if the two of you had babies, you and the German, they would be strawberry blond?' Toby went on. 'He has to be a better option than bald-patch James.'

'Pot kettle,' she fired back in irritation.

Fortunately, they were both distracted by the arrival of Filippo, who had a disgruntled-looking Siva in his arms.

'Oh my god,' said Kate, taking in the livid scratches across his throat and chest. 'What the hell happened?'

'Siva does not like her new harness and lead,' Filippo explained, more meekly than she had ever heard him sound. 'It was . . . We had a struggle to get them on.'

'Why bring her at all, you silly man?' asked Toby, who was licking his finger and dabbing delicately at the cuts.

'She was upset – crying at the window.' Filippo nuzzled his head against Siva's face. 'I think she is missing Alex,' he explained, somehow still sympathetic to the plight of the small, grey monster that had attacked him. 'I asked him to meet us here with the jeep.'

'Here?' said Kate, who was becoming increasingly edgy. The pride she had felt when the German man had admired the boat was rapidly being replaced with a very real fear that Alex would hate it.

'He's going to see it sooner or later,' Toby said, frowning as Siva let out a low, mewling growl. 'And you can be quiet, Missy. You have caused enough trouble for one day.'

'I haven't had time to get changed or even wash,' Kate went on. The shorts she was wearing were doused in paint and there were smears of the wood stain she'd used for the deck across her vest and bare legs. Having stuffed all her hair underneath a baseball cap for two days, it now resembled a haystack after a particularly savage gale.

'You and the boat are fabulous, *bambina*,' Filippo said loyally. 'Look at all these people.'

The small group of onlookers had swelled now to a moderate crowd, many of whom were asking Kate if they could go aboard and pose for a photo in the deckchair. She had taken a fair number of pictures herself, both before, during and after she had completed her modest project, but had yet to post any online. She wanted to get Alex's approval first.

Opening Instagram, she discovered that her new account, which after much mulling she had named @Unexpected_Items, had gained another few hundred followers and a flood of comments and likes. While Kate appreciated that it was crass of her to seek validation in such a transparent way, she also couldn't deny that when kind people said complimentary things about her work, it made her happy. Her @Unexpected_Items account had become the one place on the Internet into which she could disappear for an hour a day without feeling as if she was being ridiculed or criticised. There was nothing lurking ready to bite; it was a safe space. Kate had spent more time scrolling through interior design feeds than she had on James's social media accounts this week, and that alone felt like a victory.

Taking a few steps away from the others, she stared out across the sea, blinking as the dancing sunlight reflected off the surface of the water, blinding her momentarily. Another boat had pulled up alongside Alex's now, its occupants lined up along one side to get a better look, and once again she felt an uneasy tug of concern.

Would Alex be angry when he saw what she'd done?

'I might go back to the hostel,' she told Toby and Filippo, overwhelmed suddenly by an urge to be anywhere but here. But as she turned to go, Kate saw the jeep pull up on the opposite side of the road and froze. Instead of getting out, Alex merely opened the driver's door and hoisted himself up so he could see over the heads of those that were gathered. Kate tried in vain to read his expression – as far as she could tell, he looked completely impassive.

'Hey,' she said cautiously, making her slow way towards him.

Alex's pale-blue gaze moved from his boat down to her.

'Hmm,' he said, his fingers drumming on the soft roof of the jeep.

'Surprise,' she said lamely, bringing up her hands in lacklustre celebration.

Alex pulled at his beard. He seemed to be chewing over his words and Kate braced herself for a telling-off.

'You hate it, don't you? Shit. I'm so sorry, Alex. I thought that I would – that it would be nice if I—'

'Trespassed and defaced?' he suggested, his tone so flat that she could not decipher whether he was joking or not.

'The plan was simply to clean it,' she told him, dropping her gaze to the dust that coated the jeep bonnet. 'But then I thought, why not use up some of the leftover paint and add a few extra touches to make the place more homely?'

'Homely?' he repeated.

'I can take the plants down,' she hurried out. 'And paint it all white, if that's what you prefer? I was honestly trying to do a nice thing. You've been so kind to me, and I wanted to repay the favour.'

'Right.' Alex sighed. 'Listen, it's all right. I'm fine with it. It's only that I prefer it if—'

He rubbed at his eyes in agitation. 'I know you meant well.'

'You hate it.' Kate could not hide her dismay. 'God, Alex – I'm so sorry.'

He shook his head. 'No, it's fine. You caught me on a bad day, that's all.'

'Is everything OK?' she asked, her voice softening. 'Has something happened?'

Alex squinted as he looked at her, his expression still unreadable.

'Nothing,' he said. 'Nothing you need to worry yourself with anyway. Here,' he added, clambering down and pressing Filippo's keys into her hand. 'Can you pass these on with my thanks?'

'Sure.' she said, 'but aren't you going to come and say hello? See the boat properly?'

Alex stared down at his feet. 'Not now. I have to be somewhere. In town. I'm meeting Joe, you know, my old friend with the kayaks. I'm late, as it happens. I'll catch up with you later, right?'

'But I—?'

Alex had already turned to go, and he did not look back. Not at the boat, not at the crowd of people with cameras and not at her. She had tried to do something nice and it had backfired. Worse than that, it had annoyed someone she liked, someone who had been nothing but sweet to her, had accepted and helped her.

In trying to get closer to Alex, all she had managed to do was push him away.

25

Kate barely left the hostel over the next few days in case Alex came back. But he didn't. Nor was there any sign of his boat in its usual spot when she ventured down to the cove early one morning, hoping to catch him before he went off for the day.

Having convinced herself that she was solely to blame for this disappearing act, Kate fretted so often and so intently that the usually unflappable Toby ended up snapping at her.

'You're more annoying than a daddy longlegs trapped in a shower cubicle,' he grumbled, shooing her out from behind reception. 'Go and sunbathe or something.'

'But what if he never comes back?' agonised Kate, nodding hello to Nika as the hostel's office manager strolled in through the open front door. As always, she looked impeccable in a crisp white shirt and pencil skirt, her long dark hair pulled back into a neat plait.

'Is there anything I can help with?' she asked her hopefully. 'Any cleaning to do?'

'Ana and Roko will be here at eleven to do the rooms,' Toby interrupted. 'As you well know.'

Kate scrunched her toes in frustration.

'Have you been to the Fortica yet?' asked Nika, whose excellent English made Kate's pathetic attempts to speak Croatian all the more embarrassing. 'The view from up on the battlements is beautiful.'

'I haven't actually,' said Kate, brightening a fraction. 'I suppose I could head over there. But only if you're sure I can't help out here?'

'Go,' urged Toby. 'Please. I love you, sis, but you are doing my head in today.'

'Fine,' she said. 'But if Alex happens to come back then—'

'I'll tie him to a chair and call you. Now scram.'

There was bound to be a backstreet route that would get Kate to Hvar's vast fortress far more quickly than the more obvious path that began down in the main square, but she was not in any hurry. It was too hot to walk at anything other than the most leisurely pace and the nape of her neck felt damp before she had reached the end of the first road.

Now that June had arrived, the temperature on the island was reaching a scorching peak, while the nights were becoming thick and muggy. Kate dithered as she walked, stopping to inhale the scent of baked earth, flowers and fresh herbs that wafted out from every garden she passed. As she drew closer to the harbour, she found neatly manicured trees hunched in pots alongside vast containers of basil, the rich green leaves making her yearn for a fresh platter of tomato and mozzarella, doused in pepper and slippery with olive oil.

The hub of the town was well populated, yet remained quiet, and Kate suspected this was due in part to the tall buildings that lined the narrow lanes. Sound floated upwards to be immediately muffled by thick stone; an echo made mute before it gained momentum. There was also a sense that people here had time; they weren't all in a rush, tripping over each other in their haste to reach work, attend a meeting or hurry home. Nobody stood on your foot in their haste to push in front of you or elbowed you out of their way; there was no tutting in cramped spaces, no passive aggression or barely concealed anger. Hvar was serene in that way, holding its visitors in an open palm rather than a fist curled tightly shut. Not for the first time, Kate wondered how much of a struggle she would find it to acclimatise once back in London.

When she reached St Stephen's Square, she weaved through the separate groups of people at speed, her well-practised feet finding easy purchase on the marble cobbles. The fortress was perched grandly atop the hillside above her, its outer walls splayed down like stony roots into the town. Kate had assumed it would take the best part of an hour to climb all the way up, so she was pleasantly surprised to find herself at the entrance to the outer grounds less than fifteen minutes later.

The path that snaked ahead of her was curled like a dropped ribbon, while crickets sang in unison amidst dust that hovered and swirled. The cactus plants here were even larger and more alien-like than their prickly cousins along the coast, the pine trees crooked spider carcases. Wooden benches had been placed at intervals along the route and there were a handful of pop-up stalls offering cold drinks, ice creams and souvenir sprigs of lavender. When the treeline cleared, the view of Hvar Town spread out below Kate was impressive enough to stop her in her tracks, and she stood for a few minutes, gazing down at the red rooftops and the flawless blue sky beyond.

Sweat had begun to bead on her top lip; her hair was now damp beneath her hat. Kate removed it, shaking out her dark-red tendrils as she did so. She smelt of the coconut shampoo she had brought with her from home, the last of which she had squeezed out of the bottle that morning. James used to gather handfuls of ringlets up and bury his face in them. 'You smell good enough to eat,' he would say, and she would fill up with love for him.

The young man she remembered from the early days of their relationship was so different to the James who had stood in that dingy pub corridor on the night of her party. They used to be so playful and silly, optimistic and upbeat, their mid-twenties spent on a carousel of parties, pubs and passionate nights where sleep did not so much as occur to them. They had explored and enjoyed one another without shame or agenda – no trace then of a nagging voice that whispered 'maybe this time. Maybe this time you will make a baby'. If she was honest with herself, it was that carefree era of her relationship that she mourned the most – not the grown-up part that had come later, not those feelings of such inadequacy. Kate was beginning to realise that if she stripped away all the pain of being rejected, and the hankering for a time when everything was easier, long before the love she felt for James had been tarnished by his disappointment in her, then the life which remained, the one she was living right now, was essentially a happy one. She was essentially happy.

Feeling a vibration in her bag, Kate dug out her phone, her suddenly hopeful heart lodged in her throat. But it was only a message from Robyn, confirming that she would be over to visit the following week and asking if Toby would collect her from Split. Kate smiled; this was great news. She could not wait to show her best friend around. Tapping out a quick reply and adding a gif of a sunbathing cat for good measure, Kate continued along the path only to stop again a few seconds later.

There was a figure sitting on a bench up ahead that she recognised.

Just as the deckchair she had nailed to the roof of his boat made it stand out from the rest, so Alex's untidy thatch of dreadlocks made him impossible to miss – or mistake for anyone else. Turning as Kate crunched over the fallen pine needles towards him, Alex smiled in what looked to be genuine pleasure before standing up to greet her.

'I can keep on walking past if you still hate me,' she said, gripping the brim of her hat in both hands.

Alex frowned. 'Hate you?'

'I wouldn't blame you if you did,' she said, watching as he folded his arms across a vest top that might once have been black. 'Not after what I did to your boat.'

'Don't be silly. You did a nice thing for me there, so no, I don't hate you. I promise,' he added, seeing her doubtful expression. 'Thank you, is what I should be saying, and what I didn't say before. I am grateful to you. It was a bloody tip and I'd been meaning to repaint the poor old girl for months.'

'You were?' Kate let out the breath she'd been holding in. 'Oh, thank god. I've been so worried. I honestly thought I'd annoyed you. It would be just like me to do something like that after all.'

'You say some right silly things,' he replied.

'But I thought, when you didn't come back, that I'd offended you.'

Alex scratched behind his ear. 'Well, that's on me, I guess,' he said. 'It wasn't like that.'

'Where have you been?' she asked. 'I mi— I mean, all of us have missed you. Siva especially. Filippo is having to hand out earplugs to the guests because she cries all night.'

Alex responded with a small laugh. 'The poor deluded thing. Although, I guess it's nice to feel wanted.'

'Wanted and missed,' Kate clarified.

Now that she believed he wasn't cross with her, she felt better – happy.

'I'm going right up to the top,' she told him, pointing. 'Do you want to keep me company?'

Alex considered, his hand stroking his beard. 'All right,' he said.

He'd not answered her question about where he'd been all week, and Kate repeated it as they rounded the next curve of the pathway.

'I was helping Joe out with something,' he said, apparently unwilling to elaborate further. 'I'm only in Hvar tonight, as it happens, and then I have to go away again.'

'Oh?' Kate was surprised by how much this news deflated her. 'Where to?'

'Brač,' he said, again not offering her any further explanation.

'For how long?'

A shrug. 'As long as it takes.'

Kate sighed with exasperation. 'Are you always this ... evasive?'

'I prefer the word mysterious.'

'An international man of mystery?'

'Well,' he countered lightly, 'not quite. A European man of mystery, I'll give you that much.'

'So, not James Bond? More Austin Powers?'

Alex glanced down at himself disparagingly. 'Nah – he has way better chest hair than I do.'

'Ja— my ex, he couldn't grow any at all,' Kate told him. 'He hasn't got so much as a single nipple hair. And he's going bald,' she added disloyally. 'He would be so jealous of all your hair.'

Alex pulled self-consciously at a few of his dreadlocks. 'There is quite a lot of it.'

'Do you ever think about cutting it all off?' she asked hopefully.

Alex gave her a sideways look. 'No.'

'What about the beard?'

'No.'

'Doesn't it feel hot, though?' she pressed, fanning her own sweltering face with her hat. 'You know, having all that hair on your face and head?'

Another shrug. 'Not really. I've lived here long enough now to have acclimatised.'

'How long is long enough?'

This time, it was Alex's turn to sigh in exasperation. 'Are you always so . . . what's that word again? Oh yeah – nosy.'

Kate laughed. 'I think the word you meant to use was "interested".'

They'd continued to walk as they talked and now found themselves at the fortress entrance. A bored-looking woman offered them a lacklustre smile from inside a small kiosk, but as Kate drew closer, Alex hung back.

'You're not coming in?'

'I've seen it before,' he said, 'and I need to save my pennies now to maintain my boat,' he went on. 'Can't have all those freshly painted stripes wearing thin now, can we?'

'It's my treat,' she said. 'Least I can do, given the fact that those stripes are down to me and my random redecoration project.'

She did not say as much to Alex, but it felt good to be able to pay for something. Being the higher earner, James had more often than not picked up the tab when the two of them went out for a meal or to see a show. He had far more disposable income, so it made sense – at least that's what he always told her. And Kate had accepted it, although it had always made her feel a pang of shame on every occasion. When someone else was paying for an experience, you couldn't really say if you hadn't enjoyed it, if your chips were cold or your steak overdone.

Kate paid for the two tickets and passed one across to Alex.

'Please,' she said. 'For me.'

She could not be sure, but it looked an awful lot like Alex was rolling his eyes at her.

'Nosy was the wrong word after all,' he said, taking the slip of paper with a grin. 'I should have gone for bossy.'

*   *   *

Unlike the rest of Hvar, which was quirky, quaint and quietly beautiful, the Fortico was grand, vast and sternly impressive. It made sense, though, Kate noted to Alex, that an island so precious should have a guardian this strong to watch over it.

When they had explored every turret and winding stairway, the two of them made their way up to the battlements at the front and peered over the outer wall.

'That is quite some view,' said Kate, her gaze drawn far out to sea.

'I think I can see Filippo over there,' said Alex, pointing north-east. 'Sunbathing nude on the roof terrace.'

'Where?' Kate exclaimed in delight, only to scoff as Alex began to laugh.

'Very funny,' she deadpanned. 'Didn't your mother ever tell you that it's cruel to mock the dumb?'

Alex merely shook his head, still triumphant to have tricked her so successfully.

'Gullibility is one of my many talents,' she informed him. 'Along with singing out of key, being sacked from jobs and getting dumped. Oh, and collecting wrinkles,' she added. 'I swear there are three or four more every morning.'

Alex ran a hand along the smooth shaft of a huge cannon – one of a number that were aimed out over the bay – and scrutinised her face.

'You look fine to me,' he said. 'Nothing wrong with a few lines anyway.'

'I hate them,' she moaned, dragging the skin taut across her cheeks. 'As soon as I have enough money, I'm going to get Botox.'

'Is that the stuff that freezes you up like an ice pop?' he checked, and Kate nodded. 'Don't go getting that.'

'But I need it,' she replied, pushing up her eyebrows and leering at him for comedy effect. 'I'm on a one-way street to Saggy Town.'

'What a load of nonsense.' Alex moved around the cannon and came towards her. 'Give me your hand a minute,' he said.

'Why?' Kate knotted her fingers into a fist and pressed it against her chest. 'What are you going to do?'

'Just trust me, OK? I want to show you something.'

Kate unknotted.

'Right,' he said, taking her hand and leading her across the battlements. 'Touch this,' he instructed, placing Kate's hand flat against the stone wall of the fortress. 'Now, tell me how it feels.'

'Rough,' she said. 'And cold – which is a miracle on a day like this.'

'And do you like it?' he asked. 'The roughness?'

'I do,' she agreed, as he removed his hand from hers. 'I like the way it looks, too, all jagged edges and general cragginess. It's atmospheric.'

'Exactly,' he said.

'Are you saying I resemble an old ruin?' Kate replied. 'Because if so, I would agree with you.'

'No,' Alex said patiently. 'What I am trying to say is that wear and tear can be a positive thing. Imagine if this wall here had been plastered over – it wouldn't be quite so captivating then, would it?'

'No, but—'

'It's the toughness of the stone that is so enthralling,' he continued. 'It tells of history and of a life lived. To plaster over the cracks would be to erase the truth, and the beauty.'

'I guess so.' Kate rubbed at the wall until dust began to fall. 'But this is a building, not a human face. It can't speak and tell us its stories in the same way a person can.'

'Sure,' he said easily, 'but I would argue that a face left to age naturally carries far more intrigue and individualism than one full of chemicals that turn it into a mask. Those plastic-faced people don't interest me at all, but you—'

'I what?' said Kate, glancing up in time to see his cheeks redden beneath his beard.

'You're interesting,' he said. 'And your face is more than fine exactly the way it is – you don't need to mess around injecting poison into it.'

'Can't afford it anyway,' mumbled Kate, but she was smiling.

They did another full circuit of the battlements, Alex pointing out each of the Pakleni Islands and telling her the names of the various beaches.

'How many islands are there in Croatia?' she asked, her eyes widening in surprise at his answer. 'Over one thousand two hundred? No wonder everyone owns a boat of some sort. Speaking of which,' she added, 'I don't suppose you'd let me visit yours again so I can take a few photos?'

'Photos? What for?'

'For my Unexpected Items Instagram account,' she explained, digging out her phone so she could show him.

Alex looked nonplussed. 'Fine by me,' he said. 'We can go there now, if you want. Unless . . .' He paused, his mouth moving as he contemplated what to say next.

'Unless?' Kate echoed gently, watching as a shadow of what looked to be uncertainty passed across his face.

'This job I have in Brač, it's a hotel clearance. The previous owners sold it as it stood, full of furniture, and the new buyer wants the place emptied. I don't suppose you'd like to—'

'Come and help you clear it out? Yes, please!'

'I'll do all the heavy lifting,' he assured her. 'But you can go through the bits and pieces, take anything you like the look of – well, as much of it as will fit on my boat.'

'And the buyer is happy to just throw it all out?' she said. 'How wasteful.'

He nodded. 'All the more reason to come, in that case. You'd be doing a good thing by rescuing some of it. You like rescuing things, as I remember it. Mirrors, gnomes, cats . . .'

'Haha,' she said. 'Are you sure you want me?'

'Well, you know,' said Alex, 'if you're going to make a man's boat an object of ridicule, then the least you can do is sail along on it with him.'

26

Kate was waiting outside the hostel when Alex strolled down the wide shaded street at a little after seven the following morning.

'Nice day for it,' she said, in answer to his solitary hand of greeting. He was wearing the same frayed denim shorts he always seemed to be in, but today had pulled a red hooded top over his habitual vest. It was already warm, but the breeze coming in off the water carried enough of a chill to raise the hairs along Kate's arms. She'd opted for a mustard-yellow pinafore dress over a plain white T-shirt, thinking she would change into her tatty decorating ensemble when they reached Brač.

Alex had tied back his dense swathe of dreadlocks today and tucked as many of them as he could underneath a baseball cap with the word 'Croatia' threaded across the front.

'That it?' he asked, glancing at the rucksack beside Kate's feet. It was Toby's and, given that she had crammed it seam-splittingly full of her belongings, weighed almost as much as he did.

'I didn't know what to bring.'

'So, you brought everything you own, plus a bit extra for luck?'

'If you think this is bad, you should see my suitcases.'

'Suitcases plural?' Alex clenched his teeth. 'Blimey.'

There it was again, thought Kate – that trace of an accent she could never quite place.

'You know we're only away for one or two nights?' he went on, his bemusement mounting as he tested the weight of the bag.

'You can never be too prepared,' Kate said, then, when he went to pick it up. 'I can manage.'

With a Herculean effort, she lifted the rucksack and managed to get both her arms through the straps. When she bent forwards to retrieve her second, much smaller bag from the floor, however, she almost toppled right over.

'Here,' said Alex, squatting down in front of her. Kate was about to lurch away, but he was only doing up her waist strap. As soon as each side was correctly adjusted, the weight on her shoulders eased and she sighed in relief.

'Toby didn't bother showing me how to wear this thing,' she told him, tutting good-naturedly as the two of them set off down the hill. 'He was probably amused by the idea of me staggering around like an overburdened camel.'

'Camels don't tend to stagger very often,' said Alex. 'I would go for a donkey – one of those poor sods that trail up and down rainy British beaches carrying blokes in "Kiss me quick, squeeze me slow" hats.'

'Gee.' Kate groaned humourlessly. 'Thanks.'

Alex had moored his boat not far from the church that Kate had hurried past in tears the day she found out Nika was pregnant, but she forced herself not to think about that. Thanks to having had a decent amount of practice when she was redecorating, Kate was able to clamber over the side of the freshly repainted vessel with far more grace than she had the first time. Alex busied himself with wedging her rucksack through the gap and down into the small cabin area at the front of the boat, while Kate zipped up a life vest and tried her best not to notice the large grubby footprints they'd both left all over the immaculate deck.

'It shouldn't take us that long to reach Brač,' he said. 'We'll leave the boat at the port in Supetar then drive out to the hotel from there.'

'Sounds good,' said Kate, speaking loudly in order to be heard over the clanking chain of the anchor. 'Whereabouts is it – the hotel, I mean?'

'Škrip,' he said, readjusting the peak of his baseball cap. 'It's a small village with a big history. Most of the tourists that visit Brač head to Bol in the south, but we'll be up in the north.'

'I've heard of Bol,' she told him. 'That's the place with the famous long beach.'

'Correct,' he said, firing up the engine. 'You can go there this afternoon, if you like there are buses.'

'No, no. This is a business trip, not a leisure one,' she said, easing into the seat across from his as they began to move slowly away from the harbour. 'I'm not work shy,' she added, pushing her glasses further up her nose. 'James used to accuse me of not "applying myself" enough, but it was never the hard graft part that put me off.'

She was doing it again – *James, James, James.*

'As a wise friend once told me, it's all about finding the right fit,' Alex said. 'And it's nice that you're coming with me today – I mean that – but truth be told, I do work better on my own. I prefer to knuckle down and get the job done, snappy like.'

'Snappy like a crocodile sandwich,' she joked limply, at which he laughingly shook his head.

'If you say so.'

They had left Hvar behind now and the sky was a tepid forget-me-not blue. The wind that had been the merest whisper that morning gathered pace the further out to sea they sped, and Kate was glad that for once she had left her straw hat behind.

'Do you know all these people?' she asked, as the third boat they passed had its horn tooted by a friendly operator.

'No,' he said. 'They're honking in appreciation of the deckchair. Ever since you nailed it up there, I've been forced to fend off attention all over the island – a girl even wanted to take a photo of me the other day, as if I was a bloody celebrity or something.'

'Oops,' said Kate, grimacing as she raised her eyes to the cabin roof. 'I did wonder about that flapping sound.'

'Yeah,' he said. 'Quite loud, isn't it?'

'It sounds like you're being applauded by a huge crowd of people,' she declared. 'The faster we go, the louder they clap.'

'In that case,' said Alex, and he opened the throttle.

With the rumbling drone of the engine, the flapping canvas of the deckchair and the thudding slap of the waves as they crashed against the boat, it was too noisy to continue talking. Kate settled into her seat, her gaze going from the view to Alex's broad shoulders beneath the red hoodie. With his dreadlocks tucked away for once, he looked almost handsome – not her type, exactly, but definitely attractive. She recalled Robyn's Dothraki comment and wondered if her friend's initial interest would gain pace when she met the man himself. That was if Robyn got to meet him. Kate could never be sure where Alex was going to be from one day to the next, and neither, it seemed, did he. If she hadn't happened to bump into him up by the fortress, she may not have seen him again for ages and that would have been a shame. Time spent with Alex was good time. Kate felt comfortable around him for reasons she could not quite explain, and she trusted him, too, in spite of his refusal to answer half the questions she fired at him. She still had no idea where he was from, what his family situation was or why he had left the UK in the first place – but it bothered her far less than a lot of things did. In fact, when she thought about it, really thought about it, Kate realised that she was closer to being relaxed here in Croatia than she ever had been in her life. If she could only fix the James issue – *and the fertility issue,* whispered a cruel voice – then life would not be too bad at all.

It had been weeks now since her near-panic attack on the roof terrace, since she had given in to what she was feeling and let it consume her, and that version of Kate Nimble felt far away now – a dark outline at the very end of a tunnel.

Alex had just said something to her, but Kate had missed it. She imagined his words being whipped away from them by the wind, torn up and scattered across the water. How strange to think of all those uttered phrases floating about, weightless and unanchored. So much of what people said was instantly forgotten.

'What did you say?' she called over the thrum of the engine, and Alex pointed ahead.

'Land ahoy,' he said, smiling at her with such warmth that Kate was sure she could feel it.

'Aye, aye, captain!' she retorted, hopping off her seat as the boat began to slow.

Alex stared at her; his expression turned so abruptly blank that Kate wondered if something inside his mind had short-circuited. Then, almost the same moment she had registered his change in mood, Alex seemed to reboot, and laughingly tipped the front of his cap.

Was he, like her, pretending to the world that everything was fine when, in reality, something far darker was lurking beneath the surface? Perhaps if she had not become such an expert in glossing over this blackness herself, then Kate would not have seen it. But she had.

And if the Alex smiling at her now was concealing some deeper truth, then who, or what, was he hiding?

27

'I thought you said we were driving?'

Kate gawped in horror at first Alex, and then the moped he had just dismounted. Promising he'd be back to pick her up within ten minutes, he had left her and the overstuffed rucksack waiting in the shade of a pomegranate tree, the fruit from which matched her sunburnt shoulders. Kate had envisaged him driving up in a jeep like Filippo's, or at the very least, one of the small hire cars she'd seen parked all over Hvar. This rickety-looking contraption was neither.

'Generally, you do have to drive scooters,' he said. 'They don't have a self-steer function yet, though I would be willing to bet that somebody is working on it.'

'We can't go anywhere on that thing,' she exclaimed. 'Where will all the stuff from the hotel go? Where will my bag go? Where will I go?'

'You're behind me,' he said. 'And as for your stuff . . .' Alex extracted a key from the pocket of his shorts and opened the moped's cracked leather seat. There was a small storage hatch in the space underneath containing two coiled straps.

'We can tie it on the back. Unless you feel safe wearing it?'

'I don't feel safe about any of this,' Kate said fretfully. 'What if I fall off?'

'You won't, not if you're holding on,' he replied, picking up her backpack as if it weighed nothing and fixing it securely in place. His own bag, which was less than a third the size of hers, fitted neatly in the footwell. Kate rocked from one white

Converse to the other as she watched him, chewing distract-edly at her nails.

'Are there no cars available?' she pleaded, glancing around the port in the hope that one might somehow appear.

Alex straightened up and handed her a helmet. 'Scooters are cheaper,' he said. 'And better for the environment.'

'And death traps,' she added, to which he raised both eyebrows.

'The new owner told me he's happy to drive any furniture you want back down here in his van,' he assured her. 'Come on, don't look like that – you might even enjoy it. You were fine in the kayak and you don't even have to steer this thing, only hold on.'

Kate pulled a face.

'I've been driving mopeds for years now and I tell you what, they're a lot easier to handle than a boat. I got you this far in one piece, didn't I?'

'You don't have the best history with scooters, if I remember rightly,' Kate pointed out, recalling the scars he'd shown her on his elbow, but she accepted the helmet regardless. Once on, it pinned her ears flat against her head and caused the arms of her glasses to dislodge. Not that she wanted to be able to see the landscape rushing past at an alarming speed. What was exhilar-ating on the water felt much scarier on dry land. And if you fell into water, you wouldn't end up with a tarmac tan.

Alex got into position first, holding the bike steady as Kate clambered into place behind him, her feet finding the small metal struts with relative ease. It was the closest physically that she had been to Alex, and as she shuffled forward in an attempt to get more comfortable, she became immediately aware of how warm his body felt through the tattered red hoodie. She would have preferred not to have her thighs pressed quite so snugly against his, but with the bag strapped behind her, there was no room left to wriggle.

'Ready?' Alex said, one hand holding the brake and the other easing back the throttle. Kate could feel the vibration of the engine through the seat and tried not to think about how many small moving parts she was relying upon to keep them safe – not to mention how dirty, dusty and oil-stained she would be by the time they reached their destination. Wearing this dress had been a mistake; she should have got straight into her old leggings.

'Ready as I'll ever be—'

The last word came out as a high-pitched shriek as the moped surged forward, and Kate shut her eyes as they zoomed off along the main road.

'Fun, right?' he shouted, just as Kate sneaked a peek in time to see a flurry of tourists darting out of their way.

'No,' she yelled back, wrapping her arms more tightly around him as they nipped between cars, motorbikes and a vast, fume-belching coach. One of Alex's dreadlocks had broken loose from the constraints of his helmet and Kate spluttered as it flew into her open mouth.

They were following the road that ran along the coast, but all Kate could focus on was the blur of the trees, the wasp-like drone of the engine, the flash of grey asphalt speeding beneath the tyres and the banging of her heart inside her chest.

Alex, by comparison, seemed totally at ease, his body slouched as if he was in an armchair.

I must try to relax, Kate thought, releasing some of the rigid tension in her shoulders. It was not so bad; she was coping fine. Alex seemed to know what he was doing, but there was no way he would stay in the seat if she happened to fall. Kate was holding onto to him so tightly now that if she fell, he surely would too – a thought that offered minimal comfort.

The further they drove, the more Kate's initial fear was replaced by something closer to pleasure. She began to appreciate the feel of the warm air cascading across her bare arms and the comforting bulk of Alex pressed against her.

'Still OK back there?' he called.

'I'm great,' she replied, pleased to discover that she was. 'Once you get past the constant fear of a violent and bloody death, it's not too bad.'

Kate felt his stomach muscles contract beneath her hands as he laughed.

The narrow lane they were zooming along banked sharply uphill, the companionable blue curtain of the sea disappearing from sight as neatly packed houses sprung up on either side. Dust swarmed around them, the pitch of the moped's throttle reaching a high note of effort as the slope steepened further still. Kate was just wondering if they would make it to the top at all when Alex briskly applied the brakes, skidding them to an untidy standstill beside a set of sandstone steps.

'Sorry about the emergency stop,' he said, as Kate lurched sideways off the seat. 'I thought the hotel was further up. I haven't been out here in a while – not since the spring.'

'Just when I was starting to trust this thing as well,' she replied, giving the bike a stern look as she dismounted. It felt strange to be on solid ground again, her legs trembling in time to the moped's dawdling engine.

Alex removed his helmet and slipped it over one of the handlebars, so Kate followed suit on the other side, her hand going up automatically to ruffle her flattened hair and rearrange her glasses. The owner had left a set of keys in a coded lockbox beside the front door, and she watched as Alex leapt nimbly up the steps to collect them.

'The skip is out by the pool,' he told her, waiting by the now-open doors. 'Why don't you see if there's anything already in there and I'll get cracking with the clearing?'

Kate made her way into a dark reception area and stared around, blinking as her eyes adjusted to the gloom. The hotel was dated, with heavy wooden furniture and a seventies colour palette of rusts and browns. Alex had already explained that the man who'd bought the place had grand plans to update it and wanted everything painted either white or grey. Remembering this now as she took it all in, Kate wrinkled her nose.

'Your face is a picture,' Alex told her, clearly amused.

'If the new owner opts for sterile colours in here, it's going to end up looking more like a hospital than a hotel,' she said, stepping into what appeared to be a lounge and admiring the Artex ceiling. 'They'd do better with something warmer – and these walls are so high, there's scope to do some exciting things with the decoration.'

'Should I call him?' Alex offered, his ancient Nokia already in his hand. 'He's Danish, but his English is not half bad. You could tell him your ideas.'

'No, no.' Kate flapped an embarrassed hand. 'I was just thinking aloud, that's all. It's his hotel; he can do whatever he likes. I'm sure he knows better than me anyway.'

'Are you sure? I've only met him once, but he seems quite laid-back. I don't think you'd offend him, if that's what you're worried about.'

'He's rich,' Kate reminded him. 'He can pay to hire a professional interior designer.'

'Or he can pay you.' Alex was leaning against the door-frame, his arms folded and his Croatia baseball cap back in place.

'But I'm not an interior designer. I'm an amateur at best.'

Alex cocked his head to the side and stared at her.

'Why are you looking at me like that?'

'I was just thinking about that conversation we had a while back. You know, about the importance of finding the right fit. Have you not ever wondered if interior design might be yours?'

Kate had wondered that. She'd been wondering it more and more. But it was ridiculous. Anyone could match colours, choose artwork and follow a YouTube tutorial on how to create light fittings from old jelly moulds if they put their minds to it. What she had achieved at the hostel and on Alex's boat was fluke. Nothing she could turn into a viable career.

'Who was it that said that again?' she asked. 'Your wise old friend Yoda, wasn't it?'

Alex shifted a fraction. 'Josh.'

'That's right,' she said lightly. 'But I think you give him too much credit.'

'What do you mean?' Alex's expression was unreadable.

'I think,' she said, 'that's it you who's the wise one.'

28

It wasn't until the light began to fade that Kate realised she had not seen Alex for a while. He'd left her outside by the hotel's empty pool, surrounded by her piles of collected treasures, telling her he had a quick errand to run. But that had been at least an hour ago.

She'd been listening to a true crime podcast while she examined each of the items she'd salvaged, but now the silence seemed to ring. In the hostel, there was always noise, the footfalls of guests and the music drifting down from the roof terrace, while up here in Škrip, she couldn't hear any signs of life. Even the crickets had fallen silent, their chorus dimmed, as the sun had been, by the passing of day into night.

Kate picked up her phone, thinking she would call Alex, then realised she didn't have his number and sent a message to Toby instead, asking him to ping it across. How absurd that she hadn't asked Alex himself yet; they'd known each other for weeks now. But then again, he wasn't the sort to engage in text exchanges. He was more of a face-to-face man – when he deigned to show up, that was.

Kate heard what sounded like twigs cracking and stood up abruptly from the rusted sunlounger she'd been perched on. The pool terrace was walled in, but she still felt exposed out here by herself.

Perhaps listening to a true crime podcast hadn't been the best idea. Grabbing her smaller bag, she hurried towards the double doors at the back of the hotel and went inside. There were no lights on, and it was so dark that Kate had to use the torch function of her phone to search the walls for a switch.

'That's better,' she said aloud, as the room was illuminated once more, and after closing the outer doors, she made her way into the reception area. The ancient desk that had been there that morning was gone, broken down into pieces by her and Alex and stacked in the skip, but her rucksack was where she'd left it, balanced against the wall.

Kate jumped as her phone vibrated with a message. It was Toby.

'Al's number to follow. Filippo says, don't do anything he and I definitely would.'

Kate's lip curled as she took in the winking-face emoji he'd added at the end. Idiot.

Alex didn't answer when she called, but before she could type out a text message to him, one arrived. *Sorry. Errand took longer than expected. Back soon. A.*

So, he had her number then. That must be Toby's doing.

Kate looked and felt bedraggled in her stained T-shirt and leggings, her once-pristine white Converse streaked with dirt from a day of moving furniture. There were plenty of bathrooms upstairs; surely the new owner wouldn't object to her having a quick shower?

Alex hadn't yet shown her which room she'd be sleeping in, so Kate chose the first she came across, which contained a bedframe but no mattress and a single lamp with a cracked porcelain base. There were no towels in the en suite, of course, but Kate had brought along two of her own, plus a washbag full of products, a first-aid kit – you could never be too sure – and a clingy black dress on the off chance that she ended up somewhere fancy.

Not much chance of that.

Peeling off her clothes, Kate switched on the water and stepped gingerly into the cubicle only to leap out backwards with a yelp. It was cold. Freezing cold.

'Don't do this to me,' she begged, reaching in to fiddle with the lever.

It was no good; there was no hot water.

She had two choices: either she remained in her current sweaty and grimy state or she brave the chilly deluge. Dirt was not an option, though, so really she had no choice.

Gritting her teeth, Kate ducked under the shower and scrubbed herself as hard and as fast as she could, her teeth chattering and her shoulders up to her ears. Unable to face washing her hair, she angled her head out of the way and edged the other parts of herself forwards one at a time, realising as she did so how utterly ridiculous she must look. A few weeks ago, this situation would have upset her; it would have been another in a long line of disasters that always seemed to befall her and only her. But today, Kate found that she didn't mind so much. If anything, it was funny. Typical, yes, but also amusing.

She began to laugh, chuckling at first, then eventually giving into great hoots of mirth as she shimmied around in the small enclosed space. Executing a perfect pirouette, Kate's bar of soap flew out of her hand onto the wet tiles, and as she bent over to grope for it, she heard a voice.

'Kate? Kate is that you? Are you all rig— Oh!'

'No, no, no!' she yelped, just as Alex burst through the open bathroom door. Swinging around, Kate's foot found the dropped soap and she slipped over sideways, crashing through the flimsy cubicle door and landing wetly in Alex's arms.

Utterly mortified, she struggled to gain purchase on the damp floor but only succeeded in falling further towards the ground. In his attempt to put her right, Alex's hands found the underside of her boobs. It was the merest touch, barely more than a graze, but it triggered a sensation in Kate that she had not felt in some time – an urgency that flooded her cheeks with heat.

Heart racing, she staggered away from him.

'Are you OK?' he asked. Now that his hands were free, he slapped one of them over his eyes.

'Sure,' she said, voice wobbling as she snatched up her towel. 'I mean, I'm closer to death by embarrassment than I've ever been before, but other than that . . .'

'Sorry,' he said, gingerly lowering his hand as Kate gave in to hopeless laughter. 'I thought someone was torturing you up here – what the hell was that noise?'

'That was me,' she said indignantly. 'Laughing.'

'Really?' He looked genuinely astonished. 'Wow. I honestly thought you were in pain.'

'You're lucky I wasn't singing,' she said, stepping past him into the bedroom. 'That would probably have taken the windows out.'

Her heart was still crashing away, an internal percussion of total and utter humiliation.

'I should get dressed,' she added, when he made no move to go. In truth, she'd never felt more naked, only not in a way that made her feel uncomfortable. She thought cold showers were supposed to douse feelings of arousal, not stir them up.

'Oh, yes, I'll get out of your hair.' Alex for once appeared unsure of himself and Kate watched as he strode towards the door and disappeared from sight.

Could he tell that her goosebumps had little to do with the temperature of the water? Was he aware of the crackling energy that had sprung up between them?

Shaking her head, Kate unzipped the rucksack and pulled out the first item of clothing that came to hand – her black dress. The underwear she'd been wearing all day was on the floor in plain view, but Alex had seen a lot more than her knickers; he'd also seen her naked body – had touched her bare, wet, naked body. But far from feeling upset, ashamed or even regretful in the wake of this unexpected event, Kate was surprised by how little she minded. Now that the initial embarrassment had subsided, she could not stop giggling, and she continued to smile, at the memory of falling into his arms, at the sense of humour that fate continued to display, while she dressed and brushed her hair.

Alex was out on the terrace when she made her way back downstairs. He'd lit a number of tea lights and placed them along one edge of the empty pool, and there were two large sofa cushions on the ground beside a paraffin camping stove.

'Hey,' he said, glancing up from where he was crouched over a frying pan. 'I hope you like fish?'

'I do,' Kate said, the hot sensation she had felt in the bedroom burning every bit as brightly as the candles.

Alex held up a small glass bottle.

'There's a saying in Croatia that the fish here swim three times – in the sea, in olive oil, and in wine. I can't offer you the last one I'm afraid, but two out of three isn't too bad, is it?'

'Shame about the wine,' she said, lowering herself down onto one of the cushions. 'I could use a drink after what just happened.'

'I do have some water,' he offered, not meeting her eyes.

Kate poked him with a finger. 'That's OK,' she said. 'I swallowed quite a lot in the shower – that's what happens when you laugh open-mouthed, like I do.'

'I'm glad you were finding something that funny,' he said. 'What were you so amused about anyway – you never said?'

Kate removed her glasses and began cleaning them with the bottom of her dress.

'Oh, you know, life – myself,' she told him. 'The water was freezing, and I was just . . . It doesn't matter. It's stupid. I'm stupid, you should have worked that one out by now.'

Alex shook his head. He was no longer wearing the baseball cap and his dreadlocks were obscuring his eyes. He didn't smell like a man who had done a hard day's work, and Kate noticed that the fingers he was now using to sprinkle herbs from a small packet across two silvery fish were spotlessly clean.

'You're not stupid, Kate.' His voice was soft, yet firm.

'Oh, but I am,' she said, twisting open the bottle of water he passed across. 'And the ironic thing is, I came to Croatia to escape ridicule. Only apparently, it's followed me here.'

Alex was rooting through his bag now, and Kate watched as he removed first a handful of tomatoes, then a neat red onion.

'Would you?' he asked, motioning towards a wooden chopping board and knife. 'I have to keep an eye on the fish, make sure it doesn't singe.'

'Sure.'

Happy to have been given a task, Kate sat forward and started to slice.

'There's some bread in there, too,' he added, nodding towards the bag. 'By some miracle, I got to the bakery a few minutes before they shut.'

'You've thought of everything,' she said, smiling at him. 'Thanks.'

'I was away a little longer than planned,' he said, resting his chin on his raised knee. 'Fish weren't biting; I had to move around a bit.'

'Hang on.' Kate paused in her chopping. 'You're saying you caught those?'

'Of course I did.'

'As in, just now, from the sea?'

'Well, unfortunately they don't grow on trees.'

'That is impressive,' she said, cutting into the onion. 'If I tried to fish, the only thing I'd be likely to catch would be a cold.'

'Do you want me to do that?' Alex asked, as Kate's eyes began to stream.

She shook her head. 'It's fine. It's actually nice to be crying over something other than James for a change. Sorry,' she added, as his expression clouded over. 'I know I talk about him too much. It must be tedious. In fact, I know it is – Toby makes no secret of the fact.'

'He means a lot to you, this James fella?'

Kate nodded.

'Then of course you want to talk about him.'

Was that right? Did she keep talking about James because she loved him, or was it simply that she wanted to make sense of what he had done to her? Kate had come to the conclusion recently that it was more to do with the latter, but perhaps Alex was right, and it was the love she felt that was spurring her on, not the pain.

Because she did still love James. Didn't she?

'Have you ever had your heart broken?' she asked, reaching for the oil and drizzling some of it over the salad. The bread he'd bought smelt fresh and steam escaped when she broke a piece off.

'Not in the way you have,' he replied. 'Not like that.'

The fish was almost cooked, and Alex was busy preparing plates and cutlery. His small satchel appeared to have Mary Poppins carpet-bag dimensions, and Kate made admiring remarks as he arranged everything on the floor between the cushions.

'Do you mean that nobody has ever dumped you?' she said, smiling as he passed her a plate.

Alex paused for a moment before replying. 'Not really, no.'

Getting information out of Alex was like sifting through coal dust for diamonds. She would have to choose her moment to push him for more information, because this was not it. The two of them were about to share a meal that he'd prepared, and Kate did not want to say or do anything that might make him feel uncomfortable.

She wondered if he had a girlfriend – or maybe even boyfriend – tucked away on a neighbouring island. Certainly he gave no indication that this was the case, but he wasn't the type to offer any real titbits about his private life. He wouldn't necessarily discuss his personal relationships with anyone, although Kate liked to think that the two of them were friends now. And friends shared things. They talked and supported and let down their guard around each other. Might it be that all Alex needed was a nudge from her?

Perhaps if she led, then he would follow.

29

'God, that fish was delicious.'

'You're still not over it, two hours later?'

Kate smiled and rubbed her stomach for effect. 'I may never be over it,' she told him. 'You may have ruined every other fish supper I have, from now until the day I die, because none of them will ever measure up.'

Alex raised his eyes from the fan of playing cards in his hand. They were on their seventh game of Rummy, and having won three rounds each, this was the decider.

'You're going to hate me,' he warned, as he placed the King of Hearts down on the top of the pile.

'You've bloody won, haven't you?' she groaned, rolling over onto her side as he lowered the rest of his hand with a flourish. 'I knew I'd peaked too early with my triple victory at the start.'

'You should have stopped the game there,' he said. 'Generosity gets you nowhere.'

'Says the man who cooked the fish,' she countered. 'The man who caught the fish, who brought me here, who continues to put up with me.'

'Oi,' said Alex, frowning hard to beat back a smile. 'Less of that. I demand, as this evening's overall Rummy champion, that you not say anything else bad about yourself, or apologise, for at least twenty-four hours.'

'Twenty-four hours? But . . . but . . .'

'You're lucky I didn't say twenty-four years.'

Kate sat back upright and began to shuffle the cards. The tea lights had long since burned out, but the moon above them was full. She could hear the drone of a mosquito, but found she had no desire to shoo it away. There were worse things in life than the odd bite and her limbs felt leaden with complacency. It was not a feeling that came to her often, and Kate luxuriated in it now, this unfamiliar sense that nothing mattered all that much, that everything would somehow be all right.

'What do you want to play next?' she asked. 'Or, should I say, what would you like to beat me at next? Unless you're too tired?' she added, as Alex stifled a yawn. He'd fished a silver coin out of his pocket and was flicking it with his thumb into the air, catching it each time without so much as a sideways glance.

'Back in a sec,' he said. 'I just need to check something.'

Kate stared after him as he made his way inside, the coin glinting as it was tossed up and down, the hood of his jumper bouncing as he hurried up the steps. Almost as soon as he had disappeared from view, she felt a chill, and putting down the cards, reached for her cardigan.

A light went on in one of the first-floor windows, then was promptly switched off again, and a few moments later, another glow shone out from the floor above. Was it too much to hope that Alex was raiding the minibars? She was still hankering after a drink, but when he eventually returned it was not with alcohol, but more cushions and a blanket.

'I know you said that you weren't the type to sleep out on the deck of a boat,' he said, 'but how about on the terrace of an empty hotel? It's a bit creepy in there, if you ask me, and out here you'll be able to see the stars.'

'I don't know.' Kate eyed the boundary wall warily. 'What if bears get in?'

'Bears? There are no bears. This is Croatia, not the Canadian Rockies.'

'Snakes, then? What if snakes slide under the covers?'

'You'd be unlucky to find a snake all the way out here,' he said.

'Murderers, then? Murderers are everywhere.'

Alex fixed her with a look. 'I'll stay out here with you, as your protector against any bears, snakes or murderers that happen to pass by.'

'Aren't there any mattresses inside?' she asked, but Alex shook his head.

'You go indoors if you want to, but I prefer to be out here. I don't mind,' he added. 'I just figured it made more sense for us to stay together.'

'In case a killer comes to get us,' she pointed out. 'Admit it.'

'What is it with you and being murdered?' he laughed, tossing her the blanket and dropping the extra cushions onto the floor. 'I'm merely trying to be companionable.'

Alex built himself a makeshift bed and lay back, one arm hooked under his head and the other resting across his chest.

'Don't you need a blanket?' Kate asked, arranging her own cushions. She should go inside and clean her teeth, wash off the make-up she had put on. But she didn't want to; she couldn't find the energy.

'I'll be fine, don't you worry yourself.'

Kate wanted to take off her bra before she lay down, but would Alex read that as some sort of sign? He'd given her no indication that he was interested in that way and she had no reason to think that he was, but then there had been that undeniable heat in the bedroom upstairs; and he had been the one to suggest they sleep out here. It had been so long since Kate had been alone with any man but James that she worried she could be reading the situation all wrong. The last thing she wanted was more humiliation – for either of them.

She was just about to gather up the bedding and head inside after all, when she heard Alex murmur something.

'What was that?' she asked, lowering herself down onto one elbow.

'I was admiring the moon,' he said, his gaze focused up at the sky. 'I've always been a big fan.'

Kate shuffled herself flat, the blanket covering her bare legs.

'I suppose I haven't ever taken the time to properly look at it before,' she confessed. 'I guess, she's always just been there – a constant that I was happy to accept but never question.'

'I like that you do that,' he said. 'I like that you think of the moon as a she.'

'I don't know why I do.' Kate kept her eyes fixed on the smooth white pebble above them. 'Perhaps because I associate loneliness with being female.'

'You see the moon as lonely?'

His tone was one of surprise, and Kate turned her head to find him watching her.

'Well, she is. There's nothing else up there with her, is there?'

'I think that being alone and loneliness are two different things,' he said quietly. 'There's an elegance to solitude. I've always thought of the moon as having accepted her position up there for the greater good, because people look to her to be their guide. She saves lives, by being up there, by remaining alone.'

'Spoken like a true fisherman,' said Kate, glancing away and up towards the stars once again. Away from the lights of Hvar, she could see even more of them than usual; it was a beautiful, ethereal sight.

'It takes guts to stride out on your own,' she said. 'The moon must be brave – a real Wonder Moon-man.'

Alex made a noise of amusement, but didn't say anything and again, Kate turned her head to find him facing her. The intensity she had grown accustomed to seeing in his pale-blue eyes was not there tonight, but he still looked thoughtful, as if trying to work her out.

'Trust me to make a lame joke in the middle of a deep conversation,' she said. 'There you are talking about the merits of the moon and I'm trying to turn her into a pun. And not even a good one at that.'

'Oh, I don't know,' he said, stretching his arms out and yawning with the effort. 'I've heard worse.'

'You really know how to make a girl feel special.'

Alex laughed. 'I cooked you a fish dinner, missy – what more do you want?'

'Oh, you know,' she said mildly. 'Just the moon. Maybe one or two stars.'

'It would be nothing you didn't deserve.'

There it was – that intensity. Kate could almost feel it, her blood running hot as she stared at him, and he back at her. She parted her lips and saw him mirror the gesture, a pink bud amid the dark foliage of beard. Her hands were clasped together against her chest and she slowly unfurled her fingers. He must be able to hear the ferocious beating of her heart; a thudding in the space between them.

Whatever was happening, she did not want to question it.

Kate closed her eyes, one hand going down to pull the cover higher. It was a warm night, the dark air a weighted blanket thrown across them, but she shivered, a pulse throbbing insistently from somewhere deep inside. It made no sense that she was feeling this way, that she was so stirred, but she welcomed it.

He was still gazing at her, Kate could feel it, did not need to open her eyes to know that he was there. Slowly, very slowly, she looked. Alex was close enough to touch and she moved towards him, her body holding her breath captive as the gap between them closed.

He started to say her name, but she silenced him with a kiss, and for a moment he froze, his mouth unyielding. Kate drew back, then pressed her lips against his once again, and this time he responded, kissing her quietly and with infinite care. A hand cupped her face, his fingers stroking, a curl across her cheek brushed gently away.

She wanted this, wanted him – but there was a reluctance inside her. A trace of foreboding that caused her to pause. Alex opened his eyes, searching hers for an answer, and she looked away.

'Sorry, I . . .'

'Don't be sorry,' he said. 'I understand.'

Kate sighed at his words, leaning forwards until her forehead was resting against his, trying in vain to draw strength from him, to find a way to silence the insistent whispers that told her this was wrong; that she would hurt him, or he hurt her. She could have screamed with frustration, but instead she simply breathed, her chest rising and falling as Alex moved slowly away from her.

'I'll be back in a moment,' he said quietly. 'Don't let the bears steal the rest of the bread.'

'I won't,' she whispered, unable to watch as he walked across the terrace; she didn't trust herself not to follow him. Instead, she kept breathing deeply, drawing the air into her lungs and down into the pit of her stomach, holding it there and counting to one, two, three, four, before allowing herself to exhale.

In and out. In and out.

She didn't know how long she stayed like that, her mind focused only on her breaths, but eventually the unease began to ebb away, and she felt able to come back to the present.

Alex had returned, his arm once again behind his head, the hood of his top pulled up over his dreadlocks. She could barely make out his features now in the dark, and looking up, she saw that a thick swell of cloud was obscuring the moon. The breathing had calmed her; slumber would not be far off now.

'What are you thinking?' she said softly.

It was a question that she had often asked James, much to his exasperation, but Alex did not so much as sigh. She heard him clear his throat.

'I was thinking that we're equal now.'

Kate's eyelids were heavy with sleep, her reply little more than a murmur. 'What do you mean?'

'The first time we met, I was naked. And after today . . .'

'Oi,' she interrupted drowsily. 'If we never talk about it, it never happened, remember?'

'It will be our secret,' he agreed.

'There are no secrets between us,' she whispered. 'Not anymore.'

She did not hear his reply because sleep crept in then to steal her away. But later, Kate would wonder – had she missed the words he uttered?

Or had he simply said nothing at all?

30

The last thing Kate expected to find in the hotel reception the following morning was a strange man she'd never seen before.

She'd woken on the terrace to find Alex gone and her phone battery flat, the charger still in the front pocket of the rucksack where she'd left it, coiled neatly like a sunbathing snake. Squinting up at a sky that was still muted with traces of dawn, Kate pulled aside the blanket and got slowly to her feet, stepping carefully over the discarded remains of last night's meal. Charger and phone in one hand and washbag in the other, she made her way barefoot across the leaf-strewn terrace and pushed open the double doors which led into the hotel's former dining area. Alex was not in here, but she heard a voice coming from the reception area.

'You should have woken me up – oh!'

The man lowered his phone from his ear and held up a single finger to indicate that she should wait a moment. He was tall – far more so than Alex – with thick hair the colour of butter and the sort of trendy, frameless glasses that Kate had never been able to afford.

Reaching the bottom of the stairs, she heard a creak and looked around to see Alex peering down from the upper landing.

'Hey,' she mouthed, swivelling her eyes questioningly in the direction of the new arrival.

Alex descended the stairs, drawing level with her just as the man ended his call. There was dust in his beard and a smear of something black across the front of his red hoodie.

'Hello.' The man stepped forwards and went to kiss her on the cheek. Caught unawares, Kate stumbled backwards and had to be caught by Alex.

Why was he always having to catch her?

'This is Mr Van Dijk,' said Alex. 'The new owner.'

'Bram, please,' the man said, his English heavily accented. 'You are Katy – the interior designer?'

'I . . . No. Not really.' Kate stared at her feet.

'Ah.' Bram Van Dijk glanced from Alex back to Kate. 'I must be mistaken.'

'No, you're not,' said Alex. 'Kate here is just a bit bashful, you see. I was just telling Bram about your website.'

'You mean my Instagram account,' Kate corrected, to which Alex shrugged.

'I'm not very tech-knowledgeable.'

'Can I look?' Bram Van Dijk held out his hand expectantly and Kate, realising he wanted the phone that she still had clutched in her hand, shook her head apologetically.

'It's dead I'm afraid. I was just on my way to charge it and get dressed,' she said, cringing as she clocked him looking her up and down.

'A very nice dress,' he said. 'You look like two Spice Girls mixed together – Posh Spice and Ginger Spice.'

'Thanks,' said Kate with a laugh. 'I think.'

'Shall we?' said Alex, motioning towards the far door. 'I'm just going to show Bram what we did yesterday,' he told Kate. 'Then we can get everything loaded up and head off.'

In the end, however, Bram Van Dijk was so impressed by the amount of work Alex and Kate had done that he insisted on giving them brunch.

'I have a little boat at the port,' he told Kate conspiratorially. 'I think you will enjoy it.'

'Does the Danish word for "little" translate into "monster-sized"?' whispered Kate to Alex an hour later, as they wobbled their way across a polished wooden gangplank and up onto the deck of a vast, gleaming super yacht. Alex, who had been even quieter than usual since the impromptu invitation had been issued, wrinkled his nose in reply.

'Hello,' called Bram, from the depths of a squashy leather sofa. He didn't rise to greet them, merely ushered them both into the seats opposite his own and plucked a bottle of champagne from an ice bucket.

'None for me, thank you.' Alex put a hand over the top of his allocated glass. 'I have to drive the boat back to Hvar after this.'

'Katy?'

'It's actually Kate – and go on then,' she said politely, gazing around at the shiny fixtures and fittings as Bram topped her flute up to the brim. 'This is some *little* boat you have here.'

Bram laughed, so loudly that Kate recoiled.

'It is not mine,' he told her. 'Just a rental. Would you believe me if I told you it was worth more than the hotel?'

'Yes,' she said, taking in the enormous flatscreen TV on the wall behind him and what looked to be a hot tub on the other side of the lower deck. 'And you're here alone?'

'At the moment,' he said, his voice loaded with suggestion. 'But you are always welcome, of course.'

There was a crash as Alex's full water glass hit the table.

'Sorry,' he said, as Bram Van Dijk made a lunge for his iPad. 'Accident.'

'No problem, Alex.' Bram smiled genially as a young man wearing an apron appeared and began wiping up the spillage. 'Thank you, Marko,' he said. 'It is vulgar to have staff, but Marko came with the boat,' he told Kate.

She could not be certain, but Kate was pretty sure she heard Alex mutter something under his breath.

Marko returned presently with plates of fresh fruit, fluffy scrambled eggs and bread sliced thin as tissue paper. It was delicious, as was the champagne that Bram kept pouring into her glass, but Kate had much preferred the meal she and Alex shared the previous night. She kept trying to catch his eye, to show him how ludicrous she was finding this whole experience, but Alex kept his gaze steadfastly on his food or their host, who was regaling the two of them now with his plans for the hotel – many of which sounded utterly dreadful. He did not ask about Kate's Instagram account again and she was too shy to bring the subject up. Her heart went repeatedly out to the poor old building, though, which was surely facing death by dire decor.

'We should get going soon,' Alex said, putting his knife and fork together. He had barely touched his food.

They had loaded all the salvaged items and dropped off the moped and bags already, so once they had bid farewell to Bram, who was halfway down a second bottle of bubbly and kissed Kate a bit too enthusiastically on both cheeks, Kate and Alex walked the ten or so minutes along the seafront to reach his boat. As ever, the sun was bold and bright, the water below a frenzied animation of light. Supetar Port bustled with signs of industry, while the far horizon was a shadow-puppet theatre of car and cargo ferries.

'So,' she said, when she was sure they were out of Bram's earshot, 'Mr Van Dijk is, er, interesting.'

'Like him, do you?' Alex had pulled his baseball cap down so far over his nose that Kate couldn't see his eyes.

'Like is not quite the word I would choose,' she said, mulling it over for a moment.

'He's certainly an entertaining individual; I'll give him that. Eccentric for sure.'

'And rich,' put in Alex. 'Extremely rich.'

'James would have loved him,' she said. 'He had this five-year plan that he was intent on following to the letter, and the final point was "make my first million". He would have been taking notes the whole time, asking for money-making tips.'

'What about you?'

Kate swerved to avoid a tiny lizard that had just emerged from the undergrowth. 'Me? I'll never be rich.'

'But you do want to be,' he said. 'I haven't forgotten our lottery conversation.'

Feeling a bit stung, Kate hesitated before replying. 'Honestly? It would be nice to have a bit of money, but only in a comfortable, no-outstanding-debts way, not in a super-yacht way. I mean, if Bram Van Dijk is a lesson in what happens when you earn too many millions, then I would rather not – even if his glasses do make him look like a Bond villain.'

They had reached the dinghy and Alex chuckled as he bent to unfasten the rope.

'What?' demanded Kate. 'You're always laughing at me.'

'I know,' he agreed. 'But it's always with affection.'

Having helped her into the small craft, Alex lowered the outboard motor and they set off slowly through the harbour. Kate chewed her lips, debating whether she should raise the subject of their kiss. It wasn't as if Alex was acting any differently towards her, but she couldn't deny there'd been a shift. Were they more than simply friends now, or was what happened last night just a blip? A result of being caught up in a moment that had now passed.

'Do you need to be back in Hvar right away or can you spare a few hours?' he said then.

Kate, who'd been feeling slightly despondent about the idea of their sea-and-road trip coming to an end, beamed at him.

'I most certainly can. What did you have in mind?'

'If I tell you that,' he said, treating her to a smile, 'I'll ruin the surprise.'

31

Once they had left Brač behind and were speeding across the water towards Hvar, Alex beckoned Kate over from her seat and gave her a lesson in how to operate the boat. Clammy handed with nerves, she clutched the small wheel so tightly at first that the skin around her knuckles turned white, but it didn't take her long to get the hang of it. Soon she was whooping with delight every time they bounced up over a wave.

'You're a natural,' he told her. 'I should have taught you to drive the scooter as well.'

'I much prefer this,' she said loudly, shouting to be heard over the flapping sound of the rooftop deckchair. And it was true. Kate had barely been on a boat before this summer, but she felt safe out on the water, revelling in the freedom rather than longing for dry land.

Alex did not take over the controls until they had passed the western tip of Hvar, and Kate frowned in bemusement as she realised in which direction they were headed.

'You're taking us to Jerolim,' she stated. 'Was last night's shower scene not enough for you?'

'When you call it that,' he replied, 'it conjures up images of knife-wielding murderers.'

'That would be less scary. But seriously, we're not going back to the nudist bit, are we?'

Alex laughed. 'No. Just trust me – you do trust me, don't you?'

Kate did not even have to think. 'You know I do.'

Instead of steering them towards the concrete jetty where the taxi boat had dropped her off on the day of that first, fateful visit, Alex continued around the island. Such was the clearness of the water that Kate could see the outline of every rock and stone as she peered over the side, while the shoreline was adorned with knotted trees and skeletal plants.

Alex had removed his hoodie during the journey and the blond hairs along his arms were lifting in the breeze. Drawn by an urge to reach across and stroke them, Kate shifted slightly, sliding each of her hands under her thighs.

'We'll drop anchor here,' he said a few minutes later, killing the engine and heading towards the back of the boat. 'It's only a short swim – I'm guessing you brought your costume along in that humungous bag?'

'Yes, but—'

'You can get changed in the cabin, if you like?'

This would be her first time swimming out in the open water, and she wasn't sure she was mentally prepared.

'Don't worry,' said Alex, as Kate dithered by the cabin door. 'I didn't let the bears, snakes or killers get you last night, and I won't let any sharks eat you either.'

'Sharks?'

Alex raised a comical eyebrow.

'You are in no way funny.'

Oh well, she thought, peeling off her mustard dress and pulling on her green swimsuit with its white polka-dots, if she did end up drowning, at least her body would be easy to spot.

Alex was already in the water when she re-emerged, which was not ideal, because it meant he would have full view of her bottom as she lowered herself down the slippery rope ladder.

'Just jump,' he called, as she froze with one leg over the side. 'It's deep. You won't hit anything.'

'I might hit you,' she replied sweetly, squinting in his direction. She'd taken off her glasses to swim, and now regretted not packing her contact lenses.

'Do you want me to catch you?' he asked, which was humiliating enough of a suggestion to get her other foot off the deck.

'If I die,' she told him, her arms stretched out behind her clinging on to the outer rail, 'then be sure to tell my brother that I never forgave him for the nudist beach thing. Tell him I happily took that grudge with me to my watery grave.'

Alex, who was treading water less than five feet away, shook his head slowly from side to side. 'After three,' he urged. 'Come on – one, two, th—'

Kate jumped, her yelp of fear swallowed up by the same cold water that rushed into her mouth and eyes. Spluttering, she kicked hard for the surface, bursting through to find Alex only inches away, merman-like with his wet beard trailing across his face and neck.

'Still alive?' he checked, as Kate coughed and wheezed. Her hair had come loose from its band and adhered itself to her face, and she knew without needing to look that she had a swimsuit wedgie.

'Never better,' she said, as seawater dribbled out through her nostrils. From the stinging sensation in both eyes, she guessed her mascara must have run.

'Right then,' he replied, nodding in the direction of the shore. 'Follow me.'

Swimming was not something that Kate did a lot of in London, and within a few minutes she was panting with the effort of staying afloat. Alex had streaked ahead at a crawl, but to his credit, he did stop every few lengths to check that she was still behind him. As Kate had no idea which part of land they were heading for, she focused instead on the red top of his baseball cap, which Alex was still wearing, and forced her tired limbs to keep moving. It looked as if the dense shrub that covered most of Jerolim was in even greater abundance on this side of the island, but as she drew nearer to land, Kate realised that there was a narrow cove scooped out from between two opposing banks of rock. It was towards this that Alex was steadily swimming and, buoyed by the thought of solid ground, Kate kicked her legs harder and powered after him.

'Bloody hell,' she gasped, staggering onto two feet and wincing as the sharp edges of stones dug into the soft flesh. 'I'm knackered.'

Alex grinned at her from under the peak of his cap.

'Yeah, it is a bit of a swim,' he said. 'I always think this beach is closer than it actually is – and the current can be strong when you reach the inlet.'

'Tell me about it,' groaned Kate, as she hobbled over to join him. 'I knew I was unfit, but I didn't realise things had got this bad. I might have to cross the island on foot so you can pick me up on the opposite side.'

'About that,' he said, wrapping his arms around his raised knees as Kate wrung out her hair. 'You can't reach this bay on foot. I found it by accident when I was snorkelling one day.'

'Oh,' deadpanned Kate, dismayed that she would have no choice but to swim back to the boat.

'There's a sheer drop, see,' he said, pointing over his shoulder at the crumbling rock face behind them. 'You'd have to be a fool to try and climb up that.'

'Or a goat,' she said. 'A goat could probably do it.'

'I'll be sure to bring one next time, in that case.'

'Sorry for all the silly jokes,' she muttered, stretching out her legs and staring morosely at the droplets of water on her bare toes. 'I always have loved to laugh at inappropriate moments. It's got me through many a scary situation.'

She had put her hand down on the white stones between them, and just for a moment, Alex pressed his own against it.

'You don't need to apologise,' he said. 'And I don't think there's anything wrong with cracking the odd joke, but I also know what it feels like to be scared. It's why I brought you here, truth be told.'

Kate looked down at his hand; her own felt warm and safe beneath it.

'I'm going to show you a trick that someone once taught me,' he said. 'It helped me, and I think it might do the same for you. Are you game?'

He was sitting so close to her that Kate could see the freckles across his nose. She had never noticed them before, had always been so distracted by that beard and hair, by those pale eyes of his that were fixed on her now.

'Go on then,' she said. 'But it had better be more fun than Rummy.'

'This isn't the kind of game you win,' he said. 'First, we need to find as many smooth, flat pebbles as we can.'

'Are we going to build a tower?' she asked.

Alex picked up a large round stone and Kate was reminded of the moon they had stared at together the previous night.

'This is what we're after,' he said. 'Look for as many of these as you can.'

For the next few minutes, they worked in silence, Kate discarding far more rocks than she kept. From a distance, the beach had seemed littered with these perfect pale ovals, but upon closer inspection, many of them were nearer to grey in colour and lots had scuff marks or dents.

'You don't have to be too fussy,' said Alex, who had wandered further down the beach and returned with both his hands full. There was white dust all over his chest hair and a fair amount in his beard, too.

'Whatever you say, Santa.'

'You are on fire today,' he remarked, dropping his haul of stones on the ground.

'It feels like I literally am,' she said, looking fretfully towards the sun.

'Here.' Alex pulled off his cap and plonked it on top of her damp curls. 'To stop your nose burning.'

'Thanks.' She tugged it down, adjusting the back until it fitted more snugly.

Alex sat down cross-legged and motioned Kate to join him, then pulled something out from behind his ear and handed it to her.

'Where on earth did that come from?' she said, staring at the black felt-tip pen in amazement.

'You may mock the dreadlocks,' he said, 'but they're great for storing things.'

'I don't mock them,' she protested, blushing as he gave her a look.

'You want me to rinse this pen in the sea for you?'

'No.' Kate clutched it tightly as he made a grab. Her swimsuit was finally dry, but the ends of her hair were still wet, and dribbles of cold water kept trickling down her back.

'Are we ready?' she asked, suppressing a shiver. 'How does this game work?'

'It's not a game, so much as an exercise,' he explained. 'I'll start by asking you a question, and all you have to do is answer it as quickly and as honestly as you can. Understood?'

'Yes,' said Kate, beginning to feel slightly apprehensive. 'But wha—?'

'Ready?'

She nodded; lips pursed in preparation. Alex gave her a moment to collect her thoughts, waiting until she had stopped fidgeting and was still, and then he spoke.

'What scares you?'

'Pain,' said Kate, without missing a beat. 'And germs.'

'Write each word down on the stones – one stone for each thing that scares you.'

Puzzled, Kate did as instructed, swirling her 's' and making the dot of her 'i' a smiley face.

'What else?' prompted Alex.

'Being up on a high ledge,' she said decisively. 'So heights – and numbness.'

'You mean physical numbness – when you doze off in an odd position and your arm falls asleep?'

'No,' she said. 'I mean the other kind – emotional numbness. I'm scared of being hurt, but what frightens me more than that is not caring at all, you know? Or being unaffected by love, or by hate, or even by grief. Becoming a shell.'

Alex did not say anything for a while; Kate saw his Adam's apple moving in his throat, as if he was swallowing something down. When he spoke again, he sounded unsteady.

'That was a good one. What else?'

'Centipedes,' she said, in an attempt to lighten the mood. 'I found one in my bra once – while I was wearing it. The scream almost shattered the windows of James's car.'

Alex nodded, a low chuckle escaping his lips as she selected a stone long enough to accommodate the word.

'How about you?' she said. 'What are you scared of?'

'Snakes,' he said, taking the pen from her and writing it down.

'Is that so?' she said in bemusement. 'So, when you said you'd protect me from them last night, what you actually meant was you'd run away and let me deal with them alone?'

'But I would have stayed and fought a bear . . .'

'Hmm, I suppose I can let you off then. What else?'

'Sinking,' he replied. 'I worry about my boat sinking all the time.'

'I'm not surprised,' joked Kate, grinning at his expression of pretend outrage.

'Your turn,' he said, handing her the pen, but Kate had drawn a blank. There were many things she could write on the stones, but she wasn't yet ready to share them – not until he gave away something more about his own fears.

'What are we going to do with all these once we've finished?' she asked.

Alex smiled rather wistfully. 'Throw them into the water.'

'Won't that wash away the words?'

'Exactly,' he said. 'As Josh would say: "That's what we cry for – to wash away our fears." Only, in his version, you let the sea do it for you.'

Kate was aware of a strange sensation then, as if she was hearing his words for the second time. A memory tugged, but it was too quiet; and even as she felt it, it was gone, had slipped back into the misty corners of her subconscious.

'This is Josh's game?' she said, and Alex sighed.

'He was one of life's survivors.'

'Was?' she echoed tentatively. 'You don't mean that he's . . .'

'Long gone,' he said with finality. 'Josh is long gone. Now, what are you going to write down next?'

'Loss scares me,' she said, scribbling it down. 'The thought of losing my parents or Toby, of something happening to them or to James, or my best friend Robyn. I don't think I would ever recover. I'm not strong enough.'

'People do,' he said gently. 'Death is a part of life.'

'One I want no part in,' she said, underlining the word three times to illustrate her point.

'What scares you more?' Alex asked. 'Losing someone, or dying yourself?'

'The former, of course.'

'So, your own death doesn't scare you? You wouldn't write it down on the stones?'

'No,' she said, mildly diverted by her own answer. 'Like you said, there's no getting away from it, so what would be the point in fearing it? That would make living unbearable.'

'You'd be surprised how many people would disagree,' he said.

'Well, I suppose I do fear it in some regard,' she said thoughtfully. 'Because if I were to die, the people who care about me would be hurt – although maybe not all of them,' she added, thinking bitterly of James. 'But the idea of anyone I love, anyone I remotely care about being upset,' she went on, smoothing her thumb across a blank stone, 'that does scare me.'

'Shall we add it to the pile?' he said, but Kate shook her head.

'No. You can, if you like? Unless you have something better in mind?'

Alex accepted the pen and wrote 'stubbing my toe' in compact capital letters.

'What?' he said, as Kate scoffed. 'That counts. Stubbing your toe really hurts – and always seems to happen at the worst possible time, too.'

'Yeah, but you're not scared of it, are you? The thought of stubbing your toes doesn't keep you up at night?'

'Fair point,' he agreed. 'But I'm still having it.'

They continued in the same vein for a while, each trying to outdo the other with sillier and sillier suggestions. Kate chose maggots, letters from the tax office and pterodactyls, arguing that it would only take a crocodile to be amorous with a pelican for the latter to stage an evolutionary comeback. Alex in response opted for scorpions, milky tea and asteroids. They had quite a stack now, and the ink was starting to wane.

'Two more each?' Alex said, and Kate nodded.

'Yes – but they have to be good ones. Real ones,' she added, seeing his features alight with mischief. 'I'll go first.'

'Loneliness,' Alex read aloud over her shoulder. 'Even after what we discussed last night?'

'I don't mean solitude,' she said. 'I mean ending up alone; finding myself aged sixty, with no friends and no family around me because nobody remembers me. I am forgotten.'

Very gently, Alex took the pen from her and drew a firm line through the word.

'It's not loneliness you fear, it's being lonely,' he told her, turning over the stone and beginning to write.

Kate stared at the word, at the five neat letters, so innocuous in appearance yet so catastrophic in meaning.

Alone.

'Did I tell you that I wanted to run away at the start of this summer?' she said, staring out across the water because it was easier than meeting his gaze. 'I proposed to James, you know. I stood up in a room full of our friends and family, on my thirtieth birthday, and asked him to marry me.'

Alex made a noise that sounded like 'oh'.

'Obviously, he said no. Well, he didn't say anything in fact, he just stood there, staring at me with this horrified expression on his face, his mouth opening and closing like a goldfish stranded on land. If the situation hadn't been so excruciating, it might have been funny.'

Kate waited, but there was no sign of laughter – not from Alex or herself. It was too fresh for that, the rejection still too painful.

'Someone filmed the whole thing,' she went on, closing her eyes as she recalled the blurry footage. 'Posted it on the Internet and everything. I was even famous for a while – in the way that nobody would ever want to be, would not even want their worst enemy to be. I have a hashtag, Wannabe Wife, which is ridiculous because a wife isn't what I wanted to be – not really.'

She sighed, reaching for a smaller stone and throwing it

hard into the sea. There was a splash and it vanished, swallowed by the silvery blue water.

'Why did you ask someone to marry you if you didn't want to be married?'

It was a fair question but Kate still had to bite back the tears.

'I thought it might make up for the fact that . . . That I couldn't give him, give us, the thing we both wanted the most. I hoped that if we were husband and wife, that it would fix all the things that had gone wrong since—'

Alex did not say anything; he did not need to. They both knew what she was going to say next, but now that she had come this far, Kate wanted to get the words out, needed, perhaps, to let them out.

'A baby,' she whispered. 'I can't give him a baby. That's why he's left me; that's the real reason. I've failed at things my whole life, but I just thought that if I could succeed at that, if I could be a mum, then it would make all the other stuff go away. But now, I can't even do that.'

'I'm sorry.' Alex reached across and offered her his hand. Kate stared at it for a moment, then took it, her tears falling as she felt his fingers close around her own. He could have said more, offered words of sympathy, but he didn't. Kate was thankful to him for that. He seemed to understand exactly how to comfort her and it wasn't by mollycoddling, it was simply being there and listening, taking a portion of her pain and sharing it, lessening the load she had carried for what felt like so long.

'Here,' he said, selecting one of the few remaining stones and balancing it on the bend of his knee. 'I think we should add the word "hashtags" to the pile.'

'For both of us?' she said hesitantly, and he smiled.

'No – I barely know what they are. But this,' he continued, reaching for another stone and writing the word 'fear' in large, bold letters, 'is one of mine.'

'You fear *fear*?'

A nod.

Kate added another stone and wrote 'failure' in a shaky hand. 'There's one stone left,' she told him. 'Your turn.'

The silence that followed felt to Kate as if it stretched on for ages, and she squeezed the hand she was still holding, urging him to be brave, to share a truth with her that meant something. He had helped her; now she wanted to be there for him.

Of all the words Kate was expecting to see on that final stone, none of them came close to the one that appeared, small yet profound, without so much as a murmur of explanation.

Me.

Dear Josh,

I never believed things would go this far, yet here we are.

Ten years.

You have been missing for ten years.

I have to admit, I do feel angry sometimes – frustrated with you for not getting in touch and outraged with a world that continues to keep you hidden.

On other days, I am simply sad, because you are my brother and I miss you.

But today? Today, I am determined. Because I have decided that this is the year I will find you. Whatever it takes.

I have never written down what happened between us on that dreadful day, although I rarely stop thinking about it. I go over and over it in my head, wondering how I could have said all those things to you, how I got to a point of such bitterness and resentment. Was it grief? Mum and Dad died that year, not four months apart. Do you remember how we clung to one another in the hospital? I was weeping but you were trying to be strong for me. Or maybe you had no choice. Maybe you thought that if you let that pain in, on top of everything else, it would have been too much. You would have broken.

You needed me more during those darkest of days than you ever had before, but every time I looked at you, I saw my own pain reflected back at me and I couldn't bear it, Josh – I just couldn't. Our shared loss should have brought us closer, but I allowed it to flow like water into the cracks that had long existed in our family.

Fate and the universe and death were at fault, nothing more, but I wanted something tangible, someone I could shake and scream at and beat with my fists.

To my shame, that became you.

I know you chose to go because of me; that you never would have gone had I been kinder, stronger, better. Please come home so I can say sorry, so we can both forgive. I miss you.

Love, Angela

PART THREE

32

Robyn did not so much climb out of the jeep as cartwheel over the door, such was her haste to throw her arms around her best friend.

'Look at your tan!' were her first words, her mouth split open wide with approval as she gave Kate the once over. 'Look at her tan!' she said to Toby, who was staggering slightly under the weight of Robyn's suitcase.

'You do know we have a kitchen sink here, right? A few of them in fact.'

'Ah,' sighed Robyn, gazing around happily. 'The Nimble siblings and their bizarre sense of humour – how I've missed it.'

Kate caught her brother's eye and laughed.

'Come on,' she said. 'I want to give you the tour.'

'It's so hot!' Robyn exclaimed a minute later, as she fanned her face with a leaflet advertising boat trips that she had plucked off the hostel reception desk. 'I thought it had been warm in London lately, but this place is sizzling. I bet we could cook bacon and eggs out on the pavement if we tried – speaking of which' – she looked hopefully at Kate – 'I don't suppose there's any chance of breakfast. I mean, I had a tuna melt on the flight and some Pret porridge in the airport first thing, but that was basically the middle of the night. As you know, any food consumed between the hours of midnight and six a.m. does not count towards the daily intake.'

'That rule still stands, does it?' said Kate. The two of them had come up with it in their college days, when stumbling home from a pub or club always included a stop at the local kebab or fried chicken takeaway.

Her friend grinned. 'The best ones always do.'

Once they'd deposited the luggage, toured Sul Tetto and Robyn had taken a quick shower before changing into beachwear, both women were ravenous. Rather than eat up on the terrace, which was crowded with backpackers, Kate bore her friend off to her favourite waterside café, where they ordered vast fluffy omelettes and rich, bitter espressos.

'I know I keep saying it, but you look incredible,' Robyn appraised, looking Kate up and down with such pride that she blushed.

'No, I don't. Look at the state of my hair.'

Robyn examined a stray curl, tugging it gently and watching it ping back into place.

'You've always had a bonkers barnet – it's your thing.'

'It's become even more bonkers since I arrived here,' said Kate. 'It doesn't matter how much conditioner I use; it always frizzes up as if I've stuck my big toe into a plug socket.'

'At least your hair has volume,' bemoaned her friend, rolling her eyes upwards.

'Too much of it,' countered Kate. 'Your hair is smooth and shiny and makes you look even better than Uma Thurman did in *Pulp Fiction*. You do look a bit tired today,' she allowed, as Robyn yawned for the third time since they'd taken their seats. 'But still as beautiful as ever.'

'Smooth talker.' Robyn speared a slice of tomato. 'I've been working non-stop lately. I took on three new patients and this past month or so has been real a learning curve for me.'

'Me too,' agreed Kate, who was running a slice of toast through the buttery residue on her plate.

'The hostel looks wonderful,' Robyn said. 'I know, I know – I have said it about a hundred times already, but it really does. The photos don't do your vision justice.'

'Thanks,' said Kate, sitting up a fraction taller. 'It was a lot of fun, hard work, but fun. I blagged my way through a lot of it and I hadn't a clue how to do the big stuff, such as the furniture and light fittings. I have Alex to thank for all that.'

'Ah, yes.' Robyn lifted her espresso cup and extended a theatrical little finger. 'My next question was going to be about him.'

'Oh?' Kate arranged her features into what she hoped was a bland expression.

'Do I get to meet him?'

'I'm not sure. Probably. I did tell him you were coming.'

'Is he still as good-looking as ever?' Robyn smiled wickedly.

'I'm not sure you'll be so enamoured when you meet him,' Kate told her. 'He's not your normal type.'

'Thank god for that.' Robyn rubbed her hands together. 'My usual types mostly turn out to be idiots. It's about time I tried something different. The last holiday romance I had was in Corfu when we were eighteen. Do you remember Stelios?'

'I remember the back of his head,' Kate said. 'That was the only part of him I ever saw, on account of all the snogging.'

'That's right,' Robyn said, rather wistfully. 'I had stubble rash for a full fortnight after we got back and had to pretend it was sunburn.'

Once they'd finished eating, Kate led her friend along the coastal path towards the hub of Hvar Town, pointing out various landmarks as they went. Alex's boat was not in its usual spot because he'd gone over to the neighbouring island of Vis for a few days to help a friend. Those were the exact words he had used when Kate asked – 'help a friend'. Kate had wondered if he could be going to visit the much-mentioned Josh, only to remember what he'd said about him being 'long gone'. She hoped that did not mean he'd died. Presumably Josh had been a close friend once upon a time, and she hated to imagine Alex losing someone he cared about. He should have people around him that he could rely on, who would be there to support him if or when he needed help.

At least she could pick up her phone and call Alex if she wanted to. Not that she had. And nor had Kate told anyone about the kiss they'd shared, or what had taken place on the secluded beach in Jerolim. It wasn't because she was ashamed – in truth, she felt quite the opposite – but she was concerned that in trying to explain, her words would somehow cheapen the experience or make light of it. So much of the time she'd spent alone with Alex had felt so profound, so honest, so brave and so unlike anything else she'd done. He had revealed things to her that she suspected he kept hidden from most people and she wanted to respect that. But more than that, she wanted to keep those parts of him for herself, to cherish them; not tarnish their shared moments by offering them up for debate.

'You weren't lying when you told me this place was stunning,' Robyn said, her words bringing Kate out of her momentary trance. 'This sea is something else,' she said, staring down at the crystal-clear water. 'I just want to dive in, right now, in all my clothes. Can we go swimming later? Is there a beach?'

'Yes and yes.' Kate was amused by Robyn's overflowing levels of glee. 'But you're here for a whole week so there's plenty of time – and don't worry,' she added, 'I have a comprehensive itinerary of fun planned.'

'I like this new Kate,' said Robyn admiringly. 'Look at you, taking charge and making decisions. James wouldn't even recognise you.'

'Wouldn't be able to see past all this hair,' Kate joked.

'Seriously,' Robyn insisted. 'I was worried that you'd waste away without him, but you've gone and done the opposite – you seem so happy, so confident, so free . . .'

'I don't see it as being free,' muttered Kate, stepping to the side to allow a mother to pass by with a buggy. 'I see it as being cast adrift. That's all I'm doing in Croatia – floating without course, waiting in limbo for James to come to his senses.'

Robyn did not attempt to disguise her disgruntlement.

'Don't make that face,' Kate pleaded. 'It's been so great to come and live in a new place, meet new people and spend more time with my brother and Filippo. All the interior design stuff is fun, too. I'm not saying I haven't enjoyed every bit of it, but this isn't my life, not really. The life I want most is back in London with James.'

Robyn did not reply straight away, but Kate could tell she was despondent.

'Let's not talk about James now,' her friend suggested. 'We can come back to the subject later – preferably over a few drinks.'

Kate, feeling awash with relief, agreed without a murmur.

Only a few weeks ago it had been she who'd had to follow Alex through the tangle of backstreets in Hvar Town, but now Kate was the guide. It was gratifying to be the person responsible for her best friend's many 'oohs' and 'ahhs' as Robyn gazed up in awe at the explosions of bougainvillea, insisted on having artful photos taken in front of peeling-paint doors, and went into ecstasies over the quaint cafés and bars they passed. After exhausting the bowels of the town, Kate led the way through St Stephen's Square and treated the two of them to a blueberry sorbet, which they consumed in contented silence as they set off further around the coast.

Despite having done this walk countless times in the weeks she'd been on the island, Kate remained utterly captivated by the view across the water of bobbing sailboats, splashing bathers and majestic palms. When Robyn made a remark about the deafening crickets, Kate realised with surprise that she no longer heard them. Her time in Hvar had apparently taught her many things, including the ability to tune out the resident insect orchestra.

'Can we stop somewhere for a drink soon?' pleaded Robyn, who had paused to tie back her hair. 'I feel like I'm melting faster than the sorbet did.'

'Of course.' Kate did a mental calculation. 'Hula Hula is the closest place, but will likely be busy, or we can keep walking and go to Falko, where they have hammocks under the trees.'

'I vote Hula Hula, and not just because I like the crisps.'

Kate laughed. 'And you say I have a weird sense of humour . . .'

Hula Hula beach club came within earshot long before they reached it, and Robyn and Kate exchanged a bewildered look as they drew closer and a gaggle of girls in string bikinis and high heels stumbled out, tossing their hair and muttering to each other in what sounded like Russian.

'Are you sure you want to brave it?' Kate checked, but Robyn was already making her way down the steps and across the wooden decking towards the bar, where she promptly ordered them each a bottle of the local beer, Ožujsko.

'To us,' she said, clanking her bottle against Kate's. 'And to the first proper holiday I've had in two bloody years. And to Hvar, which might be the most beautiful place I've ever seen.'

'I will definitely drink to all those things,' agreed Kate, trying not to dwell on the fact that it was barely lunchtime, and therefore inadvisable to start drinking.

The seating on offer at Hula Hula ranged from booth-style tables with wraparound benches, squat wooden boxes topped with cushions, and high stools that faced out to sea. As Kate had predicted, almost every available space was taken up, but they eventually found an empty spot halfway along the club's wide concrete jetty and took off their sandals so they could dip their toes in the water.

'Now *this* is living,' Robyn said, sighing with pleasure as she angled her face towards the sun. 'I can see why your brother chose to move here.'

'The Croatian people are wonderfully laid-back and so welcoming,' said Kate. 'That's partly why Toby fits in so well here – he's a born host, that one.'

'I would argue that the same could be said for you,' Robyn pointed out. 'Aren't you at all tempted to stay on beyond the summer?'

Kate shook her head as she took a swig of beer. 'I wouldn't want to live in a different country to James.'

Once again, her friend did not attempt to hide her exasperation.

'Have you heard from him?' she asked.

Kate shook her head before taking a determined sip of her beer. 'Not since I hung up on him that time.'

'But you still think there's a way back? You still believe he'll change his mind?'

'I have to,' she said simply. 'It's the hope that's keeping me going.'

'But look at everything you've done since you've been here,' urged Robyn. 'No way would any of it have happened if you were still in London, where James makes all the rules.'

'That's not strictly true,' Kate protested, leaning back to avoid being splashed. A rowdy group of men were taking it in turns to leap off the jetty, while towards the back of the bar, a DJ was setting himself up on a raised platform. The whole place seemed to Kate as if it was thrumming with anticipation, but she felt apart from it; an outsider peering in.

'You make it sound as if James kept me chained up in front of the telly, but if anything, he was the one encouraging me to try new things all the time. Honestly, Rob – he was forever pushing me out of my comfort zone. It's not James's fault that I lack ambition.'

'But those new things always consisted of something he was interested in,' Robyn pointed out gently. 'When did he ever consider what your passions were and act on those?'

'How could he, when he didn't know what they were,' argued Kate. 'If I don't know what I'm passionate about, how the hell should he?'

She could feel frustration tiptoeing through her now, like a sniper stalking his prey.

'He isn't a mind reader,' she added defiantly. 'You can blame him for a lot of things, but not my own shortcomings.'

'Why has he never asked you, though? Like, really asked you? Sat you down and said, "Kate Nimble, love of my life, woman of my heart, what are your passions?" Or did he find it easier to mould you into someone who had the same passions as him?'

'He didn't need to ask me,' Kate mumbled. 'He knew I was passionate about him – about our future. He knew I would have done anything to make it work – would still do anything.'

'Hold that thought,' said Robyn, getting to her feet and holding out a hand for Kate's empty bottle. 'Nature calls. I'll get us another two of these on my way back.'

Kate nodded distractedly, hunching her shoulders as she gazed down at her feet below the water. Music had begun to thump out from tall speakers and a great cry of exultation rose up around her as one of the diving men executed a perfect forward flip, while another popped the cork on a magnum of prosecco.

Alex would hate it here. This would be his idea of hell.

How often her mind seemed to stray to him lately. It was almost as if he'd become her internal antidote to James; a spoonful of Alex to sweeten the bitter taste of rejection. Is that why she'd kissed him?

'Miss me?'

Kate shrieked as a returning Robyn pressed a cold bottle of beer against her bare arm.

'Are you trying to make me fall off this jetty, woman?'

'No, but I'm up for a swim if you are?' she said hopefully.

'Maybe later. We were talking about James . . .'

Robyn visibly slumped. 'So we were.' She sat down and kicked at the water. She always painted her toenails different colours, and today's were an eclectic mix of pink, purple and blue. 'He hurt you so badly,' she said. 'Seeing the state you were in after your birthday, after that bloody video appeared . . . It was tough. I hate the idea of you ever going through that again. What can I say? I'm protective. I'm like the SPF fifty of best friends.'

'You're amazing,' Kate told her, examining her bottle before taking another large sip. 'But nothing and nobody could have protected me from being hurt. I was hurting long before I stood up on that chair and asked James to marry me.'

Robyn frowned; her expression distorted by concern. 'Is this to do with the polycystic—'

Kate nodded.

'I thought the doctor had given you tablets?'

'He did.' Kate tried and failed to smile. 'But it wasn't just that – there were other reasons.'

'Such as?'

'Another time,' she said, taking off her glasses to rub her eyes. 'This is your first night of your first holiday in two years – I insist we start having some fun immediately.'

'I don't care about that,' Robyn started to protest, but Kate lifted her Ožujsko and clanked the neck of her friend's bottle so hard that beer began spurting out. Caught unawares, Robyn had no choice but to plant her mouth over the top and swallow it down, spluttering with laughing as Kate cheered her on.

'You do realise,' Robyn choked, once she had come up for air, 'that the only acceptable punishment for a crime as heinous as that is to drink whatever shot I buy you?'

Kate grinned. There was only one direction this day was destined to go now, and for once, oblivion was a state she was more than happy to welcome.

33

There were a few blissful minutes after Kate woke the next morning in which she was able to luxuriate. The events of the previous evening were kept at bay, trapped behind the dense fog of a hangover that she hoped might somehow have passed her by.

Then she attempted to move.

Groaning with misery as her dehydrated brain seemed to push against the back of her eyeballs, she fumbled around on the floor beside the bed, desperately trying to locate a glass of water. Snatches of memory flashed up like index cards, an image of herself and Robyn spraying champagne over each other, of the two of them leaping fully clothed into the sea as the sun set, of a man's arms around her waist, lifting her into the air.

Kate sat up too fast, recoiling as a fresh wave of nausea crashed over her. Putting on her glasses, which were thankfully in their usual spot on the bedside cabinet, she peeled aside the sheet next to her to find Robyn's side of the bed empty. Had her friend even made it back to the hostel? Kate could vaguely recall the two of them singing in the streets, two slices of pizza waving between them like conductors' batons.

Her reflection, when she had stumbled as far as the bathroom, confirmed her worst fears. Mascara was streaked across her cheeks; her hair was a knotted mess, and her arms were covered in scratches. She looked like a moth that had been sucked into a jet engine.

After locating and forcing down two paracetamols, Kate stood for a while with her hands on either side of the basin, trying to quell the urge to throw up.

What the hell had happened last night?

Dressing as rapidly as her still-pounding head would allow, Kate made her way to the roof terrace, gripping the banister and whimpering all the way up the stairs. She had checked her phone already, fearing the worst, but there were no outgoing calls to James listed, nor had she sent him any drunken messages. There were, she discovered, a lot of selfies plus at least fifteen pictures of Robyn curled up on the lap of Hula Hula's resident DJ. At least, it looked like him – Kate couldn't be sure because his face was obscured in the same way Stelios's had been all those years ago in Corfu. She was extremely relieved to find no photographic evidence of herself kissing anyone, but then, it was her phone. If anyone was in possession of such material, it would be Robyn.

Kate had reached the door now and steeled herself for a moment before pushing it open. The sun was for once shielding behind a bulbous patch of clouds, but the heat that greeted her felt damp and heavy. Robyn was, as Kate had hoped she would be, perched up on a bar stool talking to Toby, the remains of a cooked breakfast on a plate in front of her. When she saw Kate staggering unsteadily towards her, she beamed.

'There you are. I was just saying to Tobes that I'd better come down and wake you up. How are you feeling?' she added, as Kate clasped the bar with a clammy hand. 'Bit rough?'

Toby eyed her with concern as she levered herself up into a seat, then made a 'T' shape with his hands.

'Yes, please,' she croaked. 'But not too much milk – I don't think I can stomach it.'

Glancing at Robyn, she groaned. 'How are you so perky? You must have drunk the same amount as me, if not more.'

'I swapped to water around ten,' she said blithely. 'I tried to make you do the same, but you were adamant that gin was a better option. You told me, and I quote, "You have to put gin in it to win it", and by "it", you meant yourself.'

'Oh god.' Kate lowered her head into her hands. 'What else did I say?'

'Well,' Robyn began, sucking orange juice up through a reusable straw, 'there were a lot of grand plans of how you were going to lure James back – although if you ask me, it's him who should be begging for a second chance, not you – and then we spent a long time chatting to that group of men about brand building.'

'We did?' Kate raised her chin. 'Why would we do that?'

'They worked for a creative agency and you made a big point of showing them your Unexpected Items Instagram account – don't you remember?'

'Kate swayed slightly as she shook her head.

'Sort of. It's all a bit hazy.'

'They were very complimentary,' Robyn went on happily. 'You insisted they all follow you there and then, and told them you'd soon be available for hire.'

Toby was back with the tea, which he plonked down in front of her along with two slices of buttered toast.

'I can't.' Kate shuddered. 'I'll be sick.'

'You need to eat,' he and Robyn said in unison. 'You're so skinny now,' her brother added. 'If those cheekbones get any sharper, I'll be able to slice salami on them.'

'My BMI is fine,' she protested, but he pushed the plate towards her anyway.

'You need some sustenance,' he said. 'How else will you have the energy to recreate the *Dirty Dancing* lift that you apparently partook in last night?'

'I did *what*?'

Siva chose that moment to saunter along the bar, her blue eyes narrowing as she clocked the newcomer.

Robyn cooed a greeting, reaching forward a hand only to snatch it hurriedly back. 'Ouch,' she said, sucking at the blood that was now oozing out from a scratch across her knuckles. 'Was it something I said?'

'Siva might look like Dobby the House Elf,' said Toby, smiling with affection as the cat nonchalantly pinched the remaining half of Kate's toast, 'but personality-wise, she is pure Voldemort.'

Kate felt she should laugh but thought it quite likely she would be sick if she did.

'How did I get all these marks on my arms?' she asked Robyn. 'I didn't try to get into bed with Siva when we got back, did I?'

'Nah.' Robyn subdued a laugh. 'You fell into a cactus – one of those massive ones by the beach. I had to rescue you.'

'This is why I should never ever drink,' wailed Kate, again putting her face in her hands.

'Clearly, you needed to let off some steam,' said Toby, who was whickering like a pony as he flicked through the photos on Robyn's phone. 'Blimey! You're twerking in this one.'

'It's one of my lesser-spotted signature moves,' said Kate, sipping the last of her tea. 'James caught me practising in the bedroom mirror once and pretended to go blind with horror.'

She had smiled as she spoke, but now her face fell. James was part of the reason she had drunk so much in the first place – him and all the associated trauma of their break-up.

'I feel sick,' she said, but the other two didn't hear her. Robyn was still showing Toby something on her phone, and Kate realised he looked more intrigued now than amused.

'Interesting,' he said, looking from the screen back to Kate. 'Very interesting.'

'What is? What now? Is it a video of me doing the Agadoo and actually shaking a tree?'

Robyn lowered her phone. 'Do you remember suggesting that we call Alex last night?'

Kate's blood came to an abrupt halt inside her veins. 'No.'

'You wanted him to come and party with us – you made that point very clear.'

'But I didn't call him, did I?' she said, almost dropping her own phone in her rush to check it. 'Look, I didn't. There are no calls or messages. I knew there wouldn't be. Hula Hula is the last place I would invite Alex to; it's so not his kind of vibe.'

'Kind of vibe,' teased Toby. 'You can take the girl out of London—'

'Hang on a minute.' Kate was looking at her friend's slightly sheepish expression. 'You didn't call him, did you?'

Robyn shifted on her stool as Toby started laughing. 'What is it about Al at the moment? One of the guests was asking about him the other day, how old he was, where he was from, how long he'd been in Hvar – I think she was trying to get the lowdown on him so she could chat him up. I had no idea he was such a dark horse.'

Kate was still looking at Robyn. 'Did you call Alex, Robyn?' she repeated, this time with emphasis.

'I may have.'

'Nooo! What did he say? What did you say?'

'Nothing.' Robyn passed her mobile across so Kate could see the call list. Alex's number was there, the time alongside it read 00:45.

'It wasn't me doing the talking – it was you.'

Kate brought up a hand and put it over her mouth.

'You told him a plant had beaten you up and that you wanted to sleep in his deckchair. Something like that, anyway, you wouldn't let me listen. But he must've said no, because then you were all stroppy and said something like, "Well, you'd better come and take me and my friend out on your boat tomorrow then" before hanging up. That's why I'm up and in make-up so early, I assumed we'd be heading out with Mr Dothraki.'

'Doth-who-y?' put in Toby, but Kate never got to reply.

The door on the opposite side of the terrace had opened, and she knew – just *knew* – who was going to walk through it.

34

'Morning, baby,' was how Alex greeted her.

'Baby?'

'Your new name, apparently. Last night, you told me in no uncertain terms that I must call you that from now on.'

'I did?'

'That'll be the teenage *Dirty Dancing* obsession coming through again,' explained Robyn, who had hopped off her stool and now offered Alex her hand to shake. 'It always comes to the surface when Kate's been drinking,' she added. 'Baby is her alter ego.'

'Right.'

Alex peered a bit closer at Kate. 'How's the head?'

'Marginally less painful than the shame,' Kate muttered, relieved to see a smile playing around his lips. 'I'm really sorry for calling you so late, for calling you at all. This is why I never drink – alcohol turns me into a monster.'

'No matter.'

A silence followed in which Kate squirmed uncomfortably.

'So . . .' Toby said, with ill-disguised relish. He was clearly enjoying this situation far too much, thought Kate. 'Where are you kids off to today?'

'"You kids",' mimicked Robyn. 'Tobes, you're five years older than us – not fifty. How old are you?' she asked, turning to Alex. 'Kate never said.'

'That's probably because I never told her,' he replied, folding his arms. 'I'm thirty.'

'Same as us.' Robyn beamed. 'When was your birthday?'

Kate glanced at Alex. Somehow, she knew instinctively that he would not like the question.

'A while ago,' he said. 'I don't go in for birthdays – lot of fuss about nothing, if you ask me.'

Robyn went to protest, but Kate got in first. 'After the disastrous thirtieth I had, I'm inclined to agree with you. And please, don't feel like you have to honour your promise to take us out on the boat today,' she added. 'I can't remember much about last night, but apparently I bullied you into agreeing?'

'I would say firmly instructed,' he allowed. 'But that's OK. I have a free day today.'

'Only if you're sure? You don't have anything you'd rather be doing?'

Alex said nothing, but when Kate's eyes met his, she could have been sure he gave her the ghost of a wink.

As Robyn was the guest, Toby declared that she must choose where they went and eventually they settled on a cruise around the Pakleni Islands. It transpired that Robyn had read about the ritzy Palmižana beach on St Klement in a travel supplement from one of the Sunday broadsheets and was keen to go. When Noa popped up from reception to ask Toby about a booking enquiry and realised they were all heading out, he offered to call his girlfriend Klementina and ask if she would watch the bar so his boss could join them.

'You never take a day off,' he said. 'Go – enjoy yourself.'

The restorative effects of the tea, toast and tablets were beginning to wane, and Kate felt increasingly as if the inside of her head was a lava lamp. It was on wobbly legs that she followed Robyn downstairs so they could collect their things, and while her friend was bursting with enthusiasm at the prospect of a full day out, all Kate wanted to do was curl up in bed – or perhaps around the toilet, she half-joked.

'No way am I leaving you here,' Robyn said firmly. 'You'll only cave in and call James – hangovers make us weak.'

'I won't,' grumbled Kate, although the thought had crossed her mind more than once that morning. It had been such a long time now since they'd spoken – what if James was forgetting all about her? Robyn had laid out three bikinis on the bed and motioned for Kate to help her choose one. 'The pink,' she said at once. 'You're lucky that you can wear that shade – if I tried, I'd look like one of those chewy Fruit Salad sweets.'

'Do you think Alex will approve?'

Kate tutted. 'I'm sure he will, but what does it matter what a man thinks?'

Robyn looked at her strangely before heading into the bathroom, leaving Kate to mull over what she had said to warrant such a reaction. It was hard to think straight when your head was pounding, and your mouth was dry. Picking up her green-and-white swimsuit, she ducked behind the wardrobe door to change and sneaked a look at her phone at the same time, hoping to find something from James. A message, a notification, a change of WhatsApp photo that would allow her some insight into his state of mind – but there was nothing.

She waited for the usual pang of disappointment to strike, for her body to react somehow to the continued silence, but she remained unmoved. If anything, thought Kate, she was becoming numb to it. Or perhaps the hangover was keeping her true feelings at bay, acting like a thin cotton layer between the naked tip of a finger and the hot surface of a stove. Her mind knew she would soon feel the burn, that the pain would come, but her heart was unable to accept it.

Was this denial, or had she somehow managed to turn down the heat?

'Ta-da!' cried Robyn, bursting back into the room and performing a *Baywatch* slow-motion run towards the door. 'Are you coming or what?'

'Sure you wouldn't be better Hoff alone?'

Robyn laughed. 'There she is – I knew you were still in there somewhere.'

'Barely,' replied Kate, but she was smiling as she said it.

They took the shortcut down the hillside to Pokonji Dol beach, Kate having to catch Robyn numerous times when her flip-flops slipped on the dry, stony path, and were boarded and ready to sail soon afterwards. The clouds that had protected them from the glare of the sun all morning had long since burned away, and Kate was relieved to feel the cool air rushing across her cheeks. It was busy out in the bay today, holiday season having reached its peak, and Alex had to steer them around a multitude of fishing boats, jet skis and catamarans to reach open water.

'Hvar feels way more decadent than I was expecting,' observed Robyn, craning her head to stare as they passed a super yacht. 'More like the South of France than the Adriatic.'

'I know what you mean,' Kate agreed. 'But I preferred it when I first arrived – back when it was quieter.'

She had been half-hoping Alex would choose a route that took them around Jerolim, so she could get another look at the hidden cove they'd swum to together, but he didn't. Instead, he headed west, his red Croatia cap pulled down and his gaze fixed ahead, making no comment as Toby, ever the amateur tour guide, called out the names of the passing islands.

'The word "Pakleni" comes from a type of pine resin called "paklina",' he told them. 'It used to be harvested here and used as a kind of varnish on ships. The island to our left now is called Marinkovac, and that's where you'll find the famous Carpe Diem Beach, as well as Ždrilca and Mlini.'

'Your brother should have been a teacher,' Robyn said in an undertone, her carefully straightened hair blowing across her face. She was wearing a life vest over her pink bikini, as well as some patterned shorts with tassels sewn along the hems. Taller and slightly broader across the shoulders than Kate, she had spent three years in her university rowing team and still had the shapely thighs to prove it, although her figure was softened by a nipped-in waist and rounded hips. Being an occupational therapist, Robyn understood better than most how important it was to look after your body, and on the rare days that she didn't work, she would head out for long runs or bike rides.

Kate had missed her friend over the past five weeks, had forgotten how good Robyn was at making her laugh and helping her find the positives when there seemingly were none. She was also fiercely loyal, yet fair with it, and always told the truth rather than attempting to mollycoddle. Kate appreciated this, even if the truth was often a dry cracker to swallow.

Toby was giving Robyn his spiel about the calcium carbonate in the water, and Kate found her eyes straying to Alex, to his messy dreadlocked bun and tatty vest, the faded denim shorts and tanned bare feet. What had compelled her to call him last night instead of James? It wasn't fair of her to keep turning to Alex whenever something went wrong, but he did have a knack for showing up in moments of crisis, his presence comforting her even if he wasn't meaning to. She had known him for such a short amount of time, yet he'd become such an intrinsic part of her life – so much so that now the thought of him no longer being there was abhorrent.

'Are we mooring up at the ACI Marina?' Toby asked, stepping towards the front of the boat.

'I was thinking that would be best,' Alex said with a nod. 'Palmižana will be packed.'

'True.'

Toby caught Robyn's look of enquiry and smiled reassuringly. 'Don't fret – the marina is on the opposite side of St Klement, but it's easy enough to walk across the island. Takes about ten minutes.'

'Can I drive the boat for this last bit?' said Robyn, getting up from the bench seat and sidling towards Alex. 'I promise I won't crash.'

'Sure.' he said, standing to one side so she could take the small wheel.

Kate stared gloomily down at the water.

'Nims.' Toby brushed a finger against her arm. 'You OK?'

Alex had one of his arms around Robyn, helping her to steer, and Kate saw her friend lean backwards against him, her head thrown back as she laughed at something he'd said.

'Do you think those two will—' Toby arched a brow.

'No,' said Kate, with enough force to cause the other two to glance her way.

'Shame,' he mused. 'They seem to have hit it off. I haven't seen Alex smile this much since I met him.'

'That's what people used to say about James after we got together,' murmured Kate. 'Smiles can be deceiving.'

'Oh, sis, don't let the fact you broke up with James taint your entire relationship with him. It was good for a long time; you *were* happy together. Things just ran their course.'

She should tell him the truth about her fertility issues, but Kate couldn't – wouldn't be able to bear the pity that would surely follow. Telling Alex had felt like dropping a stone into the water, one that had been weighing her down for months, but making the same confession to her brother would be to pick it up again. She would end up carrying his sorrow as well as her own, and she wasn't strong enough to do that. Not yet.

'I know,' she said, a grim smile being the best she could muster. 'I'm trying.'

Toby put his arm around her shoulders and gave her a quick squeeze. 'You'll get over this, Nims – I know you will.'

They had entered the bucket-shaped marina and Alex took back the wheel, pointing the boat towards the second of three long wooden jetties.

'I can see why you've been spending so much time with him,' whispered Robyn, a high colour in each of her cheeks as she watched Alex leap over the washboard at the rear and fasten the line. 'He is a real man of the earth, and of the salt, and of the wind.'

'He's not the very last of the Mohicans,' said Kate. 'He's become a good friend, and there's far more to him than simply that beard and this boat.'

'Quite a lot more, presumably—'

'Robyn!'

'You can tell me – I haven't forgotten the fact that you've seen him naked.'

'I didn't see . . . that,' Kate hissed.

Robyn grinned, her smile widening even further when Alex offered her his hand to help her over the side.

'Why, thank you, kind sir.'

'I can manage,' said Kate hurriedly, and Alex raised both his hands as if in defeat.

Any pride she might have felt at not needing his assistance for once was tainted by the gut punch she'd felt watching him and Robyn operate the boat together. A show of closeness between two much cared-for friends should have made her happy, but instead it had landed like a heavy tread on her chest.

There was no reason for her to feel jealous, but there could be no denying it either.

35

The path across the island was well worn and bordered on either side by dry palms and towering fortresses of cacti. When she looked up, Kate could see lilac jacaranda petals jostling for space amongst the pink frilly skirts of myrtle flowers, while fronds of fragrant lavender bent their fragile heads to kiss the ground far below. The air hummed with insect song, pine needles crunched underfoot, and birds chattered to one another in the topmost branches.

Just as she had the previous evening at Hula Hula, Kate heard the bustle of Palmižana beach long before she saw it, so she was not surprised when they descended a set of steps to find the narrow strip of shingle ahead of them packed with holidaymakers. There was barely space to step, let alone lay down a towel, while every table at the three beachfront restaurants appeared to be occupied and yet more people stood in queues awaiting a slot. The harbour beyond was cluttered with boats – many of which looked to be at the ritziest end of the luxury yacht scale – and Kate's eyes widened as she saw a child of no more than six zooming through the shallows on a miniature jet ski.

'So this is how the other half lives,' said Robyn, staring around. 'I always had wondered.'

Kate glanced at Alex. With both his hands in his pockets and a curdled expression on his face, he looked demonstrably uncomfortable – a fact he confirmed a moment later when he announced an intention to return to the boat.

'Oh, please stay,' begged Robyn, taking hold of his arm. 'There's some room over there,' she said, pointing to where a row of wooden cabanas had been erected along the shoreline.

'I've brought snorkelling gear,' added Toby, pivoting to show them his rucksack. 'Whoever wants to can swim out a bit from the beach, where it's less crowded.'

Alex looked towards Kate, who smiled helplessly. She would happily have accompanied him back to the boat, but that would hardly be fair on Robyn. This she attempted to convey to him now with a meaningful look in her friend's direction.

'Right,' he said after a beat or two. 'I'll stay.'

It was with reluctance, however, that he followed them down the steps and around the curve of the bay, his mouth set and his eyes two dark hollows beneath the peak of his cap. Kate, who felt responsible for his disquiet – after all, it had been she who rang and demanded this day out – apologised so many times that Alex eventually told her to stop.

Oblivious to her friend's inner turmoil, Robyn skipped ahead, her agile runner's feet helping her weave and hop around and over sunbathers. She had soon reached their destination and waved them over to a flat expanse of rocks at the water's edge.

'I should have brought a cushion,' grumbled Toby, as he lowered himself into a sitting position and started unbuttoning his shirt. Robyn, who was already stretched out with both eyes closed and the straps of her bikini top unfastened to avoid tan lines, let out a satisfied sigh of contentment.

Kate hunkered down and untied the laces of her Converse, slipping them off along with her socks and leaf-print dress. She was just reaching into her bag for some sun cream when she felt a tap on her shoulder and turned to find Alex staring down at her.

'Swim?' he said, holding up two snorkelling masks.

'Um, I don't know.' Kate poked Robyn with a big toe. 'Do you want to snorkel?'

'Nah, not yet,' she replied, opening one eye and shutting it again. 'You two go ahead – me and Tobes can look after all the bags and stuff.'

'Fine by me,' agreed Toby, who had helped himself to Kate's towel and was rolling it into a pillow shape.

Alex dropped his vest and cap and waded out into the water in his denim shorts, leaving Kate to dither in his wake.

Robyn sat up to roll her bikini bottoms down a fraction. 'Go on,' she insisted. 'Otherwise how are Toby and I supposed to gossip about you?'

'So much for subtlety,' muttered Kate, scanning the water for Alex. He'd already swum some way out and was beckoning for her to join him. The water felt wonderfully cool against her sun-baked skin, but the stones below her feet were sharp-edged. Far from making a graceful entrance, she hobbled, swore, then tumbled forwards with a splash, earning herself a hearty round of applause from the other two up on the rocks.

When she reached Alex, she tried to stand, but he had brought them out too deep.

'Is this a good time to admit I've never snorkelled before?' she asked.

If Alex was treading water, which he surely must be, then he was doing so by barely moving. There was not so much as a ripple around him.

'Well, given how much you enjoyed swimming in open water the other day, I figured not.'

'I did enjoy that,' she exclaimed. 'Eventually, anyway.'

'You've done a bit of meditation before.' He didn't pose it as a question.

'Sort of,' she agreed. 'How did you know?'

'That night on the terrace,' he said. 'I saw you counting your breaths.'

Kate flushed as she recalled what had transpired shortly before that.

'My dad taught me that trick when I was little. I was a bad sleeper back then. I used to convince myself that I would have a terrible nightmare if I gave in, so I would fight it, but then of course I was exhausted and erratic the following day. My parents tried all sorts of lights and story tapes and even bribery. They promised they would take me to Disneyland if I stopped being so silly about it, but even that didn't work. In the end, a woman from my dad's work suggested the breathing trick and to his amazement, it was a success. I've been using it ever since, whenever I find myself in a situation where I need to relax.'

'I fish,' he said. 'Something about being still and watching the water – it slows the world down for a while, helps me find my way back to myself.'

'That makes sense,' she replied, a jolt going through her as their knees connected under the surface.

'Being able to control your breathing is an important skill when it comes to snorkelling,' he said, passing across a mask and breathing tube. 'Start by putting put this on, that's right, and then tighten it there at the side. OK?'

Kate nodded.

'Right, next you need to bring round this mouthpiece here and hold it in place – don't chew it!' He laughed as Kate bared her teeth. 'You want to be as relaxed as possible.'

Kate fiddled around pulling out trapped tendrils of her hair while Alex donned his own mask, her legs under the water colliding with his as she kicked hard to stop herself sinking.

'Ready to try?' he said, but Kate shook her head and promptly spat out the mouthpiece.

'I'm not sure if I can do it,' she fretted. 'I feel like I won't be able to breathe.'

'We can practise together,' he said, putting his hands on her shoulders to steady her. 'Stop moving your legs for a minute . . . don't worry, I'll hold you, that's right . . . and now slowly put your head under the water.'

Kate made sure her mouthpiece was in place before doing as he instructed, but as soon as her face was submerged, she panicked and breathed out hard through her nose, steaming up her mask and making her eyes water. Her eyesight had already been hindered by the removal of her glasses and now she couldn't see a thing. Bringing her head back above water, she yanked out the breathing tube. 'I can't do it. My lungs just closed up. It felt as if I was suffocating.'

'You're safe, I've got you,' he soothed, giving her a moment to compose herself. 'It will feel strange at first – a bit like driving a car on the opposite side of the road. Give your brain a bit of time to adjust and you'll be well away.'

'If it's my brain, we definitely have a problem,' Kate joked limply.

'I don't believe that, not for a second.'

Somehow, they had ended up only a few inches away from each other. Kate could see the droplets of water on his lashes, the pink patches of skin around his nose where the mask was pinching.

'We'll go under together this time. Keep your eyes on mine, look right here.' He tapped the front of his mask.

Kate took a deep breath and brought the mouthpiece back up to her lips, focusing all her attention on Alex. With a single careful movement, he let go of her shoulders, leaving her only for a moment to insert his own breathing tube before taking her hands. Their fingers interlocked and Kate held on tightly, the tempo of her heart increasing as she touched him.

Slowly, so slowly that it felt as if she had barely moved at all, Alex lowered the two of them under the surface, his eyes never leaving hers as the water lifted strands of her hair. She could feel the pressure building in her throat, but told herself to simply breathe, to stop being afraid and trust that her body would know what to do, that it would not let her panic this time. Remembering to count her breaths, Kate concentrated only on the air that was entering her lungs, holding it captive until her frantic heart began to slow.

Alex had not let go of her hands, nor had he shifted his pale-blue gaze from her. She was aware of a new world emerging around them, an underwater lair thrown suddenly into sharp relief. Kate saw it all, but mostly she saw Alex; felt him not only holding on to her, but deep inside herself too – an undeniable pull that awakened her every nerve.

Alex withdrew his hand from hers and it was as if a cord had snapped. The bond between them severed, and flustered, Kate splashed back to the surface, removing her mask and turning away from him, lest he see the confusion on her face.

Someone was waving from the shoreline and she rubbed the water from her eyes. It was Toby. He was holding something up and pointing to it.

Alex had swum a short distance away before resurfacing, his expression unreadable as he lifted the goggles away from his face. 'I think you've got a call,' he said.

'I better see what he wants.' Kate motioned towards her brother.

Alex merely nodded. He seemed to be trying to get his breath back, which struck her as faintly odd, given how serene he'd looked under the water. He didn't follow when she started to swim away but turned instead, cutting through the water at an elegant crawl. Kate watched him go, torn by an urge to pursue.

'Nims,' Toby yelled, as soon as she was close enough to hear. 'Come quick!'

Robyn was sitting up next to him, her smile full beneath her sunglasses.

'What's going on?' Kate stumbled as she attempted to gain purchase on the stones. 'Who was on the phone?'

'It was a guy called Lovro,' he said. 'Apparently you know him? He owns a pizza place. Anyway, he says he's opening a coffee shop in town and, well, he wants your help doing it up.'

'You're joking,' said Kate, accepting a towel. 'As in, he wants help painting?'

'Not just that – he wants to hire you as his interior designer. Apparently, you are hot property in Hvar. He's going to pay you, obviously, and it's a generous amount.'

'You're sure he said me?' Kate narrowed her eyes. 'You're not winding me up, are you?'

'No, Nims, I'm not. I never joke about work – you know that.'

Robyn had got to her feet and was hugging her. 'This is so exciting, Kate! Your first paid gig as an interior designer. I'm so proud of you.'

'Hang on.' Kate looked at each of them in turn. 'I haven't even agreed to do it yet.'

'Ah.' Toby chewed his bottom lip. 'Actually, you have. Your assistant has already agreed on your behalf.'

'They have? And I'm guessing my assistant is—'

'Me? Yep – 'fraid so.'

'But I can't do something like this – can I? It's hardly like I'm a professional interior designer, and I'm pretty sure I can't work in Croatia without the right visa.'

'Oh, stop pooping all over my parade,' scolded Toby. 'We can sort out all the boring details later – the point is, you're a wanted woman. This is it – it's really happening for you.'

'But I . . . I don't get it. How did Lovro even know about the hostel, let alone have my phone number?'

Toby shrugged. 'Someone must have tipped him off.

Maybe that gorgeous German guy you met, who I still can't believe you didn't ask over for a drink.'

'What gorgeous man?' said Robyn, but Kate had stopped listening.

There was only one person who could have set this up, only one person who had enough faith in her to suggest it; someone who knew Lovro, who would be trusted by him. Kate turned back to the water, desperately scanning the sea for any sign of him.

But Alex was nowhere to be seen.

36

'Shall we get a bottle of champagne to celebrate?'

Robyn looked expectantly at Kate, but she shook her head. 'I can't even think about alcohol. I'm still too hungover.'

'I'm at least going to treat us all to a late lunch,' said Toby, and passing Kate her phone, he headed off along the beach to see if there were any free tables.

Kate felt strangely lightheaded and loose-limbed. It must be the shock.

'Who is this Lovro, then?' Robyn enquired. 'How come you know him if Toby doesn't?'

'I met him through Alex,' she said. 'What? Why are you looking at me like that?'

'Like what?'

'Like Mrs Bennet at the ball, when Jane was asked to dance by Mr Bingley.'

Robyn reached for her bottle of sun cream. 'I'm your best friend, Kate Nimble. I can tell when you like someone.'

'I do like Alex. In the same way I like mashed potato and forward-facing seats on trains. There's nothing more to it than that.'

'If you say so,' said Robyn, her tone making it clear she believed no such thing. 'But would it be so dreadful if you did like him more than mashed potato? Perhaps much more?'

'Robyn—'

'All I'm saying is that he's single, you're single, you clearly get on and he's a nice guy. Would it be the end of the world if you had a holiday romance? A summer fling.'

'You're forgetting one vital thing,' Kate told her.

'Oh, please don't say J—'

'Yes – James.'

Robyn lay back down on her towel and closed her eyes, effectively putting an end to the conversation. Kate was about to continue when she spotted Alex sauntering through the shallows towards her, his hair flattened and his beard trailing water.

'Were your ears burning?' chimed Robyn, to which Kate laughed a bit too loud.

'Should they be?' he asked, settling down on the rock.

'I was just telling Robyn how I met Lovro,' she explained.

'Oh, right.' Alex wrung out some water from his dread-locks. 'Any reason why?'

Ignoring a sniggering Robyn, Kate filled him in on the news about the coffee shop.

'Thank you,' she said, 'for putting in a good word. I know it must have been you,' she added, as Alex started to protest. 'Nobody else knows both of us.'

'He asked, I answered.' Alex shrugged. 'No big deal.'

But it was a big deal. It was only now starting to dawn on Kate how much of a big deal it was.

'I hope I don't mess up and let you both down,' she said now. 'Not after you put in a good word for me.'

'You won't,' he said. 'Have a little faith in yourself.'

'Hear, hear,' chorused Robyn.

Kate arranged her features into a smile, but it did little to allay her concerns. Choosing a few paint colours and repurposing some old items of furniture was one thing, but to be offered paid interior design work by a stranger was another entirely. What would happen if she messed it up, or worse

– got there and found she had no ideas, nothing of merit to suggest?

Glancing at Alex, she found him looking over her shoulder and turned.

'We're never going to get a table here,' grumbled Toby, who'd returned from his perusal of Palmižana's restaurants. 'How about a celebratory dinner tonight instead? I'm sure my delectable husband will be only too happy to cook something *favoloso* on the barbecue.'

'If there's food involved, the answer is always yes,' said Robyn, who had her eyes shut again.

'I might pop by this new coffee shop of Lovro's on the way back,' said Kate. 'It would be good to get a sense of exactly what state it's in, and how much will need to be done.'

'I'm sure Al can drop you off in town on the way,' said Toby.

Kate looked at Alex, her gaze dropping of its own accord to rove across his bare chest.

'Sure,' he said. 'Not a problem.'

They left Palmižana later in the afternoon and headed back towards Hvar Town at a leisurely pace. The plan was that Alex would drop them all off at the main harbour, then take his boat back to its usual mooring spot and return to the hostel on foot, where they'd all rendezvous for dinner. When they arrived, however, Robyn held back.

'I might come with you,' she said to Alex. 'I want to have a go in the deckchair.'

Kate paused mid-clamber.

'Fine by me,' he said, one hand on the boat's rear line.

'I'll see you two in a bit then,' she added, smiling at Kate. 'Good luck.'

'But—' Kate could not think of a suitable reason to refuse, and she had no choice but to watch in silence as Alex eased the boat away, one of his hands outstretched in case Robyn fell climbing up into the deckchair. *That bloody deckchair.* She only had herself to blame.

'Ready?' asked Toby, as Kate stared forlornly across the water.

'As I'll ever be,' she said, pulling herself together.

Kate wished she hadn't spent the morning before her first official work meeting at the beach. She had no make-up on, her hair had dried into a dandelion frizz, and she should be dressed smartly in a blouse and skirt, not a gaping sundress with a wet patch on the bottom where she'd sat in her damp swimsuit.

Lovro had texted over the address of his new business venture, which Toby recognised as one of the narrow streets that led up towards the Fortico. As they came within sight of the little shop, however, Kate feeling more nervous with every step, he drew back.

'I have a few things I need to do in town,' he said. 'You'll be all right from here, won't you?'

'You're going?' Kate was aghast. 'You can't!'

'Don't be silly. You're a professional career woman now – this is your party.'

'But I need you here with me.'

'Nims, listen to me. You don't need me; you don't need anyone – especially not when you're in work mode. I lost count of the number of times you shooed me away when we were doing Sul Tetto.'

'That was different.'

'No, it wasn't,' he said patiently. 'You need to concentrate now, and I'll only distract you. This is what you're good at – just get in there and do what you do best. It will be fine, you'll see. Have a little faith in yourself for once.'

Alex had said the same thing. *Have a little faith.* It was easy for them to say.

Leaning over, Toby gave her a quick peck on the top of her head 'for luck', and then he was gone.

Kate stood alone in the lane, waiting for her hands to stop trembling. The door to what would become the coffee shop was propped open and she could hear banging coming from within. She took a hesitant step forward only for her stomach to twist into knots.

She was being ridiculous.

This was what she wanted, what she enjoyed; it was the closest she'd ever come to a passion – so why did she feel so discombobulated? Why was she letting the fear of failure hold her back yet again?

Kate pictured herself with Alex, saw the two of them sitting together surrounded by white stones. How miraculous it had felt to acknowledge all those things that scared her, give a name to those metaphorical barriers she had constructed that held her own self-worth at bay, and toss them away to be washed clean.

She could do this; she had to do this.

Taking a final, steadying breath, Kate walked up to the open door.

'Knock, knock,' she called through the gap. If only she had the skills to greet her first client in his own language. Settling for a timid '*zdravo*', she stepped over the threshold into a dark-walled and dust-filled room. Inside, there was a long, grubby countertop, a tall shuttered window and a stack of mismatched wooden furniture. A radio stood in the far corner, plugged in alongside what looked to be a circular saw, which someone had left on a low table to her right, a stack of plain white tiles piled up underneath it.

Kate was pleased; she would be working from a relatively blank canvas. It was easier to envisage something new from a clean slate, and as she stood and stared, ideas began to take shape in her mind.

The single window would not permit much natural light – especially not on a back street as narrow as this one – so the first thing they would need were some powerful spotlights. The ceiling was crisscrossed with open beams, which would provide inspiration for an aesthetic consisting of earthy tones and natural materials. She could envisage printed menus on wooden clipboards, cutlery stacked in burnished tins, Kilner jars of coffee and teabags on stripped-wooden shelves behind the counter, not uniform but spliced into ledges and arranged at varying heights. The crockery should be plain, but the saucers patterned, the few tables adorned with succulents of different shapes and sizes, each housed in clay pots bought locally and perhaps even sold to visiting tourists. The brick walls could stay, but must be painted white, and she could see a vast pinboard taking pride of place opposite the window, somewhere to share leaflets from other businesses in the area or for guests to leave notes or photos. Upcycled bar stools could house trailing plants, mirrors could reflect light and expand space, and she could use circular picture frames or adornments to soften the rather boxy feel of the place.

It was all going to work; she could do this after all.

When Lovro ambled through from the back room ten minutes later, he found Kate busy taking photos and tapping notes into her phone. All traces of her earlier trepidation gone, she smiled warmly and shook his hand, accepting his offer of coffee before talking him slowly through everything she had come up with so far. Fortunately, Lovro's grasp of English was far better than hers was of Croatian, and he understood her vision for the place immediately, nodding away and patting the pockets of his jeans in search of pen and paper to write things down. Within an hour, they had compiled a comprehensive list of materials and agreed a workable schedule. Beaming with pride and anticipation, she practically skipped back out into the lane when it was time to go and reached straight for her phone.

All she could think was that she wanted to call Alex and tell him how well it had gone, but there was already a message from him waiting.

Had to meet my friend – sorry to miss dinner.

Ten little words, eleven devastating syllables, and one confirmation that Kate could no longer deny her feelings.

37

There was no point trying to sleep.

Kate was still sharing her double bed at the hostel with Robyn, so she inched the sheet down as quietly as possible and crept from the room. She guessed from the darkness and total silence that it must be around three a.m. – an assumption that was verified by the clock on the communal kitchen wall.

Kate filled a glass of water from the tap. As much as she'd loved the hostel when it was freshly painted and free from clutter, she felt more at home here now that it was full of guests. She liked seeing boxes of food labelled and stacked on the shelves Alex had built, enjoyed the echoes of footfall on the central staircase as people left for early flights or ventured in late after a night of partying at Carpe Diem, Hula Hula or one of the island's many other bars. It was people that made a house a home – or a hostel, in this case.

There had only been four of them on the terrace for dinner in the end, and Kate had thought she'd done a good job of pretending she couldn't care less about Alex's decision not to join in. That was, until she and Robyn headed down to bed.

'Where was it Alex had to be again?' her friend asked casually, slipping off her sandals and pushing them towards her open suitcase. Despite Kate's not-so-subtle hints, Robyn had yet to unpack properly, and a trail of clothes, shoes and toiletries were spilling over the side.

'He had to see a friend.'

'And you're not annoyed?'

Kate looked up. 'Annoyed? Why would I be?'

'OK, maybe annoyed is the wrong word. I should have said disappointed.'

'I'm not annoyed or disappointed,' Kate said, but she couldn't meet Robyn's eye. She always had been a terrible liar.

'I think it might be my fault,' Robyn said, her voice unchar-acteristically meek. 'I may have said a few things to him earlier, after we left you and Tobe . . .'

Kate paused in the bathroom doorway.

'Oh?' she said. 'What things?'

'I might have suggested to him that the two of you . . . liked each other.'

Kate felt a sensation like a bath plug being pulled out in her stomach.

'And before you get cross – hear me out! He didn't seem appalled by the idea. He didn't say much, to be honest; he just kind of smiled and shook his head a bit—'

'But what did you actually say?' interrupted Kate. 'What were your exact words?'

'I said, "Kate's nice, isn't she?" And he agreed that you were. Then I said, "She's single, you know?" And he replied, "I know".'

So far, so typically non-committal Alex.

'And then what?'

'I said that what I thought you needed was a bit of fun – and that perhaps he was the man to provide it.'

'Robyn!'

Kate put her face in her hands. 'Why?'

'Because I can tell that the two of you are attracted to each other. Honestly, the tension is palpable – it was all day. Every time I looked at you both, you were staring at each other. He may not say much, but he doesn't have to – it's written all over his face. The guy is smitten.'

'Well, obviously not, if he then decided to do a runner,' Kate retorted. 'Poor bloke probably thought I'd jump him.'

She held back from mentioning the kiss. That would only strengthen Robyn's resolve to bring the two of them together, and Kate didn't want to risk losing Alex's friendship. Nor, if she was being honest, did she want news of such a thing finding its way back to James. Because while Robyn would not set out to betray Kate's secrets, she might be tricked into giving them away – especially if goaded. And it had only been the briefest of kisses; there was little chance of it happening again. Clearly, Kate thought, as she had got stiffly into bed half an hour later, Alex had articulated that point by failing to materialise that evening.

But no matter how many times Kate told herself not to worry, she couldn't rid her mind of Alex, of where he had really gone and what he genuinely felt about her. It was why she was awake now, prowling around the hostel after dark, unable to settle.

She drank her glass of water and glared solemnly out of the window; her gaze drawn as always towards the black satin surface of the sea. She would go to it; make her way to the shore and seek direction from the stars above.

There was a hooded top of Toby's on the back of the chair in reception, and Kate pulled it on over the shorts and vest she slept in. In the lost property box, she unearthed some flip-flops a size or two bigger than her own, but that didn't matter. She wouldn't go far.

It was quiet without the usual cacophony of crickets, the only sound the soft slapping of her too-big borrowed footwear, and Kate started violently when something small and lithe scampered between her feet.

'Siva,' she hissed, as the cat stared beadily up at her. 'What are you doing out here?'

The cat raised her leg and began to wash her bottom disdainfully.

'Charming,' Kate said, bending to stroke Siva's over-large ears. 'Come on then, let's go and see if we can spot any fish.'

The street lights illuminated their way until they reached the stony slope that led down to Pokonji Dol beach, after which Kate became far more cautious, her hands poised to steady herself if she were to slip or fall. It was a treacherous undertaking in daylight hours, let alone in the pitch black, but she had deliberately chosen this particular area of the coastline. From up here on the path, the beach below appeared deserted, and there were only a few lighted windows on the opposite side on the bay. Kate scanned the harbour until she found the familiar shape of Alex's boat with its deckchair adornment, but there were no lights visible on board. Either he was asleep or staying elsewhere for the night.

Siva reached the bottom of the hill first and shot across the road onto the white stones beyond, Kate hobbling behind her in her too-big sandals. The first time she'd seen this beach, the white pebbles had reminded her of fallen petals, but tonight they were a shoal of silent fish; an echo of life that remained beautiful even in death. Pausing for a moment, she heard what sounded like purring and frowned. There was only one person who could elicit such a response from Siva, and he was –

'Hello.'

A figure had sat up suddenly on one of the nearby sunloungers and Kate let out a shriek, stumbling backwards right out of her flip-flops.

'Shit, Alex – you scared me half to death.'

'Sorry,' he said, sounding bemused. 'In my defence, I didn't really expect to see you here.'

'Ditto,' she exclaimed, not altogether truthfully.

'Sleepwalking is it?' he said, resting his elbows on his knees.

'No.' Kate trod carefully across the stones and took a seat beside him. 'I just fancied a walk, that's all.'

'At half-past three in the morning?'

'That's right.'

'I see.'

Kate smiled. It was so nice to see him; she felt immeasurably better simply being in his presence.

'What's your excuse?' she asked, bringing her feet up onto the edge of the lounger and pulling Toby's hoodie down to her ankles. 'Moon bathing, is it?'

'Couldn't sleep,' he said, tugging at the sleeves of his own hooded top. It was the same one he'd worn the night they'd stayed in Brač, and Kate was sure she could detect a faint smell of candle smoke as he shifted position. He was wearing a bandana she'd not seen before over his dreadlocks that looked blue in the moonlight. Blue to match his eyes.

'You were missed at dinner,' she said. 'I ate my own body weight in squid-ink risotto, and it turned my tongue black. Look,' she said, poking it out. 'Halloween has come early.'

His eyes flickered downwards. 'Nice.'

Kate re-inserted her tongue, wondering why she must always behave so ridiculously.

'Did you meet your friend?' she asked, to which he looked puzzled.

'Friend?'

'Whoever it was that made you miss dinner?'

'Oh. Yes. Sure I did.'

'Really?'

Alex cracked his knuckles, watching wordlessly as Siva writhed her soft body against his shin. 'I had somewhere else to be, that's all.'

'Where? Here?'

A slight shake of the head.

'Then where?'

'Are you cold?' he asked. Kate had slid her arms out of her sleeves and cocooned herself inside Toby's hoodie, her shoulders hunched, and toes curled.

'A little bit,' she said. 'But that is no reason to change the subject.'

'Fair enough.'

'So . . . ?'

'I wanted to come, but—'

'Robyn scared you off,' she prompted, and Alex turned in surprise.

'Scared me? No. Nothing like that. I guess I wanted to give you some space, that's all.'

'All of us, or just me?'

Alex took a deep breath, lifting his chin so he could see the stars. 'You.'

They sat for a moment in companionable silence while Kate absorbed this, watching the distant form of Siva as she picked her way daintily over the stones. When Alex raised two fingers to his lips and whistled, the cat came back straight away and hopped up into the empty space between them.

'She looks almost docile when she's like this,' observed Kate, as Siva curled up and began to purr once again. 'You definitely have a calming effect – on people as well as animals,' she added. 'I think I'm the opposite – my nervous energy ends up putting people on edge.'

'Not me,' he said. 'I think you have good energy. I mean' – he gestured out in the vague direction of his boat – 'sometimes it might lead you to make some crazy decisions, but— '

'Point taken.' Kate laughed, rocking forwards on the balls of her feet.

'You are cold,' he said, scooping up the cat and propping her up on his shoulder. 'Come on – my camping stove is on the boat. There might even be a blanket or two, if you haven't fashioned them into a makeshift sail or suchlike.'

'Funny,' replied Kate, getting swiftly to her feet.

Under any other circumstances, it might have felt eerie to be cutting through the dark water in the dead of night, but with Alex there beside her, Kate found the dinghy crossing a thrill. After depositing a rather disgruntled Siva on the deck, Alex insisted on giving Kate a proper leg-up over the side, which somehow ended up with her bottom on his shoulders. And was it her imagination, or did his hands linger longer than they needed to on her thighs?

The air on the boat felt alive. Kate was no longer cold.

'This way,' he said, pushing open the cabin door with his foot.

Kate followed, her heart a trapped butterfly, every nerve ending a live wire poised to spark. Alex unfolded a blanket.

'Shall we sit in here or out on the deck?' he asked.

'In here is fine,' she said, her voice high and strange. She didn't remember the space inside the cabin being so small. If she moved at all, she would touch him.

Alex laid one blanket across the floor, then passed her another.

'Get comfortable,' he said. 'I'll dig out the stove.'

'No don't,' Kate said quickly, closing the space between them and almost treading on Siva who had shot in from outside. The cat's squeal of outrage was enough to break the tension, and they both smiled at one another.

'You don't want the stove on?' he clarified.

'No.' Kate stared down at her toes, refusing to meet his gaze. There was no light on inside the cabin, the porthole windows blacked out by night.

'If you sit down with me, we can keep each other warm.'

There was a long pause.

'All right,' he said, hunkering down and folding his arm beneath his head. Kate hesitated for a moment, then took off her glasses and lay down beside him, shaking out the blanket he'd given her until it was covering both of them. Alex waited while she fidgeted around, eventually offering her his shoulder to rest her head on. She knew that if she allowed herself to get too close to him, she would be lost, but Kate was past the point of logic. As if he could sense her internal battle, Alex unhooked his arm and wrapped it around her, pulling her close against his chest and holding her there.

Time seemed to stand still.

Kate could feel the frantic rush of his heart as she lay against him, her knee over his thigh and her fingers tracing a pattern up and across his torso. She felt him swallow and lifted her chin, wrinkling her nose as it was tickled by his beard. He was looking at her, but it was more than that – the sensation was one of being seen.

Alex saw straight through the person she projected to the world; he saw her.

Kate brought up her hand and slowly slid her thumb across his lips, feeling him shiver. There was no longer any space between them, but she pressed herself further forwards regardless, telling him with her body what she was feeling, how much more she wanted to feel.

'I don't want you to give me space, Alex.'

He turned at her words, his breath hot against her cheek, and she parted her lips, closed her eyes in anticipation.

'Kate.'

A single word, full of infinite meaning.

'Alex.'

The name seemed to surprise him, and for the briefest second, Kate saw a glimpse of what looked like doubt pass across his face. There were doubtless many reasons why they shouldn't do this, but Kate could not remember any of them. Desire was too impatient an opponent to deliberation. It had already won.

Without so much as a murmur, Alex slid his hands around her waist and lifted her until she was sitting across his lap. Kate could feel him, hard against her, and arched her back as he sat up and pulled her gently forwards, his lips finding the hollow of her throat. The blanket had fallen away from them and Kate pulled off her hoodie, smiling as he followed suit, his bare chest warm against hers.

'You're beautiful,' he said softly.

'So are you,' she said. And it was true. In that moment, Kate was sure that Alex was the most beautiful man she'd ever seen.

'Are you sure?' he murmured, looking at her with such intensity that Kate felt scorched. To say anything now felt impossible, muted as she was by longing, and so she nodded instead, pushing down against him until there was no room for doubt, no need for words, no reason to stop. Alex brushed a curl off her cheek; the sensation made her tremble.

'Kate, I need to—' he began, but she silenced him with her eyes.

'Later,' she whispered, resting her nose against his. 'After.'

Alex looked down and for a second, Kate felt the connection between them falter. She waited, barely daring to move or even breathe, until he slid his hands back around her waist. There was a difference to his touch now, an urgency that hadn't been there before. Kate felt it – felt him – and it was this that gave her the courage she needed.

To finally, blissfully, press her lips once again to his.

38

Kate must have dozed off, because when she awoke, Alex was gone, and the boat was moving. He had only half-closed the cabin door and she could see through the gap that it was not quite daylight. The two of them had made a mess of the makeshift bed, but at some stage Alex must have covered her up with a blanket. Bringing the scratchy material up to her face now, Kate breathed in the scent of him, of the two of them together. Siva, who was curled up on a pile of T-shirts, opened one eye and gave her a scathing look. That was fair enough, thought Kate, given what the poor cat had witnessed.

'Morning,' she said, emerging onto the deck a few minutes later. Instead of putting Toby's hoodie back on over her shorts, she had decided to wear Alex's red one, and he smiled when he saw her.

'Hey,' he replied, pulling her towards him by one of the drawstring cords and kissing her lightly on the lips. They fitted together so well, thought Kate. She didn't have to stand on tiptoes to reach him and all the most exciting parts of their bodies were aligned.

'Where are we going?' she asked, as Alex sat up on his seat and manoeuvred her between his thighs. He was only wearing his frayed denim shorts, but his bare skin felt hot to the touch. Kate wanted him to let go of the controls so that he could put his hands on her instead.

'Somewhere we can watch the sunrise,' he said, gently

turning her around. 'Here.' He lifted her hands and put them on the small wheel. 'You can help me steer.'

'I'll end up crashing if you keep doing that,' she said teasingly, as Alex started to kiss her neck. 'But don't stop. Please, don't stop.'

The sky above them now was a steely blue, the only hint of day a narrow shaft of gold on the far horizon. The sea looked almost black, its cresting waves pale and ghostly, while the distant masses of land were huge slumbering beasts. It felt miraculous to Kate that she was here at all, with a man who had made her feel so much braver and stronger, a man who made everything so much easier somehow. When she cast her mind back to the reasons she had found herself in Hvar throughout this strange meandering summer, it seemed as if they had happened to another person; a different Kate had stood up in that pub and asked James to marry her, and a new Kate was here on this boat now. Was this always the path her life was supposed to take? A reward, perhaps, for all she'd endured to get here.

Alex had slid one of his hands underneath the red hoodie, and Kate felt her knees give as his knuckles brushed against her breast.

'You do realise,' she murmured, 'that we're just heading out into open sea?'

Alex rested his chin on her shoulder and peered down at the dashboard.

'The co-ordinates are right,' he said. 'We're on course.'

'Everything about this feels right,' she said quietly, smiling as he pressed his legs more tightly around her.

Alex, in answer, allowed his hands to stray down below the waistband of her shorts.

'Just hold on to the wheel,' he whispered, as Kate let out a small groan of pleasure. 'Don't take your hands off the wheel.'

She made herself stare out across the water, trying her best to focus on the view and not what he was doing to her, so tenderly yet insistently, until everything started to blur.

Afterwards, she turned her head and kissed him.

It was getting lighter. They didn't have long until the sun came up.

'How much further?' she asked, sidling in next to him on the seat.

Alex wrapped an arm around her shoulders. 'We're almost there – see those two outcrops of rock straight ahead?'

Kate squinted through the gloom. 'Yes, just about.'

'That's the entrance to Stiniva Cove.'

'The one that's just been voted the best beach in Europe?'

'Is that so?'

'It is.' Kate snuggled herself closer. 'I cut the article out of the paper and put it up in the hostel reception. Wait a sec,' she added, as Alex began to slow the boat, 'that gap doesn't look anywhere near wide enough for us to pass through.'

'It isn't,' he said, looking slightly sheepish. 'I'm afraid we'll have to swim up to the shore.'

'But I haven't got my costume. What? Why are you laughing?'

Alex killed the engine and clambered around, fastening ropes to the mooring line in the water and checking that Siva was shut safely below deck.

'You don't need it,' he said. 'There's nobody here but us.'

'At the moment there isn't – what if another boat turns up?'

Hopping down from the washboard, he unbuckled his shorts and let them fall to floor. 'Unlikely,' he told her, grinning as Kate's eyes roamed hungrily down the length of his body. 'But if it does, then so what?'

'Then some random person will see me naked!'

Alex shrugged. 'Lucky them.'

'Can't we just watch the sunrise from here?' she pleaded. 'From under a blanket together?'

'Tempting.' Alex stepped towards her and trailed a finger across her cheek. 'But no.'

And before Kate had a chance to protest further, he'd turned and dived over the side, his lithe figure making barely a splash as it cut through the surface.

'Wait for me!' she called, whipping off her clothes and glasses and leaving them in a pile on the deck. She was not adept enough to dive, so she sat on the edge of the boat instead, shuffling forwards an inch at a time and holding her nose before allowing herself to plunge downwards.

'It's bloody freezing!' she cried, surfacing to find Alex treading water a few feet away.

'I'll keep you warm,' he promised, and she swam gratefully into his waiting arms, their bodies slotting together without thought or hesitation.

Rather than feel exposed, Kate quickly discovered that naked swimming was exhilarating. She felt free – untethered not only from her normal life but from her normal self, too. And while she and Alex might only be two tiny dots afloat in the vast ocean of life, to Kate, it felt as if they were the only things that mattered. The rest of her life – of their lives – would have to wait.

She still had her arms around Alex but disentangled herself as the two of them began to swim towards the cove. The water surrounding them was inky black, the cliffs on either side bleached from white to pale yellow by the emerging dawn. Once they were through the gap, the sea seemed to steady, while the waves that met the white-stone shoreline did so tenderly, with barely more than a soft whooshing sound. On the hillside above the half-moon beach, Kate could just make out a bristling halo of scrubby trees.

'We should have brought the snorkels,' said Alex. 'There's a baby swordfish right underneath us.'

Kate started. 'What? Where?'

'Don't worry – it's only the size of my hand.'

'It won't poke me, will it?'

Alex, who'd raised his eyebrows when she got to the word 'poke', assured her that no, it almost certainly would not.

'I might go ashore,' she said. 'Just in case.'

Once she'd staggered across the chalky pebbles as elegantly as she was able, Kate sat down and brought her knees up to her chin, watching as Alex dived down over and over. The new day was creeping across the landscape and Kate gazed up towards a sky that was dip-dyed pink and gold. How often had she sat like this in London, she wondered – was it ever? Being here had made her appreciate how important it was to stop and look, to pause and reflect, to watch the world rather than focusing on the number of comments appearing below an online post. But it was not simply the magic of Croatia that she had to thank.

It was the person here with her now.

Alex crunched up the beach and flopped down beside her, shaking water off his dreadlocks as vigorously as a dog after a bath. Kate had never seen him this carefree and languid; he'd shrugged off his usual reserve and become more playful, rolling her onto her back so he could plant kisses all over her face.

'You're like a horny teenager,' she said, laughing as he buried his head in her chest. 'It's almost as if you've never seen a naked woman before, which I know from our first encounter is definitely not the case.'

Alex gave her a look that was loaded with desire.

'You aren't just any woman. A naked Kate is better than a naked anyone else.'

'Smooth talker,' she said, taking his hand. 'Thank you, by the way, for bringing me here. It really is beautiful – certainly worthy of an award.'

'Unfortunately, winning a prize will only make this cove more popular,' he said with a sigh. 'It's nowhere near as tranquil when it's overflowing with boats, floats and—'

'Goats?' she interrupted, to which he responded by kissing her again.

'It's going to be another blinder of a day,' she said, resting her head on his shoulder as they each basked in the mild sunshine. 'Is it bad that I don't want to go back to Hvar, to reality? I wish there was a way we could simply stay here.'

Alex picked up a stone and threw it into the water. 'We can stay if you want,' he said simply. 'But if I know you as well as I think I do, then your conscience won't allow it. You have people relying on you, a friend visiting, a new project.'

'True.'

'But if you genuinely wanted to go – to disappear for a while – I could make that happen.'

'Don't tell me you're a magician as well as a carpenter-stroke-fisherman?'

'You don't need magic to vanish,' he countered. 'You only need to want to.'

Kate sat back up and turned from the view so she could look at him. 'I don't think I ever could,' she said seriously. 'I would feel too guilty. Plus, as much as this is nice – and it is, you know, it's the nicest time I've had in as long as I can remember – there are other people to consider.'

Alex nodded, his pale eyes searching hers.

'But we can do this again. I mean, if you want to. If I haven't scared you off by flashing all my wobbly bits?'

'I told you,' he said meditatively. 'You're beautiful. I would have told you so the first time we met, if I hadn't been naked at the time.'

'And why haven't you since?' she teased.

'I wasn't sure you'd want to hear it, not from me anyway,' he began, sitting up a fraction taller. 'You seemed pretty focused on your ex.'

'Let's not talk about him,' she pleaded. 'Not here, not now. The James situation is . . . complicated. But I do feel as if I'm getting over it – over him. It's just . . . oh, I don't know.'

'Hey, Kate – it's OK.'

He wrapped his arms around her, and Kate allowed herself to melt into them. It was easier to chase away thoughts of James when she was kissing Alex, when she could give herself over completely to the feel of him, to his lips and his hands and his taste. Her body responded in such a way that left her impervious to any protestations from her mind and, for the time being at least, Kate was content to simply let herself fall.

39

When Kate tiptoed back into her hostel room several hours later, she found the bed she and Robyn shared empty and the bathroom door shut. The temptation to knock loud enough to be heard over the shower and tell her friend everything was a strong one, but Kate resisted. Robyn would have an opinion – undoubtedly a strong one. Kate had insisted repeatedly that she did not like Alex in that way, that the two of them were simply friends and, more pressingly, that she was still in love with James.

She must not think about James.

There was no reason to think that anything had changed with him and, Kate noted, with something close to satisfaction, she realised that at this moment in time, she had no desire to see or even speak to him.

Sitting down, she reached for her phone and was still scrolling mindlessly when Robyn emerged, her dark hair plastered wet against her shoulders.

'Oh, hello,' she said, wrapping her towel around her chest a fraction tighter. 'You're back.'

'I am,' said Kate, being careful to keep her tone noncommittal.

Robyn rubbed at her eyes, which were ringed black by smudges of the previous night's mascara. 'You look . . . different. Your hair's all crunchy. Have you been swimming?'

'Yes.' Kate drew the word out, stretching it like chewing gum across her tongue. It was no good, she wasn't going to be able to keep what happened a secret – not from Robyn.

'Kate Nimble,' said her friend suspiciously, lowering herself down until their eyes were level. 'What aren't you telling me?'

Taking a deep breath, Kate relinquished the smile she'd been holding in.

'Oh my god – I recognise that expression. That's a sex-pression!'

'What are you, some sort of oracle?' Kate laughed.

'Tell me everything – immediately!'

'Are you sure you don't want a cup of tea fir—'

'TELL!'

'All right, all right.' Kate held up her hands. 'But you have to promise not to tell anyone.'

Once she had finished, Robyn simply sat and stared at her agape.

'Shit,' she said at last. 'I mean wow. I didn't know you had it in you.'

'You make it sound as if I planned it,' said Kate. 'I didn't – it just sort of happened.'

'Didn't it just,' Robyn said slyly. 'I knew it. I knew about two minutes after meeting him that the two of you were in love with each other.'

'Hey! Who said anything about love – we aren't in love with each other.'

Robyn made a 'if you say so' face.

'We're not. It was a bit of fun, that's all. Sex between consenting adults.'

'Kate, be serious, it was way more than that. The boat, the blankets, the deserted beach at sunrise – it was the whole romantic movie package. If it was just about sex, he would have banged you on the sunlounger and been done with it.'

'Charming.'

'I'm right though, aren't I?' Robyn was resolute. 'About

the love. And I'm all for it – he's nice and seems like a straight-forward kind of bloke. I think your heart would be in safe hands with him. But all that is immaterial if you only see it as a friends-with-benefits arrangement. Do you? Or are there real feelings there?'

Be brave. Tell the truth.

'I guess there are some,' she said. 'I don't want to label it yet, but I do know that when I'm with him, I just feel . . . I feel like myself. Does that even make sense? As if I'm me, but a better version of me. What? Why are you looking at me like that?'

Robyn was smiling at her indulgently. 'Because you love each other.'

'Stop saying that,' Kate implored, banging her hands on the bed before burying them in her hair and tugging it down over her face. 'Bloody hell – what am I going to do? How have I managed to get myself in this situation?'

'This situation being: you like a man who likes you? What's so bad about that?'

'It's way more complicated than that and you know it.'

'Is it?' Robyn said, her tone measured yet unequivocal. 'Or is it very simple? You loved James; James left you. You came to Hvar and met Alex, now you love him instead. Sounds pretty simple to me.'

'Stop using that word! I don't love Alex. How can I? I barely know him. I don't even know his last name,' she added, the ridiculousness of that particular detail causing her to laugh despairingly. 'And he lives here in Croatia; I live in North London. How would it ever work?'

Kate got up and began pacing around the room, stubbing her toe on one of the footstools she'd rescued from the skip and swearing with gusto.

'You're freaking out and there's no need,' soothed Robyn, getting up off the bed and pulling a dress out of her suitcase. 'This isn't the Grand National of relationships. You and Alex have only had sex once – you don't have to make a decision about moving countries quite yet. Just wait and see what happens. You're going to be here a while longer anyway now, to do the coffee shop refurbishment.'

Kate stopped pacing. 'True.'

'This thing between you and Alex might only be a holiday fling, but it could be more. The only way to know for sure is to keep meeting up with him for more of the great sex and see where it leads. I am right in thinking the sex was great, aren't I?'

Kate suppressed a smile. 'It was,' she said. 'But it was meaningful, too. There was nothing cheap about it, nothing that felt gratuitous. It was . . . adult, I guess. We were in synch.'

'Uh-oh.' Robyn was smiling her proud-mum smile again. 'Sounds a lot like love to me.'

Kate put up the hood of Toby's jumper and pulled the drawstrings until her eyes and mouth were hidden from view. Love was such a big word; she didn't feel as if there was space for it in this room, let alone in her life. But if love wasn't on the horizon for her and Alex, what was the point? She was thirty years old, a grown woman. She wanted to be caught, not flung.

Robyn had begun to slowly but firmly loosen the hood around Kate's face.

'You can't hide from this,' she said evenly. 'And you shouldn't want to. After everything you've been through with James, you deserve some fun. It's what I've been saying all along. And I've seen you with Alex,' she went on, sounding more earnest now. 'I thought at first that Hvar was responsible for giving you this incredible new glow, but I see now that it's more than that. He's switched something on in you, a light that I haven't seen for a long time. With James, I always felt a bit like you were his court jester. You were always making light of things and clowning around like you did in front of the boys you fancied at school – but you're not like that with Alex. You're less jumpy, more comfortable in your own skin.'

Kate, who could not disagree with any of these observations, fell silent.

'You want my advice?' Robyn prompted and Kate nodded. 'Please.'

'Give this thing with Alex the chance it deserves. Stay here, do that coffee shop job, spend time with him, find out his bloody surname and,' she added, as Kate smiled helplessly, 'by the time you have to make a decision, you will already know what you want to do.'

'Thank you,' mumbled Kate. 'I'm sorry I'm such an idiot.'

'There's no denying that.' Robyn laughed. 'Only you, Kate Nimble, would end up having the best sex of your life with a bloody cat watching.'

40

It was with a surreal sense of happy bewilderment that Kate breezed through the rest of the day. Determined not to be a bore, she focused all her attention on Robyn, taking her into Hvar Town before treating her to lunch at one of the restaurants in the square.

She'd decided her friend was right and that the best course of action was to simply ride the wave of whatever this new thing was with Alex and not fret too much about the eventual outcome. There were so many uncertainties in Kate's life, but her feelings towards Alex were one thing she could trust. Every time she allowed her mind to wander back to the events of the previous night, Kate found herself promptly aglow with happiness, and so when a message arrived from him later that evening, inviting her to join him on the boat after Robyn had gone to bed, she could barely tap out her affirmative reply fast enough.

There was no shyness in his manner this time, and Kate returned his kiss of greeting with such enthusiasm that she almost toppled them off the edge of the coastal path into the water.

'Come on,' Alex said, when the two of them finally broke apart. 'I'm taking you on a midnight tour.'

Once they'd crossed in the dinghy and he'd helped her clamber up over the side of the boat, Kate settled herself down and watched as the lights from Hvar faded into the distance. It was a beautiful night, the sky every bit as clear as the water below it, while the soft breeze blowing in over the bow carried with it the scent of pine trees.

When she stole a glance towards Alex, she found herself smiling, and unable to resist any longer, Kate stood up and made her way towards him.

'What's so funny?' he asked, as she snuggled against his chest.

'Oh, nothing.' Kate hesitated. 'I mean, just this. Us, here together like this. I'm not laughing because it's funny, more because it's extraordinary.'

'Flattery like that will get you tossed overboard,' he remarked cheerfully.

'I'm probably using the wrong words,' she admitted. 'I'm just surprised that I don't feel more strange. It's been a long time since—' Kate stopped abruptly. She'd been about to say that it had been a long time since she'd been with anyone other than James, but she did not want to sully this night, nor this moment, by mentioning his name.

Alex must have understood her meaning, however, because he merely pulled her in for a kiss and murmured, 'It's been even longer for me.'

As they reached open water, he opened the throttle and Kate let out a yelp as the skirt of her dress was blown over her head.

'Help yourself to a blanket if you're cold,' Alex offered, but Kate said she'd rather be warmed up by him. It should have sounded like the corniest line in history, but she didn't feel embarrassed saying it. On the contrary, she felt as if she could say pretty much anything to this man. Ever since she'd first met Alex, she'd liked him for his unflappability. He was not quick to judge, as so many were. He simply took her as she was and accepted every trait, every peculiarity. Kate loved that about him. She'd become accustomed to her actions – or lack of them – being judged by everybody in her life. Alex felt like a revelation.

She nestled in closer to him as they continued on around the island, the noise from the engine encouraging the two of them to adopt a companionable silence, until eventually, the boat began to slow.

'That's the harbour at Stari Grad up ahead. The inlet that leads up to the town is not as busy as the marina in Hvar, but there will still be plenty of people about. Do you want to go in for a closer look, or are you happy to drop anchor here for a while?'

'The latter,' said Kate, and he widened his eyes, amused by the speed of her reply.

'Whatever the lady commands.'

Kate waited on the cracked leather seat while he tied the line and fetched some pillows and bedding from inside the cabin.

'I thought we could lay down under the stars,' he said, spreading out a blanket.

Kate didn't need any more encouragement.

'I bet you know all about the stars, don't you?' she said a few moments later.

Alex laced his fingers through hers, gently stroking until Kate felt her breath catch in her throat. 'I don't know which one is which,' he told her. 'Terrible thing for a fisherman to admit, that is. But what I can tell you is that each of the stars we can see now are larger than the sun.'

'Just a lot further away?'

'Exactly.'

'Would you go up into space,' she asked. 'If someone offered you a seat on a shuttle?'

'I don't reckon so, no.' Alex turned to face her. 'I reckon I have a far better reason to stay here on Earth now.'

It was on the tip of Kate's tongue to tease him for saying something so cheesy, but she didn't. Instead she bent her head and kissed him, meaning to pull away after a few seconds only to find that she couldn't bear to. The two of them fitted together so seamlessly that it felt to Kate almost as if she would be breaking some kind of rule by severing the bond.

Perhaps a rule that had been written in the stars.

Being here with Alex did feel like fate; a pre-ordained circumstance that would always have happened, no matter the circumstances. Knowing it made so much of the other stuff fall away; all the pain and hurt she'd endured had been given a purpose. Without it, she would never have found her way here, found her way to him.

James felt a long way away in this moment – a distant star next to the bright, sun-like Alex. And he *was* like the sun. He'd brought so much warmth into her life and so much heat into her heart. And into other places too, of course, Kate thought, breaking contact in order to begin unbuttoning her dress.

'Is this OK?' Alex murmured. 'Do you want this?'

Kate nodded, a smile breaking free across her face as she realised the truth.

That in this moment, with this person, right here under the stars, there was nothing in the whole world that she wanted more.

41

Kate started work at Lovro's coffee shop two days after Robyn flew home.

They'd spent the final part of her visit sightseeing, sunbathing and sampling local delicacies, while each night, Kate had waited until her friend was ready to sleep before venturing out to meet Alex. She was exhausted, but happier than she could ever remember feeling.

Getting her head back into work mode that morning had been a challenge, but once Kate had spread out her schedule and discussed it over very strong coffee with Lovro, she slipped seamlessly back into her creative role, marking out areas on the walls for shelving and hooks, ordering paint and flicking through homeware catalogues. She'd decided to dress the part in an attempt to appear more professional, but soon regretted her smart trousers and plain blouse when Lovro began feeding wood through his circular saw. Kate had to wipe sawdust off her glasses so many times that she eventually wore them on top of her head instead.

Having got to the shop a little after nine, by the time the clock reached six she was leaden with fatigue, and it was with mild relief that she said '*laku noć*' and stepped outside into the warm evening air. She and Alex had agreed a vague plan to meet at Pokonji Dol beach once Toby and Filippo – who still had no idea the two of them were spending every night together – had returned to their apartment, so Kate had some free hours to spare and on a whim, decided to pick up a bottle of something nice for the two of them to share.

The square, as ever, was alive with noise and bustle. Swallows ducked and dived between the rooftops, soaring up and around the bells of the grand Venetian tower; harassed parents pursued toddlers as they gave chase to the pigeons, both bird and child species wobbling on the uneven ground, while on the periphery, restaurant tables groaned under a cargo of food and drink, the occupants of each rosy faced after a day spent in the sun.

Kate nipped into the Tisak supermarket and spent a little more than she usually would on a local red wine, picking up a punnet of cherries and a bar of dark chocolate at the same time. The two of them had yet to drink together, and while he'd never said as much, she presumed he didn't indulge often. Every time he'd been offered alcohol in her presence, he'd refused, and she liked that he wasn't a habitual beer guzzler.

Liked most things about him, in fact.

Helplessly cheerful at the prospect of seeing him in just a few short hours, Kate breezed through the slender lanes and alleyways with a smile on her face, revelling in the natural artistry of gold stone walls set against an azure sky, and of terracotta pots overflowing with emerald vines. No wonder her creative spirit had been tempted out since she arrived in Hvar, an island that exuded dynamic beauty at every turn. The longer Kate spent in situ, the less she missed home; the days that had at the beginning of summer felt so cumbersome were now hurtling by, which both pleased and concerned her. Because while it was nice to be floating along in a bubble of happiness, there was always the fear that something might pop it.

Her phone rang.

Assuming it would be Toby asking her to pick something up from the supermarket she had just left – Alex never called, he always messaged – Kate let it ring out, giving in to curiosity only when her phone began to vibrate again almost immediately.

It was James.

Kate gaped down at the mobile in her hand, horror mounting like floodwater.

The last time she'd answered a call from James, they'd argued. She'd been upset for days afterwards, barely slept and fretted compulsively, had messaged him and been callously ignored. When she took all this into consideration, it made sense not to answer. He did not deserve an answer.

Kate answered. 'Hello.'

'Kate, there you are. How are you? Where are you?'

'Still away.'

'Yeah, well, obviously you are – I got the foreign ringtone again.'

Kate said nothing. The tote bag containing the wine, chocolate and cherries slid dolefully down her arm, but she barely noticed.

'How are you?' he said again.

'Fine.'

She did not bother to ask how he was.

'It feels like ages since we spoke,' he went on. 'I thought I should check up on you – make sure you're all right.'

Kate had reached the end of the street, but waited a moment before continuing, her arms wrapped tightly around her body despite the heat. A few weeks ago, the idea of James checking up on her would have filled her with joy, but now, that same notion rankled. Was he suggesting that she didn't know how to take care of herself? And why now – why had he become so concerned about her all of a sudden?

'I saw your mum,' he said.

Oh, that was why.

'Right . . .' said Kate questioningly.

'She didn't seem very pleased to see me,' he went on, doing his best to make light of the fact. 'Tried to shut the front door in my face.'

'Well, you did break her daughter's heart,' Kate replied, thinking how much the trailing bougainvillea petals above her looked like dribbles of paint. Perhaps a burst of colour in the coffee shop would be a good idea? One of the cacti with the bright red flowers.

'Did you ever tell your parents?' he went on. 'You know, about the fertility stuff?'

'No.' Kate was gripped by a sudden panic. 'You didn't, did you?'

'Of course not,' said James. 'You asked me not to and I'm a man of my word.'

'If you say so,' she said snippily, making her way down a flight of wide stone steps and emerging halfway along the Riva. Early evening was fading into dusk, the water in the harbour tinged gold by a sun as bright and shiny as a new penny. The lights on the yachts flickered into life as she passed, as if she was the current of electricity connecting each one to the next. She had felt like one only moments ago; had been fizzing with such hope. This conversation was draining her. James was draining her.

'Did you have a reason for calling?' she asked. 'Or was it just that you saw my mum and were reminded of how badly you treated me?'

'Now, hang on a minute,' he began, but Kate did not want to wait, did not want to be told what to think or feel – especially not by him. It was becoming apparent that the emotional catastrophe she'd been waiting for ever since she saw his name appear on her phone was not going to come. Because sorrow was no longer what she was feeling – it was anger.

'James, you gave up on me the moment we found out I was the sole reason we were struggling to conceive. You took eight

years and flushed them, just like that, as if our entire relationship was nothing more than shit. You told me you loved me
yet behaved as if I didn't matter. If you're calling to rub any
of that in my face, then there really is no need. I am only too
aware of my failings and how distasteful you find them.'

'What are you on about?'

He sounded genuinely confused, but Kate did not let that
dent her resolve. Now that she'd opened the floodgates, she
couldn't stop herself hurling accusations at him. She might
have failed to give him a baby, but he'd done worse – he'd
failed to forgive her for it.

'Kate, I don't blame you. That's what I've been trying to
say – it's why I called you.'

'Then why?' she cried, so desperately that a passing
woman veered sideways in alarm. Kate had reached the spot
where the black cat always sat and washed itself, and bending
to stroke it, she saw that her hand was shaking.

'You ended things because you didn't want to try. You
thought you could dump me and find yourself another girl,
one who was younger and more fertile – someone who could
ensure that you stuck to that ridiculous five-year life plan.
Tell me I'm wrong!'

'There is no new girlfriend,' he told her. 'I can't believe
you would even think that. We only split up about a month
ago, for heaven's sake.'

'It's been far longer than that,' she snapped, guilt over Alex
making her temper rise.

'Fine,' he said. 'Whatever. The point is, there is no one else.
I went to your parents' house because I hoped you'd be there,
then when you weren't, and your mum refused to tell me
where you really were, I got worried. I am worried.'

Kate quailed. It was time to end this call. If she didn't, she
would crack.

'I miss you,' he said. 'I want to see you.'

'Don't James.'

'I mean it. I told your mum as much – ask her if you don't believe me.'

'Please don't involve my mum in our private business,' she said wearily, trudging up the hill so rapidly that her calf muscles burned with the effort. 'And don't say you miss me just to guilt-trip me into coming home. If you really wanted me there,' she added hotly, 'you wouldn't have dumped me in the first place.'

'I broke things off because we were unhappy,' he said. 'We both were. I know you say you weren't, but I know you, Kate. I could tell you were pretending that everything was sound. I did the brave thing. But that doesn't mean I stopped loving you. Of course I didn't. I told you that.'

Kate came to an abrupt stop. 'Are you saying that you still love me?'

James started to reply, only to hesitate, tripping over his words as he tried and failed to produce a coherent sentence.

'It's a simple yes or no, James – do you love me?'

Kate knew what he was going to say and steeled herself, her shoulders rigid and her free arm clamped to her side. He felt so far away from her, yet it was almost as if he was standing right in front of her on the path, his fine hair lifted by the same breeze that was rippling the fine cotton of her blouse. As much as she tried to be angry with him, she knew there was still a small piece of her that yearned for him; longed for him to want her again.

James cleared his throat. It sounded like defeat.

'Yes, Kate,' he said, with a small sigh. 'Yes, I still love you.'

42

Kate hung up the phone, staring at it as if it might grow teeth and bite her.

James missed her, wanted to see her – still *loved* her?

It wasn't enough to have simply hung up. Kate pressed her finger down hard on the off switch, only letting go of the breath she was holding when the screen went dark. She could not deal with this now, it was too much.

The hostel was less than five minutes away, but instead of heading for home, Kate retraced her steps and returned to the coastal path. Half-expecting that neither Alex nor his boat would be in the usual mooring spot, she was relieved they were. But then she had to fight the urge to cry as soon as he turned around and saw her, his smile of delighted surprise making her feel even more like a criminal. He was not on the deck, but in the dinghy, a paintbrush in his hand and a small tin balanced in the other.

'Thought it was about time I gave her a proper name,' he called, as Kate made her careful way down the stony slope towards the water's edge. 'What do you think?'

Kate looked at the red letters and frowned. She had no idea what the word 'Okretan' meant and shook her head to communicate her ignorance.

'I'll come over,' he called, his smile drooping a bit at the corners. Kate waited as he hoisted the painting tools onto the boat, trying her best not to convey how upset she felt. She should have known better, of course, because there was no fooling Alex.

'What's up?'

'Nothing,' she said, her voice high and shrill.

Alex stepped onto dry land and reached for the line, but he didn't fasten it. 'Do you want to come aboard?' he said.

Kate shook her head, unable to meet his eyes.

'Hey,' he said, this time putting a hand on her arm. 'What's happened? You're not OK.'

'I am,' she managed, the lie running aground before she could qualify it with further explanation. 'I'm sorry,' she went on. 'I don't mean to be weird. I'm just . . . It's only . . .'

Alex didn't say anything else, nor did he step across and kiss her as she'd hoped he would. He still looked concerned, but there was a wariness in his eyes, as if he could tell that whatever was wrong with her was going to have an impact on him.

'James called,' she said, hanging her head. 'Just now. I didn't know where to . . . I'm sorry.'

She heard Alex take a breath, heard the trace of what sounded like impatience in his tone when he said, 'Right.'

Only that morning, she'd lain naked in his arms, their legs entwined and his fingers stroking her hair from her face. Now, he felt like a stranger again.

Kate held out the tote bag. 'I bought these,' she said. 'For us, for later I mean.'

Alex took it from her and looked inside. 'That was a nice thought,' he said. 'But you'll have to drink the wine yourself.'

That wouldn't be much of a problem.

'Do you still want to see me tonight?' she asked, and this time Alex wrinkled his forehead with consternation.

'Is there any reason why you think I wouldn't?'

'No, I just . . .' She trailed off yet again, staring hard at a splodge of red paint on his T-shirt. As if sensing this scrutinisation, Alex lowered the bag to the ground and folded his arms, shutting her out.

'I need some time,' she told him, hating herself more with every word. 'Some time to think.'

'Right.' Alex fiddled with the peak of his cap, pulling it down and throwing his pale-blue eyes into shadow. 'Well, then.'

Seeing him start to move back towards the dinghy, Kate darted forwards and grabbed his hand. 'Where are you going?' she said.

'Back to the boat,' he replied, as if that much was obvious. 'To give you some time. That's what you wanted, wasn't it?'

'Yes, but—'

'Well, then. You know where to find me when you're done thinking.'

'Please don't be like this.' Kate was close to tears now, but she let go of his hand. 'I want to explain. This thing with me and James, it's complicated. I need to allow myself time to digest what he just said to me. At the moment, I feel so angry with him, with the whole bloody situation, but I owe it to him to at least think it through.'

'This James is the same man you told me about? The same guy who humiliated you, made you feel worthless, left you broken-hearted?'

'He did do all those things,' she agreed. 'But he's also the man I spent eight years with, the man I wanted to marry and have a family with, the person I came to Croatia for.'

'What do you mean?' Alex looked puzzled.

'I thought if I disappeared, went missing for a while, that he would realise how much he missed me, how much he still loved me.'

Alex flinched as if she'd spat the words at him, his hand tightening on the dinghy line.

'And I'm guessing your plan worked?'

Kate could only nod.

Alex looked down at his bare feet, his face contorting.

'I don't want to fall out with you,' Kate pleaded. 'I care about you and I hate . . . this,' she said, throwing up her hands in exasperation.

Digging in his pocket, Alex extracted a silver coin. The way he threw it up and caught it each time was so nonchalant, so utterly untroubled, that Kate wanted to snatch it out of the air and hurl it into the water. She knew it wasn't fair of her to be angry with him, that he'd done nothing but be kind to her, but this pretence he was putting on was infuriating.

'You shouldn't care about me,' he said flatly, watching the coin rather than her. 'Nothing good ever came of anyone who cared about me.'

'Now you're talking in riddles,' she said despairingly. 'I do care about you – of course I do. That's why I'm confused. James is a big part of my life, I thought he was going to be my future. Then I met you and . . . well, everything changed. I love who I am with you, I do,' she said earnestly, seeing a flicker of hope transform his features. 'But I also know next to nothing about you. If you could just open up to me or share a bit more . . . I want this to feel real.'

'You know me,' he said, his voice unsteady.

'No, I don't.'

Kate waited until he looked at her before continuing.

'All I know is that your name is Alex and that you maybe, once upon a time, lived in the west of England. I know you like fishing and that you build things from wood and carry that bloody coin around like some sort of good-luck charm. I know you're angry with me right now, but most of the time you're angrier at yourself, or with the world at large, and I don't know why. I don't know your last name, or who your parents are, if you have any siblings or what you wanted to be when you were growing up. And I want to know it all, Alex, but you won't let me. Why won't you let me in?'

Kate had been speaking so quickly that she'd run out of breath. Now she wanted more than anything to gather the words back, to try and make sense of everything she'd said to him. The outburst had come from nowhere, but it must have been gathering pace in her subconscious for a while. Alex had obviously realised the same thing; he looked sad now rather than disgruntled, and Kate longed to draw him against her, to listen while he explained, to heal any wounds he might have – but she could not summon up the strength required.

'I'm sorry. I should go,' she said, stopping as he reached for her hand, his fingers squeezing hers for the briefest moment. His face was a mask, the pale-blue eyes she'd lost herself in so often now blank and unreadable. Taking back her hand, she turned to leave.

'Kate.'

'Yes?'

He looked at her then, really looked. There was a moment when it seemed like Alex was about to let her in. Then his face shuttered, and it was gone.

'Nothing. You're right. You should go.'

Biting back a sob, Kate turned away and headed slowly back up the slope away from him. Such were her mixed feelings of shame and confusion that she barely registered the faces of those she passed on her way along the coastal path.

It was only many hours later, when she was huddled alone in the darkness of her hostel bedroom that Kate remembered what Alex had been doing when she found him. Opening up the translator app on her phone, she typed in the name Alex had painted, a single tear falling across her cheek as she saw the result.

Okretan was the Croatian word for Nimble.

He had named his boat after her.

43

It took Kate a while to pluck up enough courage to switch her phone back on, but when she did, she found no messages waiting. Not from James, not from Alex, not from anyone. Not even a notification telling her she'd amassed another two hundred Instagram followers on her Unexpected Items account could rouse her spirits.

What did it matter? What did any of it matter?

Opening Twitter, Kate typed #WannabeWife into the search bar and scrolled through the multitude of comments and posts until she found the original video. Every time she'd watched it, she'd done so through self-critical eyes, ripping apart everything from her choice of words to the shape of her figure, berating and trashing and condemning both herself and her actions.

Tonight, she wanted to try something different.

The footage began halfway through her attempts to call the room to attention, the scrape of the chair as she dragged it across the floor doing most of the hard work for her. A cheer rose up as Kate clambered onto it, her guests quickly fanning out into a semicircle around her, presumably anticipating a speech about how she felt to be turning the dreaded three-o.

There had been none of that, though. Nothing about her at all, in fact. Even on her thirtieth birthday, at a party arranged by her best friend to celebrate her life, Kate had deferred to James.

'There's a very special man here tonight,' she said, and there was a murmuring from the crowd, followed by a few 'awws' as someone nudged James forward. Watching it now, Kate could see the back of Robyn's sleek shiny head. Her friend was already making her way to the front, had sensed trouble almost as soon as Kate stood up on the chair. The first time she'd noticed this, Kate had felt ashamed. Poor Robyn, being lumbered with such a walking disaster as a best friend. This time, however, she forced herself to view the situation through Robyn's eyes, and found nothing there but concern and affection.

The video played on.

Kate had told the room a few of the reasons why she loved James so much, only realising now that every single point she listed reflected her in a poor light. Poor long-suffering James, she had said, what a hero he is for 'putting up with me', 'taking care of me', 'loving me despite all my many failings'. It was not so much a proposal speech as an exercise in public self-flagellation.

Searching the crowd for James, Kate saw from his side profile that he was nodding along, agreeing with her as she lauded his capabilities and called for him to be awarded some sort of medal for having endured eight years in her company.

Nodding in agreement.

Whoever was holding the camera then whispered to the person next to them.

'What is this, the British Academy of Good Boyfriend awards?' to which their amused neighbour replied, 'Poor James.'

Upon hearing this for the first time, Kate had felt mortally wounded, but now she was simply annoyed. How dare they poke fun at her? It had been her party, her bar tab, her speech. They were obnoxious imbeciles.

'So, I should get to the point, shouldn't I?' said the Kate in the video, and this was met with a rumble of jeers and whoops. Everyone had known what she was going to say before she said it, and many were gleeful at the prospect of witnessing such a huge romantic gesture.

'James,' she began, staring down at him. Kate knew that her eyes had been watering at this point, that her knees had trembled, and her heart had felt like a trapped bird, but on the screen in front of her now, she appeared calm and composed – determined even.

'You know I love you,' she went on. 'More than anyone and anything else in this world. All I want in my future is to be with you, for the two of us to be together for the rest of our lives.'

The room had fallen silent now; only the faint sounds of the pub downstairs were audible.

'James Frederick Clifford Morrison – will you marry me?'

The person filming gasped in unison with the assembled guests. James's face turned to stone. Kate, up on her podium, continued to smile.

The heckles began.

'Start with an easy one!', 'Go on, Jimbo – don't leave her hanging!', 'Say yes! Say yes! Say yes!'

Whoever had attempted to start a chant had quickly trailed off, realising perhaps sooner than Kate herself that this proposal was not going to end well.

Wiping the tears from her cheeks now, Kate studied her small hopeful form, feeling not frustration or distaste but pity. Sorrow for a woman who had put her heart on the line and seen it torn asunder.

The video continued to roll, capturing the moment Robyn stormed through in rescue, Kate almost falling off the chair and James, surrounded by his friends, laughing nervously and wiping his brow.

'How embarrassing,' said a voice, and the screen went black.

Kate lowered her phone. She was no longer crying. After all, she knew how this story ended. Unlike the hundreds of thousands of Twitter users who had shared and viewed and laughed over this most hopeful of beginnings, she could say with confidence that the woman in the video was not 'sad', 'desperate', 'deluded' or 'pathetic'. In the weeks since she'd become the thing she feared the most – a public failure – Kate had found her passion. She had crafted and created, turned trash into treasure, called out her fears and faced her anxieties head-on. The love she'd thought was treacherous had endured, and she'd welcomed it, trusted it, believed that she deserved it – but most importantly of all, Kate had somehow learnt to love herself.

And that, she now knew, was the only thing that really mattered.

44

It was two days before Kate saw Alex again.

Two days of composing messages she then deleted and of wandering along the coastline hoping to see his boat. Torn between her guilt at having run to him in the wake of her conversation with James and frustration at his refusal to open up when asked, she'd concluded in the end that it was probably best to wait for him to reappear in his own time.

She'd not contacted James, nor heard from him. They were back where they'd been all those weeks ago – in a stalemate. Kate was still processing how she felt about his unexpected proclamation, but she'd at least realised now that it was not going to be a simple case of resetting the clock. Things between them had changed. She had changed.

Alex did not send a message or call, he simply reappeared. Kate came out of the coffee shop to find him leaning against the opposite wall, his red 'Croatia' cap pulled down and his hands buried deep in his pockets. When he saw her, he tried for a smile, and Kate did not hesitate to smile back.

'Hey, stranger,' she said, walking towards him with her arms folded. She and Lovro had been painting walls today, and Kate's dark-red curls were peppered with fine white splatters.

'Hey,' he said, meeting her gaze. 'Are you free for half an hour or so?'

Instead of heading down into the hub of the old town, Alex led her through the cobbled backstreets until they reached a wide, open pathway halfway up the hillside. An untended churchyard lay below them, its monuments overgrown with ivy and wildflowers, and a small herd of nanny goats grazed in a dilapidated paddock above. Toby had warned her that rain would be on the way soon, but there was not so much as a hint of that today. The sky beyond the rust-coloured rooftops was a dense, impenetrable blue, the heat rough and dry.

Alex crossed to the rough stone wall separating the path from the undergrowth and rested his elbows on the top, his eyes focused ahead towards the horizon. After a moment, Kate went to stand beside him, waiting in silence while he gathered his thoughts.

'I owe you an apology,' he said. 'For the way I was the other day. It was wrong and I shouldn't have been so short with you.'

Kate forced the words 'it was all my fault' back down and merely nodded instead.

'Truth is, I haven't met anyone like you for a long time,' he said.

'Like me?'

'Someone I like. Someone I care about.'

'Oh.'

Kate edged closer to him, feeling him relax a fraction.

'When you told me that your ex had been back in touch, I wanted to be there to help, to comfort you, but I convinced myself that it was easier to walk away.'

'I should never have gone running to you right after I spoke to him,' Kate said. 'That was unfair. I know that now and I'm sorry.'

'I thought you might have gone,' he muttered. 'Flown back home to be with him – but you haven't.'

'No.' Kate smiled. 'I haven't.'

'I'm glad.' Alex turned to face her. 'I might have missed you a bit if you had.'

'Just a bit?'

'Quite a big bit. A Lovro pizza slice-sized bit.'

'That much?' Kate widened her eyes. 'Now you're just flattering me.'

Alex stretched out a little finger and stroked it against hers. The lightest of touches, it caught the air in the back of Kate's throat. She could hear the insistent beat of her heart; feel the heated tiptoe of desire – or was it appeasement? Relief that he still wanted her.

'I've been thinking about what you said,' he told her. 'About wanting to know things about me, needing more from me than I have given you so far.'

'I do, but—'

Alex turned back to gaze at the view. 'You were right to ask,' he said, shaking his head as she went to disagree. 'I do want to be honest with you, but it's hard for me. Trusting people never has come easily, not since I was a child. I grew up feeling let down by a lot of the people around me.'

'By your family?' she guessed, but Alex shook his head. 'No – they were great.'

Did his use of the past tense mean they were no longer alive?

'You've probably wondered why I stage these disappearing acts every so often,' he went on. 'The thing is, you see, I get overwhelmed from time to time. I fall into this darkness and I can't always get myself out of it again – not easily anyway. Sometimes, the only way to see and think clearly again is to be by myself for a while. I don't want to be a burden, see?'

Kate took his hand. 'You're not a burden.'

'You say that,' he replied, not meeting her eyes. 'But you haven't seen me at my worst, on my very darkest days. I've always been this way; always had to survive on an endless cycle of highs and lows. It's like a bloody fairground ride that I can never get off. When I feel at my lowest ebb, the only thing I can do is wait it out and it's better I do that alone. There's no pressure then, see? Nobody there to witness it. I hate the thought of that.'

Kate's heart went out to him. 'But you shouldn't have to cope with that alone,' she said. 'And if you've never let anyone in, then how do you know that it wouldn't be better with someone else there?'

'I did try,' he tempered. 'A very long time ago. But all I felt was guilty, and that only made it harder to deal with.'

'I understand,' Kate told him truthfully. How much of her own anxiety had she kept hidden? How often during times of stress had she struggled to sleep, struggled to think straight, struggled to breathe?

Alex listened in silence as she explained this, confessing a truth of her own in exchange for a fragment of his. They were so similar, the two of them, so tied up in knots by the idea of causing anyone concern. But while Alex was still blaming himself, Kate had begun to recognise the need to be more accepting of herself. She would help Alex do the same, just as he had shown her how to master her fears.

'Why don't we agree to be that person for each other?' she said, sliding a timid arm around his back. 'Someone we can rely on to never judge us, however much we mess up?'

'I don't know,' he said, his voice muffled by her hair. 'I don't know if I can do that.'

'But you can try.'

Kate could feel the steady beat of his heart as she leant against him, read the vulnerability in his pale eyes as he looked at her.

'Yes,' he said at last. 'I can try.'

Kate pulled him gently around until they were standing face to face and reaching up, removed his cap.

'I used to think that tall, clean-shaven men were my type,' she said lightly. 'Shows how little I knew.'

'Hey,' he scolded gently. 'You'd better not be mocking the dreads.'

'Always,' she retorted cheerfully. 'And the beard, too, for that matter. I continue to live in hope of you shaving it off.'

'Does it scratch you?' Alex pulled back.

'No,' she said. 'But it would be nice to see more of your face. It's one of my favourites.'

'Only one of?'

'Stop baiting me for compliments.'

Laughing, Alex bent his head to kiss her, gently at first but then with an urgency that turned her limbs molten. Kate was all at once overcome by a delicious, insistent warmth. She felt a thrumming pulse begin to beat below her belly button and arched herself against him, needing to feel the solidness of his body, the confirmation of his desire, the wonderfully simple yet undeniable yearning they each had for the other.

It was in these moments that she felt most alive, most present, as if the world had shrunk to a pinprick of light while she and Alex floated freely amongst the stars, entwined and in tune, as nature had intended all along. He'd left her, but he'd come back; had overcome his instinct to hide the parts of himself he found lacking and instead share them with her. That was enough for now; the rest of her questions could wait for another day.

'Shall we go to the boat?' she whispered, but as Alex let go of her, his phone rang.

'It's Bram Van Dijk,' he said.

'Ignore it?' she suggested hopefully.

Alex picked up her hand and kissed it. 'I'd better see what he wants.'

After exchanging pleasantries, however, he passed the ancient Nokia to Kate. 'He wants to talk to you.'

'Hello?' she said, rather cautiously.

'Katy! Are you well? It is Bram Van Dijk.'

'I'm fine, thanks. How are y—'

'Good, good. So, I'm having a look at your Instagram and I'm impressed. Alex showed it to me because the other guy I hired . . . well, we're not seeing eye to eye.'

'Oh . . .' Kate looked at Alex and pulled a 'what the hell?' face, to which he grinned and made a show of lifting his shoulders.

'You have some ideas for interior of my hotel, yes?'

'Well, I—'

'Good. In that case, you must show me. How soon can you come to Brač?'

'I've a week or so left on a project here in Hvar, but once that's complete, I could get the boat across and—'

'Good. Send me a message and I'll make some time. Thank you, Katy.'

'It's Kate.'

'Kate. OK. Goodbye.'

'Er, bye – and thank you,' she garbled, but Bram Van Dijk had already hung up.

'Blooming heck,' she breathed, giving the phone back to Alex. 'He wants me to show him some design ideas for the hotel.'

'Is that right? Well, that is good news.'

'You did this,' she exclaimed delightedly. 'He said you showed him my Instagram.'

'I may have reminded him about it, but you're the one who impressed him.'

'A whole hotel,' she said, wonderment rapidly turning to trepidation. 'I don't know if I have what it takes to work on a place as huge as that – what if it's too much?'

'If you don't try, you'll never know,' he said. 'And you don't strike me as the quitting sort.'

'No, usually I'm more of the "gets sacked a lot from jobs" sort.'

Alex gave her a look that was more affectionate than stern.

'Do you really believe I can do this? Like, really?'

Alex pulled her towards him, his lips seeking hers. 'What I believe in,' he said, 'is you.'

45

'Does this mean you'll be staying past the summer?'

Kate was relieved to note that her brother was not horrified by the prospect. Both he and Filippo were beaming at her with undisguised pride.

'I guess so,' she said. 'Although if you're sick of me taking up the room, I can move?'

'I imagine this Van Dijk bloke will offer you space at the hotel once the work starts,' said Toby, bending to help himself to a bottle of Ožujsko from the Tiki Bar fridge. 'Although it goes without saying that you're welcome to stay here for as long as you like.'

'Thanks,' Kate replied. 'But I really should start paying rent or something.'

'*Silenzio, bambina,*' chided Filippo, folding himself onto the stool next to hers. 'We are the ones who should be paying you after everything you have done for us and this place.'

'I still can't believe it,' Kate said. 'A whole hotel. I've got so much research to do.'

There was a lot to consider, she knew, mostly boring tax-related and visa issues, but for tonight at least, all this would have to wait. Alex had kissed her lingeringly when she left him down by the water with a promise that she'd be back as soon as she'd washed off that day's paint splatters. He was going to take her out on his boat so they could enjoy an uninterrupted view of the sunset, after which Kate was planning to drag him into the cabin so she could indulge in an uninterrupted view of his beautiful naked body. The thought alone was enough to make her smile.

'I think we should open a bottle of the good stuff to celebrate,' said Toby, who had made short work of his beer.

Filippo applauded with a 'bravo'.

'Put one on ice for me,' she said, hopping off her stool just as Siva stalked menacingly along the bar top. 'I need a shower.'

Once downstairs, she set about beautifying herself, washing and blow-drying her hair, rubbing in scented body lotion and applying a subtle-yet-flattering amount of make-up. Alex would not care whether she turned up in a ballgown or a bin liner, but she wanted to make an effort for herself as much as him, and so carefully chose a floor-length olive-green dress that gathered favourably around her waist and selected a pair of plain gold hoop earrings.

'Swit-swoo,' whistled Toby, as Filippo lifted a snarling Siva off Kate's seat. 'I was about to send out a search party,' he added. 'The champagne has been on ice so long that it's basically a slushy.'

'I haven't got long,' she said, glancing up at a sky that was already powder pink. 'I . . . er, thought I'd go down to the water to watch the sunset.'

Toby and Filippo exchanged a glance, but neither said anything.

It was quiet up on the roof terrace, with only a few guests milling around sipping Toby's floor-stripper cocktails, and Kate let out a sigh of contentment as she sat down. Feeling her phone vibrate inside her bag, she extracted it expecting to see a teasing summons from Alex, but it was a message from Robyn.

Can you talk?

Short, sharp and perplexing. Kate pressed call.

'I did a bad thing,' was how Robyn answered.

Kate tutted good-naturedly. 'You haven't gone back on Tinder, have you?'

'I wish. No, this is something way worse.'

Her friend had not so much as sniggered; whatever this was, it must be serious. Kate accepted a flute of champagne from Toby and watched the tiny bubbles scurrying up to the surface.

'What could be worse than Tinder? Did you sign up for Uniform Dating dot com?'

'I saw James.'

Kate lowered her glass. 'And?'

'It was weird actually, almost as if he was waiting for me. I left my patient – you know, the one who lives down the road from your old house – and there he was, just standing by my car.'

'I spoke to him a few days ago,' said Kate. 'He called me demanding to know where I was, saying he wanted to see me. Sorry,' she added, when Robyn said nothing. 'I should have thought to warn you that he'd be on the warpath. He got nowhere with my mum and you're the obvious second choice.'

'He didn't even mention that he'd seen your folks,' said a mystified Robyn. 'He made out that him being there was pure coincidence, which threw me, and then he started asking after my family and stuff, which threw me even more. I mean, he's never been the most solicitous man, has he? But suddenly, it was all, "How's your mum been since her hip op?" and, "Your hair looks nice like that – have you have it cut?". Mental.'

'I don't see how any of this is particularly bad,' said Kate, who was itching to finish her drink and get going. 'As long as you didn't discuss me.'

There was silence at the other end of the line.

'Robyn?'

'Yes?'

'You didn't tell him where I am, did you?'

'I'm so sorry, Kate – he pulled some sort of Jedi mind trick on me with all the flattery. He even said he was happy that you were doing so well, and so I agreed naturally, and told him how proud I was of you for finally working out what it was you were good at, and how you were making a real go of it and getting hired for interior design jobs. He didn't so much as flinch, so I assumed he knew. And then he complimented me on my tan and asked how hot it had been over in Spain, so I laughed and corrected him. Now, I realise the devious little toad was fishing for information.'

Toby was waving a slow hand in front of Kate's face. 'Nims . . .'

'In a minute. When did this conversation take place, Robyn – how long ago?'

'A few days – the morning after I got back.'

Kate imagined her best friend cringing with regret.

'I should have told you sooner, but I was worried that you'd be cross.'

'I'm not cross. He was bound to find out where I am sooner or later and—'

'Nims—'

'In a minute.'

'No, Kate, seriously.' Toby reached over the bar and put his hands on her shoulders, turning her slowly around until she could see who was standing on the opposite side of the terrace.

Assuming that her friend's sudden silence was due to delayed annoyance, Robyn began to prattle out apologies in earnest, but Kate barely heard them. A long moment passed during which none of them said anything. Siva, picking up on the tension, let out a low hiss from her position on Filippo's lap.

'Kate?' Robyn sounded upset. 'Are you still there?'

'Yes,' Kate told her, watching as if in slow motion as the new arrival lifted an uncertain hand of greeting. James looked different; his face was fuller as if he'd gained weight, and there were untidy tufts of blond stubble on his cheeks. No matter how hard she stared at him, Kate could not fathom the fact that he was here, the man she knew so well yet not at all. He'd become a stranger in the time she'd been away, a player in the game of her former life and now an unwelcome pawn in the new one.

'I'm still here,' she said, cradling the phone as James began to make his way towards her. 'And I'm not the only one.'

46

There was music playing on the terrace, but Kate barely heard it. The faces of the guests had become little more than a blur. She couldn't feel the warmth of the early evening sun or smell the smoke wafting over from the barbecue. All she was aware of was James.

What was he doing here? How could this be happening?

When he got within a few feet of the bar, James raised his hands as if to embrace her only to lower them again rapidly when he clocked the expression on her face. Part of her wanted to leap out of her seat and run to him, but a larger part yearned to run away; she wanted to both hug and punch him, did not know if the sensation building inside her chest was laughter or anger. She was scared to find out.

'Hi, Kate,' he said.

'James.'

'The guy on reception told me you'd probably be up here. I left my case down there; I didn't know if . . .' He attempted a smile that Kate did not return. 'Well, what I mean is, I can always find somewhere else to stay.'

'You might have a job at this time of year,' she said coldly. 'It's peak holiday season.'

'I'm sure we can find a space—' began Toby but was silenced by a thunderous glare.

Kate took a deep, steadying breath.

'Well,' said Toby lightly. 'This is a bit awkward, isn't it?

Nims, why don't you and James pop over the road to the apartment, where you can talk in peace?'

'No.' Kate got down from her stool, her forgotten glass of bubbly abandoned on the bar. 'Here will be fine.'

Leaving the three men staring after her, she stalked across the terrace to the low outer wall and perched on the edge. The sea far below was a carpet of sparkles, the distant hills misshapen stacks of furniture draped with sheets, while the birds that dipped and dived rippled carelessly on the breeze. Watching them, she experienced a stab of envy. How blissful it would be to take off into the sunset.

'Nice view from up here,' said James. He'd brought her champagne across with him, but Kate could no more face drinking it than she could join the birds in flight.

'The whole place is pretty impressive. I haven't seen all the rooms yet, obviously, but what I did see looks great. You've done a good job.'

'We,' she corrected. 'It wasn't just me.'

'I saw your new Instagram account,' he went on, fussing with the upturned collar of his white polo shirt. Kate could see a paler area of skin below his hairline – the tell of a recent cut, one done after a weekend in the sunshine of a pub garden. She hadn't missed the summer rituals of home – the picnics on Hampstead Heath, the jingle of the ice-cream van, or lazy strolls along Regent's Canal punctuated by cold pints of cider. She'd been far too busy creating new ones.

'I can't believe you have over thirty thousand followers,' he went on. 'I bet that's earning you some decent money?'

He'd posed it as a question, which irritated her. There was a slew of messages in her inbox offering products in exchange for endorsement, but so far, Kate had ignored all of them.

'What's the matter?' she said, her tone flat. 'Worried I'll make my first million before you?'

James accepted the dig, his mouth set as he tore at the label on his beer bottle. So often in the past, Kate had picked up on these displays of agitation and been quick to offer comfort; had hated the idea of him being in distress and did whatever she could to rally him. Now, however, that door had closed. She didn't care that he was on edge.

'What are you doing here, James? I don't believe you flew all the way to Croatia just to ask me about my Instagram account.'

'No.' James looked her placatingly. 'I came to see you, obviously. I told you on the phone that I needed to talk.'

Kate met his gaze. 'So, now you've seen me. Is that it?'

'Why are you being like this – so cold all of a sudden? A few weeks ago, you were begging me to reconsider, telling me that you still loved me.'

'That was then,' she said. 'Things have changed.'

'I can see that,' he said. 'And I understand why you might be angry with me.'

'Oh, you do, do you?'

James looked at her in bewilderment, his hand going up to self-consciously stroke his Prince William patch.

'You're making out like this whole thing was my fault,' he said, in the injured tone of a toddler that's had their ball taken away after kicking it through a window.

'You're right,' she said, lifting her glass and downing half the contents. 'But that is my right, given that I'm the one who was dumped, ridiculed and publicly shamed. You seem to have come away from this whole thing with barely a scratch on you.'

'Barely a scratch?' he exclaimed. 'You think breaking up with you was easy? You think I haven't suffered too? That I haven't missed you? That I haven't got any regrets?'

Kate's determination not to become upset was starting to crumble.

'What exactly are you saying?' she demanded. 'That you've had a miraculous change of heart all of a sudden and want me back?'

'I never wanted to lose you,' he beseeched, trying to reach for her.

Kate shuffled along the wall away from him and saw the hurt in his eyes.

'I honestly thought that splitting up was the right thing. I wouldn't have done it otherwise.'

'Then what happened to change your mind so absolutely?' she said wearily. 'And why now?'

James sat down, letting out a sigh that seemed to deflate him.

'I missed you,' he said, looking at her now with such fierce intensity that Kate felt compelled to meet his eyes. They were dark and deep-set, the opposite of the pale-blue pair she should be looking into now.

Alex would be wondering where she was; waiting for her with no clue as to why she was so late. Kate had left the handbag containing her phone over at the bar, but as she went to stand, James grabbed her hand.

'Did you hear me, Kate? I said, I missed you. I do miss you. I was stupid. I made a stupid mistake. I took you for granted – I know that now. I won't ever do it again.'

He was saying the words she had dreamt of hearing ever since that fateful night in April, but they were ineffectual, pebbles off a thick stone wall. James must have been able to sense her resistance because as she leant away, he gripped her more tightly, pulling her towards him until their knees touched.

'This is you and me, Kate – we belong together.'

'That's not what you said on my birthday,' she reminded him. 'If I remember rightly, back then it was all about you and what you wanted. There was no "us" left, according to you.'

'I was being selfish,' he said, knotting his fingers through hers. She could smell the lemony scent of his cologne and see a nick on his throat where he'd cut himself shaving.

'I still can't give you what you want, though, James,' she said, staring down at their entwined fingers. 'I'm still the same person with exactly the same limitations.'

'But you aren't the same at all,' he implored. 'Look at you, Kate – you're so much more together and confident. When I walked through that door and saw this gorgeous woman sitting there, with her hair spilling all over her shoulders and her tanned body in this green dress, I thought, "Wow – who is this vision that I see before me?" And it was you, Kate. You are more beautiful now than you've ever been.'

'It's a tan, a dress and a blow-dry,' she countered lightly. 'I'm still the same reproductively challenged idiot underneath it all, even if the packaging looks different.'

'An idiot with her own design career and tens of thousands of followers on social media. Your success is ... well, really bloody sexy, to be honest. I feel as nervous around you now as I did on our first date.'

Kate smiled for the first time as she pictured the two of them sitting across from each other at Pizza Hut. Their first date had been on Valentine's Day and every other restaurant table in their north London borough had been fully booked. They had shared a bottomless salad bowl and agreed to choose an extra topping each for their pizza, only to both select prawns.

It had felt like fate.

Kate felt a welling of tears in her throat and swallowed hard. She'd missed the sunset now. Alex would think she'd stood him up.

Glancing towards the bar, Kate started in surprise. Alex was there, sitting in the same stool she had vacated not half an hour before, a glass of what looked to be water in front of him. As she stared, he turned and looked her way, his expression not one of consternation or judgement, but of tenderness and concern. Toby and Filippo were hovering, so Alex could be in no doubt of who this man was beside her. He must understand what that could mean, yet he had chosen to stay regardless.

'Let me speak for a minute, James.' Kate extracted her hand from his. 'Let me tell you what I think has happened,' she said. 'I think you enjoyed single life at first. I'm guessing you had a few dates, made a bit of a mess around the house, wore the same pants all weekend and watched sport all day on TV – but then it dawned on you that all the things you wanted, all those stipulations you reeled off your life list, weren't appearing as if by magic now that I'd gone. I think you realised that relationships take work, and that I had done most of the heavy lifting over the past eight years – at least where our emotions were concerned.'

James went to argue, but she cut him off.

'No, let me finish. The thing is, I think you're here because the alternative is too hard. I don't think you want me at all – not really. I think what you want is to not have to try. With me, you can be the one who achieves, the one with the good job, the higher salary and the perfectly functioning fertility,' she said, her voice cracking. 'Being with me makes you feel good about yourself and now it's not so easy. Am I right?'

'No.' James's tone had become surly. 'That's not it at all.'

'Then what is it? Because all this missing me stuff is not very convincing. Sorry, but it's not,' she added, as James looked stricken. 'You're right,' she went on. 'I have changed since I came over to Croatia – I've learned to value myself more. Being around people who think I'm worth something has changed things for me.'

As she said it, Kate had looked instinctively across at Alex – a move not missed by James.

'Who's that?' he said shortly.

'That's Alex. He's my friend.'

'That guy?' James squinted in disbelief. 'That hippy? I thought you liked things clean and tidy, Kate – that bloke looks as if he hasn't had a bath all year.'

'Don't be such an arse,' she retorted. 'Alex is kind, accepting and real. You have no idea how refreshing it's been to spend time with a man not obsessed with money or his career, a man who's content to simply go with the flow.'

'Just not under it,' threw back James with a hard laugh. 'And you may mock my ambition, Kate, but the main reason I want to do well and build up some savings is so we can have a family, so I can support us adequately enough to raise our children. If that makes me a bad guy, then I don't know, Kate, I really don't.'

Kate fell silent, wounded by his words and by her own treacherous tears, which had sprung out as soon as he mentioned family. It had been their plan for so long; the future she had believed that she wanted above any other. And she did want to be a mother one day, whatever it took and however difficult that may prove to be. James was here now, promising her exactly that. Could she afford to wait? Should she even want to wait?

'I don't know what to do,' she whispered, so quietly that James bent his head towards hers. At some point he must have slid his hand into hers again. Kate did not have the strength to pull away from him. All her self-righteous anger was ebbing away, and she was weakening. What she'd shared with Alex was special, but this was James – her James, the man she had, until a mere few weeks ago, wanted back in her life as her partner. She'd been ready to give up because she'd thought there was no hope, but now that had changed and suddenly the decision lay in her hands. Kate never had been good at making decisions.

'Kate, please,' he said, pressing his head against hers. 'I'm sorry for hurting you. I've been wrong about so many things. All I'm asking is for the chance to prove myself.'

'I don't know,' she said, her voice strained. 'So much has happened. Trying to get over you has been the hardest thing I've ever done – it almost broke me. I can't risk putting myself through all that pain again, I just can't.'

'Don't do it for me, then,' he said. 'Don't do it for either of us.'

Kate sat back and away from him, severing the connection of his skin against hers.

'What do you mean?' she asked, weary now. 'If not for us, then for who?'

Smiling, James pulled a wedge of paper from the back pocket of his jeans, unfolding it before passing it across. There was a heart-shaped logo printed at the top, beneath it the words Adopt North London and below that a headline that read: Children who need adopting.

'Do it for our child,' he said.

47

'You want us to adopt?'

Kate gawped first at the pages in her hands then at James.

'I've done a bit of research and I think we'd be strong candidates,' he said, plumping up with renewed self-importance as she gaped at him. 'My company offers a great paternity package and you'd be happy to stick a pin in all this interiors stuff for a few years, wouldn't you? It would be worth it,' he added, misreading her disbelief, 'for a baby.'

Toby had switched on the lantern lights that were strung above the Tiki Bar and the colours swam together as Kate stared at them. Alex was no longer there; she hoped he was OK.

'I don't understand,' she murmured, scanning the pages once again. James must have printed them out from a website. Next to stock photos of children's hands on toys or their welly-booted feet splashing in puddles, there were names and short biographies.

Charlie, five, loves dinosaurs, space and bedtime stories. He's bois-terous but loving, looking for a forever home.

Maisie, seventeen months, enjoys bath time, loves teddy bears and cuddles.

Jonas, three, has problems with his language and development but is making good progress with his foster family.

Kate wanted to adopt every single one of them, but she was also shrewd enough to recognise emotional manipulation when it was thrust under her nose.

Slowly, she folded the paper over.

'I thought you were against the idea of adoption?' she said. 'You told me emphatically that you wanted your own child.'

'I do,' said James, the words escaping like a reflex. 'But not more than I want to be with you,' he added hurriedly.

'You've changed your tune,' she said accusingly. 'This is a complete one-eighty.'

James had shredded the entire label from his beer bottle and was now picking at the glue. 'I needed time to get my head around the idea, and now I have.'

'Just like that?'

'Uh huh.'

'But why adoption? Why not try IVF first?'

'It'll take too long,' he said, plucking the printouts from her hands and unfolding them. 'Little Maisie needs a mum and dad now – she's already been born. We could buy her lovely things with all the money we'd save not doing endless rounds of IVF.'

'If we agreed to wait a while, then I'm fairly certain the NHS would fund our first try,' Kate pointed out. 'And I could still conceive naturally. I started taking the pill before I came out here to Croatia, but I could easily stop again.'

James was shaking his head as if this second suggestion was ludicrous. 'But if we opted for IVF, just think of all the tests and the drugs, all the prodding and poking – it would be horrible for you and there are no guarantees.'

'I know all that,' she allowed. 'But it would be our baby. And I would get to be pregnant.'

'Do you really want that, though? Morning sickness, droopy boobs and stretch marks.'

Kate glared at him. 'What a ludicrous and small-minded thing to say, James – as if any of that crap matters.'

'No, sorry. Of course it doesn't.'

Kate paused, astonished by this new fire in her belly. James rarely apologised – either he was genuinely sorry, or he'd undergone a complete personality transplant in the time since she'd seen him last. Her eyes strayed back towards the bar. Alex hadn't returned. She tried to imagine how she would have felt if James had shown up even a fortnight ago. Would that Kate have leapt at the chance to return home, or would she have hesitated? She had told herself so many times that a life with James was what she wanted, but while he'd been absent, she'd filled the gap he left behind with so many other things – not simply Alex, but a career, too. Being hired by Lovro and now Bram Van Dijk had soothed the sting caused by failure and rejection; it had given her a role that felt right. If she went back to London now, she would have to give it all up.

But a baby.

Kate's heart burst open at the mere thought of motherhood. She'd not forgotten her reaction upon overhearing Nika's pregnancy news, and how she had carefully avoided the dark-haired office manager since. She'd buried her feelings about it to survive, but they were still there. If she said no to James, was she consigning herself to childless future?

'I'd want to try IVF first,' she said firmly, seeing James's shoulders slouch in defeat.

'Why is that such an awful prospect all of a sudden?'

'It's not, it's just that—'

Whatever it was that James wanted to say, he couldn't seem to locate the right words. A crimson flush was creeping across his neck, his face was clammy, and his fingers were still grinding glue off the empty beer bottle.

'Are you OK?' she asked. 'You look as if you're about to throw up.'

James shook his head.

'Wait here – I'll go and get some water.'

Toby was talking to a group of guests and there was still no sign of Alex, so she ducked behind the bar and filled a glass from the soda tap. The fact that James was here at all had yet to fully sink in, and now that she'd put a small measure of distance between the two of them, Kate was able to view the situation with more clarity.

There was something important he wasn't telling her – but what?

Reaching over the bar, Kate retrieved her bag and phone, finding a 'sorry' message from Robyn followed by a stream of kisses. She wanted to ring Alex, and as she thought of him, an idea came to her. Hurrying back across the terrace, she urged James to drink up.

'What's the rush?' he asked, his face paled by the moonlight.

'I think we should go for a walk,' she said. 'There's something I want to show you.'

James nodded. He seemed glad to be leaving the busy hostel, where the prying eyes of Toby, Filippo and, for a time, Alex had been fixed on him since he arrived. When he told Kate this, she was nonplussed.

'They all saw what the break-up did to me; the mess it made of me. And I'm not saying that to be cruel to you,' she added, as the corners of James's mouth sagged. 'I'm only telling you what you already know.'

'Will you hold my hand?' he asked, when they reached the crumbling stone path that led down to Pokonji Dol beach. 'It feels weird us not touching.'

Kate extended a reluctant arm.

How could she explain that the opposite was true for her; that the idea of doing anything more intimate than a hand-hold with him made her insides churn with discomfort.

Unlike Robyn, who had splatter-gunned Hvar with super-latives during her week on the island, James made no comment as they rounded the slope, and the bay came into view below them. He did grumble about there not being 'a proper set of steps' down the hillside, only to hurriedly take it back when Kate told him she liked the more natural arrange-ment of crumbling rocks.

'You don't have to agree with me simply for the sake of it,' she told him, but James shook his head.

'No, I do. It's my new thing: trying not to be such a – what was it – small-minded arse?'

There were a few pockets of holidaymakers still on the beach, tins of beer at their feet and towels wrapped around their shoulders, so Kate led James to the opposite end of the shoreline, where they sat together on a stack of wooden loungers. He'd let go of her hand as they crossed the stones and Kate tucked her own away beneath her armpits, her knees pulled up to her chin. Everything about her body language said 'do not touch' and James received the message loud and clear.

Folding his arms, he stared gloomily out over the water, waiting for her to explain why she'd brought him here.

'There is something you're not telling me,' she said, with-out preamble.

James's features flickered with unease, but he didn't speak.

Releasing her hands and lowering her knees, Kate reached down and picked up a smooth, flat stone. She'd brought her bag with her, and now rummaged inside until she located a pen.

'My friend, that guy you were so quick to judge up on the terrace, he taught me a trick a few weeks ago.'

'You're not going to start juggling, are you?' said James. 'I haven't forgotten your ill-fated week as a trainee children's party entertainer.'

Isabelle Broom

Kate laughed. It felt like a relief to do so.

'Not my finest seven days, I grant you. Although, in my defence, it's not as easy as it looks to make animals out of balloons. But no – I'm not going to juggle. Because I don't want to, not because I can't,' she added, as he made a 'whatever you say' face. For a moment, it was as if the past few months had never happened, as if they were back on the sofa they had picked out together from the DFS Boxing Day sale, laughingly lamenting her latest work-related mishap. Before the issue of fertility crashed catastrophically into their lives, they had laughed together a lot – more often than not because of something Kate had done.

'Here.' She handed him the stone and pen. 'I want you to write down the thing that scares you the most.'

James looked as if he might make a disparaging remark, but then thought better of it.

Kate watched in silence as he carefully stencilled the word 'BALDNESS' in large, bold letters.

'Hair loss?' she exclaimed. 'That is genuinely the one thing in life that scares you more than any other?'

'Give me a chance, I'm just warming up,' he protested, selecting another stone and writing 'POVERTY' in more solid capitals.

'Right, so you don't want to end up with no hair or no money,' she surmised. 'That's fair. What about emotional fears?'

'You mean, which emotions am I scared of?'

'Yes. Does fear scare you? Or hope? Or love?'

'No.' James shook his head. 'But I am scared of losing you – can I write that?'

'If that is true. But ask yourself, James – is it really that, or is it the regret that scares you? Because if you think about it, you lost me out of choice. Now, you're starting to think that may have been a mistake and those feelings concern you because you don't know what to do with them.'

'I don't think I get it,' he said, but wrote the word 'REGRET' on the stone regardless.

Now they were getting somewhere.

'Has everything you've told me since arriving in Croatia been the truth?' she asked, as gently as she could. It was important that she soothe rather than shake this out of him. Kate wanted full transparency, not another argument. 'And before you answer,' she went on, 'I want you to know that if – and it's a big "if" – I do decide that we can try again, then I need to know everything, no matter how murky the truth and no matter how much you think it will hurt me. There's no point in pretence – we're too old for games and there's too much at stake. How can we sit before an adoption panel if we can't be honest with each other?'

James had been on the verge of scribbling down another word, but he stilled as she spoke. The internal struggle was playing out across his features, which were twisting and contorted by indecision, and as he fought his own conscience, Kate put her hand over his.

'Whatever it is, I'll listen. I promise.'

To her astonishment, James began to cry.

'Shit, sorry,' he blurted. 'I don't know if I can. It's too much.'

Kate shifted along until she was close enough to put an arm around him. 'It can't be all that bad, can it? Did you cheat on me, is that it?'

James shook his head violently. 'No, I would never do that.'

'Are you secretly in mountains of debt? Do you have a gambling habit I know nothing about?'

James's bottom lip jutted out as he muttered a 'no'. 'I wish it was something like that,' he said forlornly. 'Something I could fix.'

Kate was beginning to feel uneasy, but she had to know. She had to keep pushing until she got the answer.

'It's . . . I can't . . .'

There were tears coursing down James's cheeks now, and he pushed them furiously away with clenched fists. Kate had never seen him so distraught.

'It's all right,' she soothed, squeezing him against her. 'You can tell me – it's me. Whatever it is that you're holding on to, it's clearly upsetting, so you have to tell someone, and it might as well be me – and it might as well be here,' she said.

James lifted his head and looked at her, his dark, desperate eyes beseeching. 'It's all my fault,' he said, the words choking out over a sob. 'I'm a failure.'

'No, you're not,' Kate soothed, but his expression caused her to pause. 'What is it, James – tell me.'

'I'm the one,' he said. 'It's me who can't have children.'

48

The story about the pregnant girl at university hadn't been a lie, but whoever fathered that child could not have been James. The tests he'd undertaken for Kate, to put her mind at rest, had come back with devastating results. Results that James had not been able to bear admitting to her or even to himself.

'So instead, you let me believe it was all my fault?'

Even in her sympathy and shock, Kate was appalled by his conduct.

James hung his head, unable to meet her eyes.

'I feel sorry for you, I really do, but how could you not tell me? How could you let me believe that the tablets weren't working, that my PCOS was the reason we couldn't get pregnant? I hated myself for it, James. I hated my body and blamed myself for all of it.'

'I know, I know.' James was shaking his head, still weeping with what Kate now knew was both self-pity and self-loathing. 'It's unforgivable, I know. But I couldn't tell you. I didn't know how to.'

'You should have tried harder,' she said, close to tears herself. The agony she'd gone through, having convinced herself she would never conceive, that she would be unlikely to ever experience a first scan, or a first kick, had been palpable.

'Why did you think it was acceptable to lie to me?' she demanded, crossing the arms she'd removed from around him. 'If you couldn't say the words, you could have left the test results out for me to find; you could have written me a letter or told your mum and have her explain it to me. I would have understood, James – I still would have wanted to be with you.'

'I know.' He'd buried his face in his hands now and his words were muffled.

'But you,' she said accusingly, 'broke up with me because you wanted *your own children*. That's what you let me think. Do you know how hurtful that was, James? Do you realise the damage that did to me?'

'Damage?' He removed his hands and stared at her in disbelief. 'You were so damaged that you went skipping off to Croatia, started up a new business and found yourself lots of new friends.' He'd put a disgruntled emphasis on the last word that made Kate think longingly of Alex, of his honesty and serenity. He would never have lied to her like this.

'I'd become a national laughing stock, in case you've forgotten. It wasn't as if I ran away, I merely took some time out. I was ill, James – I was on the verge of having a breakdown and barely eating or sleeping. Coming to Hvar cured me. It cured me of y—'

'Of me?' he finished. 'So, when you told me you still loved me, that was a lie?'

Kate flushed. 'Don't try to turn this around onto me. Your lie beats any I might have told in my entire lifetime. No matter how sad I was, or scared I was, I would never, not ever, let you believe that you couldn't have a child. I don't even know what to say to you. I feel sick.'

James chewed furiously at his thumbnail, his teeth stripping it away until he tore the delicate skin beneath. Blood pooled and he sucked it off irritably.

'I behaved atrociously,' he said. 'I know that, Kate. And I agree with everything you've said. I don't know why I didn't tell you. I guess I'd become so used to being the strong one, and the thing is, I never fail, not at anything. I never have. When I found out that I wasn't up to scratch, that I was lacking in the most important aspect of all, it freaked me out. I lied to you before I knew what I was saying, and then it became impossible to take it back. The more time that passed, the easier it became to keep it a secret – but I hated myself for it. I hated what it was doing to you. Don't you see? That's why I ended things – not because I didn't love you, but because it became too hard to keep lying to you.'

'And yet, you came all the way out here with your bloody adoption printouts and absolutely zero intention of being honest with me,' she stated, calmer now.

'You always said adoption was a wonderful thing,' he said petulantly. 'That motherhood is about more than just pregnancy.'

'I did,' she agreed. 'And it is – but I should have been allowed a choice. I would happily have adopted with you if you'd told me the truth; you must have known that?'

'I panicked. I was stupid and I said the wrong thing. I didn't see how to take it back and I'm sorry, for god's sake. Do you not understand at all where I'm coming from?'

There was nobody else on the beach now. They were alone. The moon that had been so bright as they made their way across the stones was obscured now by clouds, and the water below had been thrown into shadow. What had looked so inviting earlier, now appeared formidable, as if grasping hands were lurking below the surface, waiting to drag down anyone foolish enough to wade out into the depths. Kate felt as if she were already marooned, alone on a raft of sorrow, hurt and confusion. What James had done was shameful, but she could see how it had happened – and why. Better than most, she understood what it was to fail, to feel as if your ability to control anything had been ripped away from you. And as desolating as it had been to believe she would never fall pregnant, James had been right in his assumption that she would have survived it. Kate and deficiency were long-term acquaintances, whereas he was a newcomer to the party.

She selected a stone and snatched up the pen.

'I know what you're most scared of,' she told him, removing the lid and bending to write. 'Truth. You're scared of the bloody truth.'

He did not disagree, merely gazed at her, his cheeks wet and dark eyes caverns.

'What do we do now then?' he asked sulkily. 'What was the point in all these stones?'

Kate sighed. 'You're supposed to throw them into the water and watch your fears wash away, but I'm not sure you're ready for that – or even if you deserve it.'

James slumped. 'I probably don't.'

'Is this it?' she asked. 'Is this the only thing you've been hiding from me?'

For a beat or two, he could not meet her eyes, staring out towards the horizon instead. It was too dark to see the distinctive shape of Alex's boat, but Kate took comfort from knowing it was there; that he was in all likelihood there as well.

'This is the only thing,' he said at last, his voice hollow. 'There isn't anything else, I promise.'

Kate nodded but said nothing.

'What are you thinking?' he asked, with a desperate edge that dragged through her.

'I'm thinking that I'm tired and that we're both exhausted. We could easily sit here all night, chasing this thing around and getting nowhere, or we can go back to the hostel and sleep on it. And I don't know about you, but I definitely need to sleep on it.'

'That's a good idea,' he agreed, sounding marginally less despairing.

'I'm not saying this conversation is over,' she warned. 'Because it isn't. You are not forgiven, nor am I saying anything other than I need time to think.'

'I understand,' he assured her, standing up and reaching for her hand.

Kate ignored him, wrapping her arms around herself instead. She was still wearing the green dress she'd chosen specially for Alex's benefit; the toenails she'd painted gold looked dour and grey in the darkness. Her phone had remained silent inside her bag and she hoped Alex did not think she'd forgotten about him. As James began to clamber back up the stony path ahead of her, Kate tapped out a quick text to him: *Sorry about tonight. K xx*

The reply came back as just they reached Sul'letto.

Here if you need me. Always. A x.

49

That night, Kate dreamt she was lost at sea.

All around her, black waves rose and fell, unrelenting in their tussle to claim her, while the sky above was split open by thunder and lightning, crashing and roaring with the same unbridled rage that hurtled through her veins. No matter how hard she struggled against the tide, she knew there was no way out. Nobody could save her, but on she fought; wearying limbs thrashing, trying but failing to rescue her broken heart.

She awoke in a tangle of sheets to the sound of running water. The spare mattress Toby had left on the floor for James was empty, and the bathroom door was closed. Kate rubbed her eyes and checked the time; it was early. Having erected a pillow barrier around herself the previous night as a clear signal to her uninvited guest that he should not come near her, she found most of them on the floor and guessed she must have moved around a lot in her sleep. James's phone, the charger for which he'd plugged into the wall socket behind her head, was another casualty, and had somehow ended up in the far corner of the room.

Pulling on Toby's hoodie, which she'd yet to give back, Kate scooped the phone up off the floor and was about to plug it back in when she noticed a waiting message from someone named Claire.

She vaguely recalled James mentioning a Claire from his office – another architect he occasionally collaborated with at

the planning stage of a new project – but she couldn't be
sure. He'd promised her that he'd not started seeing anyone
else since they'd split, but then, James's word had ceased to
count for much. If Kate was even going to consider forgiving
him, she needed to find out if he'd lied about anything else.
Sneaking a look at his phone felt justified, but even so, she
ducked back under the covers before tapping in his passcode.
Not being the most imaginative of men, James used the same
one as he did for their Amazon Prime and Sky TV login –
Kate would not be surprised if it matched the pin of his bank
card, too.

The message opened and Kate breathed with relief. It was
the same Claire. The most recent text was asking if his
'romantic reunion' – Kate pursed her lips at that – had gone
as planned, and poor, sweet, delusional Claire had followed it
with a string of crossed-fingers emojis. Above that was one
from James, thanking her for the 'great advice' and telling her
he'd booked a flight. They must have discussed the situation
while at work.

Kate continued to scroll through a lot of dull messages
about planning permission, buildings regulations and site
visits, only to stop abruptly when she spotted the word
'video'.

Claire had written:

*Hey, just wanted to let you know that I've told my boyfriend to
find out who posted the video and tell them to take it down. I can't
believe he sent it around to his mates in the first place, the absolute
idiot. Poor Kate, I feel so sorry for her. But maybe you'll both
laugh about it one day – play it at your wedding or something?
She was so brave to get up and propose to you like that. Please tell
her from me that she's my hero!*

Very slowly, Kate scrolled down to James's reply.

Hey Claire Bear – no worries. It's all a bit of fun, isn't it? No harm done. Kate is cool about it, so don't worry about taking it down. I'm hoping it'll hit a million views. LOL.

Kate had read both messages three times before the shower was turned off and waited in silence as James blew his nose and cleaned his teeth. The bathroom door was opposite the bed, so he saw her sitting there as soon as he opened it.

'Hey, sleepyhead. What's up?'

He'd knotted a towel around his waist and there were droplets of water on his bare, hairless chest. Kate took a breath.

'Who was it that posted that video of me proposing to you on the Internet?'

James's ears turned red, followed rapidly by his neck. 'I've no idea – one of your mad friends probably.'

'So, not a friend of Claire Bear's idiot boyfriend, then?' she said disparagingly, holding up his phone so he could see the screen.

'Kate, listen to m—'

'No. Why should I? Why should I listen to another single bloody word you say?'

James bent to retrieve a pair of boxers from his open suitcase and pulled them on under his towel.

'Why are you looking through my phone?' he grumbled. 'Those are my private messages.'

'Call it a hunch,' she said icily. 'A text came through from Claire – she wanted to know if you'd managed to win me back, although it would have been more of a coercion than a win, given what I know now.'

'I told her I was coming here,' protested James. 'She said I should make a grand romantic gesture – there's nothing going on between us.'

'I know that,' said Kate, through gritted teeth. 'That's not the issue here, the video is.'

The harshness of her tone seemed to rattle James, and he put out an arm to steady himself against the bedroom wall.

'Loads of people were filming you that night,' he said. 'Even if I had told Claire to get the video taken down, someone else would have posted another one. The damage was already done.'

'So what? Instead of defending me, instead of condemning whoever had done it, you thought you'd make light of it? Tell everyone I found it hilarious; that a video which is even now being laughed at all across England – thanks to its catchy "Wannabe Wife" hashtag – was nothing more than a joke?'

'Well, it is, isn't it?' he said challengingly. 'It's not that big of a deal, Kate.'

Not that big of a deal?

'No, no,' she agreed sarcastically. 'It's not as if I've agonised over it and driven myself almost mad watching it time and time again. I mean, of course I haven't studied it, lived and breathed it, wondered how I will ever get over the shame of it.'

'Kate, I—'

'But you.' It was almost a snarl. 'You were all for getting the views up over a million. Did you hope that me becoming the world's most famous spinster would make you feel better about having lied to me? That it would justify your decision to dump me?'

She thought he was going to deny it and a part of her hoped he would. Because the alternative was so reprehensible that Kate didn't honestly know how she'd react. There was a brief, tense moment, during which they simply glared hard at each other, and then James dropped his eyes.

'OK.' He held up his hands. 'The truth is it did make me feel better.'

'Because it proved what a lucky escape you'd made?'

'No, not that,' he said simply. 'It was my excuse to stay away, to reject you, to keep the truth about my infertility a secret – and I grabbed it with both hands. At the time Claire sent that message, only a small number of people had even seen the video. How was I to know it would blow up the Internet?'

'Two days after it was posted they played it on *This Morning* and *Loose* bloody *Women*!'

Kate clenched her jaw, closing her eyes as she recalled the cruel words written alongside that first awful post: #WannabeWife #NorthLondonLoser #ProposalFail #LeftOn TheShelf. It was designed to go viral; and a small part of James must have enjoyed the protracted attention, even if he couldn't be identified in the footage. Kate opened her eyes and stared hard at the man she'd loved so deeply for so long. He was not strong and capable after all, but weak and afraid. While she'd faced her fears and found a way to make peace with her failings, James had wallowed in shame and self-interest. He was here because he wanted her to save him – needed her to do what he could not. But, in order to do that, Kate would need to love him still, and loving James meant not loving herself. Kate could not do that anymore; she was not that person anymore.

'You look like you want to hit me,' he said, groping for his shorts.

Kate tossed his mobile down onto the bed. She could have caused a huge scene, could have thrown his phone against the wall and stormed around the room, sweeping all his belongings into his bag while she screamed and ranted. But now that she examined it, Kate found that she was not angry after all. She was simply done – with him, with their relationship, with the dishonesty – all of it.

Pushing aside the covers, she walked past him to the wardrobe and pulled out some underwear, a plain white T-shirt, and the mustard dress she'd worn the day she and Alex went to Brač. The day she'd kissed him for the first time.

'I'm going to get dressed,' she said, crossing to the bathroom. 'I suggest you do the same. Then you can start packing.'

'But what abou—'

Kate silenced him by shutting the door in his face, surprised to discover that she was smiling. She felt lighter somehow, as if she'd done a juice cleanse and dropped six pounds overnight.

When she re-emerged, James was moodily stuffing rolled-up socks into his suitcase.

'Is this it, then?' he said. 'You're throwing me out, after everything we've been through?'

Kate picked up her hairbrush. She had been thinking a ponytail today, but perhaps she would leave it loose. Alex would only run his hands through it later anyway. The thought of that was enough to widen her smile further, and seeing this, James's mood soured.

'I'm glad you're finding this so enjoyable,' he said resentfully.

'I'm not celebrating,' she said calmly. 'I'd just prefer it if you stayed somewhere else. I can help you find a place.'

The hostel was beginning to wake up. Kate could hear feet on the stairs and voices coming from the communal bathroom along the hall. Her phone buzzed with a message. It was Lovro, telling her he'd had to go over to the mainland for business and that she should take the day off.

'Kate, this can't be it. You can't seriously be throwing away your entire future over a video.'

'I'm not,' she said, reaching around him to pick up her lip balm. 'Now, where did I leave my shoes – oh, there they are.'

'Kate!' James was becoming whiney now. If there was one thing she could not stand, it was grown men that whined like toddlers.

'I'll wait for you downstairs,' she said. 'We can ask Nika to call around and see who has an empty room for you. I assume you booked a return flight, did you? I'm sure that can be altered, too, if necessary.'

'You think I'm going to go quietly?' he said in disbelief, throwing the shirt he was folding onto the floor. 'I tell you now, Kate, I'm not. I'm going to stay on this island until you see reason. I'm going to . . . I'm going to . . . I know you still love me,' he added desperately. 'I know you do.'

Kate extracted the cleaning cloth from her glasses case and began polishing her lenses.

'Did you hear me?' James shouted. 'I said, I'm not going to go without a fight!'

There was nothing, she realised. Not so much as the merest flicker of anger, nor sadness, nor affection. She did feel a bit sorry for him, for the predicament he was in and the regret he would have to contend with now that he'd lost her for good. But that was the extent of it. She'd given him every-thing already; he'd wrung out every last drop of her. James did not love her, not in the way she deserved to be loved, and Kate felt an ache then for the woman she'd left behind back in London. That confused, aimless, lost girl that she had treated so badly. What Kate should have done was love her, but instead she had given her whole heart, her whole self, to someone else – a man who had betrayed her in the worst possible way. A man who had lied.

She knew now that she would never, ever, make the same mistake again.

Kate put her glasses back on and gathered up her bag. 'I'll be downstairs,' she said, and headed for the door before he had a chance to argue.

Nika was in the back office but there was no sign of her brother or Filippo, which she supposed was a blessing. As much as she wanted James gone, she did not want his depart-ure to become a spectacle. Pushing open the hostel front door, Kate settled down on the steps outside to wait for him and was struck once again by how wonderfully free she felt. All the tightly coiled knots of anxiety were unspooling; the residual hurt and fear draining away. Everything felt softer somehow – even the sunlight that bathed the pavement seemed less abrasive.

Kate was exactly where she was meant to be, and she had become exactly who she was supposed to be too.

There was a sound behind her and she turned to see James emerge into the street. His still damp hair was sticking up at all angles and he looked despondent. Not quite beaten, but certainly subdued.

'I was going to ask you to marry me,' he said. 'There's a ring in my bag.'

Kate got to her feet. Her instinct was to comfort him, but she resisted. 'I will forgive you, James,' she told him.

Hope reignited his features.

'You will?'

'Yes, eventually. But I don't love you – not anymore. I'm sorry, but that's the truth. I don't know what else I can say.'

Her words had finally silenced him and after a moment he nodded, understanding at last that this was it; that their relationship was over.

Kate felt him take her hand, but she did not look at him, gazing instead across the rooftops and down to the tinsel-glint of water below. He had been her home once, but she had never belonged with him. They both knew that now.

James squeezed her fingers tightly one final time and then, so quietly that she would wonder later if he had said it at all, he whispered a single word.

'Goodbye.'

50

James had only just disappeared over the brow of the hill when Toby and Filippo emerged from their apartment. As it transpired, they'd been watching through the curtains, ready to rush over and offer assistance if the need arose. When Kate explained what had happened, Toby could barely contain his pride.

'I knew it!' he said triumphantly to his husband. 'I knew she would see sense and stay with Alex.'

'What?' Kate exclaimed, feigning confusion, but Filippo silenced her with one of his dropped-chin expressions of pure scepticism.

'We have known for a while, *bambina* – and we are very happy for you both.'

Kate was tempted to rush down to the marina immediately and tell Alex everything, but she settled on a text instead, asking him if he was free because she had an unexpected day off. The reply arrived less than a minute later and Toby clocked her smiling as she read it.

'I was going to offer you breakfast,' he said. 'But I'm guessing whatever Alex has on the menu is far more exciting?' Then, when Kate merely grinned. 'Off you go, then.'

She found Alex waiting for her at the bottom of the long pathway that led down to the water. There was a smear of oil across his white T-shirt and another on his cheek.

'So, guess what,' she said as she approached, 'I'm afraid our secret is well and truly out. I don't think I've ever seen my brother so happy to have won a bet in his life.'

'I'm glad he isn't the type to puff up his chest and tell me that I'd better treat you right or else,' said Alex, affecting a ridiculous thuggish voice. He'd removed his Croatia cap and tucked it into the back pocket of his shorts, and Kate could see dark roots growing through beneath the blond dreadlocks.

'Nah,' she grinned. 'He's a pussycat – although, since meeting Siva, I'm beginning to think that saying needs a rethink.'

'I've never been in the position of seeking approval from a sibling before,' Alex went on. 'I never met the extended family of the few girls I dated growing up.'

'What about since you've been here?'

'There haven't been any – not in years.'

Kate did not ask why. She'd learned that when it came to Alex, it was better to remain quiet and wait for him to explain in his own time. He preferred to consider his responses.

'James has gone,' she said, and he nodded.

'Are you OK?'

Kate's only answer was to lean in and kiss him.

The boat was moored up not far from the main harbour in town, and once on board, Alex fired up the rather spluttery-sounding engine he'd been trying to fix all morning and steered them out past the Pakleni Islands to a spot in open water, far away from the prying eyes of anyone who happened to be sailing past. Kate had missed him the previous night and could think of little else but her need to be close to him again, to give herself to him, to forget all the drama with James and simply lose herself in pure sensation.

Alex was in no hurry, however, and tempered her enthusiasm by kissing her tenderly, his fingers stroking gently through her hair, over her chest and down towards her stomach. When Kate opened her eyes, she found that he'd not closed his own, but was using them to take in every inch of her.

'It still amazes me that I can do this,' he murmured. 'That I can hold you in my arms, that I can kiss you here' – he pressed his lips softly against her cheekbone – 'and here,' he whispered, trailing his tongue across her throat. The curls of his beard tickled her bare skin, sending shivers of pleasure from Kate's toes all the way up to her shoulders.

'Well, don't let that stop you doing it,' she teased, sighing with contentment as he continued to cover her face with featherlight kisses. The pace of her heart had quietened, but her desire still burnt red hot inside. Kate knew what she was feeling was more than a purely physical need; it was an overwhelming sense of rightness, of being in the right place with the right person. She was stirred, yet safe; her once-solid wall of vulnerability little more than dust on the floor of the boat. Every sense was heightened, every colour extra bright.

'Do you feel it?' she whispered. 'Us?'

Alex nodded, his gaze more intent now. The body that had been soft and supple beside her hardening as she spoke. Just as he had the first time he'd laid with her in the cabin of his boat, Alex manoeuvred himself beneath her and put his hands on either side of her waist, lifting her up until she faced him. A moment passed where Kate thought he was going to tell her something, and for once she willed him to speak, pausing in her movements only to exhale with surprise as their bodies connected. Within seconds, she was utterly lost.

'Would you have come to find me at the hostel if I hadn't messaged you this morning?' she asked him afterwards, when they were lying together, slick with sweat, on top of the tangled blankets.

'Probably.' He grinned. 'I'm pretty sure I've left my wrench there and I need it to finish fixing the engine.'

'Charming!' Kate hooked a bare leg over his.

Alex returned the pressure. 'Truth?'

She smiled. 'Always.'

'I was on the verge of setting off when I heard from you. Truth is, I wanted to tell you to choose me, not him.'

Kate propped herself up on an elbow. 'Really?'

Reaching out a finger, Alex tapped her nose. 'Really.' He paused. 'The thing is, I don't do . . . this. I actively try not to develop feelings for people, not since . . . Well, it's been a long time. But for some reason when I met you, that changed. I tried to ignore it at first, but somehow, there you always were.'

'You make me sound like a mosquito,' she replied, buzzing gently into his ear.

'That day you came across the skip and I drove over and found you half-in and half-out of it, covered in dust and all excited over a pile of broken furniture, I knew I was in trouble. I couldn't take my eyes off you. I volunteered to help with all the interior stuff at the hostel purely so I could stay nearby. I turned down other work to do it – other paid work,' he added, seeing Kate's look of flattered dismay. 'I knew you were still hankering after your ex, but that was all right, because it meant nothing would ever happen. That I could admire you from a distance, see?'

'And then we went to Brač,' she prompted, running her hand through the soft wiry hair on his chest.

'And you kissed me,' he said, smiling at the memory. 'That gave me hope.'

'I'm sorry if I was giving you confusing signals,' she said. 'I knew there was something happening between us, but I wasn't sure what it was or even what to do with those feelings, if that makes any sense? I was conflicted, because I'd convinced myself that winning James back was the endgame. It was only after Robyn showed up and winkled the truth out of me that I knew for sure. In fact, on the subject of Robyn, I should send her a text, let her know that she can stop feeling guilty about telling James where I was.'

As she sat up and began rummaging for her phone, however, Alex leaned across and wrapped her in his arms, pulling her over until she was lying on top of him. Kate thought he was going to kiss her, but instead, he simply stopped and stared, his pale-blue eyes silver in the darkened cabin.

'If we do this, Kate,' he said softly, intently. 'I want us to do it properly.'

'This as in us?'

'Yes, this as in us.' He stroked a curl off her face with such tenderness that Kate's heart seemed to skip a beat.

'And you believe we can?' she murmured, loath to taint the moment with questions, but needing to know the answers. 'Obviously, I'm based here in Croatia at the moment, and will be for a while now thanks to Bram Van Dijk, but I'll have to go home to England at some point, even if it's just temporarily.'

Alex did not clam up as she'd assumed he would, but he did close his eyes for second, shutting her out while he contemplated his reply. 'I understand,' he said. 'There will be a lot of decisions we'll need to make further down the line, but I do want to be a part of them. I want us to work.'

Kate couldn't hold on to her tears and blinked helplessly as they tumbled down her cheeks. 'I'm only crying because I'm happy,' she whispered, as Alex caught them with his thumbs. 'I'm weird like that.'

'You are,' he agreed cheerfully, kissing her wet face. 'But I wouldn't want you any other way. You're perfect.'

'Nobody's perfect,' she protested sleepily, ready to lose herself again. 'But at least you know everything now. There are no more surprises lurking, I promise. No more ex-boyfriends likely to turn up begging for my hand in marriage.'

Alex fell silent for a moment, his expression set. 'There are things I need to tell you,' he said, and Kate could feel his heart racing below her own. 'Things you need to know about me, about my past. I want you to hear it all before you make any decisions, before you decide if this is what you want.'

Kate moved her lips to his. 'Then tell me,' she urged. 'I want to know you, Alex. I want to know everything about you.'

'I will,' he murmured, between kisses. 'Soon. I promise.'

Alex's hands stroked her back, his touch featherlight and his breath warm against her neck. Kate arched against him; she felt almost drunk with desire.

'When?' she whispered, her breath shallow as she felt him there, wanting her, needing her.

'Tonight,' he said. 'I'll tell you everything tonight.'

The boat rocked gently as the two of them became lost in one another, the water surrounding them dulled by the grey clouds above. In the far distance, a low rumble was gathering pace; sea birds called out a warning, high and shrill, while in the cabin, tools lay scattered. Forgotten.

51

Drowsy after hours of lovemaking and uplifted by a spirited phone call with Robyn, Kate made her slow way back to the hostel later that afternoon. Alex had surprised her by suggesting the two of them have dinner together in town that night, instead of cooking something over the camping stove on his boat as they usually did. A summer storm was headed towards Hvar and the sea would soon become rough – far too choppy for either of them to get any sleep if they stayed on board. So tonight, Kate had invited him to share her bed on dry land for the first time.

The wind blowing the dust along the pavements carried the cold edge of imminent rain and Kate shivered as she pushed open the hostel door and hurried upstairs to her room. Having showered and changed into cropped jeans and plain black T-shirt, she changed the bedding and gave the room a quick spruce before heading to the lounge area. The Tiki Bar and barbecue had been closed for the night on account of the incoming storm but, never one to be hampered by something as innocuous as a spot of bad weather, Toby had set up a serving station for his experimental beverages on one end of the long wooden dining table.

'Hey,' said Kate, taking a seat on the bench. There was a young Japanese couple watching something on a shared iPad a few seats away, while a dark-haired woman who looked vaguely familiar sat opposite, one of Toby's lurid-coloured cocktails in front of her. A few of the other guests were piled

in artful heaps on the sofas around the TV, chatting animated-
ly over a music channel that currently featured a lithe and
much-younger Justin Timberlake singing about a river.

'Something to wet your whistle?' asked Toby, holding up a
beer.

'No, thanks.' Kate took a half-empty bottle of water out of
her bag and waved it at him.

'Already drunk on lurve?' he joked.

'What are you, twelve?'

'Sorry,' Toby said to the woman, who was listening in
bemusement to their exchange. 'We're always like this, have
been since we were kids.'

'Oh,' she said, as understanding dawned. 'You're brother
and sister? I see the resemblance now – red hair and green
eyes.'

'We also share the same daft sense of humour,' added
Kate, wondering where she had seen this woman before. If
they'd been introduced on a previous occasion, then surely
she would have remembered her strong Welsh accent.

The woman smiled. 'It's nice that the two of you are so
close. I wish I could say the same.'

'Angela here is actually on the island looking for her
brother,' Toby explained. 'Can you tell Kate what you told
me?' he asked. 'It's quite some story.'

'Well,' said Angela, taking the paper umbrella out of her
drink and turning it over in her hands. 'My brother has been
missing for a while – ten years now, in fact – but a week or so
ago I received a message from someone who thought they'd
seen him, here in Hvar.'

A memory was tugging at the very edges of Kate's subconscious, but she couldn't quite grasp it.

'I did an interview months ago for one of those real-life
magazines, you know the ones. I don't read them myself, but
I know a lot of people do and, well, I was determined that this

year I would find him. I was willing to try whatever it took. Someone picked up that magazine here in this hostel and read my story, and then, according to the girl who got in touch, the very next day she saw someone in town that she thought could be him.'

'Isn't that crazy?' said Toby, taking a swig of beer. 'What are the chances?'

Kate was not listening; she was focused on the woman, Angela.

'So, this girl followed him around for a while, this man, and eventually asked him if she could take a photo, which he refused. She took one anyway, though,' said Angela. 'It's blurred and half his face is obscured by his hand, so I can't be absolutely sure, but I think it could be him. I think it is Josh.'

'Oh my god!' exclaimed Kate. 'That's it! I knew I recognised you,' she said to Angela. 'I read your story, too. It was probably me who brought that magazine here in the first place – I packed a whole stack of them in my hand luggage to read on the flight over back in May.'

Angela had shredded the paper umbrella; there were remnants of it all over the long table.

'And your brother's name is Josh?' said Kate, feeling a trickle of excitement. 'Can I see the photo of him?'

Toby looked at Kate enquiringly as Angela took out her phone. 'Bother,' she said, showing them the blank screen. 'Battery's gone. It's so old this thing – keeps dying on me.'

'What did he look like?' asked Kate. 'The guy in the picture?'

'Longish blond hair, tanned skin – bit like I imagine a surfer to look,' said Angela. 'It was taken on a beach – I could make out kayaks in the background. I'll just go up to my room and find my charger,' she added. 'Then I can show you.'

Kate smiled, waiting until Angela had disappeared through the outer door before turning to Toby.

'I think I might know who her brother is!'

Toby's eyes widened. 'Who?'

'You know that bloke who hires out kayaks down on Pokonji Dol?'

Toby shook his head. 'No.'

'Well, I do. He's a good friend of Alex's and calls himself Joe but sounds exactly like the bloke in this photo. The thing is, Alex has mentioned a Josh to me a few times, but always becomes a bit cagey whenever I ask any questions about him. What if this Joe is actually Josh and has asked Alex to keep his real identity a secret? That would make sense, given that he's been missing all these years.'

'If that's true then you have to tell Angela,' said Toby, but Kate wasn't so sure.

'Isn't that betraying Alex's trust?'

'If Alex were here now and could see how much that poor woman wants to find her brother, he'd want to help. No way would he stand in the way of a reunion.'

'I don't know, Tobe – what if I'm wrong about Joe?'

'If you are, then it's no harm done.'

The door from the stairwell opened then and Angela came back towards them, a phone charger clasped in her hand. As she neared the table, Toby threw Kate a meaningful stare.

'Tell her,' he said.

Angela froze. 'Tell me what?'

'If you don't, then I will.'

Kate took a deep breath, her eyes flickering from her brother's firm gaze to Angela's desperate one.

'Please,' she begged. 'This is the first solid lead on Josh I've had in over ten years. If you know something, you have to tell me.'

'It might be nothing,' Kate warned. 'I could be mistaken.'

But as much as she did not want to get Alex into any kind of trouble with his friend, Kate couldn't ignore the plight of this poor woman, her large dark eyes spilling over with tremulous tears and her clothing creased from the long flight – the one she'd booked the moment she'd received the merest hint of news about her brother.

Toby was right; they all had a duty to help.

'There is someone in Hvar who knows a Josh,' she said. 'And I can take you to him.'

52

It was with conflicting emotions that Kate led Angela towards the harbour later that evening. Having been convinced not to let Alex know in advance that she was bringing someone to meet him, she couldn't stop worrying about how he would react.

She and Alex were finally in a positive place and the first thing she'd done was go behind his back. How would he respond when confronted by Angela and all her questions? What Kate should have done was keep her suspicions to herself until she'd had the chance to ask him for more information on Josh. If she was mistaken and Joe was not Angela's missing brother after all, then she would have abused Alex's trust and raised Angela's hopes for nothing.

But it was too late now; she had no choice but to see it through.

Alex had sent her a text not long ago: *Podrum is booked. See you there in an hour. P.S. I have something to show you that I think you'll like ...*

She'd hated having to reply with a simple, *Can't wait!* It felt like she was hoodwinking him.

Angela was silent beside Kate, but feeling her gaze, she turned and smiled shyly.

'Thank you again,' she said. 'For doing this. I know I'm asking a lot of you.'

'You're not,' Kate assured her. 'And Alex is a good man. If he can help you, he will.'

'This all feels so surreal,' Angela went on. 'Nothing has happened for so long, no news, no word, no hope whatsoever – and suddenly here I am, on my way to meet someone who might actually know where Josh is. It doesn't feel real. I keep waiting for a camera crew to burst out from behind one of these plant pots and tell me it's all been a big joke.'

'I imagine there isn't much about this situation you can find to laugh about?' Kate replied, and Angela bit her lip.

'No,' she agreed. 'In the beginning, I kept thinking he would come back. Show up on the doorstep one day as if nothing had happened. I told myself that if he did, I wouldn't even ask him where he'd been, I would simply welcome him back, be thankful that he was alive.'

Her voice had caught as she said the last, and Kate waited for a few moments before she spoke again.

'I can't even begin to imagine what you've been through,' she said. 'What you're still going through. The article moved me; the way you talked about your brother and the things you said to him in that letter were so raw and honest. You must be extremely brave.'

'No.' Angela's dark hair fell across her face as she dropped her chin towards her chest. 'Not brave at all – quite the opposite. If I'd been braver, then Josh might never have left. If I'd been less selfish, perhaps . . .' She trailed off, and Kate stepped ahead of her as they passed through a narrow lane overhung with lime trees.

'If there's one thing I have learnt this summer, it's that people are responsible for their own actions,' Kate told her. 'Whatever happened to make your brother leave home, it was his decision to do so. The responsibility lies with him, not you.'

Angela nodded, but she did not look convinced. 'I have to know the truth, though,' she said. 'Even if the news is bad. So that I can move on. When someone disappears, it's far worse than when they die, because all you're left with is this lingering hope that they'll come back. The longer they choose to stay away, the deeper that yearning carves its mark in you. It starts to define who you are, the choices you make, the way in which you live your life. I can't move house in case he comes back, or writes to me and I never receive it. I can't go on holiday or progress any relationship in a meaningful way. The idea of having a child terrifies me, because what if they are born with the same problems as Josh? I couldn't help him and so how would I help them?'

Kate wanted more than anything to offer words of comfort, but every phrase she composed in her head felt useless, empty, patronising. 'I wish I knew what to say.'

'Don't worry.' Angela took a breath and composed herself. 'I shouldn't go on and on. Self-pity is such a wretched trait to be lumbered with. But I'm so fed up with feeling sad, you know?'

'I think I do,' said Kate. 'And for what it's worth, I hope that by the end of this evening, you might have discovered a reason to feel cautiously optimistic again.'

'I hope so too,' said Angela.

Kate knew where Podrum cellar bar was located, because she walked past it on the way to Lovro's coffee shop every day. Glancing up at a sky that was heavy with black clouds she could see why Alex had chosen an underground establishment as their meeting point. It was empty inside save for an elderly couple who were sharing a bottle of red wine. Feeling the need for a touch of liquid courage, Kate ordered a glass of the same for herself while Angela opted for a large gin and tonic. Under any other circumstances, Kate's eyes would have been hungrily roaming around the bar's interior, but such were her jitters that she barcly registered the neat stone alcoves haloed with amber light, the wicker vases of dried flowers or the mosaic tiles in harmonious shades of moccasin and butterscotch.

The hour was up. Alex should be here any moment.

Kate took a sip of wine, followed by another.

The air conditioning in the bar was turned up too high and she wished she'd brought a jacket with her. But it didn't matter, because Alex would soon be here to keep her warm. He would put his arm around her and squeeze her tight, not angry that she'd tricked him but relieved to be able to help. Kate was fretting unnecessarily. Everything was going to be fine.

She was swilling the last of her wine around in her glass when the door into the bar opened and a man appeared. Not much taller than her, he was dressed in a red hooded top and frayed denim shorts, a pair of beaten-up Converse on his feet.

Kate froze.

It was Alex's hooded top; Alex's denim shorts; Alex's beaten-up trainers.

But this man couldn't be him, for he was clean-shaven with very dark, closely cropped hair. As she continued to stare, the man glanced across the room and saw her, the smile that was playing around his lips promptly dropping into an expression of pure horror.

At last, Kate came to her senses.

'Alex,' she called, seeing the eyes she'd recognised as his widen in shock.

Angela's glass of gin and tonic hit the floor with a loud crash.

'Josh!'

Hurtling forwards with a sob, she threw herself at Alex, clasping his face in her both hands and gazing at him in wonder.

'Oh my god, Josh. It is you, it's really you.'

Kate opened her mouth to speak, but a rasping sound was all that emerged. She had been right the first time: this man was not Alex after all.

He was Josh.

53

This could not be happening. This was *not* happening.

Kate stood, rigid with shock, her wine glass in her hand and her heart pounding against her chest.

Alex was Josh. Josh was Alex.

She shook her head, hoping to dislodge herself from this nightmare. Because how could it be true? How could the missing man she'd read about in *Me Time* magazine all those weeks ago, an article that had been the catalyst for her coming to Croatia in the first place, be the same man she'd fallen for this summer?

Because she had. There was no point denying it anymore. She had fallen in love with him.

Angela didn't seem able to stop crying, her sobbing overwrought enough to summon the owner of the bar, who hurried over to see if he could do anything to help. Another staff member was discreetly sweeping up the pieces of broken glass around Kate's feet, the young woman's gaze straying from the floor across the room, towards the woman who was wailing and the man who had said nothing at all.

'I can't believe it,' Angela kept saying, her breath coming in ragged gasps as she clung to her brother, his body stiff and unyielding. 'I can't believe it's really you.'

It felt like an eternity before Angela managed to get herself back under control, as if the orbit of the Earth had stalled. Taking Alex's hands, she pulled him gently back towards the table. He looked ashen, utterly devoid of colour or emotion, not a man, but a statue.

Kate tried to speak but found she couldn't. Like the man now sitting opposite her, she felt as if she'd been turned to stone, and although she could see him, it was as if neither of them were there at all. Was this what it felt like to have an out-of-body experience? Had the world ended without her noticing and thrown them into an alternative reality? A place of purgatory, where black became white, good became bad, everything you believed to be true was untrue and all that was right became wrong?

Angela pulled some of the napkins from the container on the table and dabbed at her eyes. She was still clinging fast to her brother with her other hand and Kate could see the white of her knuckles through the pale skin.

'Everyone told me you must be dead,' she said, more to herself than either Kate or Alex. 'But I never believed them. I knew you wouldn't have done that. I knew you were still alive.'

Kate's mouth had gone dry. When she swallowed, it felt as if her throat was full of gravel.

At last, Alex spoke. 'How did you . . . What are you doing here?'

'She's here because of me.'

Kate was shocked by how stoic she sounded. She'd expected her words to emerge as a cry, splintered into shards by the earthquake of emotion smashing through her.

'Angela, she did an interview about you – about Josh. I read it weeks ago, but I didn't recognise you when we met,' she said, faltering as he looked away. 'But I did bring the magazine with me from England and left it out at the hostel for guests to read. Someone saw it and made the connection. But I . . . I thought that your friend Joe might be Josh. Angela had a photo of someone with long hair. He looked different,' she said to Angela. 'Until tonight, Al – He had dreadlocks and a beard.'

Staring across at him now, Kate studied all the parts of him she'd never seen: the sharp, neat cheekbones and soft, shapely mouth. It had all been hidden before because he'd been in hiding: a missing person doing his best not to be found. Jolted by this thought, Kate dropped her gaze to the table, to where her hands rested, each one shaking, alive with the same tremors that were rattling her arms and causing her feet to tap. She had gone from paralysed to skittish and it was agony to sit, to do nothing, to feel trapped by circumstance and indecision.

Alex stared at his sister. 'You did an interview about me?'

'Only because I was desperate,' Angela said beseechingly. 'I told myself at the start of this year that I would do whatever it took to find you. I never wanted to tell people what happened, I never wanted to share my innermost thoughts with some journalist. I didn't have a choice – I had to make sure people were still looking for you.'

Alex nodded, his eyes glassy and still. 'When was this?'

'In May – just after the ten-year anniversary of the day you went missing. I don't know, Josh. I guess I hoped that some-one, somewhere, would read it and recognise you – and I was right,' she said triumphantly. 'When I was contacted last week, I had a feeling. Something inside me, some sort of strong sisterly instinct – call it whatever you want – told me that I had to fly out here. I didn't question it, I just came, straight to the place where I knew the article had been seen, which was where I met Kate, who then led me to you. Oh Josh, I still can't believe it. I honestly thought I'd lost you forever.'

Kate waited for him to speak, to say he was sorry for running away, for putting her through so many years of torment, that he was happy to see her again. Instead, he turned to Kate.

'How much do you know?' he asked, in a tone he'd never used for her before; a low growl that could have been sorrow or anger.

'Hardly anything,' Kate said honestly. 'Only that you lost your parents and—' Her voice caught. It was pointless trying to stem the tears now. The owner of the bar placed a jug of water and three glasses on the table without a word, the elderly couple continued their muted conversation in the corner, and candlelight danced across the ceiling.

Kate thought she could hear rain.

'I did what I thought was best,' he said, the hand that was not being grasped by Angela rubbing at his eyes. He looked younger without a beard, while his shaved head lent him a vulnerability that had not been there before. Kate wasn't angry with him. She was compelled by an urge to protect, to wrap her arms around him and tell him that everything was going to be all right. As hard as this was for her, it could be nowhere close to the shock and confusion he must be experiencing.

He looked up then, his expression haunted.

'I was toxic, Ange – no good for anyone. You were right, what you said to me that day. Everything had always been about me and it wasn't fair on you. It wasn't up to you to fix me, just like it wasn't up to Mum and Dad.'

Pulling his hand away from Angela, he covered his face, his shoulders heaving, his body slumped over in the chair.

'I believed that you were better off without me,' he said, his anguish so palpable that Kate started to cry. 'I couldn't stand by and hurt you over and over again, not after everything I'd put you through – all that Mum and Dad had endured because of me. All my outbursts of rage, all the weeks where I refused to leave my bedroom, all that money and time and love wasted. I was so cruel to you all, so ungrateful, when all you ever did was try to help.'

'I didn't mean what I said that day,' Angela said, reaching for him. 'Do you know how many times I've been over it? So many times, hating myself for every foul word I uttered.'

Alex was shaking his head, unable to speak, and Angela turned to Kate.

'We argued,' she said. 'It was awful. It was the evening of Mum's funeral and Josh came to me, wanting to talk and needing my support. Your mood used to go in cycles,' she reminded him, and Kate recalled what Alex had told her just days ago; how he'd learnt to take himself away from the world when he was struggling. 'And this was a bad one. All you needed was reassurance, and I told you to get out, to leave me alone, to sort yourself out and be a man instead of a stupid little boy. I didn't mean any of it, Josh. I was just tired – so tired and so scared that it was just us. I never thought you would go; I never wanted you to go.'

Alex was sobbing properly now, pitifully, as he must once have done as a child. How hard it must have been for him to hold this in, for all this time. Kate should have pushed harder, could have tried harder to get through to him.

She put her hands flat on the table. 'I should go.'

Angela responded with a watery smile.

'You two need some time alone to talk properly,' she said. 'I'm sure there's a lot to say and I don't want to intrude more than I already have.'

Picking up her bag, she pushed out her chair. 'Alex?' He was still Alex to her. 'I'm going to go back to the hostel, so I'll wait for you there.'

He nodded but didn't look at her.

'He has my number,' she said to Angela. 'Just call me if you need anything – anything at all.'

'I will – and Kate.'

'Yes?'

'Thank you,' she said. 'Thank you for giving me back my brother.'

54

Outside, the rain lashed.

Torrents of it hammered down onto Kate as she ran, drenching her clothes, her hair, her skin. She could no longer see through her glasses and took them off, the deluge stripping through the trails her tears had left behind.

Thunder crashed, loud as falling timber, across a sky cut open by jagged shards of white light. It was as if her nightmare had become reality, only worse – more volatile, unrelenting and visceral. She streaked past the harbour with its juddering boats, the roar of the churning water a hoarse echo that followed her through backstreets turned glassy underfoot.

Twice she slipped, not once did she stop.

Kate had thought that Alex was her guide; the shining light showing her which direction she must take. But she'd forgotten about that other side of the moon; that which was destined to be forever shrouded in darkness. She heard again the words he'd whispered to her that afternoon, his promise to tell her everything. He'd been preparing to confess the truth about who he really was, only Kate had somehow beaten him to it.

The fact that Alex was Josh, that he'd run away and abandoned his own sister, that he'd lived within the constraints of a false identity for over a decade, rolled over Kate as she ran, the brute force of each repetitive blow threatening to bring her to her knees. He had lied to her, to the world, and to himself for so many years and in so many circumstances that the mere notion of telling the truth, of revealing how deep the well of dishonesty had run, must have been terrifying. Yet he'd been willing to do it. For her.

Swiping her key card against the hostel entrance, Kate pushed open the door and was greeted by sounds of revelry from above. Toby's mobile bar must be proving popular. She'd imagined going straight to find her brother but rapidly concluded that being around happy, drunken guests would be too jarring. Instead, she headed to her room, where she peeled off her sodden clothing and cocooned her wet hair in a towel.

The bathroom bore witness to her earlier preparation, the lid left off the perfume she had sprayed liberally over her body, the hairdryer still plugged in and a smear of cocoa butter on the edge of the basin. Methodically, Kate tidied and cleaned, the irony of restoring order when so much else had been thrown into disarray was not lost on her. It did help, though, to put things back in their allotted places; it helped her calm down.

Wind and rain howled beyond the window, and Kate shivered despite the mugginess of the small room. Finding a long cardigan in the wardrobe, she pulled it on over the leggings and shirt she'd changed into, starting as there was a bang on the door.

Kate took off her glasses and hurriedly wiped the tears off her cheeks.

'Nims, you in there?'

It was Toby.

'Is Al with you?' he asked, when the door was opened, looking around her into the room.

Kate wrapped her arms around herself. 'No, he's with Angela.'

Toby shook his head impatiently. 'Not anymore he's not. She just rang the office number; said she can't reach you.'

Kate glanced around for her bag, which she'd dropped on the floor outside the bathroom and pulled out her phone.

'Shit,' she said, tapping uselessly at the blank screen. 'It must have got wet in the rain. What did Angela say? Where the hell is Alex?'

'I don't know. But she's on her way here now,' Toby explained. 'I told her we'd wait for her in reception.'

On the way downstairs, Kate filled him in, explaining as best she could in the space of a few minutes how she'd inadvertently managed to solve a missing-person case.

'So, Alex is actually Josh?'

'So it would seem.'

'And he's been missing for over a decade?'

'Yes.'

'And you had no idea—'

'None.'

'Bloody hell, Nims.'

'I know.' She grimaced. 'It's a lot to take in. Where's Filippo?'

'Manning the bar.' Toby stole a glance towards the ceiling. 'Or trying to.'

As they reached the ground floor, Kate saw Angela standing on the other side of the entrance window and hurried to let her in.

'Is he here?' were her first words.

Kate shook her head. 'I don't understand,' she said, as a motionless Angela stood there in an appalled silence, her saturated clothes dripping water onto the tiled floor. 'I only left you two an hour ago – what happened?'

'That's just it,' moaned Angela, as Toby ducked into the back office. 'We were getting on fine. Josh seemed to get over his initial shock and we were talking, really talking, like we used to on his good days. He told me all about you.' She turned to Kate, her lower lip quivering as Toby wrapped a towel around her shoulders. 'He loves you, you know?'

Kate heard her brother exhale with shock.

'We agreed to come back here, so we could find you and talk some more,' Angela went on. 'Josh said he needed to pick up a few things from his boat first and I was keen to go along with him, but he said no, and that I would get soaked. He seemed so sedate, so completely at ease with everything, and I trusted him when he said he'd catch up with me. I let him go,' she cried, engulfed by a fresh wave of panic. 'Why did I do that? What was I thinking?'

She was bashing the flat of her hand against her forehead as she spoke, and Kate moved forwards to intervene.

'Please don't blame yourself,' she said. 'Maybe Al – Josh bumped into someone he knows and got held up?'

'In a force-nine gale?' reasoned Toby, prompting them to glance out through the darkened windows.

'I thought he was happy to see me,' Angela said, her voice strangled by wretched sobs. 'But what if he's gone? What if it was all too much for him to cope with? What if seeing me again after such a long time has pushed him over the edge?'

'No,' said Kate, more sharply than she had intended. 'Don't say that – don't even think that. Alex will be all right. He maybe just needs a few hours alone to process what's happened. I can think of a few places he might have gone. We can go now, all of us. OK? We can find him together.'

This seemed to bolster Angela and she sniffed hard, wiping away her tears with one corner of the towel.

Kate turned to Toby.

'Can you take Angela down to Lovro's pizza place? He's one of Alex's closest friends on the island and I know he trusts him. There's a good chance that's where he'd go if he needed a bolthole.'

'Good plan.' Toby darted behind the reception desk and re-emerged with a bright yellow raincoat and two umbrellas.

'Where are you going to go?' he asked Kate, who'd already reached the door.

'To the beach,' she said. 'To find his boat.'

55

There was no sign of Alex or his boat in the bay at Pokonji Dol, neither did Kate find any trace of it along the coastal path or in the town harbour.

The ongoing storm had blotted out the stars and driven dense clouds over the moon. It was almost impossible to see much beyond the shoreline. The further she searched, the more desperate Kate became, eventually wading into the shallows and screaming his name into the night. But it did no good. The wind that was buckling the sailboats snatched her cries away and buffeted them against the rocks, the swirling water shouting back a warning of its own that she must retreat. Nobody would be foolish enough to venture out in this.

Would they?

Without her phone, Kate had no idea how Toby and Angela were getting on, so she had no choice but to plough back up the hill to Sul Tetto, where Filippo gave her more bad news.

'No luck yet, *bambina*. Toby is taking Angela from bar to bar.'

'Alex won't be in a bar,' she said insistently. 'He'll be outside somewhere – I know him.'

'Stay here,' soothed Filippo. 'Let me go out and try.'

But Kate would not let him.

Again, she trawled along the water's edge, calling out his name. The umbrella Toby had given her blew inside out, its flimsy metal arms mangled beyond repair, so she hurled it into a bin, calling it all the worst curse words she knew, all the things she longed to shout at the world for doing this to her; for giving her someone to love only to spirit him away.

The storm scared her with its ferociousness. The restaurants in the town square were eerily quiet, the floodlit Fortico thrown for once into shadow. Kate wished she'd thought to put in her hated contact lenses before leaving the hostel, because it was hopeless trying to see through her glasses. She'd never known Alex to moor any further around the coast, but she set off along the wide pathway regardless, scouring the dark sea for any sign of a blue, white and red boat and yelling his name until it became a whimper.

There were no lights on the water, no movement save for the waves, no people hunched on benches or crouched hidden below the path. Kate searched every outcrop, every cove, every empty beach bar and every darkened pathway.

Alex was not hiding. He was gone.

It was well past midnight when Kate finally trudged back to the hostel, soaked through and shuddering with cold and misery. She found Angela on the sofa in the lounge area, a cup of something hot in her hands and haunted expression on her face that only became more so as she watched Kate walk in alone. Toby handed over her phone, which he'd managed to revive, but there were no waiting messages from Alex.

'I guess you've all tried to call him?' she said, and Angela sighed miserably.

'No point. He left his phone with me – probably thought it would throw me off the scent,' she said pointedly, only to crumple inwards with regret. 'Shit, I didn't mean that. Or maybe I did. I don't know. I just don't know what to do next, who to call, where to start looking. I feel so helpless.'

Kate said the one thing she'd been repeating to herself all night. 'Alex can take care of himself. He has done for a long time.'

'I know,' Angela agreed, not looking up. 'But what if he chooses not to this time?'

'Come on now,' said Toby, who'd just brought Kate a mug of tea. 'There's no point thinking like that. Al would never—'

'You don't know that,' interrupted Angela. 'When people are cornered like this, they do all sorts of awful things. It's my fault. I never should have let him out of my sight.'

'Don't be so hard on yourself,' said Toby, but he had visibly paled.

'Depression isn't temporary,' Angela went on sadly. 'You can't simply hunker down with a Lemsip and emerge well again a few days later.'

Toby started to reply, but she cut across him.

'You have no idea how many times I've had to explain that to people,' she said tersely. 'How many times Josh was told to "cheer up", like he was choosing to feel bad, like he was pretending to be afraid to leave his bedroom.'

Toby had turned very red.

She didn't look as if she was going to stop ranting now she had started, so Kate put her mug on the floor and cleared her throat.

'We're not arguing with you,' she said gently. 'We're not those people.'

Angela opened her mouth to retort, then closed it again. 'Sorry,' she mumbled. 'I shouldn't have gone off on one. You've been so kind and I'm behaving terribly as always.'

'Forget about it,' said Toby evenly. 'Does anyone want something stronger to drink?'

Both women shook their heads.

'Well, I hope you don't mind if I do? I have a feeling we're in for a long night.'

They'd agreed it was pointless to continue their search until after the storm had passed but sitting and waiting for it to end was almost worse than stumbling around in the downpour. Kate couldn't stay still and paced the lounge endlessly, clutching cups of tea and coffee that she never drank. Angela, meanwhile, curled herself up into a tight ball, scrolling through her phone and saying nothing. Toby pretended to read a novel, while Filippo, who had joined them after locking up for the night, flicked through a copy of *Vogue* that had been left behind by one of the guests.

The inside of Kate's mouth felt as if it was growing moss, so at around six, she headed upstairs to clean her teeth and re-emerged to find Siva sitting on the landing.

'You miss him, don't you?' she murmured, bending to stroke the cat. 'Me too.'

The rain finally splattered to a stop just after seven a.m. and a watered-down sun emerged from behind milky white clouds. Kate was expecting to find devastation in the streets, but there was little out of place save for a few fallen palm leaves and strewn items of rubbish. Bins had been toppled and washing whipped from lines, but such was the heat that the pavements seemed to steam underfoot, the air thick and metallic in flavour. Angela and Filippo set off to walk the same coastal path route that Kate had followed during the night, while she and Toby clambered into the jeep and drove to western tip of the island, their plan being to walk back along the shoreline from the opposite direction.

It did not take long for them to find something.

'Oh no,' Kate cried, running across the rocks so fast that she tripped, crumpling to the ground and cutting her knee and elbow in the process.

'Be careful,' yelled Toby from above, but Kate barely felt a thing.

There was an object in the water ahead of her; something she recognised but did not want to believe she was seeing. It had been she who had nailed the deckchair to the roof of Alex's boat and she who chose its bright, swirly, cactus-print pattern. Kate could not deny that it was the same chair floating in pieces before her no matter how much she wanted to.

Toby came to a halt behind her. 'That could be anyone's deckchair,' he said, but his voice sounded shaky. 'There must be loads like that in Hvar.'

'There aren't,' she said dully. 'I made this for him myself. It's the only one.'

A silence followed while Toby took this in. Kate crouched and pulled the splintered frame of the chair towards her, hauling it out from among sticks of driftwood, beer bottles, plastic carrier bags and an old blanket gently, as if it would somehow emerge with Alex attached.

'Leave it.' Toby put a hand on her arm. 'We need to go, Nims – we need to call the coastguard, put an alert out.'

'It's all my fault,' she whispered, holding tight to what remained of Alex's boat. 'I should never have taken Angela to meet him – I should have checked with him first.'

'Kate, we have to go.'

'I did this, Toby, don't you see? He ran because of me and now he's dead.'

'Don't say that. You don't know that.'

'This is his boat,' she cried, starting to shake. 'This chair, that blanket, all this stuff. He wanted to fix the engine yesterday and I didn't let him. I distracted him. It's been playing up for ages, since we went to Palmižana that day with Robyn, remember? What if he tried to go out in the storm and got into trouble? What if he smashed into the rocks?'

'That's why we have to go.' Toby tugged at her arm again. 'We need to start searching the sea.'

Kate couldn't move, could no longer speak, could hardly breathe. She was numb.

Toby led her away, his arm around her shoulders as he told her over and over again that everything would be all right, that they would find him, that she would see Alex again.

If only she could believe him.

56

The rest of the day seemed to pass Kate by in a blur.

She was aware of calls being made and received, of Angela's anguished tears upon learning of the smashed deck-chair, of Toby's tireless attempts to comfort, and of Siva's claws digging into her bare thighs as she sat, motionless with dread, in the apartment opposite the hostel.

Alex had run away, that much was obvious. But how far had the storm allowed him to go?

Kate had been all for renting a boat and going out to look for him herself, but Toby, via the Maritime Search and Rescue team, had told her gently but firmly that she was better off waiting by the phone.

'But have you told them?' she'd pleaded. 'About the secret cove on Jerolim and the beach at Stiniva?'

'They know,' he had assured her. 'They are going to look everywhere.'

Sundown arrived and there was still no news. Nobody could find a trace of Alex or his boat, but there was no sign of any additional wreckage either – a fact that Filippo repeated so often that it became a mantra.

'No news is good news,' Toby kept saying, until Kate could take it no longer.

'Where are you going?' said Angela, who was hollow-eyed and twitchy. Kate wanted to comfort her but felt it would be dishonest to make assurances she couldn't keep. She was unable to shake the feeling that this entire mess was her fault, and the guilt was in danger of consuming her, one greedy piece after another.

'For a walk,' she said. 'I need some air.' Then, as Angela looked at her in desperation. 'It's OK. I won't be long. I'll take my phone with me.'

'We will look after you, darling,' said Filippo. 'Why don't you try to eat something?'

Angela shook her head and Kate understood why. Food was an impossibility. Even sipping water was a struggle. Her stomach was bound so tightly in knots that it felt bruised.

Where was he?

Kate left the apartment and headed east, her trainers making little sound as she walked.

A whole day since she had seen him; twenty-four hours since he had run.

It felt like longer.

She hadn't set out with a destination in mind, but the water was calling to her, beckoning her down as it always did to the white-stone beach not far from the hostel. So many times she'd walked this route on her way to meet Alex, a smile of anticipation playing around her lips whenever she saw him there, waiting by the shore, eager to see her, to touch her, to wrap her up and kiss her. So strong was the memory that a part of Kate allowed herself to believe she might find him there. But there was nobody. Only the stones and the water; the moon and the stars; the emptiness and the disappointment. Kate had never felt more helpless in her life.

Stooping, she picked up a pebble, turning it over in her hands as she thought about all the things she'd been through to get here; her spiritless start, when she was broken down and riddled with anxiety, when she'd cowered inside a chrysalis woven from dejection only to emerge like a butterfly as her creativity flourished. The heart she'd thought shattered had mended, now larger and fuller than ever, the confidence she'd sought for so long gained pace alongside her ambition. Kate had made wishes that were granted, possibilities once stolen were returned, but as she gazed out now, across a sea that swayed in time to its own beat, all she could think was that she would trade all of it. Every bit.

For him.

She sat for a while, staring but not seeing, the stones below her cooled by a night that felt darker than most. Noticing something small glinting in the shallows, she knelt forwards to retrieve it, giving in to a hopeless smile as she saw what it was. A silver coin, a lucky charm, a reminder of the man she'd found. And lost.

Tossing the coin up into the air, Kate caught it in the flat of her palm, closing her eyes before she could see which way it had landed.

Heads he comes back; tails he doesn't.

She hardly dared look.

There was a whisper of sound behind her and Siva appeared, her soft grey body warm as she snaked between Kate's knees, purring with pleasure.

'What are you doing all the way down here?' she said, softened by such an uncharacteristic display of affection.

'She came with me.'

With a gasp, Kate swung around, her cry of surprise breaking into a sob.

Alex was standing just a few feet away, his hands by his sides and an expression on his face that looked both tortured and happy.

'I'm sorry,' he said. 'I'm so sorry.'

Scrambling to her feet, Kate ran to him, banging her fists on his chest again and again.

'Where the bloody hell were you?' she cried. 'I thought you were dead.'

Alex caught her arms, forcing her to stop. But when he tried to hold her, Kate pulled away.

'You scared me,' she said in anguish. 'I thought you'd been killed in the storm, I thought I'd never see you again.'

'I know, I know.' Alex tried again to comfort her. 'I'm sorry.'

'I need to call Angela,' she said, her hand clamping around his wrist in case he ran again.

'It's OK. I saw her a few minutes ago at the hostel.'

The adrenaline that had surged through Kate when she saw him was receding, and she felt ragged and unsteady on her feet.

'I just . . . I don't know what to say, Alex. Can I even call you Alex?'

'Well now, Joshua Alexander Dawson is the name on my birth certificate,' he said, his tone measured and calm. 'But my friends call me Alex.'

'I should be furious with you,' she went on. But she wasn't; she was simply overwhelmed with relief that he was safe, that he was here, that she was able to touch him, to see him. 'Shall we sit?' Kate let go of his wrist.

As soon as Alex lowered himself down onto the stones, Siva padded over and curled up on his lap.

'She doesn't want you to run away either,' said Kate, wrapping her arms around her scuffed knees.

Alex ran a hand across his shaved head. He had no hair nor beard to hide behind anymore and Kate was still getting used to how he looked without them. He was the same, yet different, still Alex, but also Josh.

'Must feel strange,' she observed. 'All those dreadlocks being gone.'

'In a way,' he agreed. 'But it's also quite nice, truth be told. I wanted to find out how it would feel to look like my old self again, and it wasn't as scary as I thought it would be. And that's because of you.'

'Me? Why me?'

'You made me want to be brave,' he said simply. 'I knew that in order to deserve you, I had to be honest. After everything you'd been through, I couldn't keep lying to you or to myself. It was time. You set the example – all I had to do was follow it.'

'So, you were planning to tell me?' she said. 'About being Josh, about your past, about all of it?'

A nod. 'My plan was to tell you first, and then to get in touch with Angie. The last thing I expected was for her to be sitting there in that bar with you,' he said, and Kate thought she saw him wince as he recalled it. 'It was such a shock. I didn't know what to do with myself, and then you left, and I worried that I'd lost you. I thought to myself, she won't want anything to do with me now. Your ex had caused you so much pain by telling lies, and there I was pretending to be someone else. My falsehood was far bigger than any of his.'

'But you knew how much I cared about you,' she protested. 'I told you that.'

'It was all such a shock,' he said again. 'I couldn't think; I didn't know how to make sense of it all. And so, I guess I did what I always do when things become too much. I ran away.'

'To the boat?'

'Where else?' He smiled sadly. 'Of course, I hadn't got that far when I realised something.'

Kate had moved closer to him without really being aware of it; she needed to feel the comforting warmth of him.

'What?' she asked. 'What did you realise?'

Alex didn't speak for a moment and Kate rested her head on his shoulder, waiting.

'I realised there was nothing to run away from anymore. You see, when I left England, I did so thinking that I had no other choice. I was weighed down by guilt at what I'd put my parents through, what I'd put my sister through. She wanted her life back and didn't need me hanging around with my moods and my problems. I knew Angela had lashed out because she was grieving, but all the same, I managed to convince myself she'd be better off without me and I kept on telling myself the same lie. Have you ever done that?' he asked. 'Have you ever told yourself a story so many times that it started to feel like the truth?'

Kate opened her eyes and lifted her head from his shoulder. He was staring at her, his pale eyes the same fluid silver as the coin in her hand.

'Mine was always about me being a failure,' she said. 'Until I came here and met you, there was only one part I ever played in the story of my own life. I didn't know that I could choose another one. But you made all those fears I'd held on to for so long feel irrelevant – not that they didn't matter, but that they shouldn't. At least not enough to stop me believing in myself.'

'You say that,' he said, smiling at her. 'But it wasn't me that made you realise what you were capable of. You did that all by yourself, Kate. I was just the bloke lucky enough to stand beside you and watch as it happened. In the beginning, I admit, I was driven by a desire to look after you, but I soon realised you didn't need me to do that – you didn't need anyone except yourself. You might think you're not strong, Kate, but you are.'

She was shaking her head now. 'I'm not,' she mumbled. 'I found that out when you disappeared and I quickly realised that without you, everything else felt pointless. I know it should be enough, that I have more than many – but what if I still want more? What if I want you, too?'

'You still want me?' he said. 'Even now, after everything I've done?'

Kate smiled.

'Well then, that is good news. Because the truth is, I love you, Kate Nimble. More than those stars up there and these stones, more than the voice that whispers to me that I don't deserve you, the one that told me to run away. Loving you is the reason I turned back, because it makes me feel able to tackle everything else, no matter how hard that might be.'

'Stop,' she said tearfully. 'Just stop.'

'I don't want to stop,' he told her, taking her hand in his. 'I want to tell you every day. Every minute. For all the moments I didn't tell you and for all those yet to come.'

Kate couldn't say anything else because she was crying again, struck anew by what would have happened had he not come back, had he kept on running.

'I thought you were dead,' she wailed.

'You know I've been plotting to get rid of that bloody deckchair for ages,' he joked. 'But it honestly wasn't my fault – not that part of the story anyway. What happened was, I went to the boat purely to collect some things and it just all hit me at once – the fact that my sister was here on the island, that you knew my secret, that everyone soon would – and I didn't think, I simply did. It was as if my body had a mind of its own. But then, as I reached open water, the engine stalled and I couldn't get her to start again, not for love nor money. The wind had become so strong and the deckchair had started to come loose. I clambered up to try and secure it only for the wood to splinter in my hands. If I hadn't let go when I did, I reckon I would have been swept out to sea along with it.'

'Thank goodness you weren't,' she said aghast.

'I kept on trying to get the engine going for a while after that,' he told her. 'But eventually I had no choice but to bunker down and allow the boat to drift. The sea was pretty choppy, as I'm sure you know, and I wasn't all that far from Brač by then, so I did what I could to steer the old girl into shore, but it took most of the night to reach it. I was wet through and fed up. I didn't have my phone or any money, so

I left the boat and I walked around the island to the port, where I knew Bram moored his yacht.'

'Bram Van Dijk?'

'The very same.'

'Why didn't he call me? Or ring the hostel?'

'Well, I didn't know you'd seen the deckchair. I thought Angie would assume that I was away clearing my head, not that I had perished in the storm. And I figured by the time Bram brought me back to Hvar this evening, you would have had a bit of time to think. It's a lot to take in, all this. I'm not trying to pretend that it isn't. But then, when I got to the hostel just now, I thought Toby was going to knock me out.'

Kate sat back in surprise. 'My Toby? That big softie?'

'He was pretty miffed.' Alex scratched absently behind Siva's big ears. 'Told me the next time I went missing would be because he'd murdered me and buried my body at sea.'

'Wow! And then what? How did you know to come here?'

'This little madam wouldn't stop mewing at me,' he said, as Kate reached across to stroke Siva's silky fur. 'I could tell she wanted to show me something and I hoped it would be you.'

Kate tugged down the drawstrings of his red hoodie.

'Sorry I thumped you,' she said. 'And shouted at you.'

'I deserved it.'

'No, if anyone should apologise, it's me. I'm the reason your sister turned up here. I'm the one you should blame for all this coming out before you were ready.'

Alex was shaking his head. 'No, Kate.'

'And I want you to know that whatever it is that causes you to have these dark days, whether it's depression or anxiety or something else entirely, then I want to help you manage it. I want to be there, so you don't have to go through it all alone anymore. I'm not afraid,' she said, reading the doubt on his face. 'And I'm not going anywhere. I stand by what I said to you on the boat. I want us to work. I want to be with you.'

'Are you sure?'

Alex's tentative smile did not reach his eyes and Kate wrapped her hands tightly around his, watching as his features constricted with fear.

'It's OK,' she murmured. 'You don't have to be afraid, not anymore, because I love you, too. I love your tatty shorts and bare feet, I love your calloused hands and your big heart, your stupid boat and your soulful eyes. I love that you build things, I love that you make me stop and look. I love how everything seems more beautiful when you're there, how you cook fish and help me breathe under the water. I love all that you are, all you have been, all that we will be. Whatever life has in store, we can overcome it together, as long as we have each other; love each other.'

For a moment, Alex said nothing. His expression had not changed as she spoke, but his eyes, like her own, were wet with tears. Leaning forwards, Kate kissed him, just once, feeling him slacken beneath her touch. It was then, like the sun coming out from behind a cloud, that happiness broke through, and they smiled at each other in wonder.

Neither one was lost anymore.

EPILOGUE

A woman stands by the water.

She has come to the shoreline to seek refuge, a moment's calm in a day that has been frenetic with celebration. Summer has arrived in all its sizzling glory, the sea below her lit up by sunshine; a thousand glistening stars.

A new hotel is open, its terrace adorned with balloons; a party to honour the occasion that will likely tinkle on until dawn. Music strays down from the hillside; she can smell the smoky scent of grilled fish and smiles at the soft pop of a cork being eased from a bottle.

In this pause, the woman pictures herself as she was just one year ago, frantic to disappear from the endless corridor of a life with no open doorways. Today, there is light; there is space; there is chance – the world is open, and she is free to roam. Yet she does not need to; she has found her home.

Turning, she starts to make her way back up the hill, to where the others are waiting. They are all here, those who count; new friends and old, parents, a brother and a sister – she who has been so brave and forgiven so much, who has found space in her heart for a whole new family. Her loneliness is a chapter completed, the future a story she is free to write.

Pale-blue eyes greet the woman as she makes her way inside; his lips lift into a smile that she softens with a kiss, her hand over his as it falls to rest between them.

She was adrift when she came here, as was he; but now each has the other.

And soon, they will be three.

ACKNOWLEDGEMENTS

As I sit and write these acknowledgments, it is a year to the day that the country went into lockdown for the first time. I was not actually in the UK to watch Boris "bad thatch" Johnson address the nation. Like any good escapist fiction author, I was away travelling – in New Zealand no less. Not a bad place to be trapped during a global pandemic as it turned out, but I came home anyway. Eventually . . .

I had taken myself abroad to escape for a while. Life had become exhausting, work was relentless and my health – both mental and physical – had borne the brunt. As soon as I reached New Zealand, however, I felt at peace. The multiple tabs that had been open in my mind for so many months began to close one by one, leaving my imagination the space it needed to recalibrate. And while I did not set out on that trip with the view of plotting a novel, I was not surprised when an idea began to flourish.

A story about two lost souls. A love story. A *life* story.

I feel hugely privileged to have written this novel during lockdown. Not only did it provide me with an often much-needed escape from the everyday doom-scrolling, but it served as a constant reminder that life would return eventually, that we would all be free to set off on adventures again, and that taking the time to focus on yourself can never be a bad thing. I hope you have enjoyed Kate and Alex's story, and that you have added Croatia to your list of must-visit countries. It genuinely is as beautiful as it sounds. I cannot recommend it more.

And now to my thank yous. I must start, as always, with my readers, without whom I would be a very sad author indeed. Please know that I cherish every single one of you and always will. To all those who read early proofs and shared reviews, it is thanks to you that new readers take a chance on new authors. You are the beating heart of this industry and I love you all.

To my agent Hannah Ferguson and the whole team at Hardman & Swainson, thank you for continuing to champion me and my stories – and for ensuring they find an audience not just here in the UK, but all over the world.

To my editor Kimberley Atkins, I continue to bow down to your brilliance and enthusiasm. Without you, this book would have far more unnecessary adjectives – and far less sex(!). To Myrto Kalavrezou, Alice Morley, Amy Batley and Kay Gale – publicity, marketing, editorial and copy-editing angels respectively – thank you for all you do and for believing in this book. To Catherine Worsley, Sarah Clay, Rich Peters, Iman Khabl and Lucy Howkins – aka Sales Team Extraordinaire – you are all incredible and as soon as I can do so safely, I WILL kiss you! It goes without saying that I am proud beyond measure to be published by Hodder & Stoughton – and I could not be more thrilled to be writing books 9 and 10 for you.

I'm fortunate enough to have far too many author friends to list here, but I would like to send a special thank you to Katie Marsh (for everything), Cathy Bramley (for Corfu and infinite wisdom), Paige Toon (for garden cuppas and laughter), my Book Camp crew Cesca Major, Katy Colins, Holly Martin, Liz Fenwick, Basia Martin, Kirsty Greenwood, Rachael Lucas, Pernille Hughes, Jo Eustace, Emily Kerr, Tasmina Perry, Cressida McLaughlin, Alex Brown and Ali Harris (for WhatsApp heroics), my Nearest and Dearest chums Sara-Jade Virtue, Louise Candlish, Fanny Blake and Claire Frost (for books and LOLs) and Chris Whitaker, Tom Wood and Lisa Howells (for all the love and hilarity). Writing can be a tough and lonely job at times. You all make it much less so.

To all the reviewers, bloggers, influencers, Book Tokkers, tweeters and newsletter subscribers, thank you for all you do and for all your support of this book.

To Edward Oliver (@cgmichaelsillustration), for his beautiful artwork and postcards.

To my friends, you're all bonkers. But that's OK, because so am I.

To my family, ditto.

And to Mum – it's still you I do it all for. Every single word.

Love can be found in the most unlikely places . . .

Discover Isabelle Broom's sweeping romance *Hello, Again*.

'A dreamy, romantic, irresistible treat'
Lindsey Kelk

'Emotional, enthralling and exquisitely written'
Cathy Bramley